ERF WORLD CREATIONS LLC

PRESENTS

THE PATH OF JA'BRAHMA
BOOK ONE

ASSASSINS' FATE

BY
E. RAMON

ERF World Creations, LLC

13337 South Street # 824

Cerritos, CA 90703

© copyright 2024 ERF World Creations

ISBN

979-8-9915307-05 (eBook)

979-8-9915307-1-2 (Paperback)

979-8-9915307-2-9 (Hardcover)

THANKS & DEDICATIONS

There is no way to fully explain all it took to bring this impossible dream to reality. Because before I could make it happen another impossible dream had to happen. So, this is dedicated to the indomitable spirits who refuse to quit no matter the circumstances.

Special thanks to Jaime Delgado who helped cut, peel, and apply envelope glue strips as I wrote the original manuscripts. So many hours using pudding to bind the chapters and never showing a doubt in the vision.

To Jelo and Aunt Daphne. Outside support at every turn. Not surprising I actually wore down that typewriter!

To my mother for teaching me to set the highest ambition. To Mikey & Ray Ray for supporting the dream and keeping my memory alive.

To everyone else who supported me in any fashion, especially JLH aka Mr. Bat Nuts who taught me how to fix the technical issues I had.

The Path Of Ja'brahma

BOOK ONE

ASSASSINS' FATE

1) The Contract	1
2) The Choice	35
3) The Hunt	65
4) The Harbingers	97
5) Assassins' Honor	131
6) The Elves	163
7) The War	205
8) The Harlequins	251
9) The Keepers	291
10) Ancient Heroes	333
11) The Avatar	365
12) The Hilt	403
13) The Paladins	447
14) The Return	473

Written
by
E. RAMON

INTRODUCTION

Long ago, the Creator created two gods (Eloh and Rakaar) to influence the world. However, Rakaar wanted to rule the world not just influence it. He made his servants stronger in magic and made Haar (an elf hating human) his champion.

Yet, it was his queen, not Haar, who helped him enter the world.

Rakaar being in the world forced Eloh to make Ja'Brahma (an elf druid who had no fear of Rakaar) his champion. That changed things in the world, so much so that after Rakaar was defeated, Eloh instructed his servants to act against Ja'Brahma.

That ended what would become known as the First Champions' War.

Since then, the world has followed the Path of Ja'Brahma with each god choosing a champion to oppose the other.

Eloh's champion is called the Gideon. Rakaar's champion is called the Chosen Servant. The gods' servants follow the champions during what have become known as the Champions' Wars.

Although the original champions are believed dead, the gods' top servants know the truth. The Champions' Era is almost over. It is time for the Path of Ja'Brahma to end.

CHAPTER 1

THE CONTRACT

Alena stood staring through the window at the bottom of the last flight of stairs. She had intended to go to the top of the tower, but when she noticed a group of novices running toward the tower she stopped. The group had caught her attention because very few novices were allowed to work inside the palace.

Dressed in gray peasant dresses (as is custom), the novices ran with abandon. Even from high above them, she could see their smiles. They had obviously enjoyed the bright warm day, which is typical weather for southern Anazi.

She turned her attention to the city. Anazi Falls is massive. The biggest city in Anazi. Bartizans line the outer walls with a fortress in each corner. The center of the city is spacious. To protect its secrets, it is surrounded by a labyrinth. Fields of crops take up most of the space, but there are a few other buildings besides the palace.

The Order of the Flame, of which Alena is a member, controls the wells throughout the city. It is no secret only members of the Order of the Flame live in the center of the city. It is not something that is openly discussed, but people appreciate how things are.

The Order of the Flame serves the god Eloh and stands against the god Rakaar. Alena has been a member for forty years. She is well versed in its structure. Three entities make up its leadership.

The Conclave, the human leaders, is based in Anazi Falls. The Gully Council, the dwarf leaders, is based in Gully. The Canopy, the elf leaders, is based in Alf-Heim.

Together, they wage a not-so-secret, secret war against those who serve Rakaar and or his magi. They are highly organized. They follow the three keepers: the Blue Keeper, the Red Keeper, and the Yellow Keeper who are equal in every way, but the Blue Keeper usually has the final say.

At the bottom of the Conclave's ranks are the novices. All novices who can wield magic are trained to become siblings. Those who cannot are trained to become bulwarks. Bulwarks act as spies, guards, and or soldiers in the Anazian armies. Some become siblings by mastering wizardry.

Thinking about this made Alena smile because it made her remember Razial, her longtime love. He is an assassin and dislikes the gods. He only has one good thing to say about the Order of the Flame. He admires how they keep their structure without infighting. She is worried about him because two keepers had called her to the palace and the only thing, she was told about the meeting is that it concerns Razial.

In her mind, the meeting might be about the belief Razial had assassinated the Arapian prince years earlier in the center of Anazi Falls.

To the public, the prince's death was an accident. However, the keepers have information that Razial had killed the prince on his own accord without a contract. Now, it seems as if the keepers are ready to act!

Worrying about that is what had made her come to the tower. She wanted to be alone to try to avoid thinking about Razial, but seeing the novices led her to think about the Order of the Flame's structure which led her to think about Razial.

"Sister," a bulwark called to her.

She looked over the rail and saw him standing several flights below her.

"You are wanted in the Flame Hall. Also," he added. "I was told to inform you that Ariel has arrived."

"Thank you, brother." She replied.

She had expected that. As she descended the stairs, she told the bulwark to inform Ariel she wanted to talk to her. He nodded while agreeing to do this. She quickly made her way to Flame Hall.

The heavy wooden doors slowly opened. Alena smiled as Araceli exited the hall. They are close friends. Araceli had helped her get accustomed to life in the Order of the Flame.

Physically, they are opposites. Alena has toned yellow skin, long dark hair, curvy hips, and like all elves she is short. Araceli, on the other hand, is tall with long red hair, pale skin, and is thinly built.

Mentally, they are alike and enjoy being around each other. Araceli is almost twice her age but appears young. They had not seen each other in months. They embraced, while Araceli said.

"Your turn."

They smiled at each other. Araceli winked, then she was off. Alena entered the hall. As usual, it is dimly lit. Eight druid-siblings (members of the Conclave) sat around the flame-shaped black and gray marble table. At the head of the table is Lela the Yellow Keeper and Tu'ani the Red Keeper. Alena looked at the druid-siblings as she approached the table. With the hoods of their gray cowls magically hiding their faces, they appeared evil. Their cowls used to intimidate her as a child, so she understood why many people were afraid in their presence.

"Be at ease child." Lela said.

Her pale white skin seemed grayish in the dimness of the hall. Her long white hair hung down her back. Her wrinkles do not begin to hint at her true age. She has the appearance of someone in their sixties or seventies. Alena does not know her exact age, but she knows all the keepers have been alive since the fourth Champions' War which ended a thousand years ago!

"Alena." Tu'ani called. "What is worrying you?"

"Nothing Keeper Tu'ani. I am simply curious about why we are meeting about Razial." Alena replied.

The two keepers smiled, then simultaneously explained they wanted her to find Razial and bring him to Anazi Falls. She became defensive and asked why.

"To offer him a contract." They answered.

That puzzled her. They have countless capable killers at their command. They do not need Razial.

"Choose another sibling to accompany you, but only you are to know what you are doing until you encounter Razial." They said, ignoring the confusion in her eyes.

She nodded saying she would send her elfin hawks to search for Razial.

Elfin animals trust Razial. They call him Hawk's-Blood and they will only reveal his location to those he trusts. The keepers had obviously tried to find him and failed.

"Would Razial ever serve Rakaar?" Daniel asked.

Alena recognized his voice. She has never seen his face, but she has talked with him many times. He has influence in the Conclave, which is why he is present.

She told him Razial would never serve Rakaar.

"How can you be so sure?" Daniel asked.

"If you knew Razial, you would not bother to ask such a question." She answered firmly.

Another druid-sibling asked if Razial enjoys killing.

"He does not kill for the sake of killing." She said, stronger than she wanted to.

"When you reach him, ask him why he killed the prince of Arapia." Tu'ani said.

Her long curly brown hair hangs like a mane. There is no doubt she is Tuyakan Menna. The dimness makes her tan skin seem darker than it actually is. Like Lela, she does not appear to be ancient, but she is.

"I will try Keeper Tu'ani." Alena stated.

With that, the meeting ended. Alena exited the hall. As she walked the hallways making her way to where she knew Ariel would be, she wondered why the keepers wanted to hire Razial.

***

The moon sat high in the cloudless sky, so visibility was good as Razial and Kalvin rode toward the city of Sahkar. The two of them have traveled, together, for almost five years. They had met, by chance, in the capital of Anazi. Kalvin had happened to rob the same nobleman Razial was there to assassinate.

Razial had seen Kalvin but paid him no mind until their paths crossed again-the day after the assassination.

Kalvin's partner had doubled crossed him. The two of them fought. The partner was fatally wounded. Razial helped Kalvin escape the city and the two of them have been together ever since.

Unfortunately for Kalvin, his partner had been part of the Children of Doh. (A guild of thieves.) Razial had hoped they would have forgotten about Kalvin but while in Vin he discovered the man Kalvin had killed was the prince of thieves which is why the Children of Doh have marked Kalvin for death!

As a member of the Society, Razial has nothing to worry about. The Society is feared. They control the city of Fulancia, and it is no secret the Children of Doh cannot stand against them. That is why he is going to have one of his leaders negotiate a safe end for Kalvin.

In the beginning, he did not like Kalvin enough to do this. Now, Kalvin is his friend. They have gotten in and out of some serious situations. After all their travels, (they have been to Uliv, Winnin, Ruug, and Vin-twice) Kalvin has proven to be two things: a survivor and a loyal friend.

Although Kalvin knows Razial is an assassin, he has no idea he has been traveling with the infamous assassin known as the Avatar of Death. He thinks Razial is a low-ranking assassin. Razial knows Kalvin is about to learn how high ranking he really is.

"Finally, the last of winter." Kalvin smiled.

"What? You're not going to miss winter in the Coilu lands?" Razial laughed.

Razial's voice was full of sarcasm. Kalvin was born in the city of Anazi and has spent most of his life in southern Anazi. He hates the cold and winters in Coilu are only second to those in Nibel, in harshness.

"I never want to spend another winter in Coilu again." Kalvin shook his head while dismounting his horse.

"Not even for all the coin we made?" Razial whispered.

That made Kalvin think. He looked at the pouch tied to his saddle. Inside the pouch are stolen gems and jewels from the city of Vin. He looked back at Razial and said there is no need to go back to Coilu.

They paid the toll to enter the city with no problem. They led their horses by the reins as they made their way through the city. The two of them are opposites. Kalvin is tall, with shoulder length blond hair, light olive skin, blue eyes, and a playful expression.

Razial is short, with long brown wavy hair, narrow brown eyes, golden olive skin, and a solemn expression. Like every other person who has tan-dark olive skin, he is recognized as a Tuyakan, which in his case is half true because his mother was Tuyakan. His father was an elf.

As an assassin, going unnoticed is an asset so he rarely discusses his bloodline. Seeing a Tuyakan is nothing to take note of. People remember half elves.

"Let us find an inn with two rooms so we can rest. I will meet with my contact and exchange our bounty tomorrow." Razial said, keeping his voice low and eyes on all passersby.

***

The next day, Razial took the jewels and gems to meet with the contractor of Sahkar. In every major area, the Society has a retired assassin who handles contracts and gathers information. Each contractor has a cover. Usually, they act like merchants or traders. In Sahkar, the contractor is a jeweler.

As Razial entered the small well-kept room of the shop, he was greeted by a servant. She kept her head down saying the contractor would meet with him shortly because he is with another client. She asked his name. He could sense her scanning him for weapons while acting meekly. That made him smile, mentally.

While handing her a gold coin, he said he had a delivery from Fulancia. She understood the code and hurried off while he sat.

He mindlessly rubbed the hilts of the daggers he keeps hidden in his sleeves. (He rarely carries a sword but keeps two daggers, one on each hip when he travels.

"Avatar." Vernon said as he entered the room.

He has been the contractor in Sahkar for years. He and Razial are not close, but they know each other well. He gestured for Razial to follow him. While they made their way to the back of the shop, Vernon asked.

"What can I do for you?"

"Give me what you believe is fair for these." Razial answered while handing him the pouch with the jewels and gems.

Vernon inspected the pouch before pouring its contents onto a table. He smoothed the pile. Then looked back at Razial before saying.

"Two hundred gold coins and one hundred silver pieces."

"Make it two hundred coins and fifty pieces." Razial said.

Vernon left him alone for a moment, then returned with the payment. He told Razial several witches from Ocia and several spies from Danou are in Sahkar and that the Order of the Flame is behind the king of Osam wanting to meet with the king of Sahkar. That made Razial remember Alena was in the area looking for him. His mindset changed when Vernon said there is a group of thieves looking for someone who had killed one of them years ago.

Razial thanked him. Then left in a hurry because he must find Kalvin before the thieves did.

*

Kalvin walked confidently through a street full of people trying to buy food to restock their shelves. It is the beginning of spring, but it feels like summer to Kalvin. Winter in central Coilu has made him appreciate being in northern Brahma where he used to hate being during winter.

He walked by a group of children begging for a bowl of grain. A merchant cursed them holding up a hand to hit the oldest child- a girl.

"Hit her and I will hit you." Kalvin growled.

The man looked him up and down. His attention returned to the sword hanging on Kalvin's hip. Kalvin looked at the children. Two girls and a boy. They are thin from hunger. He feels sad for them. He knows they are orphans. He took out two gold coins and told the merchant to give them a sack of beans and a sack of oats each.

"They'll each get a sack of oats but only one will get a sack of beans unless you have more coin." The merchant said while checking the coins Kalvin had given him.

Kalvin handed the man another gold coin. The man stepped into his shop. The children thanked Kalvin. The youngest, a girl, gasped when an ancient elf tapped Kalvin on his shoulder. Kalvin turned to look at the elf who was completely bald. He was the first bald elf Kalvin had ever seen. The elf only has all white elflocks that hang in front of his ears. To Kalvin's surprise, the elf knew his name. Looking into the elf's red right eye and yellow left eye, Kalvin stood with a confused expression.

"Kindness is a rare trait for those in your profession. Razial shall find a place for the children to live." The elf said then added. "Later tonight, ask yourself if you were two priceless ancient gems where would you be. Ask yourself this and you shall find them." The elf smiled.

Kalvin stared in amazement before asking who he was. The elf told him Razial knows who he is. Then, he told him not to allow the fight to make him forget about the gems. He turned and walked away. Kalvin intended to stop him, but the merchant had returned.

"What fight?" Kalvin asked.

"The one those thieves are about to start with you."

The elf's voice echoed in Kalvin's head because he had used telepathy to answer him.

Kalvin looked around. He saw four men making their way toward him. Passersby seemed to move in slow-motion. He quickly reached for his daggers while he watched the men maneuver around people between them and him.

"Always remember, you and Razial did not meet by chance. Fate brought you two together." The elf thought to Kalvin.

Kalvin heard every word, but his attention was on the men moving toward him. A stream of people crossed between him and the men. He began throwing his first dagger just before the last person cleared the first thief's path. Immediately, he began throwing his second dagger. The first dagger struck the first thief in his chest. His second dagger slammed into the second thief's stomach. Kalvin had expected him to duck, but he did not. The two other thieves drew their swords. Kalvin drew his. People quickly scattered away giving them room to fight. The men moved to engage him, but the oldest girl threw dirt into one of their eyes. Blinded he had to back up while Kalvin prepared to engage the other man.

As Kalvin moved in, he saw sunlight reflect off metal before a dagger bit into the back of the man's head. He looked around and saw Razial finish off the second thief. He quickly drove his sword through the blinded thief before he could recover.

"Get the dagger." Razial said.

He picked up two sacks of oats and two sacks of beans while telling the children to follow him. Kalvin picked up the other sacks and quickly followed them.

***

That night, after Razial had arranged for the children to be sent to Fulancia and had explained to Kalvin that he had met Priato, a well-renown elf. They made their way to a town just southwest of Sahkar.

The town is centered around a small fortress where the baroness of Sahkar lives. They sneaked into the fortress and made their way to the third floor. Razial had made it clear he was there for an assassination, so they split up.

Minutes after they split up, Razial killed two guards. He felt sweat roll down the side of his face while he used the swords, he had taken from the dead guards to lift the bar from the hinges on the closed door.

With little space between the door and the doorway, Razial had to slide the bar as far as he could to the left, then hold it with the swords while raising it until it cleared the hinges.

After it cleared the hinges, he pushed the door open while lowering the bar to the floor. He quickly made his way through the chambers until he came to the baroness' bedroom. He saw her asleep on her back. She laid naked next to the governor of southern Sahkar.

As he scanned the room, the dark patch between her legs and her brown nipples stood out against her white skin. A passing sense of arousal past through him, but he focused on a leather strap next to the bed. It obviously belongs to the governor, his target. He wrapped the strap around his hands, then slid it around the governor's neck. In one fluid motion, he yanked the governor off the bed and rolled him on to his stomach. He put a knee against his back as he pulled with all his might. The man gasped, but only for a moment. The strap was wrapped just above his Adam's apple, so he quickly passed out.

Razial drug him around for a moment while he looked for something to steal. Then he left the lifeless body in the middle of the room.

*

Kalvin smiled when he saw Razial. He held out his left hand to show him a fist size diamond. Then held out his right hand to reveal a fist size ruby.

"We're more than rich. That crazy elf was right!" Kalvin whispered excitedly.

Razial smiled and followed his friend out of the fortress.

***

The next morning, Razial and Kalvin ate breakfast at a tavern. Kalvin did his best to explain away Priato's knowledge of the gems he had found. Razial told him he had found himself in the middle of something worldly. He teased Kalvin because Kalvin has always wanted to be involved in something worldly.

To Kalvin, Priato had gotten lucky. Razial quickly corrected him saying.

"Kalvin trust me. A'Priato is a legend. Everything he told you; you can trust is true."

Razial finished eating. He wants to give Alena time to find him. Kalvin does not need to know that. So, they agreed to leave after he looked around and got his hair cut.

*

Alena watched as Razial exited the tavern. Her elfin hawks had met with him. He had used them to send her his plans. After informing the keepers, they told her to be sure to bring Kalvin to Anazi Falls as well. They did not give a reason. They simply told her it is important for her to do so. She had shared this with Ariel who was puzzled by the keepers instructing them to return with Kalvin as well.

Wearing gray burnooses, she and Ariel approached Kalvin. She wanted to talk to Kalvin before she met with Razial. They smiled at Kalvin as they approached him. Ariel pulled back her hood so he could see her face. Alena had brought her because, even though she and Razial do not get along, she knows how to handle Razial and how to deal with the danger that usually surrounds him.

"Hello Kalvin." Ariel grinned.

"Caught at a disadvantage by a tall, beautiful redhead. What can I do for you?" Kalvin asked.

Ariel and Alena struck up a conversation. After a short while, Ariel convinced him to talk in his room. He had gotten the wrong idea about them, and Ariel took advantage of that.

Alena followed them up the stairs to his room. Ariel continued flirting with him. She is good at flirting, and she is not above laying with a man to get what she needs for a task.

Upon entering the room, Ariel looked around. She made her way to the back of the room. Kalvin closed the door behind Alena, who stopped in the center of the room. She removed her hood revealing that she is an elf.

"I am Fa' Alena," she said.

"Alena?" Kalvin frowned. "As in the Alena who moved away to Anazi Falls?"

Alena smiled and nodded. Razial had told him about her which means he trusts Kalvin. Showing he is more astute than he appears, Kalvin asked her why she had waited until Razial had left before approaching him. Alena smiled because she knew she must convince him to help her convince Razial to accompany her to Anazi Falls.

Hours later, things in the town changed drastically. The baroness had ordered the arrest of all foreign swordsmen. Guards had tried to arrest Kalvin, but Ariel convinced them that he was her guard. She told them she has another guard, Razial. The guards' leader told Ariel she could claim Razial in the morning if he is arrested. Until then, they are to remain inside the tavern to avoid further problems.

They passed the time by talking. Kalvin asked why she and Ariel do not simply use their powers to make him and Razial go with them.

"Because Razial would never forgive me." Alena said.

"Well, we might as well go to sleep and claim Razial in the morning." Ariel said as she sat on the bed.

Kalvin frowned at her. He could sense she dislikes Razial. He told her the town's guard would never catch Razial. She asked him how he could be so sure. What he revealed made Alena realize why Razial trusts him enough to reveal that he is half elf and to tell him about her.

He told them how he and Razial had escaped Winnin and Uliv. They stared at him in disbelief.

Winnin is in the Gnor Valley where everyone worships Rakaar. It is home to Rakaar's first temple where Rakaar's eternal flame still burns. Few people who do not worship Rakaar dare travel across the Gnor Valley. For many, entering Winnin is borderline suicidal!

Going to Uliv is not as bad but dangerous, nonetheless. It is in northwest Danou and home to Rakaar's second temple. It is not as feared as Winnin because it is under the control of the

Theocracy, an entity that openly serves Eloh, but its leaders secretly serve the magus Cas, one of Rakaar's magi.

The Theocracy is careful about who gets into Uliv, so their true agenda is not discovered.

Ariel told Kalvin he had been foolish to go to Winnin and Uliv. He dismissed this but Alena could sense he had reservations about going to Winnin. Looking at him, she realized who he really was.

"You are Kalvin with a K." She whispered. "You are wanted in Cozik."

Ariel's eyes widened in recognition. She glanced at Alena who nodded.

"My sister, Araceli, is searching for you to find out who killed a Cozikan trader who had settled in central Anazi." Ariel pointed at Kalvin.

Kalvin shook his head in disappointment. He quickly explained he did not kill the man. He had only gone to Cozik with his ex-partner to steal some jewels and that he believes his ex-partner was involved in killing the Cozikan trader. Ariel asked where his ex-partner was.

"Dead. Five years now." Kalvin said.

To change the subject, he asked why they have so many friends whose names begin with the letter A.

"Araceli and I are sisters. Our parents thought it was a good idea to give us names that start with the same letter. Alena is our friend. Now you have your answer." Ariel said to go along with his change of subject.

Before anything else could be said, they heard someone approach the door. Alena moved with confidence to the door while Ariel stood ready. Kalvin wondered if they had drawn their powers. He wishes he could sense when a magician draws magic.

Looking at his sword and dagger, he remembered when Razial had given him the weapons. The weapons were forged with magic so he could use them against anyone-even if they have their powers drawn.

Not wanting to let the others down, he drew his sword in case they must fight.

The door opened. Razial stared at Alena as he entered the room with a shocked expression. He glanced at Kalvin and Ariel before his attention returned to Alena. They embraced. She kissed him softly then frowned while rubbing his freshly cut hair.

"Something different." He referred to his hair cut.

Alena likes his hair long but does not mind it short.

"What is going on out there?" Ariel asked.

"The baroness believes two witches from the Order of the Flame killed the governor." Razial answered.

He explained that two witches from Ocia had tracked Alena and Ariel and that these same witches have the baroness' confidence so he tried to get close to them so he could kill them but could not. Alena then told him why she had come to meet with him. They began arguing in elvish. Kalvin turned to Ariel to see if she could understand Elvish. Her expression revealed that she could not.

Hearing a group of guards entering the tavern stopped the argument. They all looked at each other. Alena and Ariel drew their powers when the guards made their way up the stairs. Kalvin took note of how calm they all remained. That made him remember when Razial had said.

"Meet danger calm enough to play but serious enough to slay."

Ariel made her way to the window, then gestured for Kalvin to follow her. The door swung open. Alena struck the guards who rushed in stopping them in their tracks. Ariel sent the shutters splintering into the ranks of the guards standing in the street. She leapt through the window and Kalvin followed. Behind Kalvin, leapt Alena and Razial who ran off while the others fought. He returned with horses. The others quickly mounted the horses, and they all raced off. Razial's only concern was how long will they be chased.

***

Pam is not a typical coven leader. She is not old for a witch (only two hundred eighty-five) nor is she prone to useless sacrifice and she does not rule by fear. However, she has two things all coven leaders must have: powerful magic and powerful allies.

She sat alone in the courtyard of Suce's palace. She is enjoying the spring weather, something she could not have done in the past.

Before, she would have still been at war with other covens that serve the magus Mel.

Although they are known as the Sisterhood, the witches of Ocia were in a constant state of war which made them the weakest of the entities that serve a magus. However, that all changed five years ago. That is when all the covens united. There is no more in-fighting. The thirteen strongest members of the Sisterhood formed a new coven. Forming another coven is forbidden. Some had to learn that the hard way.

The Sisterhood has prospered. It is no longer the weakest magus entity. The Fellowship-the entity that serves the magus Bal is amid a power struggle-thanks to the Sisterhood. Still, the Theocracy remains the strongest of the Magi's entities.

Drinking from her silver goblet, Pam heard several people approach the courtyard's door. She put her goblet on the table as the door opened.

"Your sister, Lisa has arrived." Her protegee said.

Pam still cringes at the mention of Lisa's name. Although they are coven members, that does not change the past. They were once worse enemies. For decades, they had waged war against each other for control of Suce. Now, they live peacefully in Suce.

She watched Lisa and Tammy (Lisa's protegee) walk across the courtyard. They walked confidently as they should. Lisa is as powerful as she is beautiful. Her long wavy brownish blond hair hangs over her shoulders and down her back. She has cat-like eyes that match her olive skin.

Many are fooled into believing she is Tuyakan. She is not, but Tammy is. No one understands why Lisa chose Tammy as her protegee. Some even protested Lisa choosing her. Where their protest of Pam's protegee-was because of her protegee's age, their protest of Tammy was based on real merit. Tammy's mother was an enemy to all members of the Sisterhood.

"Magus Mel be praised." Lisa said to Pam.

She eyed Pam and her protegee. The two of them could pass for sisters. They have long curly brown hair, light eyes, and full pink lips. Their toned complexion is more typical of southern Ocia. They are not as pale as most northern Ocians.

"The greatest of all magi." Pam responded.

This is customary for those who serve Mel because Mel had made it a rule for all leaders to say this.

"I have news from the Ancient." Lisa said.

"Do tell." Pam replied.

Lisa then explained that the Ancient had sent news that the Order of the Flame wants to stop the Fellowship from taking control of all Coilu and that they have discovered that there are high level spies in their ranks.

After that, she explained that the Order of the Flame would hire an assassin to help them in the Coilu lands. That made Pam frown.

"Will we have to change our plans?" She asked.

"No. The Ancient says that no one knows that we are behind the Fellowship's actions." Lisa answered.

Pam began to think. The Ancient is a powerful sorceress who controls Tunez. Although the king of Tunez still reigns, he does so at the Ancient's leisure. It was the Ancient who facilitated the end of the in-fighting between the Sisterhood. She not only made the thirteen scepters that each member of the Sisterhood's coven can use to take power from male magicians and or from other enemies, but she also provided the agents who have made the Sisterhood a lot stronger. She had gotten all that done by threatening to kill all who stood against the Sisterhood's unification.

"What does the Ancient want us to do about this?" Pam asked.

"Nothing. She wants us to continue as planned. That is why I am here." Lisa answered.

***

Two weeks after Razial and the others had escaped the town, Razial decided that they no longer needed to cover their trail because they had lost their pursuers. A small town ahead of them is the first town they have come across in days, so they have no choice but to stop there for supplies.

As they rode along, Kalvin continued to ask questions. Most of Alena's and Ariel's answers were either half-truth or roundabout facts. Still, while Kalvin asked his questions, they did their best to learn more about his and Razial's travels. Razial had told Ariel not to reveal he is the Avatar of Death. (Alena already knew not to.)

"Is it just me or is it hot for spring?" Kalvin asked.

They are about a hundred miles east of Anazi. To the east of them there seems to be no life in the dense thicket Razial had decided not to enter. The regrowth makes it too difficult to pass. Alena had wanted to use the thicket to cover their trail, but Razial said there was no need to.

Riding alongside of Razial, Alena finds it humorous (as does Ariel) that Kalvin has no idea he is the Avatar of Death. She has managed to piece together that Razial was involved in the assassinations of the ruler of Winnin and the ruler's son. Razial refuses to acknowledge any of this. He also refuses to discuss the prince of Arapia's death.

"It's only going to get hotter the further south we travel." Razial said in response to Kalvin.

*

Hours later, they bathed and eaten. Razial sat at a table watching Alena as she crossed the inn's dining room. She sat to his left. Although she is wearing her burnoose's hood, he is sure many can see that she is an elf. He caressed her arm hoping no one would cause any trouble.

"Where is Kalvin?" He asked.

"In the room. I believe he will try to lie with Ariel." Alena answered.

"And she feels what about this?"

"She will let him get close, but he will have to wait until we reach Anazi Falls."

Razial did not respond. He knows she had come to press him about going to Anazi Falls. He asked her how she feels about Kalvin. She told him she likes Kalvin. She asked him why he had not settled the issue Kalvin has with the Children of Doh.

"I will when we reach Fulancia." He stated.

He asked her how many siblings are like Ariel.

"Quite a few. It is a lonely life we live-very lonely." She teased.

He scowled at her. She laughed. She had made him jealous like she had intended. He noticed this and smiled.

"I am not like that, and you know it. Come around more..." She trailed off.

His eyes left hers then returned. She knows he has noticed everyone who might be a threat to them.

"I am going with you." He stated.

"What has changed?" She asked.

"Your safety."

"How many are there?" Alena asked this with a smile.

She feels happy cause he will accompany her to Anazi Falls. Her mood quickly changed when they sensed several magical strikes on the second floor.

She raced up the stairs. Razial sprang to his feet-dagger in hand. He saw a wizard stand and chant attempting to strike Alena. His dagger tumbled once before it slammed into the wizard's back. Two men moved to engage him but stopped because they had expected the wizard to survive his dagger. Their delay cost their lives.

Razial tossed a chair at the first man who easily deflected the chair. Unfortunately for the man, a dagger followed the chair. It struck true into the man's throat. The second man charged. He could not avoid the dagger Razial threw at his stomach. He winced in pain but still swung at Razial who ducked pulling the dagger free. He hit the man across his face causing him to stumble. He ignored him after that and collected his other daggers.

Sensing no more magical strikes, Razial watched the stairs as Kalvin, Alena, and Ariel descended the stairs. Ariel's hands are covered in blood.

"This was supposed to be a trap. A group of wizards will arrive soon." Ariel said angrily.

Razial did not respond. He simply followed the others out of the inn. They gathered their horses and supplies. He hopes an enemy is foolish enough to follow them.

***

In Anazi Falls, Tu'ani and Lela entered the telepathic realm. Since keepers' powers link in each other's presence, they are not worried about being attacked. They contacted Priato who was happy they did. They explained many other leaders of the Order of the Flame disbelieve Razial is fated to become the Gideon and Kalvin is fated to become a paladin.

They explained most go along with their plans out of respect. Priato thanked them, then explained the Harbingers- a group whose cause threatens the Order of the Flame, are behind what is going on in Coilu.

"They have kept us in the dark. I was too busy trying to figure out if Goraan is a Harbinger while the Harbingers hid themselves and prepared for this war." Priato thought.

As Eloh's seer, Priato is allowed to see and know certain things that the keepers do not know. Long lived, Priato loses himself to bouts of senility, at times, but he is sure Razial is fated to become the Gideon, Eloh's champion and Kalvin is fated to be a paladin, one of eight who will act as the Gideon's generals.

This Champions' War (the fifth) is different than the others. Usually, most paladins are found and trained before the Gideon is found. Priato told them the fact Razial is an assassin, and Kalvin is a thief means nothing.

"Tell the others to stop worrying about that. They should be worried about the fact Razial was born with sorcery and cannot wield it." Priato thought strongly.

"A'ja'Priato. How long has the war been going on?" Lela asked.

"For quite some time. Razial is sixty years old. Events took place when he was young that led him down the champion's path." Priato thought.

He then explained that soon Ja'Brahma's daggers would find their way to Razial. That puzzled Tu'ani and Lela, but neither said a word. No one has been able to find the ancient daggers that once belonged to the ancient elf druid Ja'Brahma, Eloh's original champion. The daggers were lost at the end of the Fourth Champions' War when the last Gideon was killed. Still, they know Priato would not have said this unless he had seen it.

"Any idea what path Razial will walk, A'ja'Priato?" Tu'ani asked.

Priato told her that he does not know which path Razial will walk. Then he ended their connection. Lela and Tu'ani decided to contact Zelia.

*

Zelia lay awake on her bed. She had never expected to be involved in such an important task so soon. Unlike her twin sister, Xochi, she never embraced being the great, great granddaughter of Tu'ani the mighty Red Keeper. She had always taken odd tasks trying to build her own path in the Order of the Flame. Along with several other siblings, she undertook the task of trying to stop the Fellowship from spreading their influence across western Coilu.

In the beginning, it seemed like the perfect task for her to gain recognition on her own. Now, all of that has changed. Her task has become the most important task the Order of the Flame has at the present time because of what is going on.

The king of Mohr has agreed to abdicate his throne in return for forty thousand gold coins and the marriage of his niece to the imperial prince, who will not only get married in Mohr but remain to rule the city. Already, an imperial army has arrived to secure the city.

Acting like a servant to the captain of the palace guard, Zelia had discovered that the imperial prince is under a spell and that the Fellowship intends to use him to invade Nibel after they have defeated the Partisans, a militia made to act as a buffer between Coilu and Nibel. Zelia relayed all this news to Tu'ani and Lela when they contacted her. When she finished, they told her about their plan. Their plan puzzles her. She does not understand why they want her to make plans for the assassin's arrival when he has yet to accept the contract they intend to offer him.

Rolling on her bed, she tried to figure out why they even wanted to involve the assassin.

***

Sixteen days after they had avoided the trap, Razial and the others arrived in Anazi Falls. Kalvin rode next to Ariel while Razial and Alena rode behind them. Ariel had cleared up all the misconceptions Kalvin had had about Anazi Falls. She had made it clear he is to never admit to outsiders that she and Alena are siblings. She had also explained the Order of the Flame allows people to be confused for being members of their order because it makes it easier for their real members to go unnoticed.

As they made their way to the labyrinth, Kalvin looked back at Razial wondering why he was so nonchalant about entering the labyrinth.

"I guess you want me to believe you've been in the labyrinth before." Kalvin smirked.

Razial laughed. Ariel told Kalvin that Razial is the reason there is a night patrol in the labyrinth. That made Razial scowl at her. Alena smiled at Kalvin's reaction to this news. She knows Ariel had referred to the assassination of the Arapian prince- something Razial does not want discussed around Kalvin.

"I thought that was an accident." Razial said.

"That was our public response." Ariel responded.

To change the subject, Razial told Kalvin the only city he has not been inside of is Gnor.

"And that is because it is sealed." He winked.

"How is it you have been to Alf-Heim without Alena?" Kalvin asked.

Alena could sense this is not the first time they have had this conversation. She told Kalvin that she and Razial had been born in Alf-Heim. Ariel then told him Razial's parents had been members of the Order of the Flame. Alena glared at her. Ariel had gone too far.

Noticing Alena's displeasure, Ariel said no more about his parents.

*

Hours later, Alena and Ariel sat inside Flame Hall. Four druid-siblings sat across from them. Tu'ani and Lela sat at the head of the table. They had explained Alena and Ariel are to head to Mohr and meet with Zelia. They then told them there are spies in their ranks, so they must keep things as secretive as possible.

"Razial and Kalvin are very important." Tu'ani said.

She stared at Alena and Ariel. She has always had an aura of power, but at that moment she seems more powerful-as does Lela, who joined Tu'ani in saying.

"Keep them alive at all costs!"

Then, speaking simultaneously, they told them to convince Kalvin to accompany them to Mohr. After that Alena was sent to bring Razial to the hall.

Dressed in all black, Razial has on loose-fitting pants and an oversized pullover shirt with a V-neck collar. He had expected to meet with the keepers in a private chamber not in the Flame Hall.

Standing at the end of the table, he ignored the druid-siblings and kept his focus on the keepers.

"You are welcome to sit Ja'Razial son of A'Ashiek." The two keepers said.

With Alena next to him, Razial thought about how if she had not asked him to come to Anazi Falls he would not have come. He noticed they had used the A' prefix with his father's name to show respect and honor. He has no idea if they did that for him or if they truly feel his father deserves such an honor.

"I want to stand. Thank you." He replied.

He wondered if Alena had told them he dislikes it when others bring up his parents, especially members of the Order of the Flame. His parents died serving Eloh. To him, serving the gods is foolish and makes one a puppet.

"Very well." The keepers said.

A scroll floated to him. Alena watched his expression change as he read the scroll. Wondering what brought about the change, she began reading the scroll.

"You cannot be serious." Razial said.

"We are quite serious." The keepers said.

They want him to go to Mohr and bring the imperial prince to Anazi Falls. They also want him to assassinate the prince's fiancée and serve the Order of the Flame for three years. They want all of this for four thousand gold coins.

"I do not accept this contract."

"You would refuse four thousand gold coins?" Daniel asked.

"Do not forget who I am. I am a prince of Fulancia." Razial said.

Alena wanted to smile. Razial is a master assassin. Other master assassins stand in awe of him. To act against him is to invite the Society's full wrath. The society's treasury is open to him. He wants for nothing. Four thousand gold coins does not impress him.

"Besides, I hate this prince. I intend to kill him soon. He ordered the hunt of wolves throughout Coilu." Razial barked.

His tone caught Alena off guard.

"He is under a spell. Bring him here and we shall free him. Do this and we will show you how to return the elfin wolves' ability to become invisible." The two keepers said.

"Do not mock me." Razial warned.

"Accept the contract and we will do this now, Hawk's-Blood." Tu'ani and Lela said knowing they have intrigued him.

"If you can do this, why have you not done it already?"

"Because we cannot. This is something only you can do. We only discovered this weeks ago."

Razial stared at them in disbelief. Lela grew tired of the standoff. She walked over to the back window with a wand in her hand.

"Come." She gestured with the wand. "We shall do this, but now the three years do not start until you return from Mohr."

Razial walked over and took the wand. She began teaching him an ancient chant in ancient elvish. Alena watched him recite the chant.

All elfin animals are linked to certain individuals, usually an elf. If that individual dies before another link is in effect, the elfin animals connected to that link lose their ability to become invisible until another link is discovered. She thinks it is only right that he is the elfin wolves' link.

When Razial finished the chant, a large flash lit the sky. The wand turned to dust. Razial looked at Lela in disbelief. She just smiled and said.

"Sign the contract Ja'Razial. We shall send two thousand gold coins to Fulancia."

*

Kalvin was drunk half dressed in his room with the door open. He had experienced Ariel's flesh and was happy he had. She had left after seeing the flash across the sky.

Seeing Araceli walk by, he thought she was Ariel. He moved to the doorway and called out to her. Araceli stopped and faced him. She demanded to know who he was because he only had pants on. He made the mistake of approaching her. She prepared to strike him, but Razial called out to her.

"Araceli?" Kalvin frowned.

Araceli and Razial greeted each other. He explained who Kalvin was before he led him back into his room. He knows that Araceli is a lot less tolerant than Ariel.

"Kalvin. Araceli is not as playful as her sister. Be glad I arrived when I did, or you would have been sorry." Razial warned.

***

The next morning, Tu'ani and Lela talked with Tina, a member of the Conclave. Unlike the others who do not know, Tina is not worried about why Razial is so important. (Although the Conclave knows about the plan in Mohr, only the Canopy knows why Razial was hired.) Tina's concern is securing the six ancient crowns and keeping the few descendants of the Six Heroes alive.

She trusts the keepers so instead of asking about Razial, she has made her own plans.

Lela and Tu'ani sat listening to her explain the plan she and Barthus, a legendary bulwark had made. They will go to Danou to get the ancient crown of Danou and the Danouan descendant of the Six Heroes. While they do that, they want others to take action to get the other crowns. Lela told Tina she would have Daniel see to the other actions to get the other crowns. Tina likes that a lot. She left with a smile leaving Lela and Tu'ani alone.

"If we cannot get this imperial prince-Paul, into the fold with us, getting the crown of Coilu will be that much more difficult." Lela said.

"And if his father recovers, we must have Razial end his life. Do you agree?" Tu'ani asked.

Lela simply nodded in response. Neither enjoys ordering the death of a non-enemy, but as keepers this is sometimes part of their roles.

Lela's mind went to Razial. Things would be so much easier for them if Razial were in the fold with them. Getting him to leave the Society is an impossible thought. He is a loyal assassin.

Although Alena cannot reveal much about her life in Fulancia, she had made it clear that Razial is loyal to Anjia, Binu, and Goraan: three elves who are high ranking members of the Society.

Goraan is known to all the keepers-personally. They would like nothing more than to imprison him, but as a member of the Hilt, the five leaders of the Society, Goraan is all but untouchable.

Binu has crossed paths with Ulina (the Blue Keeper), but extraordinarily little is known about him before he became an assassin. The fact he leads the Hilt and not Goraan is all they need to know about him.

Anjia is the least known to the Order of the Flame. They know she is at least half elf and so prolific as an assassin she is known as the Lady Avatar.

According to Alena, Anjia grew up with her and Razial and that Goraan had tried to convince them not to become assassins. Because of the oath she took before joining the Order of the Flame, Alena could say no more.

The one thing she has discussed repeatedly is Razial, Anjia, Binu, and Goraan, form a close family unit that includes Alena. That is enough for Lela and Tu'ani to accept that Razial will not leave the Society even though he is fated to become the Gideon.

***

Razial and Kalvin stood in Kalvin's room. Razial had tried to convince Kalvin to stay out of this mission but failed. Kalvin has a look of determination in his eyes. Razial can sense there is no way Kalvin will not stay out of this mission. He thought about asking Alena to have the Order of the Flame keep Kalvin in Anazi, but Kalvin revealed that that would not work.

"The Order has given me five hundred coins!" Kalvin said excitedly.

Seeing the gold angered Razial, but he remained stoic. Before that moment, he had thought the Order of the Flame had only wanted Kalvin to come to Anazi Falls to make it easier for him to come. Now, he realizes they have plans for Kalvin-plans that he distrusts. He told Kalvin he should return the gold. Kalvin shook his head saying.

"This is worldly Raz. The Order wants us to help them. And they want to pay us. How could you ask me to stay out of this? We went to Uliv and Winnin. Mohr will be nothing."

Razial smirked. He admitted he had taken Kalvin to Winnin because he did not like him that much back then.

"What? Now you're worried?" Kalvin frowned.

"Something seems wrong. Before, we were in control. This will be much different Kalvin. You do not need the coin. You can go to Fulancia and exchange the gems. You could move your family there. No-"

"On whose word? Yours?" Kalvin cut him off.

Razial smiled. He tried to explain that he had enough influence to allow Kalvin to move his family to Fulancia, but Kalvin continued to be sarcastic with him. He shook his head. It is his fault Kalvin does not believe him.

"Very well. Leave the gems and the coins here. We will not need them."

Kalvin did not want to leave the gems. Razial convinced him to trust Alena.

"If she loses them, you owe me a noble title." Kalvin said.

"You want to go, so you can spend winter in the Coilu lands." Razial teased.

Kalvin's expression changed. He had forgotten about that. They laughed.

CHAPTER 2

THE CHOICE

Beulah sat in a telepathic trance. She contacted the Master, the unknown leader of the Harbingers. He had recruited her when she was young. Her enemies had pushed to remove her from the throne in Ino-Heim. They had made it seem as if the Harbingers had killed her father-Bahkez the legendary elf who had led the Boar clan out of Alf-Heim.

When the war against her enemies became too dangerous, the Master helped her escape to Alf-Heim while staying behind to wage the war against her enemies. For almost a century, the Master battled her enemies.

During this time, the Fourth Champions' War began. Beulah made the choice to help Eloh's servants. The Master did not protest this decision. Instead, the Master and others joined her in helping defeat Rakaar's servants. However, the damage to Ino-Heim had been done. The sorcery that keeps Ino-Heim healthy has been failing ever since. Now it is at the point of no return. The Boars need a new home.

"I am here little sister." The Master thought to her.

Her mind returned to the present. She explained she has decided to kill the king of Tunez. The Master asked if she was sure she no longer needed the king. She told the Master, she was sure.

"Very well, so long as this does not jeopardize our plans for Coilu and the Fellowship." The Master thought.

She asked if he is sure letting Razial live is a good idea. Unlike some Harbingers, she does not want to kill Razial nor is she sure killing him will make their goal more attainable. The only thing that concerns her is Razial joining the Order of the Flame. The Master is sure that will not happen. The Master had given all the Harbingers the same order about Razial.

"Take no action against him except those we have planned. He is more useful to us alive than dead." The Master said.

Before ending their connection, the Master told her to be careful. He warned her that the Order of the Flame would not hesitate to imprison her if they find proof she is a Harbinger.

She did not respond. She thought about how in ancient Elvish the word imprison can also be used to say cause shame. (She thought about this because the Master usually communicates with her in ancient elvish. Something elves do to those they are close to or to show respect. He has no reason to respect her in such fashion but has always treated her as if they are close.)

Standing, she is unfazed by the darkness of her room. She walked across the room and opened the door. She walked through the hallway that leads to the stairs. Inside the palace of Tunez, she has no worries. The top floor is hers. Only her maidens are allowed on the top floor. The floor beneath hers belongs to her warriors. Like her maidens, they all cover their faces when they leave their floor. She does not want it to get out that she is an elf. That would cause her a lot of problems. Being ruled by an unknown sorceress who takes care of them is acceptable to the Tunezans. Being ruled by an elf is not no matter how well she takes care of them.

"A'fa'Beulah." Bri'ina and Sa'ami bowed in respect.

The two sisters have cared for her all her life. They are very loyal and their commitment to her is absolute. She smiled at them when she reached the bottom of the stairs. Without anything being said, they fell in stride with her. The warriors she had them call to join them during the meeting with the king brought up the rear.

When they approached the king's chambers, she could see the king's guards tense up. She looked into their eyes and only saw intimidation. They know something is about to happen. Tunezans have come to recognize her signature black cowl that magically hides her face. She knows people fear it when they see it. The guards tapped the butts of their spears to signal for the door to be opened. She had thought about using her powers to blow the door open, but her maidens had told her not to. They had also told her not to change too many things after she kills the king.

"Feed the peasants and reward some generals with nobility to replace the nobles we kill." Bri'ina had said.

Sa'ame had agreed with this. (They rarely disagree.) She then told Beulah not to disband the palace guard saying.

"It keeps them from joining those who will oppose you."

The chamber's door opened, and Beulah's mind returned to the present. She entered the chambers without missing a stride. The king sat near the back of the room. His eyes are full of concern. He knows he has angered her. She had told him not to kill one of his bannerman, but he did it anyway.

She ignored the others in the room. She had had them called to the chambers so they could witness her killing the king.

"I was told" she drew her powers making her hands glow. "-long ago that one should never make a choice one cannot live with or is unwilling to die for. So, when one makes a choice, one should be willing to live with it and die for it."

She took hold of the king magically squeezing him and lifting him into the air.

"You made a choice, a bad choice, but a choice, nonetheless. My response is simple. Live with it. Die for it."

The king's men thought about trying to save him but only for a moment.

***

Peter had been a young low-ranking general when he had first encountered the Master. Dressed in his red Harbinger cowl, he had intimidated Peter. Peter was given a dingus book which was unlike any other dingus book. Where wizards must study their dingus books daily, his dingus book allowed him to learn and memorize chants. That allowed him to master simple wizardry in five years!

In time, his powers grew stronger and slowed his aging process, which could have been a problem had the Master not shown him how to reinvent himself. Now, only those who are loyal to him know how long lived he truly is.

Just as the Master had instructed him to do, Peter built a following in the imperial army of Coilu. He has few enemies and all of them are members of the Fellowship-which he has infiltrated for the Harbingers.

For thirty years, he has risen in the Fellowship's ranks and secretly created a rift in the Fellowship's leadership. One faction-Peter's faction- wants peace with the other entities that stand with the other magi. The other faction opposes this. Both factions want control of all Coilu. Peter does not care which faction wins. He has gained the confidence of the other faction's leaders and has convinced them to plot to invade Nibel. Now, he only has one problem. His meteoric rise in the Fellowship has made others jealous. By Bal's law, no member of the Fellowship is to act against another member without permission from the leaders. Peter's distractors have violated this law. That is why he was given permission to act against them.

With three men behind him, he walked through the short corridor that leads to the private chambers of the imperial wizards. Each of his men is a captain, the captain of the city's guard, the captain of the palace guard, and the captain of his army. Each has sworn fealty to him. To them, he is the top imperial general. He intends to reward them after this action. He knocked on the door. One of the wizards asked who was knocking. He identified himself. A moment later, the door was opened.

"Peter. Has the emperor's condition worsened?" a wizard asked.

"No." He answered.

He looked around the greeting room. Decorated with plush floor pillows and lavish drapes, the room is fit for a king instead of three traitorous wizards.

"Then what is wrong?" The second wizard asked.

Before Peter could respond, the third wizard entered the room. He appears to have been asleep.

"You seem preoccupied Peter." the third wizard said.

In the past, they had all been friends. They had planned to take the imperial throne together, but they grew jealous and greedy and want Peter out of their way.

"I have news of a plot to kill me." Peter said.

All three stared with shocked expressions. The first wizard told him they would stand with him. Peter told them not to worry because he would handle the matter. That seemed to put them at ease. He smiled then threw a pouch of powder in the air. They stared at him with puzzled expressions. Before either could say a word, they began to choke and cough. Blood began to stream from their eyes and ears. The poison had been designed just for them. It is harmless to everyone else. They fell lifeless to the floor. He told his men to take their dingus books. His mind then went to how he should proceed. With Paul in Mohr, several generals have made it clear they will support him if he pushes for power. He knows making himself emperor would be a bad move. He has nothing to gain. So that is not an option.

"True power lies in the shadows unless you can rule on your own."

The Master had said to Peter when he asked him why he did not want to rule openly. The Master had explained that a ruler who needs others to rule, is just as much their servant as they are the ruler's servants.

Following that philosophy, Peter has made many decisions including his decision not to become emperor. He has bigger plans than that.

***

After two weeks of fast riding, Razial and the others slowed their pace as they neared the great forest of northern Anazi. They intend to rest for several days so they can ride hard through Gully.

Although Ariel dislikes that the keepers had told her and Alena to allow Razial to control the group's movements, she has kept it to herself. According to the keepers, Razial's fate affects many things. They did not say how or why, but Ariel and Alena understood that they did not say this lightly.

Kalvin and Razial sat by a tree drinking water while Ariel and Alena sat several paces away. The day is bright, and the air is fresh. Razial explained to Kalvin how to use elvish prefixes and suffixes because Kalvin had asked why he and others use the prefix A'ja when they refer to Priato.

Razial explained that Ja' is for male elves and Fa' is for female elves. Both express respect and or formalness. Then, he told him that using them at the end of an elf's name expresses care by the speaker.

"A' by itself expresses honor and respect. Adding it to Ja' or Fa' is like a superlative. Using it as a suffix is done by a spouse or a parent. A spouse uses it when talking about one's spouse and a parent does it when talking to one's child." Razial said.

"Or when an elder talks to someone much younger." Alena added.

Kalvin noticed the way Razial winked at her. She smiled back. That made Kalvin think how he is the youngest in their group by far. At thirty, he is only half Razial's age who is the same age as Alena. Ariel is one hundred thirty-seven and blends in well with them. She appears to be in her late twenties or early thirties to all who look upon her. All of that came to his mind because seeing Razial and Alena smile at each other made him remember them saying that they had been in love for decades. (That is when he learned all their ages.)

"Something is wrong." Ariel stood.

They all looked around. The horses are tethered to trees. Kalvin looked at Alena because she stood with her head tilted and her eyes closed. He turned to look at Razial, but Razial was gone!

"Elfin wolves." Alena said when she opened her eyes.

She explained Razial had gone off to greet a pack of elfin wolves that had sensed her and Razial. That put the others at ease. She then thought about how for most of his life Razial has killed those who hunt elfin animals and any non-game animal.

Several kings died for hunting elfin wolves and Razial made it well known why they had died. He was so prolific at killing hunters in the lands of Giaour that no one there dares openly discuss hunting non-game animals. Kalvin asked how she communicates with elfin animals. She told him by using mental images and her thoughts along with her emotions. She told him it is easier for elves to communicate with elfin animals of their own clan.

"But you have pet hawks, and you are a Wolf." Kalvin said.

"I raised them, so it was easy for me-a Wolf- to communicate with them. Also, my father was a Hawk, which makes it easier." Alena said.

Seeing that Kalvin was confused, she explained clan lines are maternal in elves. Naturally, he asked about Razial because Razial's father was an elf not his mother. She simply told him half elves are an exception to the rule.

With that Kalvin's curiosity was sated. Razial returned and said it is time to move on. His mood had changed, but he did not say why.

***

Acting like a servant is the perfect cover. As a servant, Zelia is ignored. She moves around unnoticed and can listen to others converse while she cooks, cleans, and or serve those in the house. She can also go about the city unnoticed, which allows her to pass and receive information a lot easier than she did before.

Carrying a small tray with sliced ham and potatoes on it, Zelia walked toward the table where Sidney-the captain she serves in Mohr, and his guests sat. As fate would have it, Sidney was sent ahead of Paul to secure the city before Paul arrived and Zelia was fortunate enough to become his servant. When she heard him say he wanted to hire outsiders to guard Paul, she told the keepers, expecting them to send a sibling. Instead, they told her to mention the assassin to Paul. She disliked that.

"Thank you, Zelia." Sidney said politely.

Zelia smiled as she placed the tray on the table and put a plate in front of him and in front of each of his guests.

"Are you sure your cousin will arrive in time?" Sidney asked.

"He will arrive soon." She replied.

She had told him Razial was her cousin and assured him he would not find anyone better as a fighter. He told her he will have Razial tested when he arrives. She told him Razial will have no problem with that.

"I hope he is as good as you say he is." Sidney said.

"Trust me. He will not disappoint you." Zelia responded.

One of the guests asked where Razial is from. Without thinking, she answered truthfully.

"Fulancia?!"

The other two guests asked simultaneously. The second guest stated every fighter he has met from Fulancia has excellent skills.

"Because they were probably all assassins." The first guest said.

Sidney eyed Zelia but she remained stoic. She knows she should have lied just to avoid this line of thought. She picked up the tray while assuring Sidney Razial would do all he could do to protect Paul. With that, she left the room.

She returned the tray to the kitchen, then returned to eavesdrop on Sidney and his guests. They talked about how the imperial wizards had been killed and how it was Peter who had killed them. To them, that proves Peter is not part of the Fellowship. Zelia knows better.

She continued to listen while they talked about how Peter can still make a push for power. After that, they began talking about Paul's fiancée. They think she is part of the Fellowship.

Zelia was surprised to hear the third guest say he thinks the fiancée is behind the rumor that she has been targeted for assassination. Zelia knows that is no rumor.

"What is this?" A woman whispered. "An eaves...dropping servant?"

Startled, Zelia stood straight up and turned around. She saw a tall thinly built woman who stood in front of four men. Two of the men moved to flank Zelia. The other two held their crossbows aimed at her.

"Scream and I will kill you." The woman said.

Zelia cursed herself for not paying attention while she eavesdropped. Her eyes widened when a fifth man walked from behind the woman.

"I am a wizard and so is he." The woman pointed at the fifth man. "Now call to your master."

Zelia turned around and knocked on the door while calling out to Sidney. She almost laughed when the men lowered their crossbows away from her. Now, all she needs is room to fight. Two men pulled her back as the door swung open. She did not see who had opened the door. The wizards charged into the room lashing out with their powers. Surprising them and Zelia, Sidney's second guest is a warlock!

Zelia could not see them fighting but she sensed them. She pulled the two knives she keeps under her apron and stabbed the two men who had held her. Then, she ran into the room. She saw Sidney fighting one of the swordsmen. The first guest lay dead near the door. The second guest struggled against the wizards while the third guest fought the other swordsman. Immediately, she decided what to do.

She ran over and stabbed the man who fought Sidney. She drew her powers and struck the wizards while running over to stab the other swordsman. The male wizard fell and was stabbed by the second guest. The female wizard knew she could not defeat her so to Zelia's amazement, the woman stabbed herself with a horn shaped dagger refusing to be captured alive!

*

An hour later, after the house was cleaned, the bodies disposed of, and all wounds healed, Zelia and Sidney sat talking. His warlock friend is sleeping. The third guest had been fatally wounded and could not be saved. Zelia had tried but she was not strong enough.

Although Sidney is convinced, she is a member of the Order of the Flame, she refuses to admit it. She thought about how he meets several criteria for recruitment; he stands against their enemies on his own, he is motivated by revenge, the Fellowship killed his father, and most importantly he is a marked enemy of the Fellowship.

After he had told her all he knew about what was going on, Zelia explained why he was wrong about Peter. She told him that Peter is most likely heavily involved in the power struggle that is going on in the Fellowship. She then told him that the Partisans had nothing to do with the Fellowship.

"The Fellowship started that rumor." She stated.

"Are the Partisans part of the Order?" Sidney asked.

"No. They are allies." She answered.

Sidney nodded before telling her he would not mind joining the Order of the Flame. Her response was simple.

"Be careful what you ask for."

***

Priato sat in the back of a wagon. Along with several bulwarks and a sibling-who is driving the wagon-and four female spies, he is going to Anazi Falls. He had met with them in Jedan to prevent something horrible from happening to them.

With Razial en route to Mohr, he must take more action. He contacted Ulina. She had told the Canopy to patrol the telepathic realm to stop the Harbingers from communicating so easily. He wants to know if she has learned anything new.

"A'ja'Priato." Ulina thought.

He greeted her then asked her what she has learned about the power struggle in the Fellowship. She told him that both factions seem to have accepted the lull in their power struggle.

She told him Gwen of Dax-the former undisputed leader of the Fellowship is still a threat even with Frauter-her right hand being the only one with her.

"She will continue to oppose peace with the Sisterhood." Ulina thought.

"As she should." Priato thought.

Ulina then told him that she had found no trace of the Harbingers in Coilu. Priato sensed that bothered her. He told her the Harbingers are behind what is happening in Coilu. He then told her she must stay in Coilu so she could save Razial when the time came. She was intrigued by what he said but said nothing. Instead, she asked if they should send Razial to Alf-Heim to be trained.

"Not until I have talked with Goraan." He thought.

"We cannot allow Ja'Goraan to influence him." Ulina thought.

She knows Goraan is more than a mentor to Razial. Her concern is Goraan trying to guide Razial down the wrong path. She explained that if Goraan is a Harbinger and Razial obtains Ja'Brahma's daggers things will turn out bad for them.

"Allow me to judge Goraan's reaction to Razial being fated to become the Gideon." Priato thought.

Ulina allowed the matter to end there.

***

Just over a week after their encounter with the elfin wolves, Razial and the others led their horses by their reins along a trail through the densely forested hills of southern Gully.

Ariel had assured Kalvin that Gully dwarfs would not attack them. Kalvin is still not sure. A lot of humans are afraid of Gully dwarfs for good reason. Gully has been the end of many invading armies. It is home to many elves and dwarfs who like to travel the human lands. However, most of the humans who live in Gully are Tuyakan-almost all of them practice Tuya-Kan.

Kalvin is not worried about them. He simply wants to avoid problems with the Gully dwarfs who live in the hills.

Gully dwarfs are shorter than other dwarfs, but they are just as stubborn and in many ways they are meaner. Like their cousins in

Nibel, they have an aversion for riding horses and a love for strong drink. Fierce fighters, their greatest warriors are the jolems, Gully dwarfs born with the ability to pass through and affect soil at will. (They use this ability to build, modify, and or seal the tunnels Gully dwarfs live in.) Kalvin hopes to see a jolem. He asked why they had not come across any fortifications.

"Because Gully dwarfs hate forts." Ariel said.

Their conversation then moved to Tuyakans. Ariel explained there were three tribes of Tuyakans: the Menna, the Gully, and the Denari.

Razial was surprised she knew that. He listened to her tell Kalvin that each tribe was named after a daughter of Tuya and Kan and that most people called Tuyakans today are basically descendants of Menna and or Gully who had stopped practicing Tuya-Kan long ago.

She then told Kalvin how Tuyakans were the first humans to stand with elves and dwarfs against Rakaar. Kalvin asked her why a lot of people believe Tuyakans used to stand with Rakaar.

"That is because of the Tuyakan Betrayal." Ariel said.

She explained how nations evolved from each clan and how some Tuyakans perverted the way of Tuya-Kan betraying those who served Eloh. Her words made Razial wonder if she knew the whole story or if she had left out certain details on purpose.

"What kind of Tuyakan was your mother, Raz?" Kalvin asked.

"My mother was a true Tuyakan. Her mother was Gully, and her father was Menna. They both practiced Tuya-Kan." Razial answered.

Knowing Razial does not want to discuss his mother any further, Alena told Kalvin many bulwarks are Tuyakan and how bulwarks are made. Kalvin was surprised to learn that a keeper gives each bulwark a day's worth of magic that grows with time. The magic is how bulwarks heal faster, sense magic, and eventually become able to wield magic.

"Tell him about the side effect." Razial said.

"It will make you very energetic for days." Alena smiled.

As they continued to walk, the horses became nervous. Razail stopped when he sensed elfin wolves. He cursed himself for allowing Alena's elfin hawks to fly off.

"Tether the horses." He said as he ran off.

With so much foliage, it was difficult for Razial to see far ahead, but he continued at a fast pace. He could sense the wolves trying to avoid whoever was chasing them. Behind him, Alena ran trying to catch up to him. She is angry with him for running off. Behind her Ariel and Kalvin-who had his sword ready, ran side by side.

Kalvin heard Razial fighting before he saw him. He moved around a tree and saw Razial fighting several swordsmen, Ariel exchanging magical strikes with two wizards, Alena striking several other men, while all around them, elfin wolves made themselves visible as they attacked those fighting Razial and the others.

"Behind you, Raz!" Kalvin shouted.

He was not overwhelmed by the fighting. He saw two men trying to sneak up behind Razial, so he did what any friend would do. He ran to engage the men. The men did not hesitate to take him on. He parried two swings as he moved back. An elfin wolf tackled one of the men. The man's throat was ripped open before he hit the ground. Kalvin took advantage of the other man's pause and ran him through. Before he could move on, two other men targeted him. He stood his ground.

An elfin wolf took one of them down. That allowed Kalvin to press the fourth man. They fought until another elfin wolf tackled the man.

Kalvin spun around and saw Razial fighting four men. Razial used the foliage to avoid being surrounded. Razial's skills with a sword and dagger impressed him. He will never tease Razial for choosing a machete style sword again.

"Help Alena and Ariel." Razial said to Kalvin.

Unlike Kavin, he can sense the difference between wizardry, magic, and sorcery. He knows a powerful warlock had joined the fighting.

Alena had been attacked from behind by the warlock, who had even struck a tiring Ariel. Ariel had to deal with the wizards and their swords, or she would have pummeled them. By the time she was ready to finish them, the warlock attacked.

Alena rolled over the grass and staggered to her feet while Kalvin ran behind the warlock. She lashed out at the warlock to distract him. Kalvin brought his sword down across the warlock's neck. The warlock stumbled forward before falling to his knees. Alena looked around and saw the fighting had ended. She saw Razial carrying a wounded elfin wolf. Knowing he wants her to heal the wolf, she said.

"I will have to link with you to heal him."

He told her to heal all the elfin wolves. She agreed. Although he cannot wield his powers, others can link with him to use his powers. It is a rare thing for someone to be born with sorcery. She has no idea why he is one of them.

***

Three weeks after the fight, Razial led the way along the bottom trails of the Axe Peaks-the southernmost mountains of the Great Nibel Range. Alena's pets continue to scout around them. Sometimes, they soar high in the sky, but now they are flying low to better see through the foliage.

Razail thought about how after Kalvin had heard about Araceli and four bulwarks being sent to Mohr to help them Kalvin insisted on being told more. That is why Alena had shared that their foes should not even know they are heading to Mohr. Razial told her there is a high-ranking traitor among their ranks. Kalvin agreed.

After sharing more about what they are doing with Kalvin, Alena told him about Razial being born with sorcery. Razial disliked that but did not make an issue out of it.

Traveling with the six elfin wolves they had saved, made Kalvin wonder if it was because Razial was born with sorcery. He does not understand why Razial is unable to wield his powers yet but to him it explains why elfin animals are close to Razial.

A group of elfin wolves approached them. Razial decided to go hunting with them. He told the others to rest. He grabbed his bow and a quiver of arrows. He put an arm around Alena and kissed her on her forehead. She playfully pushed him away.

With the sun high in the sky, the air is still cool. Although it is the beginning of summer, it feels like early spring in northern Anazi. Alena told him to hurry back then asked.

"Do you think Scar will discuss his name?"

They had named the alpha male Scar because of the large scar on his neck and shoulder. Alena named his mate She-Scar because she has a similar scar. Neither likes having a name, but they have accepted them.

"Not unless I call out to him." Razial winked.

As he walked off, the other wolves informed him and Alena that there are other elves and dwarfs in the area. Alena told Ariel and Kalvin the Partisans must be close by.

***

The next day, after the other packs had left, Alena's pets warned her that a group approached. She and the others finished getting ready to leave until a dwarf wobbled toward them. He asked who they were. Alena explained who they are without saying they are siblings. The dwarf read between the lines. He told them the Partisans had fought a major battle and that many of them needed to be healed.

"Fogi Red was captured during the battle." the dwarf said.

Razial read about Fogi Red, the king of the mountain dwarfs. He read Fogi Red lives among the Partisans because the king of the lowland dwarfs is trying to assassinate him. According to Goraan, Fogi Red is a member of the Order of the Flame.

"Take us to your camp" Ariel said with authority.

Kalvin watched as the dwarf led them to other Partisans. A few of them are elves. A lot of them are dwarfs, but most of them are humans. He noticed no dwarf was riding a horse. Still, they had no problem keeping up even after they picked up the pace.

Before, he used to think dwarfs could run the dwarf-run because of magic. A dwarf in the city of Anazi had explained that dwarfs are born with the ability to run the dwarf-run.

"Humans are born with height and the ability to reproduce quickly, but they live short lives. Elves are born with power, immortality, wisdom, and patience. Dwarfs are born with strength, great craftmanship, and the dwarf-run." The old dwarf had said to Kalvin.

Watching the dwarfs run, Kalvin realized the dwarf had forgotten to mention that dwarfs are also born with long lives. Thinking about that made him think about his father because his father had been present when he had talked with the old dwarf. His father would be proud if he knew what Kalvin was doing with Alena and the others.

When they reached the Partisans' camp, an elf named Raal came to greet them. Bandaged from head to waist, Raal explained that he wants to lead a full-scale assault against Mohr so he could free Fogi Red.

"Do that and they will know how important Fogi Red is." Razial said.

Raal did not argue. He understands Razial's point. Together, they came up with a plan to free Fogi Red. Raal had talked with

Razial as if he is a member of the Order of the Flame. He did not realize his mistake until Razial corrected him but that was after they had finished making their plan.

Ariel and Alena joined them after they finished healing the wounded Partisans. Kalvin was surprised by the fact neither voiced any disagreement with the plan Razial and Raal had made.

The plan is simple. Razial, Kalvin, and Alena will go to Mohr while Ariel and Raal stay with the Partisans to coordinate their actions with what is going on inside Mohr.

*

Later that night, Razial, Alena, Kalvin, and Scar's pack entered Mohr's eastern gates. (To avoid suspicion, they had ridden around Mohr then doubled back.) The city is still abuzz with talk of the battle against the Partisans. Razial told Alena to take Kalvin and five of the elfin wolves to meet with Zelia while he goes to meet with the city's contractor. Alena did not argue because the elfin wolves cannot remain invisible for too much longer.

Razial had a difficult time explaining domestication to Scar because in the wild other animals can sense when a wolf is on the hunt. They are cautious but not skittish like the animals that sensed him even though he is cloaked to non-sorcerers.

When Razial reached the smith shop, he tethered his horse and held the door open so Scar could enter.

"Hey you! Close the door. I'm losing heat." A tall blacksmith shouted.

Razial watched him hammer a fiery piece of steel. He is not sure if the man is the contractor's son or nephew because both act as his apprentice.

"You are much too small to stare at me like that." The man said.

Razial does not seem like a threat to him. He took notice of how the man stands and noticed the man has no sense of balance. Scar projected that he is uncomfortable and dislikes the man's emotions.

"Tell your boss that a messenger from Fulancia has arrived." Razial said firmly.

He almost laughed when the man's expression changed. All his bravado was gone. He stumbled to the back room leaving Razial and an agitated Scar alone. The fires and heat bothered Scar. Razial told him they were going to leave soon.

"Avatar." The contractor said.

He moved across the shop to bar the front door. Razial could see it in his eyes that he had heard about how he had been greeted by the other man.

"My nephew is a bit testy-"

"His size will be his downfall." Razial said to cut him off.

The contractor nodded in agreement. Razial told him to forget about what had happened. The contractor nodded before telling him all that was happening in Mohr. Razial was surprised to hear several other assassins are in Mohr including Vishnu the Weapon of Death.

"Pam from the Sisterhood hired the Weapon to do the opposite of your contract." The contractor said.

He then told Razial that the Children of Doh have put a standard twenty-coin contract on Kalvin. Razail was angry with himself. He had waited too long to settle things for Kalvin. Vishnu is above standard open contracts, but he would act against Kalvin to spite Razial. He had been in Vin when Razial and Kalvin were there. He knew Razial liked Kalvin and since he and Razial cannot fight he will take out his anger with Razial on Kalvin.

Razial thanked the contractor, then exited the shop. Scar is going to lead him to the others.

*

Alena, Kalvin, and Zelia sat around a table. It did not take Alena long to find Zelia after she had met with the Order of the Flame's spies in Mohr. Upon her arrival, Zelia informed her about Sidney and the change in plans. She told Alena that Ulina had contacted her and said they must free Fogi Red and keep him alive and well.

The elfin wolves entered the room and made themselves visible while thinking to Alena that two men are approaching the house. She told this to Zelia who stood and moved to the door. She is expecting Sidney and his friend.

A moment later, Sidney called out to Zelia. She opened the door, then introduced Sidney and his friend to Alena and Kalvin. Alena stared at Sidney. His blue eyes seem cold. He is taller than Kalvin but not tall for a Coiluan. He is big but not muscular. She has no doubt he can hold his own in a fight. They moved back to the table. Sidney told them an army had been sent to engage the Partisans. The former king has decided to push the Partisans as far back as he can. Sidney then revealed Fogi Red is being held in the dungeon's lowest cells being fed slop once a day. Before he could say more, the elfin wolves exited the room. They are happy but Sidney and his friend do not know that.

"The wolves are with us!" Alena said when the warlock drew his powers.

A moment later, Razial and Scar entered the house. Speaking in elvish, he told her about the contract on Kalvin. He told her Vishnu is in Mohr, so she must be vigilant around Kalvin. He then switched to common asking if the fiancée was in Mohr.

"She is due to arrive soon." Zelia said in elvish.

She opened the back door so Scar could go eat and drink. (She had put out food and water for the other elfin wolves when they arrived.

"I am not a lost Menna Ja'Razial." She said with a grin.

She can tell by the way he looked at her he knew that. Still, she wanted him to know she truly practiced Tuya-Kan and does not simply descend from the Menna tribe.

"You could have been a lost Gully or Denari." Razial said in elvish.

"Gully? Maybe. Very few Denari have our appearance." Zelia said.

By looking at her, Razial could see she is most likely Menna. Her cinnamon skin is smooth. She has long wavy brown hair and cat-like hazel eyes. He finds her attractive and he knows many other men do as well.

They informed him about what Sidney had told them. He told Alena to send her hawks to warn Ariel saying she and Zelia should contact the keepers. He told Sidney he needed a tour of the palace. Sidney said that would not be a problem. After that, Razial decided to tell Kalvin about the contract on him.

***

Days later, Razial was made Paul's personal guard. He had impressed Paul by defeating three guards at once inside a hallway. The fiancée had arrived along with a Danouan priestess which is strange, but no one challenged the fiancée's choice of maidens.

Reports about the battles fought between the Mohran and imperial armies against the Partisans have been mixed. Both sides suffered heavy losses, but the Partisans still held. The fiancée is bothered by the reports. She distrusts Razial and wants Fogi Red's head cut off on her wedding day. None of that bothers Razial. His mind is on having to stay because the keepers want the former king of Mohr dead. He has to stay in Mohr longer than he wanted to. He had passed the time by staying close to Vishnu, who had been in the palace as much as Razial had.

"You cannot be in two places at the same time. I will kill Kalvin or Paul." Vishnu had said.

Razial pushed the thought out of his head. He had finally managed to get Zelia alone with Paul so she could find out how Paul had been bewitched. He opened the door to the small room he had left Paul in. He let Zelia enter first then closed the door while he stood guard. No one will pass until Zelia exits with the hood to her black burnoose drawn over her head.

Kalvin and Alena returned to Sidney's house. Alena's hawks had communicated that Ariel had been captured during the last battle. With Araceli due to arrive any day, which was not the kind of news that Alena wanted to hear.

A noise from the back of the house drew their attention. Kalvin's hand went to his sword's hilt. With Scar's pack out searching for a scent of Ariel, no one should be in the house. Alena moved with confidence as she drew her powers. She sensed Sidney's friend draw his powers as he called out to Zelia then to her. She responded as she released her powers.

"Now is not the time to be creeping around." Kalvin said.

"I just chased two men out of the house." The warlock said.

Alena's attention went to the door because she heard a knock. She asked who was knocking. No one replied. She sensed three individuals draw their powers-a warlock and two wizards. She drew her powers and told Kalvin to draw his sword. Sidney's friend drew his powers just before the door splintered open. The two wizards stormed into the house with their swords in front of them. Alena and Sidney's friend struck them stopping them and knocking them back. That is when Vishnu entered the house lashing out accurately. He targeted Sidney's friend, then Kalvin until Alena engaged him. The two of them know each other well. He had watched her grow up. Before she decided to join the Order of the Flame, they used to be friends. He could seriously hurt her, but she can sense he does not want to-not out of fear but respect. Each member of the Hilt likes her. Although he is well within his rights to harm her, he knows the Hilt would look down upon him for doing so.

"Finish the target." Vishnu said.

With control over limited sorcery, he is stronger than Alena. He is simply keeping her busy while his apprentices go after Kalvin. The problem is the warlock with them is keeping Kalvin alive. Having no reason to hold back, Vishnu decided to kill him.

He struck the man and charged him. He sensed Alena fighting his apprentices, but he stayed focused on his target. He quickly overwhelmed the man with ease then ran him through before cutting his throat open so he could bleed out.

"Run Kalvin." Alena ordered.

Kalvin did not listen. Breathing hard and fast as he backed up so he could reset, he saw Vishnu kill Sidney's friend. Wounded and tired, he feels hopeless. The other two assassins are coming for him. Suddenly, a dagger slammed into one of the assassins' hands. Zelia struck Vishnu repeatedly while Razial stopped the other man from reaching Kalvin. They fought like experts. Their swords rattled, but it was a kick to the chest that ended the fight.

"That is enough!" Razial shouted.

Zelia refused to stop. She is angry. Kalvin is wounded, Alena is hurt, and Sidney's friend is dead. She wants to kill Vishnu.

"Zelia." Alena said.

Unlike Zelia, she understands the severity of the situation. Razial has just made a choice that has put him in grave danger!

*

Hours later, Razial had returned to the palace and Alena had explained to the others-including Araceli, who had arrived with the bulwarks escorting her, why Razial had to stop Zelia from attacking Vishnu. They had all been shocked to discover that it was Vishnu who had attacked Kalvin and Alena. Zelia was impressed by how much respect Vishnu had shown Alena.

After that had settled in, Alena told the others about Ariel being captured. That saddened Kalvin and Araceli, but Zelia asked to hear more about Razial's predicament.

"So, why are you worried about Razial saving Kalvin from his assassin brethren?" Zelia asked Alena.

"Because no Society member is to act against another member to prevent an assassination of a contracted target. The Society shall hunt him for this violation." Alena replied.

"But why?" Zelia frowned. "He did not harm this, Vishnu."

Alena sighed to remain calm before saying.

"When an assassin breaks the wrong law, that assassin must return to Fulancia for one day. The Society informs all of its members said assassin has been unwelcomed in Fulancia for three years. Every member who wants to hunt the assassin has to get a red sash and the hunt begins the day after the marked assassin has left Fulancia."

After her explanation, the others realized the danger Razial had put himself in. Kalvin feels guilty. Araceli noticed this and quickly scolded him saying.

"You are no more at fault for Razial's choice as I am for my sister's capture. We have a task to complete. We cannot afford to feel guilty."

***

Beulah and the Master were linked telepathically. He praised her for getting Pam to foolishly put the contract on Paul. He then explained that Razial will be the Magi's problem, but Beulah has reservations about freeing all three magi at once. The Master told her the longer Alf-Heim keeps the elves out of this Champions' War the more likely the Order of the Flame will succeed. He is out to force them to take bold actions since he is so far ahead of them. She asked him about his plans to free the prisoners he wanted to free.

"I will do that soon. The traitors inside the Order of the Flame are making this easy." The Master thought.

He has no idea who the traitors are, but he intends to use them until he cannot. He told Beulah to continue with the plans in Coilu and that he was close to success in Danou. He will use the Theocracy whose clergy are great manipulators.

Little do they know that long ago he falsified a prophecy about elves. They are waiting for a group of elves who will stand against Alf-Heim. At present, many of them believe this is about the elves who live in the Tetra Mountains, but they are wrong.

Sensing others drawing close to them, they ended their connection.

CHAPTER 3

THE HUNT

Dressed formally like a high-ranking soldier, Razial walked out of the dance hall. He dislikes the red suede jacket he was forced to wear. Paul had insisted his men wear red formal jackets and black pants. He had also tried to convince Razial to switch swords, but Razial told him the machete style sword is better than the cutlass, rapier, long sword, and the broadsword. Paul disagreed but he accepted Razial's decision.

On his way out of the hall, he had made eye contact with Sidney, who had asked why he is so sure Vishnu will try to kill Paul on his wedding day. As expected, the wedding ended without any problems. Nothing had happened during the early dances. However, Paul and his bride had gone off to be alone. Razial told Sidney to watch the priestess while he goes to guard Paul.

"I am sure of two things." Razial had said to Sidney before leaving the hall. "First, the bride and priestess will begin to plan Paul's downfall. Second, Paul will have to survive an assassination attempt tonight."

His words had made Sidney frown. Unlike Sidney, he knows the Fellowship and the Sisterhood did not put Paul under a spell and gets one of their agents to marry Paul to let Paul stay alive and rule. The sooner Paul is dead, the sooner they can forward their cause. It does not matter to Razial that the Fellowship is divided over the issue of peace with the Sisterhood, but he is sure the Hilt has plans to deal with them if they do make peace. The Society cannot allow them to control all the lands of Ocia and Coilu.

Thinking about this as he climbed the stairs, his mind went to the plan that Alena and Araceli made to help him escape Mohr with Paul. Zelia found out the medallion Paul wears is how their enemies put Paul under a spell. They must take him to Anazi Falls so the keepers can remove the medallion without Paul dying.

Razial does not mind kidnapping Paul or saving Fogi Red, but he dislikes the plan that Alena and Araceli made. They have ordered Raal to attack the city in the morning when Fogi Red is scheduled to be executed. He would rather kill his target, take Paul while Sidney frees Fogi Red, and they all escape through the secret passage that leads out of Mohr.

As he neared Paul's chambers, he crept to the door. He put his ear to the door and listened. He heard Paul's wife giggle. He could smell the wine they had obviously spilled on the floor. His pulse quickened when he heard someone else walking through the chambers. He drew his sword and kicked open the door. Paul's wife gasped acting as if she was afraid. She stood completely naked at the back end of the room. Her large breasts heaved in excitement. She smiled at him. He thought about killing her then and there.

"What are you doing?" Paul demanded.

He stood trying to pull up his pants. His shirt is on the floor with his bride's dress-both stained with wine. With several candles burning, the room is still not well lit.

Razial ignored Paul's questioning eyes. Vishnu had entered the room. Had Paul made it to the back room, he would be dead.

"I said. What are" Paul stopped when he noticed Vishnu.

Vishnu's shoulder length black hair is pulled back as usual. His full beard matches his hair and is always well kept. Taller than Razial, he stands above medium height. His dark blue eyes seem to turn colors when he is angry. With his long sword held before him, he stared menacingly at Razial. They charged each other. Their swords crashed repeatedly.

"Get back Paul." Razial warned.

He and Vishnu put on a masterful display of swordsmanship. They moved with precision. Paul stood dumbfounded. He had never seen such a display of skill, speed, and precision before.

"Help him." Paul's wife said.

Razial took note she wants to play her role to the end. Vishnu spun around and in one fluid motion threw a dagger at Paul. Razial had no choice. When he saw what Vishnu was about to do, he prepared to throw his own sword.

Paul stood frozen in fear as the dagger tumbled toward him. He was amazed to see it deflected by Razial's sword.

While Paul felt flushed with relief, Razial struggled to keep Vishnu at bay. Using two daggers, he fought fiercely. Guards could be heard racing toward the chambers. To Razial's dismay, Vishnu's apprentices ran up behind the guards. It only took several moments for the two assassins to finish the guards but that was enough time for more guards to arrive. That angered Vishnu. He drew his powers and knocked Razial down with a magical strike. He had wanted to defeat Razial without using his powers. That is what cost him this opportunity to kill Paul. He ran away angry.

"Go after the assassins!" She snapped at him.

"My job is to protect Paul. Not leave his side during danger." Razial growled.

***

The next afternoon, Paul's wife argued for Razial to be punished for being insolent. Sidney could sense Paul trying to resist her. The priestess, who is never far from Paul's wife, agreed with her. It took all of Sidney's patience to remain silent. He could not believe they would dare think about having Razial imprisoned just after an attempt on Paul's life. He wants to shout but so long as they believe he is not part of Razial's plans the better it is for him because he can continue to learn about their plans.

"Very well," Paul sighed. "One week in the dungeon should rid him of his insolence."

His wife liked hearing that. The priestess nodded. Dressed in her white wimple and white gown, Sidney has no idea how she appears without her veil. All he knows about her is that she is tall. Her voice is strong, and she always speaks with confidence.

"We should go with Sidney to arrest him now. To make sure all goes well." The priestess said.

Paul nodded. He told Sidney he wants six guards to go with them to escort Razial to the dungeon. Sidney did not respond. He knows why Paul wants so many guards.

*

Zelia sat talking with Razial. No one pays attention to her visiting with Razial when he has free time. They had met up after he had checked the palace. When they reached his room, he told her he wanted to change Araceli's plan. They began discussing the pros and cons of Araceli's plan.

While they talked, they heard a group approaching his room. He gestured for her to answer the door. At first, she did not move, but she realized that for appearance's sake she has to answer the door because she is a servant, and he is Paul's guard.

Sidney led the group into Razial's room. He was not surprised to see Zelia open the door. Paul's wife was.

"Watch your servant, Sidney, or she will be with child soon." Paul's wife said.

Zelia did not respond. She kept her head low and her eyes down. She listened while Paul explained that Razial had to sit in the dungeon for a week. She knows her enemies are behind this. She remained quiet while Razial told Paul he had put himself in more danger. She does not understand how he can be so calm about this. He is acting as if he is in total control.

"He has other guards." Paul's wife spat.

Razial ignored her. He told Paul he was ready to serve his sentence. Zelia looked at him. He winked at her. She let the guards take him without saying anything.

*

Kalvin and the four bulwarks who had arrived with Araceli had missed the fighting with Vishnu because they had been made dungeon guards so they could look after Fogi Red. After being told Paul had pushed back Fogi Red's execution, Kalvin does not expect anything to happen until they act to free Fogi Red, kill Paul's wife, and kidnap Paul.

Until Mohr, Kalvin had never been inside a dungeon. It is just like all the stories he has heard. It is poorly lit and has many foul odors that mix and make the air taste bad. The torches flicker and cause strange shadows. The walls are stained, and he does not understand why the guards never clean them.

"Is there any more mead?" Fogi Red asked.

Kalvin stood in front of his cell. He had delivered food and drink to the other prisoners not just the Partisans. That kept the other prisoners quiet.

Looking down at Fogi Red, Kalvin thought about how even in the dimly lit dungeon his red hair and beard appear bright. His frizzy beard seems more unkempt than usual.

"That is all for tonight." He spoke. Then, he added. "Besides, you do not want to wake up with a hangover."

Fogi Red smirked at him. They have made fast friends.

"I am a dwarf. I do not wake up with hangovers." Fogi Red said.

Before Kalvin could respond, a bulwark whistled to signal others had entered the dungeon. All the prisoners quickly hid the extra food Kalvin had given them. Kalvin walked the tier to make sure there were no signs of any of the weapons he had given them.

By the time he returned to Fogi Red's cell, the real guards were leading a bound and shackled Razial to the tier. He was shocked to see this. The captain told him to put Razial in a cell with another prisoner.

"It does not matter which cell." The captain added.

Kalvin led Razial into Fogi Red's cell. The captain and the other guards left as soon as Kalvin had locked the door. He asked Razial if he wanted out of the cell.

"No. Tell the others to stick to the plan. I will kill my target at the first sound of fighting." Razial said confidently.

"You make it sound easy." Kalvin said.

Razial winked, then he introduced himself to Fogi Red, who seemed unaffected by all this.

The two of them began to talk. Razial discovered Fogi Red is just as confident as he is. They talked until it was time to rest.

The next morning, Alena and Araceli watched the elfin hawks soar over the city. The Partisans have arrived and there is no sign of danger. Alena and Araceli walked toward the western gates. Their plan is simple. They must keep the gates open and make sure archers do not line up along the western wall's battlement. The Partisans do not have to hold the streets. This is a simple raid. Still, Alena knows they will suffer heavy losses.

"Are you ready?" Araceli asked.

Alena can sense her anger. In Araceli's mind her sister is being tortured somewhere near Mohr. Alena could not change her mind. Since her arrival, Alena has only seen her smile once and that is when she heard about Razial allowing himself to be put in the dungeon so their plan could succeed.

"I will deal with the archers." Alena said.

She inhaled slowly as she drew her powers and made her way to the stairs that led to the top of the wall. Araceli drew her powers and walked toward the guards who man the gates. She will kill them all. She cannot afford to show any mercy.

*

Raal sensed when Alena and Araceli drew their powers. Along with the rest of the Partisans with him, he had crept to the edge of the woodland that surrounds the city. To confuse the Mohrans, he sent several units to charge from the east, south, and north.

Looking at the city, he took in the scene. The sun is at its noon peak. It is warm and will get warmer. Thin white clouds are scattered across the sky. Alena's elfin hawks dove signaling for him to charge. He kicked his horse to a charge. He watched as the gates opened. The dwarfs among his ranks sped ahead. They will get their fill of blood.

*

Zelia stood behind Sidney, who stood next to Paul. On the opposite side of Paul, is his wife and her priestess. All of them are on the balcony that overlooks the courtyard. Paul had

called for Fogi Red and the others to be executed. Zelia knows his wife and her priestess can sense the magical strikes near the western gates. She almost smiled at them as they struggled to remain stoic. The priestess seems to know she is more than a simple servant.

"I shall see to the dwarf." The priestess said.

A second after she entered the palace, the alarm bells rang. Paul and his wife looked around. The people who had gathered to see the executions became nervous.

"We should go inside." Paul's wife said.

"The others can, but you have to get by me." Razial said.

His voice was cold. He stepped out onto the balcony sword in hand. Paul's wife drew her powers. Zelia drew hers. Sidney and the two bulwarks who followed Razial on to the balcony attacked the guards who tried to act against Razial. Zelia gasped when Razial was struck by a magical blow. Still, he charged his target.

"Get Paul out of here." Razial said to Zelia.

She struck Paul knocking him unconscious. Sidney picked him up and they ran off. Razial knows that Zelia wanted to help him, but he had given her a look to signal that it is best for her to head to the rendezvous.

Fighting his target, he looked into her eyes. She seems confused by the fact he can sustain her powers. She is a witch, but she is not strong enough to really harm him. He used his sword to put her out of her misery, cutting her throat open before he drove his sword into her head. His mind then moved to helping Kalvin and the others.

*

Fogi Red fought with impressive power. Like most dwarfs his weapon of choice is an ax. Along with Kalvin and two bulwarks, he led the prisoners through the palace. The freed prisoners made him think of an old saying.

"In battle, desperate people fight with great focus or with reckless abandon-ready to die fighting."

The prisoners proved this to be true. They pressed the palace guards who had recovered from the initial surprise of the attack. The echoes through the hallways make the fighting seem more chaotic than it is. Kalvin threw his helmet at a guard forcing him back. With fighting all around, the guards simply fell back to hold all the palace's doors so no one could escape.

"We have to get out while the others are still fighting." Fogi Red growled.

Kalvin could not agree more. He ducked a swing from his opponent then kicked him in his chest. He saw two enemies fall from ax inflicted wounds. All around him, Partisans fought with discipline. They methodically pressed ahead. From a connecting hallway a group of freed prisoners joined them. They had obviously been turned back after trying to find their own way out. The guards could not hold. Then, the priestess joined the fighting.

"The dwarf is mine." The priestess said.

With powerful bursts of magic, she struck all near Fogi Red. It did not matter if they were friend or foe. Her gown is covered with blood. She had fought her way to this area. The Master had told her to capture Fogi Red if she could. She does not want him harmed or killed accidentally. She struck all in her path until Kalvin crashed against her with his shield.

"Damn you, thief!" She cursed.

She struck Kalvin causing him to writhe in pain. He saw her lift Fogi Red into the air and a sense of panic filled him. He knows Fogi Red is important. Struggling to his feet, he saw two daggers tumble past him. The priestess was forced to deflect them. She spun around and was forced to deal with Razial.

"The elfin wolves are waiting Kalvin. Get them out of the palace!" Razial said excitedly.

His sword cut across the priestess' magically shielded hands. That allowed two Partisans to drag Fogi Red to safety. The palace's foyer is littered with bodies. The prisoners' desperation drove them to push forward. The guards could hold the front doors no longer. Kalvin, Fogi Red, and others reached the doors. Razial saw them. As he prepared to try to finish the priestess who is stronger than he had expected, he was rocked by a magical blow. The priestess spun in the air. While she did, her gown became a bright red cowl. He swung his sword at her.

"Run Raz!" Kalvin shouted.

Fogi Red looked up at him wondering why he had shouted. The courtyard is bright. The sunlight made his eyes water. Squinting, he saw the guards trying to regroup to close the courtyard. Some Mohrans joined the guards. When they tried to charge, Scar's pack revealed themselves and attacked. The people and the guards panicked.

"Come on. We have to reach the others." Fogi Red said.

Razial had to abandon his fight against the Harbinger. He stumbled out of the palace after stragglers from the dungeon attacked the Harbinger. Some of the prisoners paid severely for attacking the Harbinger while others followed Razial out of the palace. He does not know why the Harbinger tried to capture him and Fogi Red, but it does not concern him for now. He knows enough about the Harbingers to know they do not act lightly. He began thinking about his contract. Taking on the Fellowship and the Sisterhood is an acceptable challenge. Taking on the Harbingers requires more information.

*

The fighting inside Mohr turned against the Partisans. Raal had all their magicians follow the dwarfs while he had set up several defensive formations around the gates. He held while Alena and Araceli led a group to reach Fogi Red's group. The problem is the Mohrans are regrouping, and the Partisan magicians are tiring.

"Where is Razial?" Alena asked Kalvin.

"He told us to make the rendezvous." Kalvin replied.

Alena stopped running and looked around. Due to her lack of height, she could not see very well. She spun toward Araceli who said she saw Razial running toward them.

"Arrows!" Araceli snapped lashing out with her powers.

Alena joined her in deflecting the arrows. Archers had lined up on the rooftops of the buildings along the streets to the western gates. Walking more than running, Alena saw an arrow slam into an archer just before her pets drove their talons into two other archers' necks. The sound of horses charging toward the gates drew her attention. She thought to Scar and asked him to deal with the calvary riding toward the gates. Another arrow slammed into an archer.

"Razial." Alena thought.

She and Araceli linked their powers. They covered Fogi Red and the dwarfs charging the calvary. She is no longer worried about Razial because she saw him running through the street.

Razial saw the former king of Mohr trying to cut down Fogi Red, so he stopped running and took aim. The prisoners who ran with him kept running. They stayed close to the buildings to avoid being targeted by the archers. He heard arrows whistling toward him. His body tensed in anticipation of being struck by an arrow. He fired his arrow just before the elfin hawks shrieked as they snatched the arrows headed for him. They flew past him as he stood watching his arrow fly across the distance between him and the former king of Mohr. The former king raised his sword to strike Fogi Red just before the arrow slammed into his back knocking him off his horse. Razial did not see Raal kill the former king. He mounted a horse then made sure Alena, Kalvin, and the others were safe before riding hard and fast toward the gates. He made eye contact with Raal and told him to tell Alena he is going to meet with the others who have Paul. He smelled the oil that Raal had poured around the gates. He heard Raal call for a retreat. He smiled mentally when he heard the flames spring to life so the Mohrans could not give chase while the Partisans and others retreated.

*

Zelia had used her powers to keep Paul unconscious. Sidney had tied his hands and legs before carrying him off. With two bulwarks helping him they had made good time.

Just over a mile long, the passage is nothing more than a dark damp and hard packed underground tunnel after one passes the paved portion.

As they drew near the end of the passage, Zelia could smell blood. She slowed her breathing so she could remain calm. She whispered to the others that something was wrong. The bulwarks handed Paul to Sidney then drew their swords. She kept her torch in front of her. She squinted so dirt would not get in her eyes as she turned sideways to exit the tunnel.

She wondered how the battle was going or how it went. The sunlight burned her eyes. The exit is near a small hill with boulders hiding it. She rubbed her eyes and gasped.

"You again?!"

Sidney heard Zelia say. He laid Paul on the ground. He heard swords crashing so he drew his sword and ran to join the others. He saw several bodies on the ground. He assumed they had been killed while waiting for him and the others. Breathing hard and fast, he threw his torch at a man fighting one of the bulwarks. He charged the man who spun to face him. The man is extremely skilled. Sidney was hard-pressed to hold his ground against him. Moving backwards, he saw the other bulwark fighting a skilled fighter while the bulwark he had helped tried to help Zelia against Vishnu. That is when he realized they are fighting the exact same men who had killed his friend when they tried to assassinate Kalvin. That made him angry. He became flushed with adrenaline. He pressed his opponent-a mistake. The man parried his thrusts with a backhanded swing then cut him across his stomach.

"Find the prince and kill him. These bulwarks are worth nothing to us." Vishnu said. "Enough of this!"

He hit Zelia across her face, but she fought back. He heard a rider approaching. He knew whoever it was, was there to help his rivals.

"Stand down!" Razial shouted.

Vishnu ignored him, then he heard the elfin wolves growl. He began to think how when the Partisan charged the city, he knew Razial would use the secret passage to get Paul out of the city.

He had killed the men who had been waiting near the end of the passage. Everything had gone as he had expected until Razial's arrived with the elfin wolves. He had heard Razial riding but not the elfin wolves with him.

"Do not make me join the fighting." Razial threatened.

Vishnu surveyed the scene. The elfin wolves were ready to fight even though several were wounded. Sidney appeared ready to collapse and the bulwarks need to be healed. Still, Paul is too far from Vishnu for him to keep fighting. The price would be too high. He told his apprentices to step back. Razial told Zelia to stand down so they could leave in peace. Unlike the last time she did not argue.

"I shall see you in Fulancia." Vishnu led his apprentices away.

Razial ignored him. He told the others to get Paul because the former Mohran king was dead and the Mohrans wanted blood.

***

Days later, Tu'ani and Lela walked through the palace's garden. It is a typical hot summer day. The sun is high in the sky warming the land. Hundreds of flowers are in bloom. Tu'ani noticed this while she and Lela talked about how they must stop the Harbingers.

After Ariel and Alena had explained what had happened in Mohr, no one doubted Priato anymore. Having to trust an assassin makes many in the Order of the Flame nervous. Ja'Brahma's daggers finding their way to Razial causes great concern.

"Fate shall return the daggers when the champion's enemies are close to being freed."

The prophecy is clear. It means the Magi are close to being freed! The Order of the Flame is too far behind whatever game the Harbingers are playing. The keepers-all three of them, had sent two jolems to guide and guard Razial. Things have taken a serious turn, and they must find a way to stop the Magi from being freed.

"All of this and we still have to stop Ja'Razial from walking the path of Ja'Brahma." Lela sighed.

"And the hunt shall make things more difficult." Tu'ani added. "We must change the tide of this Champions' War."

***

Three weeks after the battle in Mohr, Razail, Kalvin, Alena, and the others rode along the hills that mark the border between Gully and the Axe Peaks. Fogi Red and Raal had been told to ride to Anazi Falls with them. That intrigued Alena, Ariel, and Zelia, who intends to have Sidney embraced as a bulwark. The three of them had tried to figure out why the keepers want Fogi Red in Anazi Falls but came up with nothing. It was plain to see that Fogi

Red does not want to go to Anazi Falls. For days, he ranted about having to go to Anazi. He did not give the siblings any problems until they asked him to ride a horse.

Alena and the other siblings had been informed that actions had been taken to make it seem as if the former king of Mohr was behind the assassination attempt on Paul and that Paul's wife had been part of the plot. The decision to have Razial arrested will be used against the dead wife.

The keepers had also informed them that Paul's father-the emperor had died. Several factions have formed. The city of Bassar has declared that it shall support Paul until he is proven dead.

With so much going on, Araceli was surprised by Bassar's action. She told Paul about all that was going on throughout Coilu. Riding in a cart with Fogi Red, Raal, and Sidney, Paul made the mistake of accusing Araceli of standing with the Fellowship. She made sure he did not do that again.

Razial found no advantage in knowing any of this. Before leaving Partisan controlled land, he had sent a message to the contractor informing him about the Harbinger and telling him to terminate the contract on Kalvin. He knows the Hilt will approve his request, but it will cost him a lot. He also knows Goraan will be extremely interested in the news about the Harbinger, especially because the Harbinger had tried to capture him.

"What are you thinking about?" Alena asked.

She rode to his left. They are riding at the rear of the procession. Her pets are flying above them, and Scar's pack is off hunting. The weather is warm and as expected the weather is growing warmer as they travel farther south.

They had argued earlier after he had told her he was going to ride to Fulancia when the jolems joined them. She knows what fate awaits an assassin who tries to avoid a hunt. She accepted his decision, but still disagrees with it.

"The Harbingers and how Goraan will respond." Razial said to answer her question.

"I would not doubt it if they have not already sent an apology to Fulancia." Alena said playfully.

"Doubtful. To the Harbingers I am a member of the Order of the Flame." He responded.

"And when they find out that you are an assassin?"

He stared into her narrow eyes. They smiled at each other. He told her the Harbingers would most likely stop trying to capture him when they find out he is a member of the Society.

"Sometimes, being an assassin has its benefits." He grinned.

Alena agreed. She looked around. Everything is green. She began to wonder how homesick Fogi Red was. As the son of the former king-Fogi Black, Fogi Red is the true king of Nibel, but his uncle-Lodi Gold, took the throne refusing to give it up saying Fogi Red was an elf puppet.

With so much mystery surrounding Fogi Black's death, tension between the dwarf clans rose quickly and civil war erupted. Most of the lowland clans sided with Lodi Gold while most of the mountain clans sided with Fogi Red. For fifty years they battled to a standstill until a peace was reached. After that, they tried to outmaneuver each other for decades. Then, another wave of bloody battles erupted. The second wave lasted another fifty years. The fighting only stopped for two reasons:

Nibel's population had suffered greatly, and Lodi Gold was winning!

"Do you think your leaders have finally decided to end the conflict in Nibel?" Razial asked.

His question brought her back to the present. She turned to look at him wondering if he knew what she was thinking about. She told him she did not know. Then, she began wondering why he was so important to her order.

***

The Master remained in the telepathic realm after the other Harbingers ended their connections. He had contacted four other Harbingers. He told them to meet him in Winnin. He had sensed his rivals' presence and had no doubt they had heard his message to the others. However, they do not have any way to stop him. They have few spies in the Gnor valley and none who can match him.

"You play a dangerous game." Priato thought.

Of the members of the Order of the Flame, only Priato could match him.

"You are moves behind A'Priato. Like always." He thought back.

"True. But I am getting closer." Priato replied.

That made the Master smile mentally. He and Priato have been at odds for many generations. They would never face each other in battle, but they have schemed and plotted to stop each other since the first Champions' War. At times, they have helped each other, but their positions are clear. He wants to achieve his goal and Priato is out to stop him.

"Until our paths cross again." The Master thought, ending their connection.

***

Kalvin sat with his back against a tree. He and the others had camped close to the trail. They had eaten lunch and are enjoying a short rest. The sun is still high in the sky. The summer heat in central Gully is not noteworthy, but it is hot. He no longer feels like a student with Sidney around. It is Sidney's turn to ask a lot of questions and learn what he can about what is going on. Still, Alena had told Kalvin that he must watch what he says around Sidney because he has not been accepted into the Order of the Flame, yet.

"Not everyone can be trusted like we trust you." Alena had said days earlier.

Zelia is puzzled by how Alena and Araceli treat him. Although she has convinced Alena and Araceli to vouch for Sidney, Zelia herself keeps Sidney in the dark about a lot of things.

As for Fogi Red and Raal, they are another story. They are members of the Order of the Flame. Fogi Red openly told his story, but he kept the fact he is part of the Order of the Flame from Sidney.

"Razial." Alena called playfully.

She is several paces in front of Kalvin. Razial sat at her feet with Raal to his right. Araceli, Zelia, Sidney, and Paul are close together to Kalvin's right. Fogi Red is to Raal's right. He frowned at Alena who stood acting like she was challenging Razial.

"You two should get married." Fogi Red growled.

Alena frowned at him. She moved to playfully hit him, but Kalvin startled her when he suddenly scrambled to his feet and drew his sword. Immediately, her eyes moved to see what he was looking at.

Kalvin had watched in awe as two jolems rose from the ground as if they had floated through air. Dressed like gnomes, the jolems wear Phrygian caps, oversized shirts and pants-all gray in color. They stared up at him dismissively as if they dared him to act against them.

"Adini and Havi. I should have known." Fogi Red said.

"Get your human before we do." Adini said, nodding toward Kalvin.

Adini's skin is more toned than Havi's and he has a goatee. He also has short hair. Havi is bald with a pointy nose. They both began to make their way to Fogi Red. Kalvin put away his sword. The two jolems sat down and called Razial. Kalvin can sense by the way the others defer to the jolems they have rank in the Order of the Flame.

Adini and Havi drew everyone's attention. Then told them Priato would join them soon. Zelia asked why. They said they do not know. They did not discuss why they had been sent to join them. They told Razial if he wants to go to Fulancia before returning to Anazi Falls then he must take Kalvin with him. Razial argued but they made it clear that was the only way he was leaving their presence. Kalvin stared at Razial wondering why he is accepting this. To him, Razial has respect for the jolems. He made a mental note to ask Razial about this.

"You know I go to start the hunt." Razial said.

The jolems nodded. Adini told him that is the way Priato said it must be.

"Something about events must take place." Havi stated.

Where Adini's voice is firm, Havi has a squeaky voice. He looked back at Kalvin and said if Razial is going to leave he must leave when Scar's pack returns. Razial nodded in understanding. He knows Priato had seen what must happen for him to reach Fulancia safely. He looked down at Havi then to Adini. They stared back knowingly. Something serious was going on and fate had placed him in the center of it. He looked away taking in the scenery. The forested hills of Gully stand in all their glory.

"I have always hated fate." Havi winked at Razial.

***

Six weeks after leaving Gully, Razial and Kalvin approached Fulancia. Known as a haven for assassins, Fulancia is feared. The Hilt does not dominate the city, but they control it absolutely. Unlike most major cities, Fulancia does not have an outer wall. Fortresses sprinkle the city that sprawls for a mile east to west and a mile south to north.

Razial had explained most of what Kalvin had heard about the city is true. Strangers are stopped in the streets, and he is never to try to enter the Stronghold without an escort. Kalvin stared at the Stronghold as it grew larger in the horizon. It took up most of eastern Fulancia. The city grew from the Stronghold because in the past the Stronghold-before it became known as the Stronghold, was all there was of Fulancia. Razial did not reveal how the Hilt turned Fulancia from a fortified town into one of the strongest and most feared cities in all the lands. He explained that only members of the Society roam freely inside the Stronghold. He also told Kalvin that when they enter the Stronghold's fortress he is never to go up or down any staircase without an escort. He told him doing so would cost him his life!

Kalvin looked around them when Scar's pack revealed themselves in the street. According to Razial they can stay invisible for over an hour. Their presence drew little attention.

"Does this happen every day in Fulancia?" Kalvin asked.

"What?"

"Elfin wolves escorting two riders into the city."

"No. But this is not the first time. Cover your head now. Oh, and Fulancians know to respect elfin wolves."

Razial's calmness seems unusual. Kalvin does not know how his friend can be so calm facing the hunt.

*

An hour later, Kalvin sat in his room. He had been surprised when they had entered the Stronghold. It is like a city within a city. Farmhouses and other wooden houses take up most of the central and southern areas. The fortress takes up most of the northern part of the Stronghold. It is four stories high and well built. He had never expected the inside of the Stronghold to be so organized.

After Kalvin was settled in his room, Razial revealed he is the assassin known as the Avatar of Death. At first, Kalvin disbelieved him. Razial remained stoic when he tried to playfully dismiss it.

That is when he realized Razial was not playing. They talked for several minutes after that. He understands why Razial had kept that from him. Razial then left because he had to meet with his leaders. A knock on the door drew Kalvin's attention.

"Enter." He replied.

Razial had assured him that no one would try to harm him while he was inside the Stronghold and that the contract on him had been negotiated away.

"Once the hunt begins, I will be priority." Razial had smiled.

"This coin is for you." Anjia said entering the room.

Kalvin stood as she tossed a bag full of coins at his feet. Short with long black hair, she has narrow almond shaped eyes and full lips. Her tanned, yellow skin is common in elves. Her body is slim, but her hips and breasts make her curvier than most female elves. Her auburn elflocks frame her face. She exudes confidence. Kalvin looked at her then down to the bag.

"Who are you?" He asked.

"You are lucky my love likes you. I am Fa'Anjia. I am sure I do not have to tell you to keep my name to yourself." She said coldly.

She had tried to stop herself from sounding cold. She knows it is not his fault Razial is to be hunted, but part of her still blames him.

"I have left an escort outside your door. If you want to be with a woman, he will take you. Razial shall pass the night with me when he is finished with his meeting." She smiled at him. She had wanted to threaten him but that would have been wrong.

*

Razial and Binu sat alone in the back room of Binu's private chambers. They are sitting on plush floor pillows. The room is well lit because the entire back wall is covered by mirrors that not only make the room seem bigger but reflect candlelight making the room brighter. The other walls are adorned with poems, drawings, and sayings written in ancient elvish. They give the room a relaxing feeling. Binu always calls Razial to this room whenever he has something serious and or secretive to say.

After hearing about all that happened in Mohr, Binu said the Order of the Flame is hiding its true reason for hiring him. Razial agreed with this, and they began to talk about several contracts Goraan and Rogelio had sealed so only the Hilt will know who paid for them.

"Something is going on in the shadows." Binu said.

In elvish, this saying means something dangerous is happening close to them but is unseen. It is a warning to watch one's surroundings. Razial stared into Binu's slanted eyes. Short, with long black hair, Binu has long brown elflocks that hang down the sides of his oval face. He is thinly built with an aged beige skin. He has a fragile appearance, but Razial knows better.

As a magician, Binu is an elf druid. Goraan says he is his equal in power. Razial knows how rare that is and where assassins must kill three nobles to become a master assassin, Binu's moniker is the Killer of Kings!

"Goraan is allowing too much to happen at once. I would have preferred for you to have been here helping us complete our plan to take over all Giaour." Binu said.

He then explained that a group has been eliminating those who would get in their way of taking control of the Giaour lands. Razial listened to the feats of his peers. Their actions were well planned, but he knows they are still several years away from taking over all Giaour.

"This hunt for you shall hinder our efforts. And with the Shadow imprisoned in Tali." Binu shook his head.

Razial asked why there is no plan to free Donald the Shadow. Binu explained that Carpio wanted Donald to sit in Tali's dungeon for a short while because Donald had gone against Carpio's orders not to take revenge on the marquise of Tali until the Society had completed its first wave of opposition removal.

"The Dagger knew the Shadow would disobey him. He allowed him to be captured." Binu grinned.

"The Dagger and his rules." Razial said.

"If he captures you, he will not give you an opportunity to earn your way out of his service. You will serve the ten years."

"That is why I will be sure to avoid him."

Binu did not respond because Goraan arrived with their dinner. Very few people would dare enter Binu's private chambers without knocking. Goraan is one of them. Binu gave him permission to do so long ago.

Goraan and Binu are opposites. Where Binu is stoic and calm, Goraan is more energetic. He is quick to anger, for an elf, but he is far from being a hothead. The major difference between them is cross Binu and he will hear you out. Cross Goraan and he will kill you!

Razial and Binu helped Goraan with the food. They set the plates on the table that stands only inches above the floor. Binu got the cups while Razial and Goraan prepared the plates. The smell of the food filled Razial's nostrils. The pots steamed. The rice, the beans, and the chicken vegetable soup smell good. He began to salivate.

"I have informed young Razial about our progress in eastern Giaour." Binu said.

"You do know this hunt will hinder our progress." Goraan said to Razial.

Short, with almond shaped eyes, Goraan has reddish elflocks that contrast with his long black hair. He has golden yellow skin. When he is angry-like he is now, his eyes fill with a coldness so others can see he is angry. The hunt has disrupted his plans, and he wants Razial to know how angry he is.

"And all of this for this human." Goraan hissed.

"He is my friend. You should get some." Razial said.

"For what purpose? I have you and many others at my disposal. Be glad I agreed to negotiate the contract on this Kalvin. You- "

Goraan paused because someone knocked on the door. Before any of them could respond, Anjia identified herself and entered the room.

"As I was saying." Goraan continued. "You should go to Doh; kill the king and make yourself the leader of the Children of Doh. Now that you are a master thief."

"Ja'Goraan please. Sarcasm does not fit you." Anjia said.

She smiled at Binu as she sat next to Razial across from Goraan. She waved at Goraan then kissed Razial on the side of his mouth.

Although she is Goraan's daughter, she is usually angry with him. Goraan was hard on her and Razial. He had tried to send them to Anazi Falls with Alena. Anjia did not like that. She knows Goraan feels as if had Razial not become an assassin she would not have become an assassin. Few outside the Hilt know she is Goraan's daughter. To Razial, it is humorous that he and Anjia rose quickly through the ranks of the Society because of the tasks Goraan had given them trying to dissuade them from becoming assassins.

"Anjia'fa." Binu scolded her.

"Never mind her brother. Respect does not go with her personality." Goraan said.

He does not want to focus on Anjia formally calling him which is considered a slight in elf society. He explained that he had wanted Razial to go to Alf-Heim to learn how to use his powers, but he had been informed that would allow the Harbingers to dominate the world until they are forced to deal with each other.

"Who could have- "Anjia stopped herself. She realized that Goraan had obviously been told this by Priato.

"The Order of the Flame is hiding something from you. With the Harbingers around, I want you to be careful. Three years is a short period of time, but a lot can happen in three years. Whatever the Order of the Flame asks you to do-try to learn all you can." Goraan said stoically.

Anjia could see it in Goraan's eyes. He is worried by something. That made her concerned. She knows few things worry Goraan. For a moment she felt sad for him, but then, like she always does when she wants to be angry at him, she reminded herself that he had tried to abandon her.

She thought about how it had been Binu who had brought her to Fulancia along with Razial and Alena. The only thing Goraan told her about her mother is that she was from the Bear clan. When she had pressed for more, Goraan told her the cold truth.

"Your mother betrayed me, and I killed her." He had said.

That still haunts her which is why she refuses to act like a loving daughter to him.

"So, when will you leave?" Goraan asked Razial.

"Tomorrow afternoon." Razial answered.

"You should spend another day with my daughter." Goraan said.

Binu quickly agreed. Anjia pressed against Razial. It does not matter when he leaves. He will be given a day's head start. Then those who hunt him will chase him. He agreed to stay another day. Anjia told him she had left an escort with Kalvin. Binu brought up Scar's pack saying he intends to run a night run with them. Anjia took Razial's spoon and ate some of his food. She asked if Binu or Goraan would hunt him. By law, Hilt members must get a sash, but they do not have to hunt him.

"No." Binu answered.

Anjia's went to Goraan, who said.

"Hug me before he leaves, and I will not."

With that, they began talking about times past and what had happened while Razial was away.

***

Kalvin walked alongside of Anjia, who had gone to his room to escort him to the hall where Razial was meeting with Binu and

Goraan. Anjia had been at the meeting. After Goraan had said that he and Rogelio will deal with the Fellowship and the Sisterhood, she was asked to escort Kalvin to the hall.

Seeing Goraan leaving the hall as she approached, she slowed her pace. She felt strange as she opened her arms and embraced Goraan and called him father in elvish.

"Thank you, my daughter." Goraan said in ancient elvish.

Anjia pulled away slowly. Goraan said they should hug more often. She smirked at him. He smiled then looked up at Kalvin and spoke in common saying.

"You must be remarkable for Razial to risk himself for you. Good tidings to you."

He walked off after that. Kalvin looked down at Anjia and asked her who Goraan is.

"Goraan the Merciless and you are about to meet Binu the Killer of Kings." Anjia answered.

Kalvin followed her into the hall. He felt strange when he was introduced to Binu, because although he is much bigger than Binu, he knows Binu could kill him without much effort. He tried to gauge Binu's age but could not. Binu could be any age.

"Here Kalvin." Binu used his powers to make a sword float to him.

He tried to hand the sword to Kalvin, but Kalvin refused. He smiled in understanding. He told Kavin that he can accept the sword so long as he does not draw it. Kalvin looked at the sword. It is made of blue steel and the double-edged point was forged at about a twenty-degree angle. The width of the blade is equal to three of his fingers. He tested its balance and was impressed. Its hilt allows him to use either one or two hands. Its cross guard is wide enough for him to grab each side with a whole hand. The pommel is shaped like a flattened sphere.

"Why is it so light?" Kalvin asked.

"Because it was forged by sorcery. It will never dull and can cut through anything." Binu answered.

He bid Kalvin and the others farewell then exited the hall.

"He will miss you." Anjia said.

Razial smiled and kissed her passionately. She hugged him then waved to Kalvin.

"Does she know about Alena?" Kalvin asked.

"Of course."

"You really are lucky."

"Hopefully, I remain so, for the next three years."

Razial made a gesture for Kalvin to hand him the sword. They walked out of the hall. As they reached the fortress' front doors, Kalvin asked if Anjia would hunt him.

"Of course."

"What do you mean of course? Isn't she the-"

"Yes Kalvin." Razial cut him off before he had said Anjia's moniker.

They exited the fortress. Their horses waited for them. Each is fully supplied. Scar's pack is standing around the horses. At that moment, Razial came up with a plan to reach Anazi Falls. The gates to the Stronghold were opened when they mounted their horses. Razial tossed Kalvin the sword and said.

"Kalvin, I have finally figured out which one of us is dafter."

Kalvin frowned at him. Razial explained their current situation.

"And?" Kalvin asked.

Razial galloped through the gateway while saying. "You are dafter. You are doing this by choice."

***

Standing atop the Stronghold's fortress, Goraan watched the city, his city, Fulancia. His mind for the first time in a very long time is racing with uncontrolled thoughts. His friend had informed him that Razial is in for many trials. He knows she is not talking about the hunt. Something is going on that has made the Order of the Flame hire Razial and until he knows what that is, he must busy himself finding out.

"Is Razial in danger?" He had asked his friend.

"You have made him an assassin. He is always in danger." His friend had said, refusing to say why Razial was hired.

He put thoughts of taking over all Giaour to the back of his mind. That will happen. For now, he has to find out what is truly going on with Razial. The fact his friend will not even reveal what is going on means it is very serious.

With his mind focused on the present, Goraan watched as the first wave of assassins with sashes leave Fulancia to hunt Razial. Accepting what was happening, Goraan exhaled then went about forwarding the Society's cause.

CHAPTER 4

THE HARBINGERS

Winnin is a massive sprawling city. It has no outer wall, but it remains quite formidable. Throughout the city, many barracks have been built to house its soldiers who are known as Rakaar's Own-Winninans who willingly risk their minds to serve Rakaar.

Each year, thousands of them ingest the potion the clergy produces to transform them from free thinking individuals with their own wills to tireless, fearless, and mindless fighters who are completely loyal to whomever rules Winnin.

As time passes, Rakaar's Own age slower, live longer, and eventually regain more of their own minds. They rise through the ranks until-if they live long enough, they join the clergy as magic wielding priests or priestesses. A risky gamble many Winninans are willing to take every year. It is this type of dedication that allows Winnin to always have a powerful military-a military few are willing to challenge.

In the center of the city, an ancient temple stands. As the first temple dedicated to Rakaar, it is sacred to all who worship Rakaar. The founders of Winnin made the temple so all who worship Rakaar have a unifying symbol. Atop the temple burns a large fire made up of white flames. The fire has burned for millennia.

It was created to honor Rakaar's defeat and as a sign of his imminent return.

The fire is where the clergy sacrifice their victims. To reach the top of the temple, one must pass through the hall that makes up the temple's top floor. Very few are strong enough to enter the hall. Those who built the temple made sure of this.

The ironic thing about Rakaar's capital-as Winnin is known, is it was founded by individuals who did not worship Rakaar, and when it was partially destroyed during the Third Champions' War, it was rebuilt by the Master-led Harbingers.

Standing inside the temple's hall, the Master thought about all this. With him stand four other Harbingers. This will be the first time the others discover each other's identity. The Master thought about how they must appear. The five of them dressed in magical red cowls-the Harbingers' trademark, standing in a huddle near the middle of the dimly lit hall. Even if one knows nothing about the Harbingers, it would be obvious that there is something foreboding about them.

Their cowls are blowing in the wind. With four large windows and an open doorway in each wall there is no protection from the wind.

"You may remove your hoods." The Master said in Tuyakan.

He stood perfectly still while the others pulled back their hoods. There is no way for them to reveal their faces while they are wearing their hoods. That part of the cowls' powers cannot be commanded.

To his right, is Beulah, his right hand. She has no idea who she is to him, but he shall reveal this soon. She is the shortest of the group. Her narrow almond shaped light brown eyes took in the others. Her eyes blend with her golden yellow complexion and her black hair. Her reddish-brown elflocks frame her face.

To the Master's left, is Tonige the uncontested leader of Winnin. Taller than average, Tonige has a medium build. He is bald with a graying mustache and beard. His brown eyes usually have a cold grimness in them.

Next to Tonige, is Peter. He is the tallest of the group. His blue eyes took in the others. They were full of curiosity. That is what the Master likes about him. Before making a move, Peter does his best to gauge where he stands in a situation.

Between Peter and Beulah is Ariel. Her fiery red hair is blowing in the wind. She has been a Harbinger for decades. Before that, she was one of the Master's prize recruits. She sympathized with the Harbingers' cause without knowing it. She was a young woman when she first caught his eye which was shortly after the Order of the Flame had killed her parents!

Before he introduced them to each other, he thought about revealing the identities of the other Harbingers-something he always thinks about but never does. Harbingers survive off their secrecy. That is why only Beulah knows about the imprisoned Harbinger.

Peter and Ariel were surprised to find out Tonige is a Harbinger. Tonige was shocked by Beulah's presence. He is the only one old enough to remember when she roamed the lands learning about the dynasties that ruled the masses. It was his expression that made Ariel realize just who Beulah really is.

"Beulah? As in Beulah of Ino-Heim?" Ariel asked, looking at Beulah.

Ariel's eyes moved from Beulah to the Master, who smiled mentally. He likes the fact she knows enough not to reveal that Beulah is the queen of the Boar clan to Peter. Although Peter is a Harbinger, he should not be. The Master only made him a Harbinger because he has become an integral part of their plans in Coilu.

In times past, Peter would have been given a magical red robe instead of a Harbinger cowl. The problem is the Harbinger who possesses the power to make the magical robes is imprisoned in Anazi Falls. That is why Peter is a Harbinger instead of a Herald-like he should be.

"The very one." The Master answered Ariel.

Peter sensed that Ariel had just talked around him, but he does not feel slighted. He stood listening as the Master explained his plans to release the Magi not once but twice. Beulah and Tonige dislike his plans. They debated several details. The Master heard them out but did not change his mind. Ariel asked several questions. After receiving answers, she did not state how she feels about the plans to release the Magi.

"Why must you release them twice?" Tonige asked.

He knows the Master has made up his mind, but he is curious about why the Master wants to release the Magi twice. He has been a Harbinger for a long time. He and the Master had come up with the plan to get rid of his brother-the former king of Winnin, and to kill his brother's son-which was all Tonige's idea. Truth be told, he did not expect the Avatar to succeed. He is glad he did.

"The Magi are a plague. This shall be their last Champions' War." The Master said.

Ariel likes the idea of killing the Magi. Still, she is worried about Razial.

"What if the assassin becomes a problem? The Order of the Flame has given him the authority to lead those with him." She asked.

"Ariel. The Order of the Flame did not kidnap Paul just to keep him alive. They intend to use him to obtain the ancient crown of Coilu."

The Master's response made her think. Acting as if she had been captured was only the beginning. She has a lot to do to complete the Harbingers' plans in Coilu.

She listened while Peter explained his plans to have his son become the new emperor of Coilu. His plans sound good, but she knew the Order of the Flame intended to put Paul on the imperial throne. She stated that a civil war was likely in Coilu.

"Which will only help our plans." The Master said to her.

"But the assassin will most likely lead those with Paul." Ariel countered.

She dislikes Razial but she is not foolish enough to allow her feelings to make her think less of him. He is a threat. That is why she wanted him eliminated, but the Master had plans for him, plans he would not discuss yet.

"The assassin is not our concern. He is the Magi's concern. Stop worrying about him. We need him to make sure we succeed against the Magi and their servants." The Master said.

With that, the meeting ended. Tonige made sure the others all left without notice. Ariel and Beulah will talk about several things the Master had told Beulah to reveal to Ariel. He will talk to Peter about his plan to deal with Gwen. He had told Peter not to join those out to kill Gwen. Peter had told him that he wanted to move up the Fellowship's ranks. His response was simple.

"It is better to be the least among the Harbingers than the greatest of kings."

***

Razial and Kalvin had been in the city of Giaour for two weeks. After leaving Fulancia, Razial turned east. He sent Scar's pack to Anazi Falls to help hide the fact he rode to Giaour's capital. He has no doubt had he tried to race to Anazi Falls he would have been caught.

Upon arriving to Giaour city, Kalvin suggested they take the first ship they could to Cozik. Razial told him they must remain unseen for as long as possible. He knew if word reached those who hunted him there would be crews of assassins waiting for them in Cozik. When Kalvin asked why he was so worried by lessor assassins, Razial recited an ancient saying.

"The rule of facing a superior-come with an advantage in numbers sufficient enough to overcome your lack of skills."

As time passed, Razial kept more of a lower profile. He kept close watch on the docks waiting for his chance to leave unnoticed by the Society's agents. After two days, he talked with a slaver headed to Cozik after he made a stop in Arapia. Razial liked the fact the slaver only cared about coin and even told him about a priest from the Theocracy. Although the Society is not at war with the Theocracy, they are not allowed to spread their cause in Giaour. The Society had made that very clear several times.

Sitting in the room he shares with Kalvin, Razial focused on the hay that was thrown on the floor. The air is cold and stale. It smells like seawater. The room is on the second floor of a wooden servant's house. That is why he keeps the hay on the floor. It controls the moisture that builds on the floor.

Looking at the hay-filled sacks that had served as their beds Razial stood, ignoring the tension in the room. Kalvin is angry with him because he had decided to kill the priest. Kalvin told him he is too calloused. He told Kalvin he is not calloused enough.

"When you can kill a woman without feeling guilty, you will be ready to live the worldly life you want to live." Razial said.

His words angered Kalvin because Kalvin has a problem with men killing women-a sore spot for him. Razial had told him that killing the priest is a matter of principle to him. Kalvin quickly exited the room. He will meet Razial at the slaver's ship.

***

Ulina thought about how busy she had been tracking what was going on with the Fellowship and the Sisterhood. She had found a trail that leads to the Theocracy, but she knew it was a false trail. Whoever is behind the alliance between the Fellowship and the Sisterhood remains in the shadows. She had been unable to prove Beulah was more involved than just keeping the peace. So now she must look for ties between Beulah and the Harbingers. She thought about that while walking the snow-covered streets of

Dax where she tracked a man who was an unknowing servant of the Harbingers. He thought his master was part of the Fellowship.

She had overheard him talking about his master's red cowl. That was how she had figured out his master was a Harbinger. That was enough for her to act against him.

Dressed warmly, she is walking at a leisurely pace. Her elfin burnoose is wrapped tightly around her and hangs just above her ankles. Her elfin boots keep her feet warm, and her elfin scarf hides the fact that she is an elf.

The city of Dax is a haven for the Fellowship. It is the only city where members of the rivaling factions do not act against each other. It is also very anti-elf. That is why she must act soon. The short winter day will soon become a long winter night.

She watched the man approach a house. As she had hoped, he opened the door. She quickened her pace and whispered a short chant. As a druid, she can wield wizardry without drawing her powers. She caused the man to tumble through the doorway. She entered the house. The man's blue eyes were full of fear and curiosity. He did not try to move while she closed the door. A witch ran down the stairs with her powers drawn. Ulina drew her powers and struck the witch knocking her down the stairs. She took hold of the witch and the man using her powers to squeeze them.

"I cannot be patient with you two. Anger me and I will cause magical flames to slowly burn your skin off." She spoke.

Keeping her voice full of venom, she asked them about their master's whereabouts and plans. After several moments, it became clear that they knew very little. However, the woman revealed she was ordered to gather information about ancient maps and scrolls.

"For what purpose?" Ulina asked.

"He seeks the location of an ancient dolmen." The witch answered.

The man then explained he had been ordered to spy on Gwen and Frauter as well as on those who stand against Gwen's faction. That made Ulina smile mentally because spying on both sides is standard practice for the Harbingers.

"Tell me what you have learned." She said coldly.

He told her that several leaders want to kill Gwen, but Peter will not join them, so they are going to try to kill Frauter.

"Gwen and Frauter seek favor with Bal by killing Gideon. They intend to use" He frowned as he struggled to think of what he wants to say. "Gideon's shadow to kill him."

Ulina released them. Her mind raced as she hurried out of the house. The Harbinger has people searching for Bal's dolmen which means the Harbingers intended to free Bal. That news by itself is cause for concern. It was made even worse by what the man had revealed. Although he had misunderstood what Gwen and Frauter intended to do, she understood Gwen and Frauter have started the process of releasing a shadow-tracker so it can track and kill Razial!

They do not want to kill a man named Gideon. They want to kill the Gideon. Ulina quickened her pace. The sky is growing dark, and Dax will close its gates soon. She must inform the other keepers about what she has just learned before the gates are closed.

***

The ship ride from the capital to Arapia was a smooth one. It went by without any problems. Razial and Kalvin were the only passengers besides the crew. They remained aboard while the slaver delivered his cargo.

The sky is partly cloudy, but the air remains warm. Other boats and ships are anchored around them. Rowboats move back and forth between the shore and the larger vessels carrying whatever the different crews are selling, trading, and or buying. Kalvin watched the slaves look around with different expressions. Some are afraid. Others seem curious. He knew by the unfazed expressions some have they have been through this before. That made him think about those who sell themselves to survive or to get out of a dungeon.

"If those children are slaves, I am going to kill the slaver." Razial said in a low growl.

Startled, Kalvin followed his line of vision. He saw the slaver, who had sold them passage, at the front of a rowboat while four of his men rowed in unison. In the middle of the rowboat sat four children huddled around a woman. They are all chained and shackled. Kalvin felt a sense of anger growing inside him. He disliked seeing children being bought and sold. He thought about how Razial had told him that Arapia is home to many shady individuals.

"Many perverted nobles come to Arapia to satisfy their perverted desires in secret." Razial had said to him years earlier.

He did not reveal that he had killed the prince of Arapia for this very reason. He was already planning how to deal with the crew after he has killed their leader. Kalvin stood staring at the rowboat just behind the slaver's rowboat. Razial had already decided that rowboat has supplies in it.

Moving away from Kalvin, Razial watched the four crewmen as they prepared to help their leader board the ship. One of them began lowering a rope ladder while two others began to hoist the sail.

"You do know there are more of them than us." Kalvin said.

Razial thought about killing the four crewmen while they are distracted but decided against it. He must wait until the children are aboard the ship.

"Be ready." He said in a whisper.

"Be ready?" Kalvin asked.

He realized Razial was going to act. He told him to think about the hunt and giving away their location. Razial smiled and spoke.

"I have already thought about that."

Moments later, the slaver made the decision Razial wanted him to make. He sent the woman and children up first. Razial put a dagger against the slaver's throat as soon as his foot touched the deck. Kalvin moved to stop the crewman holding the rope ladder. He put his sword against the man's chest. Razial told the other two crewmen to have the others send up the supplies first. The men hesitated. That angered Razial. He cut the slaver across his chest then kicked him to the deck.

"Challenge me and I will kill you along with your captain." He spoke.

Kalvin watched as the men's expressions changed. They can sense Razial is not bluffing. He has no doubt they can also sense his confidence. At that moment, he remembered what his father had told him while teaching him how to throw a knife.

"No one who is not used to fighting wants to fight someone who is trained to kill." His father's voice echoed in his mind.

His father had told him he would be able to avoid fights by being confident and showing skill. Kalvin had used this to avoid some fights. However, at that moment, he realized that this advice worked on those who can fight as well-not just the unskilled. He has no doubt the sailors have been in several fights, but it is obvious by their expressions that they believe Razial would kill them if they challenge him. Having no choice, the crewmen did as Razial said. The crewmen still on the rowboat disliked that so one of the four leaned over and shouted.

"Captain's orders!"

The slaver crawled away from Razial-who walked after him while he tried to call out to the other crewmen in the rowboats.

"Don't lis-"

Razial stabbed him in the leg. He wants the man to suffer.

He moved in to inflict another wound, but the woman pleaded.

"Please sir, don't" She ran before him with her hands held out in front of her.

Razial frowned at her. Kalvin kept his sword ready. One of the crewmen tried to run across the deck. Razial threw a dagger. It was buried into the man's buttocks.

"Please sir. I beg you. Do not kill them. This man bought us all as a favor. He could have separated us. I-"

"Silence yourself woman!" Razial growled between clenched teeth.

The woman is his height. She is thin with a full bosom. She has green eyes, blond hair, and white skin. Razial glanced at the children: two boys and two girls. In his mind, she is obligated to the slaver, and she should not be.

"Who are you?" He asked her.

"I'm Ofelia." She answered.

"You can remain his slave but not the children. I can provide them with somewhere to live."

Ofelia looked down at the captain. He had agreed to buy her and the children so long as she agreed to become his house slave in Cozik, and the children help take care of his estate. She did not want to agree to this, but it was the only way to keep the children together.

"No. I want to be free, but-"

"Call your men. You."

Razial pointed at the man he had hit with his dagger. He turned to Ofelia because she had drawn her powers. She is a witch, but he can sense by the way she is holding her powers she does not know how to wield her powers very well. She stared at him. Their eyes locked and she realized he can sense she is a witch.

"Put the chains on the crewmen. I will not kill them." Razial said to ease her mind.

***

Days later, Kalvin slept. They had released the slaver and the four crewmen they had chained together. Razial gave one of the men twenty coins to stay on the ship and sail it. The man agreed even though Razial kept him in leg irons.

"Kalvin." Ofelia called softly waking him.

Squinting, he looked up at her. It is early. The sky is still dark. Still groggy, he asked her what she wanted. She handed him a small scroll while saying.

"Razial said to give you this."

Kalvin frowned. He took the scroll and read it. Razial left the ship. He had sailed close to shore and took a rowboat to southern Anazi. He told Kalvin that he had left Ofelia two hundred gold coins in case she did not want to accompany him to Anazi Falls. He told Kalvin he had to separate from him to lose those who have undoubtedly picked up their trail.

"You will be watched. Do not forget that the Children of Doh still want you dead. Also, Ofelia cannot wield her powers well, but she is a witch so do not make her angry. See you in Anzazi Falls." Razial had finished.

Kalvin shook his head in disappointment. Ofelia stood next to him. She asked what was written on the scroll. He handed her the scroll. A sad expression came over her face as she said.

"I cannot read."

He stared into her green eyes. He thinks she is naturally pretty. He can sense she has been through a lot. She seems lost by the kindness he and Razial have shown her.

"Well, while you are with me, I shall teach you how to read. If you want me to." He smiled.

"I would like that, Kalvin." She replied.

***

Beulah stood watching Peter and Ariel ride off. They will ride until midnight so they can reach Coilu sooner. Around her, are twenty of her Boar warriors wearing black hooded cloaks that match her black cowl. They are in the forest that separates Tunez from Svelt northwest of Tunez city.

During the ride from Winnin, Beulah had revealed their true plans to Ariel explaining that they do not care about who wins the civil war in Coilu saying.

"We want two things from our actions: the ancient crown of Coilu and Paul's death."

She then told her that she had sent Lisa to Coilu city to help Peter and sent Pam to Ocia city with three other coven members to take over the city.

"I did this to prepare for the next phase of our plans and to make sure Peter does not accidentally harm Ja'Razial."

Ariel had agreed with her taking the actions she had taken. She had been surprised to hear that Peter was supposed to be a Herald instead of a Harbinger. However, Beulah did not tell her why the Master could not make Peter a Herald.

Beulah had liked spending time with Ariel. She had taught her how to use low levels of sorcery and told her that she must make herself stronger. She also explained that Peter is too attached to those outside of the Harbingers' inner circle. Ariel did not need to be told that is why Beulah disliked him.

With her mind on the present, she inhaled deeply. The air is fresh. The trees are full of foliage. She mounted her horse and thought about how things are about to intensify. After years of scheming, she and the Master are about to make sure this Champions' War is different than all those before it.

***

Razial stood staring at his room door. It is dark in his room. The only light is coming from the bottom of the door. He had made his way to a small inn about a hundred fifty miles southwest of Anazi Falls. The inn is owned by a contractor. Contractors can play no role in a hunt. The only thing they are allowed to do is provide information about the Society's enemies to a hunted assassin. They can say nothing about the hunted assassin's whereabouts.

The contractor had told him about the dead priest in Giaour city. He made it clear he had killed the priest. After that, the contractor treated him like any other patron.

For the first night, all went well. On the second night, the contractor's son, Rick, made the mistake of revealing that Razial is in the inn to another assassin. Razail had overheard Rick talking so he quickly made his way back to his room. He hoped the other assassin looked outside first.

Hearing his fellow assassin climb the stairs, he prepared to fight. He does not want to kill any of those who hunt him, but if he must, he will. For some reason, he thought about what Ofelia had told him before he left the ship.

"You have a lot of good in you, Razial. You should not kill just because it makes things easier." Ofelia had said.

"Every enemy you leave alive only adds to the danger you face in the future." He had replied.

A grimness came over him when he saw the assassin's shadow stop in front of his door. He could see the man's shadow lean toward his door. He calmed himself. He will have to fight. The door swung open. He did not hesitate. He threw two daggers and moved to engage the man. His daggers were deflected by the man's sword. However, he could not reset his feet before Razial reached him. With the light in his eyes, he could not see the man's face. He had no idea who the hunter was. Still, he went for the quick kill because he sensed magic. Others may be around, and he must reach Anazi Falls. He blocked a sword thrust with his right dagger and stabbed his opponent with his left dagger. The dagger bit into his chest, but the man fought on. He whipped his sword with one hand. Razial was forced to block the one-handed swing with both of his daggers. Critically wounded, the man should give ground so Razial could run. Instead, he pressed Razial. Hearing other patrons scrambling around in their rooms, Razial ducked a powerful two-handed swing then stabbed him in his chest and throat fatally wounding him. He picked up his thrown daggers and began to walk away. That is when he saw who the man was. He was one of Tollok's pupils. Seeing that he still has life in his eyes, Razial said.

"The Sword will hear how you died fighting."

"Thank you, brother."

Razial nodded in response. He will not be haunted by his death, but he disliked that it had happened.

Walking down the stairs, he saw the contractor at the bottom of the stairs. He sees the concern in his eyes. In his day, he was a well-respected assassin. As a contractor, he was just as respected.

His son: however, has made a critical mistake-one that could cost him his life.

"Your son needs to learn our ways." Razial said coldly. "He is young and got lost in the excitement of being around you, brother."

"I shall return to Fulancia after the hunt. I want him there ready to recite our laws and rules. Bury our brother and Rick is to leave within two months."

Razial said this while walking toward the door. He saw Rick in his peripheral vision and decided to end the matter then and there.

"Speak of this no more." He exited the inn.

***

The first thing Kalvin did when he entered Cozik was pay several guards to get rid of the warrant to have him arrested. What he would discover a day later is Xochi-who had been in Cozik, had already settled the matter. She did not tell him how she had managed to find him. All she had told him was that she would be ready to leave within a week. That was four days ago.

As Zelia's twin, one cannot tell them apart by appearance, but by mannerisms it is easy to tell them apart. Xochi is strict and formal. She told him that news about them taking the slaver's ship had reached the Society within days.

"The assassin acted wisely by separating from you."

Xochi had said as if giving Razial a compliment pained her. When she found out that Ofelia and the children would accompany them to Anazi Falls, she began treating Ofelia like her student. She praised Kalvin for teaching Ofelia the basic alphabet in common. Then, as is her way, she berated him for releasing the crewman. Ofelia told her that he had to keep his word.

"Never give your word to a scoundrel." Xochi had replied.

Walking through a street, Kalvin smiled as he thought about that. He had finally sold the ship. The day is chilly. He is going back to the tavern where Ofelia and the children were waiting for him. He was wearing a long wool coat because unlike the rest of southern Anazi, Cozik gets cold. Not only is it a coastal city but it also sits on the Doh-Line. (The point marking where it no longer snows south of except high in mountains.) Frozen breath rose from his mouth, but he had other things on his mind. He had crossed paths with a thief who will undoubtedly inform the Children of Doh that he is in Cozik.

*

Ofelia watched the children play in the street. Like her, they were all dressed warmly in new clothes. Kalvin was in his room. He has been inside since returning earlier. To her, he is a spy for the Order of the Flame. She had never said this to him or to Xochi when Xochi is around, it is just what she feels is true. Razial and Kalvin's kindness and the fact they were going to Anazi Falls is proof enough for her.

Looking to the sky, she rubbed her hands together for warmth. Her attention went to Anjia, who was walking toward her. Anjia was not the first elf she had seen in Cozik, but she was the first elf Ofelia had ever seen dressed in all black.

There was an aura of danger around Anjia. Her confidence makes Ofelia feel insecure. She accidentally drew her powers. Anjia stared into her eyes. Her almond shaped eyes made Ofelia look at the children. They are safe.

"Kalvin is in danger Ofelia." Anjia said.

She can sense that Ofelia does not know how to wield her powers well. She looked into her green eyes and saw only curiosity and confusion.

"Kalvin is up in his room. All is well." Ofelia frowned.

She had no idea who Anjia was. She did not know that Anjia had come to watch how Razial dealt with those who waited for him in Cozik. She was happy Razial had fooled those who hunted him. The reason she stayed to watch Kalvin was because he was Razial's friend. That was why when she noticed the crew of thieves going to the tavern, she decided to act.

"Who are y-"

The sound of swords crashing made Ofelia stop asking her question. She ran after Anjia. Other people stared at them as they ran up the stairs. The other patrons simply want to see if the fighting will move down the stairs. Ofelia paid them little mind. When she reached the top of the stairs, she saw that Kalvin's room was where the fighting was. His room's door is open. Anjia startled her when she drew two short swords while drawing her powers. She led Ofelia into the room. They saw four men trying to get around Kalvin's sword and dagger. The man Anjia targeted saw her in his peripheral vision. By the time he turned to defend himself, her sword drove through his chest. His eyes widened in fear.

Ofelia saw none of that. She was so panicked that she lashed out with all her powers. The three men who still tried to reach Kalvin were slammed against the back wall. Her strike even knocked Kalvin back several paces. Anjia was surprised by Ofelia's strike. She heard the men's bones snap from the magical blow. She knows Ofelia had even surprised herself.

"Finish them, Kalvin." Anjia said.

She sheathed her swords and smoothed out her coat. Kalvin stared at her. He does not want to kill the men while they are defenseless. She shook her head in disappointment. She walked toward the door while saying.

"You should be on your way before more thieves arrive."

"Thank you, ma'am." Ofelia said to Anjia.

She turned to Kalvin who had put a hand on her waist guiding her out of the room.

"Who is that woman?" She asked.

"Anjia. She is an assassin." Kalvin answered.

He can still hear the men moaning in pain. Ofelia looked at him as if he is mad.

"Are you sure?" She asked.

"Trust me. Now let us get the children and leave."

He checked his belt to make sure he had all his coins. Ofelia told him he needed to be healed. He told her they must leave first. She did not argue. He ignored the people's staring eyes, but he could not ignore Xochi's glaring eyes.

"What happened?" Xochi demanded.

Hearing guards racing toward the tavern.

"Kalvin. Go with them." Xochi pointed at two horsemen. "I shall bring Ofelia with me."

Kalvin did not hesitate in taking her horse. He watched as Ofelia walked toward the children, who were still playing near the tavern.

Galloping behind the two men who he was sure were bulwarks, Kalvin winced as the cold bit into his wounds. He sighed and asked himself.

"What have I gotten myself into?"

***

Alena smiled at Razial while he slept. He had arrived late, the night before. She had been in her room, in her bed when he knocked on her door. He entered her room and lay in the bed with her. They enjoyed each other for most of the night. Then, fell asleep. He is obviously tired. He rarely falls into deep sleep outside of the Stronghold.

Watching him sleep made her feel warm inside. She has loved him for most of her life. Some believe she had left Fulancia because of jealousy between her and Anjia. However, although their rift was centered around Razial, it is not about jealousy.

"Razial'ja." She called softly.

She rubbed his head. His eyes popped open. She smiled and kissed him warmly. The blanket fell off her shoulder. Her breasts reacted to the chill in the room. That made him stroke her waist. He kissed her while turning her on to her back. She kissed him back, then pulled away saying.

"We have to bathe and meet with the keepers."

Razial pouted as he laid on his back. He asked about Kalvin. She told him Kalvin was still enroute to Anazi Falls and she will tell him when something has changed.

"Now let us bathe." She pulled him off the bed.

During the meeting, Razial listened to Tu'ani and Lela explained that he faces great danger and that is why Adini and Havi will guard him. He asked why they are centering so much around him.

"Because your destiny is great, and our enemies know this."

Lela had answered. She and Tu'ani explained that he would have free reign to return Paul to the imperial throne. He asked why they are so concerned about him if they truly believe in his destiny.

"That is the thing about destiny, it is controlled by fate; I am sure you have heard that choices control fate." Tu'ani said to him.

He nodded. He knows they are hiding a lot from him. They seem to realize this. They told him they would reveal more as time passes. They told him the Harbingers meant no harm but that could change. Then, they told him how they had the gems he and Kalvin had brought from Sahkar moved. He asked why.

"You have heard of the Stones of Honor have you not?" Lela and Tu'ani asked simultaneously.

Their question answered his question. He knows they would not have brought up the Stones of Honor unless the ruby and diamond were part of the five ancient gems the Gully dwarfs once possessed.

Not expecting an answer, he asked them if they had found the other gems.

"We now have them all." The two keepers answered.

They asked him if he had plans to deal with the hunt while he is under contract. He gave them no specific answer. His mind was on why they hired him and why they were concerned with Paul. He then began thinking about what Binu had said about them hiding something serious.

"I will play your game, for now. Soon, I will have several questions. You all better have answers." He spoke.

With that, the meeting ended. He exited the hall and Alena joined him. They spent time in her room talking.

***

Days later, Kalvin and the others arrived. Zelia had joined their group two days after they had left Cozik. Kalvin was glad she did because Xochi needed to be stopped. She was too strict with him before Zelia had joined them. Xochi dislikes that Kalvin and Razial are involved with the Order of the Flame, and she does not hide it. She told Ofelia that Razial is an assassin and Kalvin is a thief. The news had shocked Ofelia, but she did not change toward Kalvin. She defended him every chance she could. At times, Zelia had to defend Ofelia when she was too hard on Ofelia during their practice sessions. It was during one of these tirades that they found out that Camri the youngest of the orphans with Ofelia is a witch.

Kalvin had enjoyed spending time with Ofelia when she had time to talk. She had expressed a desire to join the Order of the Flame and asked Kalvin how he felt about joining. He did not get a chance to answer because Zelia had heard the question and told her that he had already been on several tasks with her already. She then told Ofelia about what had happened in Mohr. She had no answer when Ofelia asked why Xochi treats Kalvin so poorly when she knows what Kalvin has done.

Entering the inner city's palace, Kalvin sensed how nervous Ofelia feels. She has the excited children close to her. After years of roaming around begging to survive, they had finally found a home. They will all join the Order of the Flame. Their lives had forever changed. Walking through a hallway, they were led to a small hall. They were served lunch. Zelia and Xochi left them alone. Sidney, Fogi Red, and Paul joined them. Kalvin introduced them to Ofelia and the children. While they ate, Havi and Adini wobbled in.

"Roasted duck." The two jolems rubbed their hands.

Their expressions changed as they turned on each other. They shook their fists at each other. Fogi Red burst into laughter. Raal laughed as well. He had entered just behind the jolems.

Kalvin had no idea jolems are very superstitious when it comes to saying the same thing at the same time, so he was puzzled.

"I see you two have not changed. Jolems and their superstition goes on." Raal said as he sat at the table.

Adini ignored him while Havi snarled at him revealing tiny sharp teeth. Ofelia prepared plates for the children while Fogi Red complained about only having ale and no mead. Camri asked if the jolems are baby dwarfs. The jolems stared at her, but they did not stop eating.

"No." Havi answered.

"And we are not giant gnomes either."

"We are Gully dwarfs." Adini smiled.

After a short while, Razial and Alena joined them. Razial did not eat while Alena ate a little beans and rice. After Kalvin introduced her to Ofelia, Alena was confused by Ofelia's reaction.

"So, you are the first A name." Ofelia smiled.

"You know Alena, Ariel, Araceli, and Anjia." Kalvin said.

Alena nodded in understanding. Razial then asked about Cozik. Kalvin told him all that had happened in Cozik. Razial was shocked by how badly he said Xochi had treated him.

"The only person I know she dislikes more than me is you." Kalvin said pointing at Razial.

"Me? I do not know her." Razial scowled.

"She dislikes the fact that-" Ofelia lowered her voice and leaned closer to him. "-you are an assassin."

Razial did not respond. He knows Xochi was the one who had told Ofelia he is an assassin. Ofelia could sense that bothered him. She assured him that her opinion of him had not changed. He smiled at her. They all continued to talk until the keepers arrived. Ofelia and the children were led away so the others could discuss their plans.

*

Hours later, Kalvin met Ofelia. They said their goodbyes and promised to see each other in the future. After that, he made his way to the top of the tower where Razial waited for him. With the sun setting, they watched the city. Razial feels as though the setting sun is the perfect metaphor for their lives because the sun is setting on their old lives. They will no longer roam the lands freely. They are in the middle of the Order of the Flame and its enemies. He should have realized this would happen when Kalvin had told him about Priato telling him about the gems. At first, he thought only Kalvin's life would change. Now he realized he was more involved than he had expected.

"I take it they told you about the gems." Razial smirked.

Kalvin shook his head in dismay. The keepers had explained to him about the Stones of Honor. He was so impressed by the tale that it made him stop feeling bad about missing out on all the coins he could have made. He shared that with Razial, then asked.

"Did you know about the Stones of Honor?"

"Kalvin. I was raised by Goraan and Binu. I was taught all of the ancient tales that shaped the world." Razial answered.

Kalvin smirked at him. He smiled-still not looking at him. He can sense Kalvin is not bothered by losing the gems at all. Wanting to warn his friend, Razial said.

"Things will get worse, Kalvin. This is not an adventure. Unless I can find and kill those who lead the opposition against Paul, we will be part of a civil war. Those who oppose us will be the magus Bal's strongest servants."

"Raz. In case you don't remember, I was in Mohr. I don't know everything, but I do know this is worldly. My family is going to be brought to Anazi Falls." Kalvin replied.

Razial turned to look at him. He knows his friend can handle himself, but he knows Kalvin has to become more calloused before he gets used to killing without regret something bulwarks must learn.

"Very well. Now, about the hunt. When I say run, do not argue. If we cross paths with the wrong crew, we cannot stay and fight. Listen to Alena, Mister Bulwark." Razial teased.

Kalvin smiled. They know he will become a bulwark. Razial knows Kalvin is fated to play a role in the Order of the Flame's war against its enemies. The question he had was how Kalvin's role is connected to his own role.

***

In the keepers' chambers, Alena, Araceli, Xochi, and Zelia sat before Tu'ani and Lela. Behind the keepers is Ofelia. That puzzled the four siblings, but neither said anything. Only Alena knows Tu'ani had her give Ofelia the gems that Razial had asked her to hold. What she and the others do not know is that Priato had told the keepers that Ofelia is fated to become a paladin and that is why Lela decided to fast track Ofelia's time as an apprentice.

With Alena and the others ready to leave within hours, the keepers decided to meet with them with Ofelia present so she could hear their plans for Coilu. After explaining they want Razial, Kalvin, Fogi Red, and Paul protected, they told the siblings that Paul is only important until they have the ancient crown of Coilu. That puzzled the siblings.

"Why until we obtain the ancient crown?" Araceli asked.

"Because Paul is the last of Coilu's heroic-line. Until we possess the crown, protect him. So long as he lives, our enemies cannot remove the crown from the city of Coilu unless he is in the city." The keepers answered.

"So, Paul matters more than the assassin?" Xochi asked.

"No. Protect Razial above all-even Fogi Red!"

The keepers' response stunned them all. Ofelia stood listening and watching. Hearing the keepers talk simultaneously seems odd to her. She is still confused about why she is present. Another thing that is bothering her is the fact Xochi continues to refer to Razial as the assassin.

"Now listen carefully. Once you all have reached the throne room in Coilu, destroy the throne." The keepers said.

"Destroy it? How?" Zelia asked.

"With your powers. We cannot allow the Harbingers to free Bal in the capital. You all will learn more. Trust Havi and Adini. Do not be fooled by their personalities. Remember what you read about them during the last Champions' War. They are the same warriors they have always been."

After that, the keepers told them about the shadow-tracker. For Ofelia's sake, they explained that it is a magically altered troll that tracks its target's shadow cast by the moon.

"Why would Gwen of Dax release a shadow-tracker after Razial?" Araceli asked.

"Because she knows what you all do not know. Be careful all of you. It is time for you to be off. Remember," The keepers said with added emphasis. "-Ja'Razial leads your group. Do not tell him about the shadow-tracker and keep him out of the moonlight."

With that, the four siblings bid the keepers and Ofelia farewell. After they left the room, Lela told Ofelia to stand in front of her and Tu ani. Lela told her to show them the gems.

"What you hold are two of the five gems that make up the Stones of Honor. All five gems were lost during the Tuyakan Betrayal. The onyx was found immediately. It is now in a war-helm."

Ofelia sensed there was something hidden about the onyx.

"As time passed, the emerald and the sapphire were found. Now, with the diamond and the ruby, we have them all. We shall give you a scroll to study. We will test you in the future. Do not disappoint us by not believing in yourself. Tell no one you have the gems unless they know already. And for anyone to ask for them-without us being present means we are dead. Put away the gems and return to your group. We shall call on you regularly."

With that, Ofelia excused herself. She exited the chambers and looked back at the flame that had been magically charred on the thick wooden door. Her heart pounded inside her chest. Her mind raced with thoughts. She could not come up with a reason why the keepers trust her so much.

As she walked through the hallway in her gray peasant dress, she nodded in respect to a sibling and druid-sibling she passed by. Her mind went to Kalvin. Although she has only known him for seven weeks, she feels close to him. When they had said their good-byes, he had kissed her softly on the lips. At that moment, she could feel that kiss. She cannot wait to see him again.

***

Binu sat opposite Rogelio inside Rogelio's chambers. They rarely meet without other Hilt members present. Both have only recently returned to Fulancia. The Hilt had decided to deal with some things in eastern Giaour-each member went on his own mission. Carpio had returned only a day ago and left the next morning. Goraan and Tollok have yet to return.

Staring into Rogelio's blue eyes, Binu thought about how he and Rogelio are usually on opposite sides. Rogelio usually sides with Goraan. Strongly built, with shoulder length reddish brown hair that matches his full beard, Rogelio is taller than him, but he is not tall for a human. He is a great fighter and his moniker, the Fist, is well deserved.

On the table between them, is a dagger wrapped in an expensive cloth and a small scroll that is really a map. Binu wants to trade the map for the dagger.

"First you acquire the other dagger from Carpio. Now, you want mine. Why?" Rogelio asked.

"I have my reasons." Binu answered.

"Like keeping them from Goraan. Are you afraid he would eventually master the daggers?" Rogelio asked.

Binu remained stoic. Of the five members of the Hilt, only Goraan can wield the daggers, but he will never be able to master them-even Goraan knows that. The daggers once belonged to Ja'Brahma. It had shocked Goraan and Binu that Goraan could wield the daggers. They had explained to the other Hilt members that the daggers can only be mastered by the one who will become the Gideon. How Carpio and Rogelio obtained the daggers does not matter. Binu and Goraan had made it clear that if the Order of the Flame finds out that they have the daggers it would mean war, so they know to keep their secret.

"This is your chance to acquire the map brother. Accept my offer or I shall give it to Carpio, and you know he will destroy it. My reasons for wanting the daggers do not concern you." Binu said firmly.

He has Rogelio in a bind. The map is only a piece of the whole map of Ino-Heim, which Rogelio had wanted for decades. He has the other two pieces and wanted to sell pieces to Winnin or to Anazi Falls. Carpio felt it is too dangerous to allow Rakaar's servant to have even a piece of the map. Rogelio argues they could help the Order of the Flame stop Rakaar's servants from freeing Rakaar. Binu must admit helping Rakaar's servants get closer to finding the location of Rakaar's prison is risky. Truthfully, Carpio's position is the best position. He is correct in saying that traitors in the Order of the Flame could steal the pieces Rogelio sold to them.

"Goraan will not like this. You know how badly he wants the daggers." Rogelio said.

"I also know how bad you want this piece of the map. Either way, someone will be disappointed. You have the chance to make sure it is not you." Binu wanted to, but he remained stoic.

Rogelio sighed in defeat. He knows Binu would give the scroll to Carpio who would destroy it. He must accept the offer.

"Very well. You have a deal." Rogelio sighed.

Although his voice remained even, Binu knows he resents being put in a bind.

"Whatever your purpose for wanting two daggers you cannot wield, I hope it makes you happy. Just tell me do you intend to sell or trade them to the Order." Rogelio said.

Binu stood and put the dagger under his belt.

"No. Although that would be a good idea. That might get one of you off their list."

Rogelio smiled. The Order of the Flame has wanted him for a very long time, but they were not willing to pay the price for acting against him. The same is true for Goraan who has been wanted for centuries.

Rogelio watched Binu leave. He nodded when Binu said.

"Have Tollok visit me when he arrives. I have things to discuss with our brothers."

CHAPTER 5

ASSASSINS' HONOR

For five weeks, Razial traveled for stealth instead of speed. That took a toll on his group. Xochi constantly argued with him about his pace and his choice of direction. She wanted to travel north through Anazi and Gully then on to Mohr. Razial chose to cross the Goraan Mountains before turning north toward Sahkar.

Things were made worse by the weather. The farther north they traveled the colder it became. Winter not only brought snow but more bickering between Razial and Xochi and more pestering from the jolems.

As they approached Sahkar, it began to rain. The rain only made them more miserable. The elfin animals had left them just before the rain began. The elfin wolves had made riding through the snow easier by taking the lead. Without them, the group's horses had to pass through deep, unbroken snow. Razial is leading the group. Kalvin is to his right. The jolems are just behind them. Alena, Araceli, Sidney, Paul, and Raal are behind the jolems. Fogi Red is off to the right of the jolems. To him, he is punishing his horse by having it break through the snow on its own. Zelia, Xochi, and four bulwarks are bringing up the rear.

Kalvin watched Fogi Red lead his horse back onto the trail. Shaking his head, he took in the scenery. The day is gray. The snow that covers the grassland south of Sahkar is melting and the clouds are pouring rain from low in the sky.

"From rain to snow to rain." Havi squeaked.

He and Adini refuse to share a horse. Even though they appear to be toddlers riding horses, they handle horses very well. They enjoy irritating the others. It is difficult for Kalvin to imagine them as deadly warriors, but the others assure him they are legends in the Order of the Flame.

"I doubt the Society has any traps in Sahkar." Havi said referring to Razial saying the Society has set traps around Anazi.

Kalvin knows Razial is not bothered by what Havi said. After news of the Partisans joining Paul's forces reached them, the others' point that they must hurry became mute in Razial's mind. With Bassar still neutral and winter bringing the fighting to a standstill, time is on their side. The fact that Peter II has become emperor helps them because many throughout western Coilu refuse to accept him.

"Do not be so sure Havi. By now, many have figured out that I am not in Anazi." Razial said.

He then told the others they will rest for two days then head to Osam.

"Osam?!" Xochi snapped.

"Trust me. I have a plan. I need you all to send a message to Anazi Falls saying we are headed to Brahma city so Paul can ask the king for his assistance." Razial said.

"For what purpose?" Xochi asked.

Alena understands he is trying to find out how infiltrated the Order of the Flame is. She explained this to Xochi. Then, Araceli said they will do as he suggested. After that, he told Xochi and

Araceli to search the city for enemies. He told Zelia to find a place to stay for two days.

"Anything else, Master?" Xochi asked sarcastically.

"Yes. Split up. You go with your sister. Fogi Red, Raal, and the jolems form your own group while Kalvin and I ride with the others into the city." Razial said.

Zelia asked what his plan was if something happened. He told her they were to meet up at the safe house the Order of the Flame has in Sahkar.

"You are smart assassin. At first, I thought you were just lucky." Adini said.

*

After splitting up, they all made their way into Sahkar. That night, Alena stood by the window in her room watching the rain. Zelia and Araceli were asleep. Xochi had gone to relieve herself. Although she had tried to be quiet, she had awakened Alena, who decided to await her return.

The inn Xochi and Zelia chose is an old wooden inn. It is the only inn that could accommodate their group. The bulwarks are all in the same room. Paul, Sidney, Raal, and Fogi Red are in the same room while Razial, Kalvin, and the jolems had to sleep above the stables. Although it is cold and squeaks a lot, the inn is a good spot because the owners are an older couple that is trusted by the Society, and they are great cooks.

Lightning flashed several times illuminating the city. Even though it is still dark, Alena knows it is close to dawn. She rubbed her arms for warmth. She heard Xochi slowly closing the door, but her attention stayed focused on the muddy street. Three hooded figures are making their way toward the inn. She looked in the opposite direction and saw a group of men walking toward the inn.

"Wake the others." She whispered.

Xochi stopped in the middle of the room. She still has on her long coat. Alena knelt to wake Araceli while telling Xochi to only have the others get ready. Xochi nodded before leaving the room.

"What is it?" Araceli asked.

Alena quickly explained what she had seen. She then went to inform Razial.

Razial crept across the kitchen with a dagger in each hand. It is dark, but he can still see. Behind him, the jolems stand ready to act. He had Paul and Kalvin sneak to the stables in case they had to fight and run. The others are in their rooms. If they can get through this without fighting, it will be better for them.

"No. None of my guests seem strange."

The innkeeper said to the people who had entered the inn. All Razial knows for sure is the hooded figures are powerful in magic. He knows this by the way they speak with authority and confidence. One asked about him and the others. Although she did not use any names, it was clear to the innkeeper that she was talking about Razial and the others.

"No large group arrived. Some arrived in groups of threes or fours." The innkeeper said.

Several others could be heard entering the inn's front door. Razial listened, trying to count how many people had just entered the inn. His pulse quickened when he heard Vishnu's voice.

"Some of them may be here; however, if Paul and my brother are not here, it is not worth the hassle." Vishnu said.

The woman did not respond at first. She thought for a moment. Then, said. "We shall eat breakfast with your patrons."

Razial's mind began to race. He cannot afford to reveal his location just yet. Vishnu would not lose track of him without a fight and other hunters would pick up his trail.

Thinking of a way out of this, Razial signaled for the jolems to stay in the kitchen while he went to the stables. He came up with a plan. He can already hear Alena berating him when she catches up to him. He smiled mentally.

*

Kalvin saw the fury in Alena's eyes. Razial had told him to wait several minutes before he informed Alena about Razial's plan to rejoin them in Osam where he was taking Paul. She understands why he did this. The problem is he does not know about the shadow-tracker.

"Kalvin you should not have agreed to do this. Your friend plans well but not this time." Xochi said.

Looking over Alena's head, Kalvin stared into Xochi's catlike eyes. He can sense she is serious. She is not just being disagreeable because it is Razial.

"Is this the same assassin who tried to kill Kalvin?" Zelia asked referring to Vishnu.

Alena explained that it is.

"Then we owe him." Xochi hissed.

"No. We owe him nothing. Vishnu will not act against us. He has no reason to." Alena countered.

"If he threatens us, we will fight." Araceli said firmly.

Kalvin sensed Alena's concern. She told him to bring the bulwarks so they could eat.

*

Vishnu sat eating with his apprentices, who are out for a little payback after what had happened in Mohr. One of them has a permanent scar on his hand from Razial's dagger. Vishnu watched as Alena descended the stairs. He looked at the dining room. The stairs end in the middle of the room. There is not much room to fight. He looked at the witch and two warlocks traveling with him. They had surprised him when they told him they had spies inside the Order of the Flame and could track Razial's group.

"It's Alena." An apprentice said.

"I see her. We are here for the Avatar." Vishnu said.

He locked eyes with Alena who took in the scenery before she and the others sat together. He looked back at the witch, who is obviously impatient. She signaled to the swordsmen traveling with her. She told them to search the inn. The innkeeper told her no one else was in the inn.

"You lie." A warlock snapped.

"Who are you fools?" Xochi asked.

Staring at her and Zelia, Vishnu tried to figure out which of them had attacked him in Mohr.

"We are not Eloh's whores." The witch said coldly.

The bystanders in the inn sensed the tension and moved out of the way. Vishnu knows by Alena's expression that Razial is not present. He was going to tell this to the witch, but Xochi stood and said.

"Bal be damned. Cas be damned. Mel be damned!"

That angered the witch and warlocks. They drew their powers. The siblings quickly did the same. Vishnu's apprentices looked at him. He finished his food before saying.

"It is not worth it. Paul is not here."

"But four of Eloh's whores are." The witch responded.

She stood and the warlocks did the same. Xochi did not hesitate. She struck the swordsmen closest to her then lashed out at Vishnu. He drew his powers and battled back.

Araceli's red hair flowed behind her as she leapt over a table to engage the witch. Alena saw Kalvin and Sidney fight the men closest to them while she knocked several men to the wooden floor. The bulwarks raced to join the fighting. Swords crashed. The tables and chairs were overturned. The fighting became chaotic. The warlocks tried to overwhelm Zelia, but she kept them at bay. Havi saved Xochi from Vishnu while Raal picked her up. Fogi Red battled the apprentices while Adini ran around killing swordsmen.

Vishnu had never fought a jolem before. He was impressed by Havi's ferocity. He had to give ground to avoid being wounded. He saw Alena help Zelia, and a bulwark killed. Seeing Fogi Red and Raal fighting his apprentices, he wanted to help, but Havi is too dangerous to turn his back on.

Araceli and the witch were surprised by the fact they are equals. Fighting near the doorway, the witch saw Alena and Zelia kill the warlocks. She called for a retreat. She could have kept fighting, but that would have been useless. She ran off glad her enemies let them leave without pursuit.

Zelia gasped with her hands on her hips. She leaned over in pain. Looking around, she saw Araceli sitting on the floor with her back against the wall. The fight had drained them all. Had Xochi not involved Vishnu and his apprentices, they could have driven their enemies off without much effort or loss. Zelia thought about scolding her sister but decided not to. However, Alena was not in a forgiving mood. She told Xochi that she had started the fight, and that the bulwark's death is her fault. Raal, who stood over Xochi healing her, told Alena to calm herself. Alena quickly rebuked him saying that he should heal those who deserve to be healed. At first, Raal did not obey her which caused Adini to snap at him saying that if he continues to heal Xochi there would be another fight.

"Listen to him Raal." Fogi Red said.

Xochi even told him to obey Adini. He stood and walked over to Araceli. Unlike the others, he is not that powerful. He did not use his powers except to shield himself.

He dislikes that the others are angry with Xochi because to him it is always correct to fight their enemies.

***

Ofelia cleaned the front room of the keepers' chambers. She had adapted to being a novice, but still felt out of place. She had little time to herself. She spent most of her time learning how to use her powers. To her surprise, she was much stronger than she had thought.

When she was not learning how to use her powers, she was learning how to read and write in common and in Tuyakan. (All important messages are sent in Tuyakan.) It was rare for a novice to be taught Tuyakan, but the keepers instructed her teachers to do so. She still had no idea why they had so much interest in her, but she was happy they did because whenever a sibling sees a novice with nothing to do the sibling quickly gives that novice something to do. Ofelia avoids that by cleaning the keepers' chambers where she can rest sometimes.

"Ofelia." The keepers called from another room.

She shook her dust towel. Then she straightened her dress. She made her way to the room where the keepers sat before a fireplace. They did not turn to face her which made her nervous.

"Calm yourself." Lela said in her assuring voice.

Ofelia likes it when they talk individually to her. When they talk simultaneously, it intimidates her. Something about them speaking in unison made her feel as if some greater force was speaking through them. She began rubbing the gems tucked near her waist to calm herself.

"We have been informed that you are quite powerful. How is it no lessor coven ever discovered you?" The keepers asked.

She became perfectly calm. It was time to tell her story. She told them at birth she was sold to a coven. Her mother acted like her wet nurse. One day the coven was attacked by the Theocracy.

Only the children were left alive. She joined a band of thieves in Danou city. Tears filled her eyes as she told them about the day a group of Danouan soldiers attacked her and her friends. The boys were killed while the girls were taken prisoner. An emptiness came over her eyes while she explained they began to beat and rape the girls. She trailed off trying to push away the pain of the memory.

"I did not mean to kill them, but I had to!" She forced the words out.

She explained that while struggling against the men who were trying to rape her, she lashed out with all her power killing them. Then, got up with her powers still lashing out striking only the men who were trying to rape or were raping her friends.

"I killed them all then ran away to Giaour where I roamed for years looking after orphans. I was captured in Arapia because I had no coin, no husband, and no home. I would still be a slave had Kalvin and Razial not freed me and the children." She finished with a smile.

Kalvin and Razial have changed her life for the rest of her life. The keepers stood and faced her. They too smiled. She told them that it was a very fortunate coincidence that Kalvin and Razial had been on the ship owned by the same slaver she had convinced to buy her and the children.

"That was no coincidence." The keepers said. "Choices control circumstances. Circumstances control fate. Fate controls destiny. Fate has brought you to us, so we can prepare for the war against Rakaar's servants."

That made Ofelia frown. The keepers dismissed her uncertainty. They told her to accept that she has a great destiny. In Ofelia's opinion, she was there because Razial's honor would not allow the slaver to transport children while he was on the ship.

***

The Master sat in a dark room. He is in a telepathic trance. He had just instructed Ariel to drag out the civil war. She is close to locating the map to Bal's dolmen. Beulah already has the maps to find Cas and Mel. He despises the Magi, but he needs them to confuse the Order of the Flame and weaken Rakaar. That is why he is acting to free them.

He knows his rivals patrol the telepathic realm, so he kept his contact with Ariel short. She knows his plans cannot succeed without Razial, so he did not discuss that. He finished by warning her to keep Peter from falling for one of Gwen's famous traps. After ending contact with Ariel, he called out to Beulah. He told her to leave for the rendezvous in four days.

"This seems dangerous. Are you sure you can control them?" Beulah asked.

Never a blind servant, she always asks questions. That is a good thing, but he does not have time to discuss things with their rivals getting close.

"It will be easy. To control them, I only have to control their leader. That, I can easily do."

After thinking that, he told her to remain silent. "Priato." The Master thought. "This Gideon shall walk the path of A'Ja'brahma."

"He will come for you if you try to control him." Priato thought back.

"As he should. This war shall change things forever. Until our paths cross."

He exited the telepathic realm knowing Beulah had done the same. He knows Priato will soon begin to figure a lot of things out. He had kept Razial hidden from him for decades, but there was never any doubt that Priato would eventually discover Razial is fated to become the Gideon.

He knows soon his Rivals shall figure out that he is out to free the elves who are magically sealed in the city of Gnor, but that does not deter him.

***

Razial lay on his side staring at his room door. He had been asleep when Scar awakened him. With Paul still asleep and the six elfin wolves sniffing the air near the door, he prepared to fight. When the wolves relaxed, he realized they sense someone familiar to them. He rolled to his feet. He had arrived in Osam that afternoon. He and Paul had eaten at the contractor's lodge. He was given meat to feed Scar's pack before making his way to a tavern that is a haven for shady individuals.

The three-week trip from Sahkar to Osam had been exhausting. Upon reaching the small windowless room, Paul fell fast asleep. Razial managed to snooze, which was good for him. He held his daggers ready while he looked at Scar. It took him a moment to figure out Scar's thoughts-the pack senses Binu near the door. He moved to open the door so by the time Binu stood in front of his room, he had opened the door.

"Uncle." He whispered in elvish.

He gestured for Binu to enter the room. He closed the door while looking back at Paul who remained asleep. Binu noticed, so he kept his voice low. He explained that the war in Coilu would be an uphill war and that the Fellowship will not simply allow the Order of the Flame to take power throughout Coilu-the lands that the Fellowship calls its own. He then told Razial the Sisterhood wants him dead.

"In the future, we shall punish them for that." Binu stated.

Paul awakened. He remained silent because he had no idea what was being said. Binu paid him no mind. He told Razial he had come to give him a gift.

"A gift?" Razial asked.

All he had been thinking while Binu talked to him was how had Binu tracked him. He handed Razial daggers wrapped inside of a cloth which Razial quickly unwrapped. He stared at the daggers in disbelief while Binu lit the candle near the door. Razial remembers the daggers from the Hilt's treasure room. One belonged to Carpio. The other to Rogelio. They are said to possess sorcery. Their blades are made of white gold while their hilts and cross guards are made of platinum. Their pommels have large sapphires embedded in them and there are four knuckle sized sapphires in each cross guard.

"These are worth at least two crowns uncle." Razial said.

"They are priceless Razial'ja. You are in possession of Ja'Brahma's daggers." Binu said seriously.

Razial stared into his slanted eyes. Binu's elflocks dangled in front of his hood. He told Razial to try to wield the daggers. Razial noticed the cloth as it floated to the floor. He thought about picking it up, but before he could move, the sapphires sparkled, and the daggers disappeared!

Paul sat up quickly causing Razial, Binu, and the elfin wolves to turn and face him.

"What happened to the daggers?!" He asked excitedly.

Binu ignored him. He told Razial that the daggers have bonded with him, and no one can ever take them from him. He explained that the daggers can cut through anything, and the blades will never dull. Razial stared at him with confusion in his eyes. He knows the daggers' history and knows that the daggers binding with him mean that he will gain possession of Ja'Brahma's powers!

"How did this happen?! How did you know?" Razial asked.

"I did not. I wanted you to give them to the Order of the Flame so you could bargain on our wanted brothers' behalf, but thinking about how much the Order of the Flame is hiding about your contract I figured asking you could not hurt. Now, you can better avoid those who hunt you." Binu said.

He then explained that only Goraan could wield the daggers. Razial did not need to be told to keep that to himself.

"This is what the Order of the Flame was keeping from you. There is no way A'Priato did not know this. That is why they hired you." Binu pointed at him.

Razial nodded in agreement. His mind began to race as he tried to figure out who else might have known. Binu noticed this and said.

"Alena does not know. I am sure."

He bid Razial farewell telling him to be careful during the hunt. Razial sensed his sadness. Binu seems to know a lot of peril awaits him in the future. In his mind, the hunt is no longer his main concern. He now has to worry about being the Gideon. He called the daggers to him, and they appeared in his hands. He released them and they disappeared.

"Who was that elf?" Paul asked as he stood. "How much did those daggers cost? Is this why you came to Osam?"

"Paul. Never mind who that is. Our plan remains the same. I suggest you rest." Razial said to calm him.

*

Anjia watched as Binu exited the tavern. Then made her way to the stairs. Dressed in all black, like usual when outside Fulancia, she thought about how she had not expected to cross paths with Razial until he reached the Coilu and Brahma border. She had been tracking Razial through the Goraan Mountains when Goraan's message had reached her. He had instructed her to kill the duke of Osam. Although he would never admit it, he had sent her to Osam to separate her from Razial. A smile came over her face as she climbed the stairs. Goraan's plan has failed. By sending her to Osam, he put her in Razial's path.

She had killed the duke days earlier and would have left Osam for Sahkar had she not sensed Scar's pack. (She did not know that it was Scar's pack. To her, it is a pack of elfin wolves that is out of place.) While trying to track the wolves, she saw several crews of assassins. She watched them for several minutes then returned to tracking the wolves. That is when she saw Binu. After he spent a little time in the tavern, she knew he had met Razial.

As she approached the room where the wolves were, she sensed their excitement. The door opened and Razial stood shirtless in the doorway. He smiled at her. She noticed Paul while kissing Razial. He closed the door, and her attention went to Scar's pack. He watched her greet the wolves and glanced at Paul. He knows that Paul will not go back to sleep now. Anjia looked at Paul. He identified Paul, then asked how she had tracked him.

"I am not that good my love." She answered in elvish.

She explained how she managed to come across him. She then told him that the king of Fulancia had lost his conflict with the generals and would soon be assassinated. That shocked him. The king of Fulancia is a longtime ally to the Society.

"That is only the beginning." Anjia said.

She went on to tell him that Diana had been chosen to rule Arapia after Goraan approved her plan to kill the entire royal family. That confused him because Diana cannot rule Arapia unless she gets married. He intended to say this, but Anjia went on telling him about how Diana killed four nobles in Tali and in other parts of eastern Giaour. That gives Diana rank over other assassins. Add the fact she is the one who made the alliance with the magicians in eastern Giaour and with the Anizetos in central Giaour and Razial understands why Anjia is so concerned with how useful Diana has made herself to the Society.

He thought about how Diana is a noble born witch who has become a master assassin. Anjia dislikes her for two reasons: she stands with Goraan, and she has feelings for Razial.

"How is Goraan going to settle the issue of Arapians demanding a king?" He asked.

"I have no idea. Now tell me why Binu was here." Anjia said.

He held up his hands and called the daggers to him. She scowled in amazement. He told her what Binu had said to him. She dislikes this sudden turn of events. She began cursing the Order of the Flame which made her suspicious of Alena. He stopped her from saying anything bad about Alena. She hugged and kissed him. She is visibly upset. She wants to be alone. She had come to tell him about the Fulancian king because he liked him. A thought to ask Goraan to stop the hunt because Razial has Ja'Brahma's daggers crossed her mind, but her honor would never allow her to do such a thing. Paul took a drink of water after Anjia left. He thought about asking Razial who she was, but Razial laid down and said.

"Do not ask."

Razial's mind is full of questions. The wolves sensed the change in him. They huddled around him. He pulled the blanket up to his shoulders. Then he put an arm around his eyes to block the candlelight. He had warned Lela and Tu'ani that they better have answers for him in the future. After binding with the daggers, he has even more questions.

***

Lela and Tu'ani sat at the head of the table inside Flame Hall with many druid-siblings sitting around the table. Also present are six members of the Gully Council. They are discussing how to stop the Harbingers from finding Bal's dolmen because they know all three Magi are inside Bal's dolmen. Some druid-siblings were surprised to learn this, but they did not feel slighted. Lela told them they wanted the Harbingers to waste time searching for the other dolmens.

"They took great risks doing so and we eliminated many of their best agents." Lela said.

Although she had spoken the truth, their plan did not work as well as they had hoped. They had located and killed the last of the Heralds but not one Harbinger. Tu'ani let that settle in, before she explained that it would take the Harbingers time to translate the dolmen.

"If the Master reads the dolmen, A'Priato would be able to track him so we have time." Tu'ani said.

Gurdia asked why they are wasting time trying to track how the Harbingers have manipulated the Fellowship and the Sisterhood when they should be tracking and killing members of the Fellowship throughout western Coilu.

"Gurdia. Coilu shall be a thorn in our side for some time to come. For now, we must plan to defend the city of Brahma in case the Harbingers succeed." Lela and Tu'ani said.

"What about Nibel?" Gurdia asked.

For the last decade, she has been spearheading the push for them to take action to put Fogi Red on Nibel's throne. She knows the Magi are a threat. She also knows the Harbingers are using the Magi to distract them. She stated this and the keepers did not disagree.

Lela stared at Gurdia. Even in the dimly lit hall, it is easy to see Gurdia's all white hair that matches Lela's own all-white hair. Gurdia is old even for a dwarf. She has seen many battles, and she is aware that she will not see the end of this Champions' War.

Chivia is the leader of the jolem armies. She came to Anazi Falls with Inora and Growan (Inora's husband) who had been part of the Gully Council for a very long time. With her long brown hair braided into two braids, (to show she is a warrior) she watched the keepers while they told Gurdia that they had plans for Nibel. Without asking to hear their plans, she told them her ideas to deal with Nibel and Brahma city.

Daniel has been a druid-sibling for quite some time. He stared at Chivia. Her pretty brown eyes are always firm. He had never seen her smile. Although Adini and Havi are the legends, she is the jolems' lead general. Her ideas seem flawless. He watched her look around waiting for someone to critique her ideas. Her eyes landed on him. She cannot see his eyes because his cowl's hood hides his face.

"Chivia. Your ideas are good." The keepers said. "We shall call on you soon. For now, you and Gurdia can put your ideas in effect while we see to things in Gnor."

That caught the others by surprise and the keepers knew it. They know the Master can open Gnor and they cannot afford to be caught off guard. They told Daniel to go to Brahma city to forward their plans there.

"Things are about to get difficult. The better prepared we are, the greater our chances for success." They said.

***

Kalvin entered Osam without incident. Zelia and Xochi are leading their group. Kalvin is in the middle of their group with Raal, Fogi Red, Sidney, and the three bulwarks while Alena and Araceli are bringing up the rear. The jolems had left to join Razial a day after he left. The others remained behind until the rainstorm in Sahkar ended. They rode hard and fast for days at a time. Sidney worried the whole time. He is not convinced that Razial would risk himself to save Paul. Alena told him not to mention his doubts in Razial's presence.

"Question an assassin's honor and you better be prepared to deal with that assassin."

Alena had said to him. Sidney kept his doubts to himself after that. Kalvin looked at the sky for a sign of Alena's pet hawks. The hawks must hunt more because it is winter. They had left the group just before they reached Osam.

"So, do you think Havi and Adini will sense us?" Sidney asked.

Ever since seeing the jolems pass through soil, he has been obsessed with learning about jolems.

"No. The wolves will." Fogi Red answered.

Where Raal is dressed warmly and blends in with the others, as a dwarf, Fogi Red cannot. His long frizzy beard stands out because it is red. Sidney has no clue that Fogi Red is the true king of Nibel and that Raal is his protector. In his mind,

Raal is so protective of Fogi Red because they are both Partisans.

Zelia is bringing Sidney along slowly. She does not distrust him, but too much is going on for him to know about. Alena told Kalvin that a lot is being kept from Sidney. He understands why.

Riding through the snow-covered streets of Osam, Kalvin took in the city. It was built in sections, so if it is breached the breached area can be sealed off.

The day is bright, but there is no sunlight-only fast moving all white clouds. An old couple caught his attention. They are cold and thin. He tossed a half-filled pouch of gold coins and silver pieces to them. The old man was startled and knocked the pouch to the ground.

"That's for you." Kalvin said.

The man picked up the pouch. With gray-white hair, the man appears frail. His eyes widened in surprise when he saw what was inside the pouch.

"Thank you, good sir!" The man shouted.

Kalvin heard him say something about being able to buy his grandchildren back. He did not hear him clearly because Fogi Red asked him what the man is yelling about.

"Nothing. I simply felt like making someone happy." Kalvin smiled.

"Well make me happy and toss me a sheep's stomach full of dwarf ale." Fogi Red teased.

Kalvin shook his head. They all continued riding along at a slow pace. He looked at Zelia and Xochi and wondered why Xochi and Alena have not settled their differences yet. Alena is still angry about Xochi attacking Vishnu and Xochi seems equally angry with Alena.

In Xochi's mind, the others should have helped target Vishnu and the witch. Araceli agrees with Alena. Zelia told Xochi that she was wrong to target Vishnu, but she has forgiven her twin. Kalvin stays out of it because Xochi is quick to say that he is not yet a member of the Order of the Flame.

"We are being watched." Raal said.

Alena had already spotted Anjia who had signaled to her before Raal spotted her walking away.

"All is well. That was Anjia." Alena replied.

Raal asked if they should worry about Anjia finding Razial.

"No." She answered.

There is no need for her to say that Anjia had most likely met with Razial. That bothers her because she believes that one day Anjia will bring harm to Razial. They were once very close- like sisters, until they argued about what she felt would happen.

Zelia asked how Anjia had found them. Alena does not know. All she knows is that Anjia will stay close to Razial until the hunt nears its end. Then, Anjia will try to capture him. The others think that is why they should deal with her, but Razial has made it very clear that to do so is to act against him. Even Alena sided with him on that issue.

"I do not know but follow her." Alena told the others.

Xochi and Zelia turned to the street that Anjia had turned on to. By the time Alena had turned on to the street, Anjia had mounted her horse and was riding slowly through the street. She turned left. Alena and the others followed. Xochi made a statement about them riding through a dangerous part of the city. They all took note of the run-down buildings. Most are made of wood and cracked bricks.

The people out in the streets are all armed so one must pay attention in this part of Osam. Alena is not worried. Her only concern is other assassins finding out that Razial is nearby. She increased her pace when she sensed Scar's pack. Raal told Xochi and Zelia to stop. Alena stopped and glanced around to make sure that no one was paying too much attention to them. She told the others that she would go and talk to Razial alone.

While she walked toward the tavern, Havi and Adini wobbled out.

"Hey. Where are our horses?" Adini asked.

He twisted his face playfully while rubbing his goatee.

"We sold them-well traded them for supplies." Fogi Red said mockingly.

Alena heard them trading insults and Zelia saying something about dwarfs and their insults. After that, the people inside the tavern drowned out their voices. Her elflocks dangled out of her hood. She paid that no mind because in this part of Osam people know confrontation can lead to death.

As she approached Razial's room, he opened the door and smiled at her.

"How long have you been here?" She asked.

"Two days. How long before you all are ready to ride?" He asked.

"We need supplies, then we can ride."

She glanced at Paul. He appears refreshed. Razial had obviously taken good care of him. She greeted the wolves who were ready to leave the city. She knows they had stayed only to keep Razial safe.

"The jolems and I have come up with a plan. First, let me explain all that I have learned." Razial said.

He told her that the contractor had told him about an impending meeting in Vin. The Society does not know why Vin has called the meeting, but they know that representatives from Ruug and Suce will be present. She was surprised to hear that Vin has sent men into northern Brahma to hire as many swordsmen as they can while sending an army to the southeast of Mohr stopping Mohr from supplying its allies in central Coilu. That army also allows Peter II's allies to defend themselves in case Bassar joins Mohr.

"Why have you kept this from me?" Paul asked.

Razial ignored him. He switched to elvish while telling Alena about Binu giving him the daggers. Not knowing what was being said and feeling insulted, to him Razial has never respected his highborn status, Paul stood and said.

"I should have been infor-"

"You should be dead." Razial said with a cold calm.

His eyes never left Alena. He called the daggers to him so she could see them. They disappeared when he released them.

"I am going to deal with that army while you all get him to Mohr and prepare for the war." Razial pointed at Paul.

He opened the door then led the wolves out. The wolves made themselves invisible. Alena turned to look at Paul. He asked her what Razial had said. She shook her head and said.

"You would be wise to remember that he does not serve you. He is not your servant. You should remember that he despises nobles. Do not forget that." She said with emphasis.

She led him out while thinking about how nobles believe they are noble and full of honor while assassins from the Society must earn their rank and honor. It is their honor that drives the members of the Society. Outsiders have no understanding of assassin's honor.

***

Vishnu had searched Brahma city and found no sign of Razial. He went to Geoffrey's smithy. As the contractor of Brahma, Geoffrey can play no role in finding Razial, but he will be able to share information with Vishnu.

Larry, Geoffrey's son, greeted Vishnu. He led him to his father. The three of them sat in the back of the shop talking. Vishnu was not surprised to hear that the Hilt wants Pam dead.

She made the mistake of asking for them to kill Razial knowing he is a member of the Society.

He thought about how the witch had told him her spies had told her that they had intercepted a message saying Paul would go to Brahma city. Angry, he asked if there were any open contracts in the city.

"Two people one contract. A witch and a warlock," Geoffrey said.

He told Vishnu the person who targeted the couple had tried to remain anonymous, but he found out it was someone in the royal house. That intrigued Vishnu. He asked why the couple had been targeted.

"Something about them getting in the way of business in Pu'um. The funny thing about it is the client does not know the couple has powers. I discovered this on my own." Geoffrey said with a wink.

"How much is the contract?" Vishnu asked.

"Five hundred gold coins."

"Why so much? Are they nobles?"

"No. However, the client has tried and failed to kill them several times."

Vishnu nodded while rubbing his beard. He handed Larry several gold coins while saying.

"Mark this couple down as mine."

Vishnu stood. He complimented Geoffrey on his skills as a contractor. He told Larry he had grown a lot since the last time they met. Geoffrey told Larry to show him where the couple lives. Larry nodded. Vishnu followed him out of the shop.

They rode through the city. Larry told him he would wave to the couple when he passed them. Vishnu let him ride a short distance ahead, so it did not appear as if they were together. He watched Larry wave at the couple then keep riding. He slowed his horse then dismounted. He began walking toward the couple who sensed the danger from him. They drew their powers. He shielded himself while drawing his sword and dagger. They did not delay in attacking him. His long coat flailed as he fought. He pressed them with his weapons, forcing them to use their powers to shield themselves more than to strike him. They had obviously not expected his magical shield to be as strong as it is.

They tried to back away because his weapons drained them too much. He stayed close to them because that was his only chance to keep them from escaping. The man knocked Vishnu back, but unfortunately for him, Vishnu's long sword cut through the front of his neck. Frozen heat rose from the pouring blood. The woman struck him with her powers and made the mistake of moving too close to him. She never saw her death coming.

He spun around avoiding her while whipping his sword so that when he faced her his sword decapitated her. Her lifeless body fell to the ground. Warm blood pooled on the snow melting it. He remounted his horse. He knows he had killed them out of anger. When he released his powers, he felt the effects of their magical strikes. He made his way to where his apprentices awaited with the witch. He will separate from her and head to Coilu city where Razial and Paul must eventually go.

***

Lisa stood watching the high ceiling hall and everyone present. She was surprised by how quickly the Harbinger had set things in motion. Along with representatives from Ruug, Suce, and Vin, she has come to end all hostilities between Ruug and Suce.

For generations, Ruug and Suce have fought an on again and off again war. Even while she and Pam battled each other for control of Suce, they took actions against Ruug. That is why everyone present knows of her. Many of them know of Tammy as well. Together, they have a formidable reputation. Not even the Vinans want to anger them, and they are in Vin!

With paintings hanging on the walls, the hall is well decorated. Drapes hang from the ceiling covering the shuttered windows. Lit candles burn in front of mirrors lighting the hall. Tammy whispered in Tuyakan about several guests. Lisa nodded in agreement. Tammy told her to watch the Vinans. Lisa had told them to agree to whatever is agreed to during this meeting or they would lose their power in Vin. She knows Ariel will decide what is to be done in Vin. She does not know who Ariel is. All she knows is a Harbinger will set the terms to what they are to agree to.

She thought about how she had become part of this. The Ancient had sent her a message inviting her to join her cause.

"Lisa. In Suce, you were a leader fighting for such a small area. Stand with me and your world shall grow. You will no longer be a top scavenger in a world of predators and hunters." The Ancient had written.

Before reading that message, she had felt slighted because Pam had been sent to Ocia city. After reading the message, she showed it to Tammy. Tammy told her it is a test to find out if she knows the difference between being a major player in a small game and a major player in a big game. Lisa liked that Tammy had seen the wisdom in the test.

"Here she comes." Tammy whispered.

Lisa looked at the hall's double doors. Ariel entered with her Harbinger cowl floating above the floor while she walked. Lisa knows the red Harbinger cowl affects the others. When she had been with Peter and Ariel, she felt uncomfortable until she got used to not being able to see their faces.

"Come let us get this is over with." Ariel said.

She called them to the table in the middle of the hall. She began by stating what is expected of Ruug and Suce to make sure peace lasts. Several minor details were discussed and settled. Lisa noticed the Vinans' shocked expressions. They had not expected things to be settled so quickly. What they do not know is Peter-as the infamous general, had threatened the Ruugans. If they did not accept the terms, they would be killed.

With things between Ruug and Suce settled, Ariel asked the Vinans what they want to swear fealty to Peter II.

"Bend a knee to Peter II?" A Vinan scoffed.

"That was not part of our deal!" Another stated angrily.

"Lisa. Explain to them why bending a knee to Peter II is a good idea." Ariel said calmly.

"Because not doing so would draw the wrath of the entire Sisterhood. Suce would march on Vin and all of Vin's leaders would be targeted by all of those who stand with me." Lisa said.

At that moment, she realized why the Ancient sent her. Seeing her act subservient to Ariel makes the Vinans realize just how powerful Ariel is.

"Perhaps you all need time to talk. You have one hour." Ariel said, sending them out of the hall.

Her attitude shocked the Ruugans and Suceans. They do not understand how she can be so demanding in Vin. Ariel seems to sense this. She told them to return to their rooms and to be ready to leave in the morning. They looked around. Lisa raised her eyebrows to signal for them to obey.

After they left, Tammy sat to Lisa's right. Ariel told Tammy that if the Vinans attack them she wants her to hide until she gets a chance to kill the king of Vin.

"Do you expect them to challenge you?" Lisa asked.

"Us. Do I expect them to challenge us?" Ariel corrected her. "As we speak, they are discussing their best option-joining forces with Paul. The problem with that is they are not sure if Paul is still alive. And if he is still alive, can his forces help them against Suce."

Lisa smiled at this. She does not need to think about it. The Vinans only have one choice.

"As for your question. No. I do not expect them to challenge us unless they are fools." Ariel said.

Moments later, the Vinans returned saying they would join Peter II. They discussed several issues then sealed the deal.

After the Vinans left, Lisa asked Ariel her name.

"For now, you do not need to know that." Ariel said.

"Then how am I to know which one of you I am talking to" Lisa asked.

"Listen to our voices. If you are ever asked, I am simply an ally dressed in a red cowl." Ariel said firmly.

***

Razial watched as Anjia rode toward the camp. He knows the others dislike her staying so close to them, but he does not care. The jolems do not mind her. Sidney had suggested they draw their weapons. Alena quickly silenced that idea. Scar's pack waited for her to stop. They had been watching him and Kalvin throw daggers at a fallen tree.

"Maybe she is hungry." Fogi Red said playfully.

"She is coming to talk to Alena." Razial said.

"Me?" Alena asked.

Standing with Araceli, Zelia, and Xochi, she turned to look at Anjia. The sky is darkening. Their camp is in a sparse woodland.

"Yes. You." Anjia said from across the short distance.

Razial urged Alena to talk with her. Anjia stopped close to her. Alena mounted her horse and rode off with Anjia. Araceli asked Razial if he was sure about them riding too far off.

"They are like sisters. All will be well." He said.

*

Alena was not surprised by Anjia's anger. She had asked her if she had known about Razial being able to master Ja'Brahma's daggers. After they had talked for several minutes, they realized they are equally ignorant about what is going on and that their leaders know more than what they are revealing to them.

"This is probably Goraan does not mind me tracking Razial anymore." Anjia said.

Alena looked at her. They are riding back to the camp. It is completely dark all around them. Ahead, they can see the campfire in the middle of the camp.

"What do you mean anymore?" Alena asked.

Anjia explained how Goraan had sent her to kill the duke in Osam and how when she finished, he told her to keep tracking Razial.

"Have you told Razial?" Alena asked.

"No." Anjia stopped because Alena began shaking her head. "What is wrong?"

Alena looked into Anjia's eyes. She had just experienced a vision. Razial is in real danger and Anjia will save him!

Decades earlier, Alena had a vision where Anjia and others attacked Razial. That vision is what caused the rift between them. Only they know about this. Alena's visions only happen around Anjia. Believing she has no choice and eying the camp, Alena said.

"Give me your word, assassin's honor, that you will keep this to yourself."

"Assassin's honor." Anjia quickly whispered.

Alena told her about the shadow-tracker. Anjia reacted as expected-promising revenge.

CHAPTER 6

THE ELVES

Mantak will be four hundred years old in several months. Yet, for an elf he is not very old. As the top general of Alf-Heim's armies-the youngest to ever serve in the position, he has accomplished a lot in his lifetime. He had joined the army at a young age. Circumstances helped him after that.

During his first trip to Gully, the kings of Osam and Sahkar joined forces to invade Gully. He earned a lot of respect during that war. His captain was betrayed by their human allies, so he snuck into Osam and killed several of their leaders. For weeks, he led attacks behind enemy lines. He stole messages, cut supply lines, and killed many enemy leaders.

By the time he was forced back into Gully, he was put in command of an army and given permission to invade Sahkar while others invaded Osam. Sahkar and Osam were devastated until the rest of Brahma united to support them. Treaties were signed and peace was agreed to.

Years later, Mantak was chosen to turn back another invasion from western Brahma. When he finished, he was asked to help found the Partisans with Raal and Fogi Red. He did that then returned to Alf-Heim.

His current task is to coordinate Paul's forces. He led the overthrow of Mohr making sure the right people were killed and that the Partisans did nothing to jeopardize the peace with Mohr. All has gone well so far. His only problem is the bickering between the Mohran and Partisan generals. Upon hearing Paul is back in the lands of Coilu, the Mohrans want to attack. They also want to send a message to Bassar telling them to attack. On the other hand, the Partisans want to wait and hear from Fogi Red.

Listening to them, Mantak began thinking about how the keepers are using Razial to locate the others who are fated to become paladins and the four women who will be his keepers. Using his choices to do this is a wise move, but with the shadow-tracker tracking him it is also a dangerous gamble.

"Listen." He said to get the generals' attention.

He stared at them. They are all sitting around a table. They are all dressed warmly because the hall is in a corner of the palace, so its two outer walls conduct a lot of cold air. He can imagine how the Mohrans feel about him. He is physically unimposing. His long black hair is pulled back into one long braid. His reddish elf-locks hang regally to his chest. His pointed ears stand out and his narrow brown eyes match his golden yellow skin perfectly. Short and well built, he knows humans respect his fighting skills because he is an elf.

Dressed in a brown surplice, (humans know that only high-ranking elves wear brown surplices in human lands) he knows they know not to challenge him. Behind him are his four guards. They are dressed in all brown: jerkins over long-sleeved shirts and pants as well as hooded cloaks. Their style of dress signals to all they are Ratels-soldiers from Alf-Heim. So, if his surplice is not enough for them to respect, his guards are. The Mohrans may not like him, but they will respect him.

"What do you all think of inviting Bassar and all neutral cities to send their best magicians and most knowledgeable nobles to test Paul. That way upon his arrival we do not have to wait to plan the next action in the war.: He asked.

He knows making plans before Paul arrives is useless. Until Razial acts, it is best to wait. He is simply trying to prevent them from making bad decisions.

"So, what say you?" He asked.

They all agreed to do as he suggested. Then, as and as unceremoniously as it had begun, the meeting ended.

***

Kalvin and the others approach Mohr. A relentless cold wind is blowing. Only Fogi Red has his face uncovered. After Razial and the jolems split away from them about a week earlier, Fogi Red decided to pester like the jolems used to. However, he has not bothered anyone-because of the wind that day. He cannot enjoy bothering them because they are all wrapped up.

Looking at him, Kalvin saw the frost cake on his beard. Being from the Axe Peaks, Fogi Red is used to severe cold. He is not unaffected by the cold, but he is not as affected as the others are.

"I do not speak horse, but I believe these horses are happy to see Mohr in the horizon." Fogi Red said.

Kalvin must agree because his horse seems to be moving with more urgency in anticipation of getting out of the cold. It has been slow going ever since they entered Coilu. He looked around wondering where Anjia was at that moment. He knows Razial is sure she will not help him unless he needs her to.

"From the moment she helps me, she will become a target. A captured assassin could be taken and or killed while with the captor until Fulancia is within sight."

Razial had said when Kalvin had asked why he did not ask Anjia to help him act against the Vinans. Kalvin turned his attention to Alena. With her back to him, he could not see her face. All he can see is there is a very small slit between her scarf, which is wrapped around her face and her cloak's hood. She has not said anything to the others about what she and Anjia had talked about, and no one asked. During the weeks since her talk with Anjia, Alena has made time to talk to Kalvin. They mostly talk about the Order of the Flame and what is expected of bulwarks. She has not revealed any secrets, but she no longer treats him like the others treat Sidney. She has even asked him how he feels about certain things.

"You cannot betray us because your fate will not allow you to. We are aware of that."

Alena had said to answer his question about why she had changed toward him.

Within shouting distance of the main gates, Sidney took the lead and rode to the gates. Kalvin watched as he talked to the guards. It only took him several moments to get the gates opened. The guards began praising Paul who unwrapped his face. Kalvin maneuvered his horse behind Raal just before they passed the gates. Raal's attention went to Mantak and his guards. They are atop the buildings a short distance away. Kalvin followed Raal's line of vision but could not see Mantak and the Ratels clearly. All he could see was a group on the rooftops. He wondered who they were after Raal said something in elvish to Fogi Red.

"He's not here for me." Fogi Red said in common so Kalvin would understand him.

"He is not here for Paul either. Something is going on. Something important. Something dangerous." Raal stated.

Kalvin has no clue who they are talking about. He does not even know the individuals he sees atop the buildings are elves. He turned to Alena and said.

"Never let me forget how much I hate winter in Coilu."

Alena laughed. She remembers the stories he and Razial had told her about their travels. Kalvin hates the cold. Razial had tried to use this to dissuade him from joining them in this task. She laughed mentally then focused on the streets.

As they neared the palace, she watched as Mantak joined the other leaders by the palace doors. She does not know who he is, but she knows he has rank in the Order of the Flame. She thought about what Raal and Fogi Red had said and realized that Mantak is there for Razial!

"Fa'Alena. I am Ja'Mantak. Where is Ja'Razial?" Mantak asked.

"I shall explain while Paul meets with his men." She replied.

Paul's men began to cheer him. They gathered in the courtyard to greet him. She dismounted her horse and walked up the stairs. She can sense Mantak is displeased about Razial not being with them.

*

Paul had bathed and eaten. He had met with his top supporters for hours. A lot of promises and plans were made. They are so caught up in the drama of the story being told that they did not question him about it. They accepted the story of him being part of the Partisans' attack on Mohr. He had expected to have to do a little explaining. Not one of his supporters questioned the story the Order of the Flame had made up.

"So, what do you think Razial is up to?" Paul asked. "Probably killing your enemies." Sidney answered.

After the fight in Sahkar, Sidney no longer considers the jolems to be useless in a fight. Now, he believes all the tales about jolems.

"I trust the Order-Hell!" Paul snapped. "I have no choice but to trust them. Can you believe how quickly and easily they managed to make up this story and made it all true to those who do not know? However, trusting Razial is difficult. He is an assassin. What if someone offers him more gold to kill me?"

Sidney stared at Paul. They both have rugged beards from not being able to shave while they traveled. He has grown to like Paul, but he does not understand how his noble upbringing continues to cloud his mind when it comes to Razial. Sidney feels no sense of betrayal, hiding the fact he will become a bulwark from Paul because Paul has not changed how he sees what is happening in the world.

"Your Majesty. I cannot imagine Razial doing such a thing." He said.

Paul stared at him for several moments then said he hoped he was right. Sidney told him to get some rest. Paul nodded and they bid each other good night.

*

Meanwhile, Mantak and Alena met in his room. As she had expected, he expressed his displeasure with the decision to let Razial ride off to kill the leaders of the Vinan armies. He was shocked to hear Razial had Ja'Brahma's daggers. He asked many questions about how he had obtained the daggers. She told him Binu had given the daggers to Razial.

"He will be angry that I revealed he has Ja'Brahma's daggers. The others do not even know." Alena stated.

Mantak was shocked by what she had said but remained stoic. He asked if the jolems knew about Razial having Ja'Brahma's daggers.

"Yes."

"How could they agree to keep this from the keepers? Those two have always done as they please."

"No, Ja'Mantak. The keepers-Tu'ani and Lela, instructed us to do what Razial wanted. They say his fate controls the fate of others."

Alena's words made Mantak think. He decided to reveal some of what was really going on. He told her about how Priato was kept in the dark about Razial until recently and how now that it is known that Razial is fated to become the Gideon they must use him to find the rest of his paladins and his keepers. He knows she understands what is going to happen in the future.

Alena began thinking how the gods choose champions and how things intensify during the times of the champions. That is why these times are called Champions' Wars. She knows Rakaar servants' refusal to work together is why they continue to fail to free their god. The only thing the Magi and their servants have in common is an undying hatred of Eloh's servants and elves.

She does not understand how Eloh chose Razial to be his champion, but she knows there is a reason.

"Already, this plan has been successful." Mantak's words made Alena refocus. "We now know Kalvin, Fogi Red, and Ofelia are to become paladins and A'Priato is sure others will be revealed when Razial is finished in Coilu."

Alena felt a sense of jealousy pass through her. The thought of Razial finding four women who will be his wives bothers her. This feeling quickly faded. She focused on the fact they are far behind in this war. They not only have to find and train those who will be Razial's paladins and keepers, but they must train Razial as well. Then, she realized that Rakaar's Chosen Servant could be known to Rakaar's servants!

"What about the Chosen Servant?" She asked.

"She has been sensed decades ago." Mantak replied.

Alena nodded in response. She has never read the Conclave's archives explaining the Champions' Wars, but she read the scrolls Goraan wrote about them. Since the second Champions' War, two things happened before the Gideon was found. First, his paladins were found and trained. Second, his keepers were found. The fact Razial was found before his keepers and paladins means things will be a lot different during this Champions' War. The fact Razial does not serve Eloh is proof enough of that. Add the fact the Chosen Servant was sensed decades earlier before the Gideon was known and Alena knows the Order of the Flame has a lot to do to prepare for this Champions' War.

"How could Eloh choose Razial? He is an assassin. It makes no sense." Alena said in frustration.

"That is why so many had a difficult time believing A'Priato when he said Ja'Razial is to become the Gideon. Now, he has mastered Ja'Brahma's daggers. Assassin or not, what has happened has happened. It cannot be changed. All we can do is make the best of this situation." Mantak said.

Before they could go on, there was a knock on the door. Mantak told the person to enter. When the door opened, Alena stood in awe seeing Anjia with Kalvin beside her. With her cloak's hood pulled back, Anjia entered the room. It is obvious Kalvin had been asleep only minutes earlier by his unkempt hair and his untied boots. Anjia's dark eyes never left Alena while saying.

"Security in Mohr is quite embarrassing. I have a message from Razial."

"Where is he?" Alena asked.

"Hunting his-your, enemies." Anjia corrected. "He said the Vinan army has moved closer than expected and that the imperial forces have spies in several fortress cities."

"How did Ja'Razial learn this information?" Mantak asked.

Anjia smirked at him. She noticed the way he is dressed, but she is not part of the Order of the Flame. She does not have to defer to him. She turned back to Alena, who told Kalvin to go back to his room and that she would talk with him in the morning. Mantak dismissed his guards, who stood by the doorway. Alena waited until the door was closed before telling Anjia who Mantak was and how he was there to help protect Razial. Anjia likes that. Alena then told her that he knows about Razial having Ja'Brahma's daggers.

"So, you trust him?" Anjia asked.

"Yes. I do." Alena answered.

Anjia then explained all that Razial had told her to explain. Alena was impressed by all the Society's spies had learned. She was not surprised to hear that Razial wants Mohr to attack in a matter of days. She thanked Anjia, then offered her a room to stay in. Caught off guard by the offer, Anjia took a moment to reply.

"Thank you, but it is best for me to ride tonight."

She bid Mantak farewell while Alena walked her to the door. She and Alena stared into each other's eyes and smiled. They know they no longer carry the anger they used to carry. They will settle things soon, but it is too early to embrace.

"So that is the infamous Lady Avatar." Mantak said.

Alena nodded. He knows she will say nothing else about Anjia.

"Let us meet with the others to discuss Razial's plans." He said to end their meeting.

***

With the sun setting, Razial rode into the massive camp. He had passed himself off as a mercenary to several Vinan captains, who are looking for more men to join their invasion of Mohr. It had taken them days to ride through the snow to reach the camp. Over twenty miles behind enemy lines, the Vinan and imperial forces have gone unnoticed for weeks. They are well supplied.

Razial had not expected to see so many soldiers so well equipped and so many horses. The snow that once covered the grass melted from being trampled and the warmth of the fires spread around the camp. He surveyed the scenery. Thousands of soldiers prepared to go to sleep. The fires seem to grow brighter with each passing moment.

Riding behind the captains to meet their generals, Razial thought about how four armies had gathered. That shows him they are serious about trying to defeat Mohr with this sneak attack.

He continued to look around as they approached four large tents. He smiled mentally because he is not thinking like an assassin but more like a daring killer. He knows Adini and Havi are close, but he does not know if Scar's pack will be able to adapt to what he intends to do.

"The generals are going to love you." One of the captains said.

They stopped their horses. Razial dismounted and tethered his horse. Then, he thought better of it. He would have to leave in a hurry, so he untethered his horse. One of the captains stared at him in confusion. Razial ignored him. He saw two of the generals exit a tent. One of them called out to the other two generals. That is when the horses around the camp began to panic because Scar's pack crept closer sensing the change in him.

"What's wrong with the horses?" The third general asked. The second general noticed Razial and pointed.

"He appears a bit shor-"

Razial threw his daggers, Ja'Brahma's daggers, with deadly accuracy. The first two generals never had a chance. They were struck by the daggers, which were back in Razial's hands before the captains could react. Razial was on them. They winced each time his daggers bit into them. Others close by stood in awe not understanding how the daggers returned to Razial each time he threw them. The remaining generals and captains called out for help trying to avoid Razial and his daggers. A sense of urgency filled Razial who knows he has to finish the generals before he is forced to run.

Just as the other two generals and captain closest to Razial moved to attack him, the camp erupted into chaos because Adini and Havi began sending the fires into the air. Razial threw the daggers at the captain. The generals charged. Unfortunately for them, the daggers were back in his hands before they could reach him. He ducked then stabbed the fourth general in his leg. Then he stepped to his right to avoid the oncoming captain, who had deflected the daggers with his sword. The captain's sword hissed several inches away from Razial, who threw his daggers. They struck true, but the captain still charged. Mortally wounded, he refused to die so easily. Razial backed away and looked around. He saw the generals going back into their tents. He threw his daggers and drew his sword. The other captain joined the fighting. Razial glanced at the wounded captain. The man can no longer fight. He had managed to block one of the daggers, but the other dagger had found its mark striking him in his leg.

Fighting the last captain, Razial heard the soldiers' screams. Scar's pack is running around attacking them while the jolems are causing the horses to scatter throughout the camp and killing any and every soldier they can. The captain knew he could not out fight Razial, so he stepped back. When Razial let him back away, he turned and ran. Razial quickly mounted his horse. He saw one of the generals stumble out of his tent. Havi rose halfway from the ground. Razial knew Havi had killed the other general as well.

"Get the supply carts!" He shouted in dwarfish.

With the soldiers regrouping, it is time to go. Scar's pack is racing toward him. He stared at one of the camp's lookouts, who had run to see what was happening. Razial decided not to throw his daggers at him. He rode off with the wolves behind him. He knows they need to rest. He heard Havi and Adini shouting insults in dwarfish. That made him laugh. He must get them horses because they will be tired after they escape.

*

Hours after attacking the camp, Razial led his horse by its reins. The jolems are back-to-back in the saddle. Scar's pack is walking around the horse. With the moon giving off a bright yellow light, the woodlands are well lit. The odd shadows in the woodlands made him think. They had already decided on a plan.

A sense of relief filled him when he saw the fortress come into view.

"All right. It is time for you two to get inside the supply bags." Razial said in dwarfish.

While the jolems climbed inside the supply bags, he tried to communicate with the wolves. They are still excited about attacking the imperial soldiers. (They recognize Coilu's imperial uniforms- all elfin animals do because Coiluans hunt elfin animals.)

Sensing the difficulty that he is having explaining what he wants the wolves to do, Havi told him to use his emotions.

"Do not forget who you are." Havi said with a smile.

His sharp teeth appeared gray in the dim light. Razial mounted his horse and made sure Scar understood he wanted the wolves to wait for them outside the city.

Just like Razial had expected, the leader of the fortress city had left a message that he is expecting a messenger to arrive. He knew the only way for the Vinans to be so far behind enemy lines without being noticed was for the leader of this fortress city to be in cahoots with them.

After telling the guards he had a message from the generals, he realized they were not involved in their leader's betrayal.

He waited several minutes for the guards to receive an order to let him enter the city. He was greeted by a captain, who told him that he should have arrived an hour earlier. Razial followed him through the fortress. Tall, the man talks with a confidence he should not have.

"The witch is in there also. I hope you have a good reason for making her wait." The man said.

Razial is not surprised that others are involved. As the door opened slowly, Razial stabbed the man four times, once in his throat, once in his spine, and twice in the base of his skull. His lifeless body fell. With no guard in the hallway, he did not care to hide the body. He entered the room. An aged blonde sat at a well-crafted wooden table. He saw the candlelight flickering in her blue eyes. To his right, is a graying medium sized middle-aged man-the city leader. They took a second to notice his daggers. That is all the time he needed. He threw his daggers at the man.

He did not even wait for the daggers to strike him before charging the woman. She drew her powers as she stood. Her eyes widened in surprise when his daggers reappeared in his hands. Still, she ignored them when he threw them-a mistake, then struck Razial. Her strike staggered him, but his daggers bit into her torso. She winced in pain, staring at him in amazement when the daggers suddenly reappeared in his hands. He threw them again-still closing in on her. She shielded herself but her wounds weakened her too much. His daggers bit into her torso again. She tried to back away. He mauled her with the daggers. She died fighting.

She had obviously turned the captain and used him to help forward the Fellowship's actions.

Breathing hard, he dragged the captain's body into the room. He closed the door behind him. The smell of blood is heavy in the hallway as is the smell of burning torches. He walked through the fortress at a calm pace. He hoped the jolems succeeded in getting horses.

*

Havi and Adini watched as Razial rode toward the gates. After entering the city, they simply stole the guards' horses and waited by a building across from the gates. Seeing Razial and not hearing any alarms, they relaxed. Their problem now is getting him inside of a tent. He has been too long in the moonlight. They know the shadow-tracker is getting close. They are not worried because the shadow-tracker is on its first life. They can deal with it with help from Scar's pack. They know others dislike what they are doing. They are taking a chance, but the chance is theirs to take.

***

Days later, Paul's forces-led by Paul, engaged and routed the armies that had gathered behind enemy lines. Without their leaders and caught off guard, the Vinans and imperial soldiers had decided to fight. They fought bravely but Alena and the others used their powers and forced them to retreat.

Razial watched as the Partisans stayed organized and disciplined while the Mohrans reveled in victory. He rode over and told Paul to have his forces run down the retreating enemy armies. Paul looked at him as if he had insulted him. Sidney-Paul's second shadow tilted his head in thought. Paul told Razial that he does not want to tire his men.

"That is why you should run down those retreating now. Letting them go means you will have to face them again in the future." Razial countered.

Fogi Red and Raal joined them. They had heard what Razial had said. From behind Razial, Xochi and several bulwarks joined the group. Xochi said there is no reason to slaughter the Vinans.

"Deal with them now or deal with them later. That army will regroup, and it will be desperate. Your forces between them and their escape will have to fight them or let them pass. Run them down while you can." Razial said firmly.

"Who do you think you are?" Paul asked. "Have you forgotten who I am?"

"You are useless!" Razial growled.

He turned his back to Paul and faced Fogi Red and asked. "Do you not see the wisdom in this?"

"Of course, I do." Fogi Red replied.

"Then let us run them down."

"Razial?!" Xochi called.

Like Fogi Red, she looked to Mantak, who looked at them. He turned to Razial and spoke in common so Paul could understand what was said.

"Slaughter them."

Xochi stood agape. Mantak told her to stay with Paul. He called Adini and Havi. They rose from the ground.

"We heard" they said.

"You better stop that!" Adini pointed.

Razial smiled because no matter what is going on, jolems never forget their superstition. To them, saying the same thing at the same time is always a bad omen.

"What do you want us to do?" Havi asked Mantak.

"Gather Scar's pack and maul those at the point of the retreat. Slow them so we can scatter them to the wind" Mantak said.

*

That night, Razial and Kalvin stood in Razial's tent. Kalvin excitedly explained how Mantak told the members of the Order of the Flame to protect Razial while he will protect Paul during the fighting. He told Razial that he had heard about the daggers. He then told him about the Fellowship fighting amongst themselves because some want peace with the Sisterhood.

"We're in the middle of all of this." Kalvin nodded.

Razial laughed. That puzzled Kalvin. He does not understand how his friend is not impressed by what is going on.

"Kalvin. Do you know who these daggers" Razial called the daggers to him and held them out for Kalvin to get a good look at them. "-used to belong to?"

"How did you do that?" Kalvin asked.

Razial explained how him mastering the daggers means he will eventually gain possession of Ja'Brahma's powers. Kalvin's blank stare revealed he did not understand. Like most people, Kalvin knows very little about the Champions' Wars. All Kalvin knows is that Ja'Brahma was Eloh's champion. He believes-like most people believe, that Ja'Brahma was killed because he was mad and wanted to conquer the world. Because of this belief, many humans fear Ja'Brahma and elves.

No one outside of the Order of the Flame knows much about the Gideon. Goraan does and he taught Razial a lot about the Champions' Wars. Razial does not question Goraan's knowledge.

"Kalvin. Listen to me. I am fated to be Eloh's champion during this Champions' War."

Razial finds it difficult to believe this, but he knows it is true. He told Kalvin that Mantak could better explain what was going on. He explained all he could and made it clear that he had no desire to be Eloh's champion.

"I am an assassin. My loyalty is to the Society. There is no turning away for me."

"Are you serious?"

"I am only here because of my contract."

"Raz. This is worldly. If what you say is true, this is the worldliest thing we'll ever witness. How can you be so, so uninterested?"

"Chaos does not interest me and that is what Champions' Wars are: total chaos."

Razial could see it in Kalvin's eyes. He is happy to be part of this. He would rather be nowhere else. Goraan had taught Razial, Anjia, and Alena all the basics of the Champion's Wars and promised to reveal more if the need arises. When Anjia had asked him why he kept so many details away from them, Goraan had told them that Champions' Wars are not meant to be told all at once.

Standing in his tent, Razial told Kalvin that he had not had any targets since Paul's wife.

"Here I am waging a war for a ruler I dislike. I am being used for something and the Order of the Flame is hiding its purpose from me." Razial said.

"What does Alena say?"

"Nothing. She was surprised to discover that I have the daggers, and I am sure Ja'Mantak was not."

That made Kalvin think. He knows all that Razial had said is true. Still, he has a question.

"So how do I fit in all of this?"

"That, I do not know."

Their eyes locked for a moment. Kalvin knows Razial has asked himself this question several times. Before, he thought he could handle all this. Now, things have turned out to be even bigger than what Razial had thought, he has a feeling that he has gotten in over his head.

"Looks like I decided to join the Order of the Flame at the wrong time. Is it too late to be an assassin?" Kalvin grinned.

That made them laugh.

*

While they talked, Alena and the other siblings met inside their large tent. They managed to convince Paul to make Sidney his heir. The keepers had instructed them to do that. The keepers also instructed them to turn the tide of the war because they found out that the Sisterhood has taken over Ocia's capital, and they cannot allow their enemies to take over Coilu city also.

Alena and Zelia are next to each other listening to the others talk about how to turn the tide of the war. Zelia had suggested for them to target their enemies' military leaders. Xochi wants to press Bassar into attacking. Alena dislikes that idea but said nothing. Araceli-who is sealing the tent magically, so no one could eavesdrop on their meeting, said they can forward both plans. She said they can send Xochi to Bassar while they sneak behind enemy lines to kill their leaders.

"What about Ja'Mantak?" Alena asked.

The others turned to face her. Araceli's green eyes revealed she had forgotten about Mantak being with them. Xochi's cat-like hazel eyes appear angry. Not knowing why Razial is so important angers her. Zelia appears curious about what Mantak could do.

"We will have to ask him what he has planned." Xochi said.

Zelia nodded in agreement as did Araceli. Then, as if he had heard them, Mantak called out to them. They told him to enter the tent. Araceli released her powers. If Mantak wants their conversation kept a secret, he will say so.

"I have news to share." Mantak said.

He drew his powers and sealed the tent. He told them he and the jolems decided to have Paul put Razial in control of his forces. Xochi frowned saying that Paul would never accept that.

"Havi and Adini shall give him no choice." Mantak said.

Then explained that Adini and Havi had approached him and made it clear that they found Paul lacking as a military leader.

"I could not have stopped them if I disagreed with them. As we talk, they set off with Fogi Red and Raal. They will give Paul no choice."

Hearing Mantak say this made Zelia remember that Adini and Havi outrank Mantak. She had completely forgotten about that.

"How can they force Paul into accepting Razial as his top military commander?" Xochi asked.

"As I have said, they will give him no choice. Now, I believe that Keeper Tu'ani and Keeper Lela informed you that a lot is going on, most of it centered around Ja'Razial. Let me inform you why.

Ja'Razial has mastered Ja'Brahma's daggers. He is the new Gideon. That is why Gwen of Dax has sent a shadow-tracker after him. That is why we must protect him at all costs."

Mantak's words shocked all except Alena. He went on to explain that Kalvin and Fogi Red are fated to become paladins. He did not mention Ofelia. He does not feel the need to. Araceli asked him how Razial had come by the daggers in Coilu. Mantak told her that Razial had had the daggers since he was in Osam. He then gave them a warning.

"Remember, the Harbingers are behind all of this."

Gwen and Frauter sat across from each other. Along with three witches who serve her, they are in a small room on the second floor of a stone house. She hates her current situation. She was once the undisputed leader of the Fellowship. All of Dax was hers. Only Frauter-her protege and her right hand, could claim power with her. All that began to change just over ten years earlier. That is when the Harbingers' plan began to weaken her power. Somehow, the Harbingers managed to make a rival faction inside the Fellowship. At first, she thought the Theocracy was behind the splintering of the Fellowship. She spent a lot of time weeding out her enemies, but they were the wrong enemies. By the time she realized her mistake, the tide had turned against her. Only recently, did she find out it is the Harbingers who are behind all her troubles. They caused her rapid downfall from power and continue to weaken her allies throughout Coilu. Now, it is time for her to go on the offensive.

She is down to her last stance. If she has it her way, it will be a glorious last stance. All those who have turned against her shall pay. The Harbingers are no longer far ahead of her. Frauter has discovered that the emperor is not dead. The Harbingers intend to use him against Paul-who has the people's support inside Coilu city. She is going to take that option from them. After she does that, she goes after Peter. She and Frauter are sure he is a Harbinger.

"Their plan is ambitious and would have worked had you not discovered the emperor's location." Gwen said.

Her light brown eyes stand out against her smooth aged pale skin that contrasts with her long dark wavy hair. Like her three servants, she is dressed like a peasant. It pains her that she must go unnoticed in Dax, her city.

"I still want to know what they are up to." Frauter said.

Tall and well built, he has a strength in his eyes even when he smiles. His long light brown hair hangs past his shoulders. He is dressed like a simple swordsman. It bothers Gwen to see him like that.

"That no longer matters. We are about to ruin this plan. Then, we go after Peter, Peter II, and Peter III." She said.

"Even the grandson?" Frauter grinned.

"We will strike them all. It is war. In war, you strike all your enemies when you can. These fools have made three mistakes."

"Three?" Frauter's raised an eyebrow.

"One-" She held up a finger. "-they challenged me without killing me. Two- "She held up two fingers. "-they brought the emperor here as if Dax is no longer mine's. Their third mistake-"

She held up three fingers. "-is thinking that it is safe to bring the emperor to Dax."

Frauter nodded. He stood when he heard the warlock return. He had sent him to check the way to the emperor's location. Gwen stood and signaled for her servants to follow Frauter. It is time to act. The first of many actions if she has her way.

They made it to the house within minutes. Gwen watched as two of her servants approached the door. Along with Frauter's servant, she walked toward the house.

The street is busy with people. Although it is late spring, the snow only melted two weeks ago. People still need to restock their shelves. That is why she must act now because it will be a lot more difficult for her to go unnoticed when winter arrives.

With her head covered, she looked around. Standing behind the third witch, she took in the scenery. She noticed her servants had gotten the door open. Frauter's servant charged past her. She sensed her servants fighting inside the house. She walked calmly into the house as she drew her powers. She saw two witches and four swordsmen fighting those with her. She lashed out at her foes and moved deeper into the house. She sensed her servants still fighting when she came to a staircase. She saw two men standing at the top of the stairs. They stared wide-eyed at her. They know who she is. She walked up the stairs like a queen.

"Take me to the emperor." She commanded.

The men backpedaled with their heads down. The sound of fighting had died. She can hear her servants walking through the house. She gestured for the men to enter the room after they had opened the door. She stared at the ailing emperor while listening to her servants climb the stairs. She saw a young girl about fourteen years old chained to the back wall. That puzzled her.

"Why is she here?" She asked.

"They used her to keep the emperor alive." One of the men answered nervously.

Gwen can sense the gleipnir used to bind the girl magically. The girl's blue eyes were full of fear as she cowered near the back wall. Gwen believes the girl is an untrained witch, so they used her to sustain the dying emperor. She used her powers to break the gleipnir and the chain while asking.

"What is your name?"

"Dawn." The girl said.

"Did these men use... you?"

She did not have to explain what she meant. Dawn nodded as if she were afraid to talk. Gwen struck the men while moving over to stab the emperor. Her servants ran into the room while she helped Dawn to her feet. She told her servants to kill the men.

Walking out of the room, she heard the witch, who had stayed with Frauter, say that a group of enemies is racing through the street. Frauter told his servants to clear the way from the back of the house.

"We are leaving through the back." Frauter said.

Gwen walked down the stairs. She introduced him to Dawn he stared at her. She thought about how elves believe in fate and that is why they pay attention to those who cross their paths.

Rakaar has never placed anyone in her life unless that person has a purpose. She is going to keep Dawn close until she discovers Dawn's purpose.

***

Ariel and Peter are alone in a large room. They had arrived in Dax, separately, days after Gwen had killed the emperor. Peter believes Gwen's actions will become a problem. He was shocked to discover the Master was unaffected by Gwen's actions. Ariel was sent to help Peter search Dax for a trace of Gwen and or Frauter before she went to Coilu city to help Peter II and Lisa deal with the unrest there. Peter was told to collect a map of Svan and to set a trap for Gwen who is to be captured alive. That news had surprised Ariel. She will have to spend more time in Dax to set the trap. She does not mind this. Her concern is what is happening on the front lines of the war. All the latest reports have been bad. Peter II is losing ground. She knows Razial had killed the four generals not a sorcerer-like rumor says.

"So why do you think the Master is not bothered by the emperor being killed?" Peter asked.

Ariel cannot see the curiosity in his eyes because they are wearing their Harbinger cowls. She knows he is at a loss. He used to think they were out to take control over all Coilu and all Ocia. Now, he knows what they are doing is only the first part of the Master's plans, he wants to figure out what is truly going on.

"We no longer needed the emperor. Now that we know where Bal's dolmen is, all we have to do is get the ancient crown and kill Paul." Ariel replied.

"What about holding the imperial throne?" He asked.

Instead of thinking like someone who is secretly trying to achieve his goal, Peter is thinking like an aging lord out to make sure his family stays in power. If he does not change, that will be the end of him as a Harbinger.

"To keep the imperial throne, we need others. Your son can either remain in power after we have won this war, or he has gathered enough support from the Fellowship. Either way, it all depends on others. Do not forget, until Gwen is found, your son is a target." Ariel said firmly.

She wished she could see his eyes to better gauge his reaction to what she had said. He has done an excellent job in convincing Fellowship members-who stand with him, to accept an open alliance with the Harbingers. Now, they can move around without hiding the fact they are Harbingers. Peter has convinced them the Harbingers will free Bal and help him against his foes.

It had taken a long time to do this. The Master and Beulah had to kill a lot of Bal's top servants to eliminate all who would stand against an alliance with them. To her, it would be a waste for Peter to fail after making himself an integral part of their plans because he wants to keep his son and grandson in power.

"Gwen will not be a threat for much longer." Peter said.

He stood and walked toward the door. Ariel followed him. She doubts they will find anyone who can lead them directly to Gwen or Frauter, but she thinks they will find someone who will point them in the right direction.

Kalvin listened to Sidney talk with Adini and Havi while they walked toward the center of the camp where Razial and others are. Months have passed since Razial was given command of Paul's forces. The battles have been bloody and fierce but successful. They have pushed into the part of Coilu that is controlled by Ruug-whose forces have held.

Bassar has been so successful that Razial does not have to worry about his northern flank. However, Vin forced him to take precautions to protect his southern flank.

The emperor's death in Dax has pushed even more people to Paul's side. That is why he has decided to rest for a couple of days while waiting to hear from Bassar. He is sure their foes' advantage in numbers and disadvantage in time will force them to counterattack. Kalvin agrees with him. Winter will help them keep the lands they have taken, but their enemies will not just let that happen.

"So how do you all breath?" Sidney asked the jolems.

This is his first chance to talk to them about their ability to pass through soil.

"Through or noses and mouths." Adini said.

"No. I mean when you tunnel." Sidney explained.

Sidney has a lot of questions. Havi rubbed his bald head in frustration.

"There is no magic to it. It is simply an ability. We cannot take anyone with us. Yes, we can sleep in the ground and so long as we are not manipulating the soil it does not tire us to pass through it." Havi said.

"What about your clothes and weapons?" Sidney asked. Havi shook his head. Adini smiled before saying.

"You have heard of elfin clothes. Well, elder jolems who have learned how to wield magic make clothing for all jolems."

Kalvin smiled at that. Sidney nodded in understanding. As they continued, Kalvin watched Raal and Scar's pack approach them. Raal called to him telling him the wolves wanted him to run the night-run with them. Behind Raal, Kalvin saw Fogi Red, who had the same hardened expression that he has had since Kalvin first saw him. He is going to run the night-run. Adini and Havi teased him. He shook his head in mock anger. Kalvin bid Sidney farewell then turned to match stride with Raal who walked in the opposite direction.

"What about us?" Havi asked mockingly.

"You two do not know how to fare well." Fogi Red grinned.

"Said the dwarf who runs night-runs with wolves, humans, and elves." Adini countered.

"So do you two." Fogi Red shot back.

"But we are from Gully. What is your excuse?" Havi laughed.

Fogi Red muttered something to himself as he kept on walking. He has met with Mantak several times who has assured him that plans are being made to end the standoff in Nibel. Thinking about that made him tighten his grip on his ax. He has waited for a long time to deal with his uncle for stealing the throne. He cannot wait to return to Nibel. He has not been in the Axe Peaks in six years. He left after he had to survive two assassination attempts. He has been on the move ever since. Raal, his best friend, his elfin brother, and sworn personal guard has been with him for a very long time. Fogi Red hopes Raal can return home soon.

***

The Master and Beulah took days to unseal the ancient part of Gnor. Mounted on their horses, they are alone. Modern day Gnorans do not dare try to enter the ancient part of their city. Long ago, Gnorans built a wall around the original part of the city because it was magically sealed.

The Master began to think how, like Winnin, Gnor is in the Gnor Valley and was founded by people who did not serve Rakaar. To most Gnorans, those who are imprisoned in the ancient part of the city haunt the city at night. They have no idea the truth about those still imprisoned in the city. They know nothing about the elves he came to free or the humans who remain imprisoned.

After the third Champions' War, a group of Boars left Ino-Heim because they decided to act against those who served either god using Gnor as the base for their raids on their targets after Gnor's original inhabitants were magically imprisoned.

These Boars became known as Harlequins because they dressed in all black. Their leader is well known to the Master. He is an ancient elf who was once an original paladin's apprentice. His name invokes fear in his enemies.

"Ja'Troggo." The Master called.

Troggo walked through the street. He kept his red eyes on the Master and Beulah. His hatred for the Harbingers is plain for all to see. His long wavy red hair hung like a mane. His black elf-locks frame his face. He stopped before the Master and Beulah. His yataghans hang at his waist. His eyes are narrow but not slanted. There is a coldness to his expression that prevents him from hiding how he feels. Looking at the Master and Beulah, he shows no sign of being bothered by the fact that he cannot see their faces.

"Why have you freed me?" He asked coldly.

Although he is still weak, there is defiance in his voice. He cowers before no one. Like Beulah, Troggo is close to the Master but has no idea. Only the Master and Priato know who Troggo and Beulah are to the Master, and he intends to keep it that way until it is time to reveal the truth.

"I want you to free your brethren while I free the Magi. The one who is destined to become the Gideon has A'Ja'Brahma's daggers and has bonded with them. Be warned. The Magi shall fail, like they always do. You have made your point. It is time for you to return to your clan."

Where Troggo had spoken in elvish the Master had spoken in ancient elvish. He also said Ja'Brahma's name with honor. Troggo never heard him do either in the past. He stared at the Master's faceless cowl trying to figure out what game he was playing.

"Who are you to tell me it is time to rejoin my clan?" Troggo asked in elvish.

He refuses to talk to him in ancient elvish. He is growing angry, and the Master can sense it. Still, he has to say what he has come to say. Troggo has been fighting Eloh's servants for far too long. Every Boar-including the Harlequins knows what happened to Ja'Brahma, but where the Master knows that only by finesse can what happened to Ja'Brahma be avenged, Troggo believes he can avenge Ja'Brhama by force.

"Listen to me, Ja'Troggo. Fighting the Order of the Flame does A'Ja'Brahma no good. Rakaar is your enemy. How can you hope to avenge A'Ja'Brahma by fighting a losing fight?"

Troggo's eyes lowered as he tried to figure out what the Master is up to. He thought about saying that so long as he dies fighting those who had attacked Ja'Brahma his life would be worth losing, but he chose not to. The Master's words had intrigued him. He began to think about his last conversation with Cas.

"The only thing I know for sure about the Master is he stands against Rakaar. He is no friend of mine."

Cas had said only weeks before the Master and several Harbingers helped the Gideon imprison the Magi. The only thing Troggo knows about the Master is that he is an elf.

"Who are you? Why are you worried about A'Ja'Brahma being avenged?" He asked curiously.

"Now, you are thinking. When you stop acting against Eloh-helping Rakaar, you will remember what it means to walk the path of A'Ja'Brahma and that to serve A'Ja'Brahma one must be one's own master."

Troggo's eyes widened. Beulah smiled. She knows the Master is trying to make Troggo a Harbinger. That gives her a sense of relief. She was worried about releasing the Magi. If Troggo turned against the Master, they would have had to turn to the Order of the Flame.

"Go. Free your brethren. Act not against Eloh's servants unless you have to." The Master said.

With that, the Master and Beulah turned their horses and galloped out of Gnor beneath the hot summer sun. He told her to head to Vin to oversee the capture of Razial while he goes to help bring Giaour into the fold with them. He then told her that Priato had been in Tunez and most likely knew there are other Boars in Tunez. She asked if he would act against her.

"No. Take no action against him-ever!" He said with emphasis.

They separated with him riding south while she rode north. She has no idea how he is going to obtain the ancient crowns of Giaour and Danou, but he has plans to obtain them.

***

Standing inside Paul's meeting tent, Razial eyed all present. Paul is at the opposite end of the table with Sidney to his right. All of Paul's generals are on one side of the table opposite Alena, Kalvin, Mantak, Fogi Red, and Zelia. They are discussing the news from Bassar. The Bassarans are going to attack until they are turned back. Paul's generals saw this as an opportunity to extend their forces' rest period. They began trying to make plans for this, but Razial quickly ruined their plans by saying they shall press Ruug until they are turned back. The generals turned to Paul, who said Razial is his war commander killing the hope in their eyes. Razial dislikes being in the tent. It is a rare warm day, especially for Coilu. He wants to be outside.

"Tomorrow, at dawn, Fogi Red and I shall attack. Your task-" Although he pointed at the generals, he did not look at them. "-is simple: outflank the Ruugans. Do not relent."

He exited the tent after saying that. Paul dislikes how he had just left the tent but said nothing. However, the generals complained. Before Paul could tell them to stop, Fogi Red said.

"Why do I see fear in your eyes?! None of you will strike first and none of you are targeted by our enemies, so stop your complaining. If you think about it, this is the best action we can take.

We have to draw our foes' attention away from those who are rebelling in the east and inside the capital."

Fogi Red stormed out of the tent after that. Alena could see the generals did not expect this war to be as bloody as it has been. They have enjoyed this little respite and now Razial has decided to end it.

Wanting to ease the tension, Alena told the generals the more they trust Razial the more their men will believe victory is possible. She tilted her head in respect to Paul then exited the tent. Zelia, Mantak, and Kalvin followed her out. Zelia and Kalvin went their own way while Alena and Mantak walked toward the southeast corner of the camp.

"That was well said." Mantak complimented Alena.

Alena tilted her head in respect. The air is warm. The smell of grass filled her nostrils. She looked up and saw her pets soaring high searching for prey.

"The Blue Keeper shall arrive soon. Join me in greeting her." Mantak said.

He followed her line of vision when the hawks dove signaling, they had spotted a target. Alena turned to look at him. A sense of nerves past through her. She has never met the Blue Keeper.

Every time Ulina visited Anazi Falls, she was somewhere else. Had she not known about Razial, she would be at a loss as to why Ulina is close by. Sensing her curiosity, Mantak said.

"She has been spying in eastern Coilu. She also had to help our agents escape."

Alena nodded then turned to the left when Araceli called out to her. Araceli's red hair and height make her stand out no matter where she is. Mantak told her to invite Araceli to join them in meeting Ulina. Alena watched her approach. There is no sign of the pain that she feels. Her green eyes hide how she feels about Ariel being missing. Alena feels bad for her. She smiled at Araceli before inviting her to join them. Araceli accepted and the three of them continued.

*

Razial stood watching Scar's pack rough house with each other. Zelia is next to him. He took a drink from his water skin. He held it out to Zelia. She accepted. While she drank, he looked around. The grass on the plain has grown a lot. It is a darker green than he remembers in the past.

"So, what are your intentions after the war?" Zelia asked.

Razial looked into her cat-like hazel eyes. She has long wavy brown hair that hangs down her back and over her shoulders. He finds her attractive, but she is Alena's friend.

"That depends on how much time I have left on my contract."

His answer made her frown. She asked him if possessing the daggers had changed his way of thinking. He told her he remained unchanged. That disappointed her. She told him he should start acting like the Gideon. He smirked, then told her Eloh should have chosen someone who is not a hunted assassin to be his champion. He could see her disappointment.

"Zelia. I am an assassin. I do not serve Eloh or Rakaar."

"Why do you not serve either god?" Zelia asked.

"Because I only serve those who help me be my own master."

"And the Hilt does this?"

"Quite well." Razial smiled.

She disliked that. She asked him why the Hilt had not called off the hunt for him.

"Because I am still alive nor have, I been captured. I broke our rules. I have to pay the price."

"And it does not bother you that your brethren are out there waiting to either kill or capture you?"

Razial looked around. He knows Anjia is close by and has no doubt others are too. He is sure several crews of assassins have infiltrated Paul's forces. He cannot worry about being the Gideon. First, he must survive the hunt.

"I knew what would happen when I decided to save Kalvin. The hunt is my own doing. Some hunt me because of who I am. Some because they dislike me. Still, it was my choice that made this happen. I hold no ill will toward those who hunt me."

He playfully rubbed her head and began talking about how he intends to outmaneuver the Ruugans.

*

Kalvin had been with Adini and Havi, who both told stories to Sidney and the other bulwarks when Ulina arrived. He did not know who she was, but the others' reaction to her made him realize that she was someone important. She introduced herself then thanked them all for their service to their cause. After talking to the jolems for a short while, she called Kalvin. Along with Alena and Mantak, he followed her into an empty tent. He stood before her.

Although he towers over her, he felt like the smallest person in the tent.

"Kalvin." Ulina called.

His mind returned to the present. He stared into her soft brown eyes. She has long brown hair that hangs to her waist. Her light olive skin seems to glow in the sunlight. Her elflocks have a bluish tint and like most elves she is thinly built. He knows the fact that she has an aged appearance means she is very old.

"I have been told that you wish to become a bulwark."

Kalvin nodded. She drew her powers and explained that he would be hyperactive for several days. He had heard about that. That does not seem like a reason not to be a bulwark. She sent a flash of sorcery into his chest. She knows how becoming a bulwark affects a normal man. She has no idea what it will do to Kalvin because he is fated to become a paladin.

A moment after he was struck with the sorcery, Kalvin began to sway. Mantak and Alena helped him to the ground. He fell unconscious as soon as his back hit the ground. Ulina smiled, then she said-in elvish.

"I want him guarded at all times. Some assassins may act against him just to spite Razial. Now, Alena let us go find young Razial so I may meet with him for a short while. Mantak please join us."

Zelia spotted Ulina first. She watched Ulina stroll across the grass with Alena by her side and Mantak behind them.

Seeing Zelia distracted, Razial turned to follow her line of vision. That is when he saw Ulina leading the others toward them. He took note of Ulina's brown cowl flowing just above the grass.

Even from a short distance, he sees her attention is on him. He turned to Zelia, and half mouthed, and half whispered.

"Who is she?"

"Fa'Ulina the Blue Keeper."

Razial did not respond. He smiled at Alena, who smiled back. Ulina stopped before him and introduced herself. She asked him if it was all right to ask him some questions. He told her he does not mind. She tilted her head in respect, then asked many questions. He disliked it when she focused on his loyalty to the Hilt, but he remained stoic. When she asked what he knows about the Champions' Wars, he told her that he knows all that Alena knows.

"I do not know what Alena knows, young Razial. Would you be kind enough to tell me what you know?" Ulina asked informally.

The fact she is talking in ancient elvish is throwing him off, especially since she is talking so informally. Still, he did as she asked. He told her all he knows about the Champions' Wars. When he finished, she nodded and said.

"Ja'Goraan has taught you only the basics. I shall tell you more in the future. If you do not mind, I would like you to take a short walk with me."

Zelia stepped aside while Ulina stepped toward him. Razial took a step back to pivot so he could walk with her. While the others walked off, Scar's pack joined him and Ulina. That is when she asked him if he wanted to hear about his father.

"Only the truth." He said.

She began by telling him how when his father was young all he wanted to do was become a Ratel. As agents and spies for the Canopy, Ratels are not a clan of elves like most humans think.

One must earn the right to call oneself a Ratel. His father made himself into one of the best Ratels ever. His last task came about when he managed to infiltrate the rebels in Ino-Heim. His father spoiled plot after plot with the help of Razial's mother.

"Later, while A'Isina was pregnant with you, she and A'Ashiek discovered the trail to those behind the plot against Fa'Beulah. They joined Alena's parents in a task. Sadly, they were all killed after leaving Alf-Heim. Fortunately, Ja'Binu found you and Alena. He informed us about what had happened to your parents when he returned to Fulancia."

To stop himself from asking why she talks to him in ancient elvish, he asked. "So, my uncle killed those who killed my parents?"

"Not all of them, but most."

She stopped and looked around. Shorter than he is, she stands to his shoulders. He senses how much she cares about him. It is not just because he is the Gideon. She is connected to him somehow, but she is not ready to reveal how.

Scar's pack became excited and ran off.

"It seems they have caught She-Bear's scent." Ulina said.

Razial looked over his shoulders to see if he could see Anjia. It does not surprise him that the wolves trust Ulina enough to reveal they refer to Anjia as She-Bear.

"Razial. Kalvin is fated to become a paladin as are Fogi Red and the woman you saved, Ofelia. You may not want to be the Gideon, but you are. Be careful. I shall be around for a short while longer. Thank you for your time."

With that, their meeting ended. She did not have to tell him not to say anything about those fated to become paladins.

*

Alena smiled with her arms around Razial. They are alone in the tent the siblings share. It is growing dark. She is happy to be alone with him. She kissed him softly, then caressed his face with her left hand. Neither said a word as they stared into each other's eyes. They slowly laid atop her sleeping blanket. He removed his shirt.

"Zelia is fond of you." Alena pouted playfully. "But she will wait until I give her permission."

He shook his head while caressing her head. Then smirked. She tried not to smile but failed.

"What? I might, just to spite Anjia."

"Alena." Razial warned.

"She and I will make peace. I am only teasing."

Hearing that made Razial happy. They began kissing just before Araceli and Xochi walked into the tent. Razial laughed. He told them they had arrived just in time to hear a secret. He noticed Araceli is not bothered by walking in on them kissing but Xochi is.

"We were only kissing Xochi." He smiled.

He turned to look into Alena's narrow eyes and told her that during an assassination in Arapia he had come across the prince of Arapia strangling a little girl.

"I wanted to kill him, but I would have failed in my task, so I followed him to Anazi Falls. He liked to rape children. I acted like a servant and served him death." He said solemnly.

He kissed Alena then laid back and pulled the blanket over his shoulders. Alena looked at Araceli and Xochi. They are as stunned by Razial's admission as she is. She knows they feel as though the prince of Arapia had gotten what he deserved.

*

Kalvin sat around the fire with the other bulwarks-including Sidncy, and the others (the jolems, Raal, Fogi Red, Mantak, and his guards), when Ulina joined them. She told them many tales and answered a lot of questions. Kalvin listened when she explained that Ja'Brahma is Ja'Brahma's complete name. The ja' in his name is not a prefix. The prefix came from his name. Raal stated he did not know that. She said many have forgotten that. Sidney then asked why most humans believe elves betrayed Ja'Brahma.

"What do most humans know about Ja'Brahma besides their ever-changing tales about him? Ja'Brahma was not the perfect, infallible elf many believe him to have been. He was infallible in one way and that was being Rakaar's enemy. He was not betrayed." Ulina said in a firm tone.

"What about Ino-Heim?" Kalvin asked.

"The Boars stand against all with Rakaar. They walk the path of Ja'Brahma. There are some-the Harlequins, who stand against Eloh as well. Pray you never come across them."

Kalvin had never expected to learn so much about elves. Talking with Ulina, he had heard more than he had wanted to hear.

CHAPTER 7

THE WAR

Razial's decision to press the Ruugans was rewarded early, but as time passed and the closer, they got to Ruug, the more difficult the fighting became and the less progress they made. For three months, Razial pressed ahead. Ulina stayed for two of those months, before she went off to help those fighting Vin. The Bassarans stalled in their efforts to reach Coilu city. Razial had hoped that either he or the Bassarans would break through before winter, but neither happened. The weather has changed, and he is still twenty miles east of Ruug city.

Mounted on his horse, Razial surveyed the scene. The Ruugans have entrenched themselves before his forces. They are formidable, appearance wise, but he can sense they do not want to fight. The problem is, neither do those with him. Still, he believes if he can break the Ruugans' position it would boost morale and allow those with him to make defensive fortifications during the winter. That will allow them to hold the line they have established.

With so much on the line, Razial put Fogi Red in charge of breaking the Ruugans' southern flank. Razial watched as Fogi Red, Raal, and a group of Partisans, all dwarfs, took the lead of the Partisans' position. They will spearhead the attack against the south while Paul leads his men against the north position. Sidney and the other bulwarks will guard Paul. Mantak and his guards will guard Razial and Kalvin, who will join Razial in leading the calvary against the central positions. The siblings will help the other magicians deal with the arrows. The jolems and Scar's pack have already taken off to act as soon as Razial leads the charge.

Looking to the sky, Razial saw Alena's hawks soaring. He has no doubt they will strike every chance they get. His attention returned to the Ruugans' battle lines. He looked back at Kalvin. His friend is ready for combat. With the sword Binu gave him hanging on his hip, Kalvin shows no sign of nerves. His blond beard makes him appear more serious than he is. Razial wants to tell him about being fated to become a paladin, but he knows doing so would change the choices Kalvin makes which would affect his destiny.

Spurring his horse forward, Razial drew his sword. He sensed when the magicians in the area drew their powers. His horse began to run faster. The browning blades of grass began to blur by. The sound of hundreds of horses galloping across the plain filled his ears. The Ruugans released volley after volley of arrows. He paid the hissing arrows no mind. Mantak and his guards will deal with every arrow aimed at him. He saw Scar's pack and the jolems maul a group of archers. Panic set in. Many Ruugans tried to avoid the wolves and or the jolems while others tried to hunker down to stop Razial's charge. The Ratels lashed out at them. A moment later, the jolems targeted them.

That cleared his path. A Ruugan captain led the charge to stop him. Razial put his sword in his left hand and began throwing his daggers with his right hand. The Ruugan captain stared in amazement at how Razial threw his daggers as if he had an infinite number of magical daggers. The captain's amazement quickly turned to horror when he was struck in his chest by one of the daggers. By the time he looked down at the dagger, it had already returned to Razial. All he saw was the gaping hole the dagger had left in his chest. His hands moved to cover the wound trying to stop the bleeding. He never saw the dagger that slammed into his head killing him.

With chaos all around him, Razial was forced to parry several attempts to strike him. The Ratels positioned themselves so their foes could only reach him from one direction. Although their lines have been broken, the Ruugans continued to fight spiritedly. With little room and not wanting his horse to be targeted, Razial dismounted.

"Raz! What are you doing? Fight from the high ground." Kalvin strained.

All around the battlefield, the Ruugans have regrouped. Fogi Red has broken the southern flank while Paul is keeping the northern position busy. Razial's calvary has stalled. The Ruugans have killed tens of horses. It is time to meet them head- on.

"Dismount!" Razial ordered.

Four men targeted him. His daggers tumbled toward them. They were surprised by the daggers, but still stopped and ducked. Razial was upon them immediately. His sword forced the first man back. The second man was struck in his torso by a dagger. When he doubled over in pain, Razial decapitated him. The third man's eyes glazed over after Kalvin's sword cut through the back of his head. The fourth man's throat was opened by a Ratel's katana. Scar's pack rallied to Razial. Time felt as if it was dragging on. Razial decided to join Fogi

Red. The Partisans' ability to be as brutal as dwarfs has put those to the south on their heels. However, the Ruugans in the north are still fighting with a greater desperation than Paul's forces are. Razial had explained that both sides would become desperate and that the only difference is that their enemies have Ruug city to fall back to while they can only retreat-something he will not allow.

He saw Fogi Red leap into the air while Mantak used his powers to knock down a group of foes. With so many people fighting, it is difficult to see far ahead. That is why he did not see Fogi Red when he shouted.

"Onward! Onward!"

Fighting with a dagger and his sword, Razial and the Ratels cut down groups of enemies while Mantak and Kalvin helped them. Finally, the Ruugans began to fall back. They are keeping their weapons moving to stop the wolves from targeting them. Razial saw several Ruugans fall. Adini had cut them across their legs. He sensed the siblings using their powers. They had saved their powers. Paul's magicians are all exhausted.

As he moved to fight two men, he saw four of Paul's men trying to reach him. Their tabards are covered in blood. With his attention on his opponents, he was puzzled when he heard Zelia shout.

"Razial, behind you!"

He groaned in pain. One of the Mohran soldiers had stabbed him between his neck and shoulder blade-a miss. His arm went limp, and his sword fell. As he spun around, he sensed Mantak and Zelia lash out at his attacker. (Mantak also struck the two Ruugans he had been fighting.) The man fell lifeless, an assassin no doubt.

The second Mohran tried to spear him, but he deflected the spear with his dagger. The third man dressed as a Mohran stabbed Razial in his ribs, before Mantak cut him down.

Seeing all of this, the Ruugans in the area tried to reach Razial. The Ratels met them head-on wielding their katanas and their powers. Razial saw this while fighting the man with the spear. His right arm is useless. He threw his daggers striking him twice before he was knocked down. The man tried to close in on him only to be sent crashing to the ground by a magical blow.

Razial felt the cold grass prickling his neck while Araceli finished the man with the spear. He rolled on to his side. He sensed a warlock draw his powers, then he was hammered magically. The warlock knelt over him. He flailed his arms and his dagger. He managed to deflect the warlock's dagger-saving his life, still he was stabbed in his right shoulder for the second time.

"Aarh!" His attacker growled in pain.

Razial recognized the voice immediately. It is Dario the Unknown.

Kalvin cut Dario across his back. He stood and tried to stab Kalvin, but Kalvin blocked his swing. Dario hit Kalvin in the mouth knocking him down. Araceli's arrival saved Kalvin's life. She engaged Dario, who had to run away to avoid having to fight others as well. However, that was not it for Razial. Another assassin crept over to finish him. He wanted to call for help, but it was not in him. He threw his daggers, but they were easily deflected.

"Your time has come, Avatar."

Razial recognized his voice. Unfortunately for him, Adini and Havi heard him. They leapt from the ground. Razial seen the assassin's shocked expression before they butchered him.

Adini told Mantak that Razial needs to be healed. Mantak told Zelia to heal him.

"The battle is coming to an end. We have won the day." Mantak said to Razial.

Razial felt a sense of relief fill him. He felt Zelia use her powers to heal his wounds. He tried to gauge what was going on but could not. He is losing consciousness. He looked into Zelia's eyes. She smiled at him while moving her hands over his body.

"Fortify and hold this position." He said before losing consciousness.

***

Before Rakaar was imprisoned, he had instructed the Magi to make a magical gateway that connects the Gnor Valley with Svan. Doing this weakened the Magi, so when Eloh's servants discovered what had happened, the keepers attacked and imprisoned the Magi. Rakaar was too taxed from his fights with Ja'Brahma and others to stop the paladins from imprisoning him while Ja'Brahma killed Rakaar's queen and the Canopy along with the Gully Council finished off Rakaar's allies and imprisoned Haar. All of that had happened at the end of the first Champions' War. Still, the gateway remains. Gnor was founded around it.

Tu'ani thought about this while staring at the original part of Gnor. Lela is next to her. Behind them are five apprentices: Vera,

Niri, Lissa, Bernice, and Ofelia. Close to their group, are forty bulwarks. Lela had told them to remain mounted. After Tu'ani told the apprentices how Gnor was founded, Lela explained that they came to Gnor to find out who had freed the Harlequins.

"Take no action unless we say otherwise." Lela said.

She and Tu'ani watched as Troggo led several of his fellow Harlequins out to meet with them. Only they know how deadly Troggo is. He is ancient even by elf standards. He has been imprisoned for close to a thousand years. Whoever freed him has gained a powerful ally.

Lela stared at him. His red hair is graying but not his long black elflocks. His red eyes are full of recognition.

"Tu'ani. Lela. I never thought I would see you two again." Troggo said in Tuyakan.

Ofelia stood nervously while watching him walk closer to her and the others. Although she has to look down at the Harlequins, she feels overmatched before them. She saw the four siblings returning to join them. They had checked the area to make sure no one was lying in wait. Troggo appears unaffected by their return. He did not even watch them dismount. Ofelia did. She took note of how their dirndls flowed above the grass while they walked over to stand with the keepers. She does not know why, but she wondered why novices wear the same style of dress, but siblings do not.

"You two have proven yourselves to be warriors. I am impressed.

Still, you stand with the traitor, Eloh." Troggo growled.

Usually, she feels a sense of peace when she looks at an elf. She feels only menace from Troggo. He stands before the keepers as if he is ready to fight. A breeze blew across the plain blowing his red hair in his face. He straightened his hair and glanced around.

"We have come for an answer, Ja'Troggo." The two keepers said simultaneously in Tuyakan.

Ofelia did not fully understand what was said. She will soon. Lela had explained to her and the others that Troggo must reveal who freed him or they had the right to enter the city to find out.

"As you can see, no Denari has been freed. As for who freed me, the Master and another Harbinger did."

With that, there was nothing else to be said. Troggo spun on his heels and walked away. Lela told everyone to mount their horses and ride off. While they rode, she and Tu'ani informed Ulina about what Troggo had said. She asked how they feel about warring with the Gnorans and Winninans.

"That would be a waste. We must keep each of these wars separate until the Harbingers hand us our enemies." Ulina thought.

"The Master is distracting us. We must stop him from achieving his goal." Tu'ani thought.

"We must keep Ja'Razial away from him. He could achieve his goal if he convinces Ja'Razial to help him." Lela stated.

They all know why she had said this. No one can force Razial to give up Ja'Brahma's daggers, but the Master could ask him to accomplish the Harbingers ultimate goal-something the Order of the Flame cannot allow.

"How do we control Ja'Razial without pushing him toward the path of Ja'Brahma?" Tu'ani asked.

"We have to allow him to continue to choose for now. The hunt makes things difficult, but until we have found all his paladins and keepers, we must trust his fate." Ulina said.

With that, Ulina ended their connection. Lela and Tu'ani took the lead of their procession. Lela came up with a plan. Tu'ani likes the plan. They turned northward hoping to evade the Gnorans like they had on their way to Gnor. Lela thought about her plan. She hopes the Harbingers do not have an easy counter to it.

***

Kalvin feels strange being inside the tent with the other members of the Order of the Flame because Razial is not present. Although it had taken Razial a week to fully recover, he is well. The attack on him had shocked all who seen it. The assassins have proven to be more daring than expected.

"Should we not inform Razial about this?" Araceli asked.

Mantak had just informed them about Coilu city being put under military rule to prevent the people from attacking the army inside the city. He also told them about the rebels in eastern Coilu that have been scattered in the wind.

With the war slowing all around Coilu because of the weather, Mantak called this meeting to discuss his plan.

"Ja'Razial knows about my plan." Mantak said.

"Then why is he not here? Did you not inform him about this meeting?" Alena asked.

She lowered her almond shaped eyes. Her skin is pale due to the weather. Kalvin can sense she is curious not angry.

"Ja'Razial is aware of the meeting. Now, I propose we take the capital." Mantak said while looking at Alena and the others.

His words surprised them. They all have confused expressions. Araceli asked how they could take capital without a long-drawn-out campaign during winter.

"We sneak a small group behind enemy lines." Mantak said.

"How? Their lines are too well guarded." Araceli stated.

Xochi and Zelia agreed with her. Fogi Red rubbed his beard in thought. He asked how they could sneak behind enemy lines without first engaging their enemies.

"We cannot. Our strength lies in our ability to rely on each other and our willingness to sacrifice for each other."

By the way Mantak said this, it is clear he will ask the others to help him execute his plan.

"You want us to attack and break the line at some point so a small group can ride toward Coilu city." Raal said knowingly.

Mantak nodded in response. A grimness came over the bulwarks. Kalvin noticed that only he and Sidney remained unchanged. He knows that means they are the only ones who do not truly understand what is being asked.

"Okay. Razial is going-which means we are going." Havi pointed at himself and Adini. "We must take Paul. So, the question is besides you who else is going?"

Mantak explained that the Ratels will stay behind with Xochi and Sidney while the others accompany the Partisans to break a point in the Ruugans' northern defense lines. No one disagreed. Zelia asked if another sibling should stay with Xochi. Mantak told her that is why he is leaving his guards behind so they can take everyone else. He then told Sidney to bring Paul and his generals.

"Alena. Inform Ja'Razial." He said.

Alena tilted her head in respect. She exited the tent with Kalvin in tow. It is already dark out. He feels odd acting as Alena's protector, but that is the way Mantak wants it. Curious about how Mantak could simply ask the Partisans to take such an action, Kalvin asked Alena.

"The Partisans serve Fogi Red. Mantak helped found the Partisans. They are all sworn to two things: protecting Fogi Red and defending Nibel. They know this is the only way to keep their way of life. They will not mind this sacrifice because they know it is what is best for their loved ones." Alena said.

Kalvin nodded in response. They walked around the camp. He saw units huddled around fires. Rows of tents line the camp. All along the back side of the camp, fortifications are being built. To Kalvin, their foes made a big mistake. Paul's forces will pass the winter building fortifications so they can hold the lands they have taken and remain close to Ruug.

As they approached Razial's tent, Kalvin realized why Razial had insisted all the necessary digging was completed before building any structures: the ground is hardening with the cold. He shook his head and smiled. His mindset then went to how Alena had tried to get Razial to move his tent closer to the siblings' tent, but he refused. According to him, he can better contact Anjia and Scar's pack can come and go as it pleases.

"Razial'ja." Alena called, leading Kalvin into his tent. Razial turned to face them while saying.

"Ja'Mantak has made a decision."

Alena nodded. She shook her head because she was not surprised, he knew why she had come to his tent. He smiled at her and waved to Kalvin. He teased him about being a bulwark, so Kalvin teased him for almost being assassinated. Razial made an expression of horror as if he was dying. Alena took note of the scrolls he was looking over. He told her to tell him Mantak's plan. He listened and when she finished, he said.

"I agree with the plan, but only if we attack at night."

He and Kalvin noticed the discomfort in her eyes. Kalvin quickly expressed that he agrees with Razial. Razial knows she knows attacking at night is the best option, but something is making her not want to attack at night.

What he does not know is that she is worried about the shadow-tracker. She does not want to tell him about it because it would affect his fate.

"Make sure he understands I will not change my mind about that." He said firmly.

Alena left Kalvin with Razial. As she walked, she thought about how Mantak would respond. She realized Mantak would go along with Razial. She cursed fate for making Razial the Gideon.

***

The next day, just before noon, everything was settled. They would attack in two days. Kalvin and Mantak walked around talking. Kalvin told him about his trip to Fulancia. He was surprised by how much attention Mantak paid to what he said about meeting Goraan. Kalvin assured him that when he had met Goraan he heard Anjia call Goraan father while they hugged.

"I don't speak elvish, but Raz and Alena taught me how to use the prefix and suffix when someone is talking to a parent." Kalvin said.

He can tell Mantak is thinking about something serious.

"Forgive me for doubting you, but are you sure?" Mantak asked.

"She called him dad while she hugged him. By the way Goraan acted, she does not do that that often." Kalvin answered.

Mantak picked up his pace. Kalvin knows he is looking for someone, so he asked who he is looking for.

"Ja'Razial. I cannot talk with Alena about this."

"About what?" Kalvin frowned.

"Fa'Anjia being Ja'Goraan's daughter."

"You act as if that is important. I'm sure that Raz and Alena could have told you this a long time ago."

That made Mantak stop. He looked into Kalvin's eyes and asked if Kalvin had told either Razial or Alena that he knows that Anjia is Goraan's daughter.

"No. Why would I? I'm sure they know." Kalvin frowned.

"Kalvin." Mantak smiled. "Alena is forbidden to even discuss Fa'Anjia with anyone from the Order of the Flame. You have just revealed one of Ja'Goraan's greatest secrets. Fate allowed you to discover this and fate has allowed me to be the one you revealed it to."

Kalvin knows Mantak is happy, while he on the other hand is worried. He doubts Razial is going to be pleased by the fact Mantak knows something about Anjia he should not know.

***

Inside Coilu's imperial palace, Lisa and Ariel are in Ariel's private room. Ariel's cowl has a strange appearance. It seems alive in the dim light-only one candle burns in the room. Although the cowl's appearance is at the front of her mind, she feels quite relieved. She had come to the room expecting to argue in support of Tammy, but she did not have to. Ariel just told her that Tammy was right to have killed the men who had tried to help the nobleman Tammy had scarred for trying to force himself on her.

"Always stand with those loyal to you." Ariel said.

Lisa nodded in response. Ariel asked her where Tammy was. She told her that Tammy was in her room. Ariel left it at that. Lisa listened to her explain that she had to leave the city to deal with Gwen. That made Lisa think. She does not understand how Ariel could talk about facing Gwen as if she is talking about facing a novice magician. To her, it is shocking because she has only feared two individuals in her life: the Ancient of Tunez and Gwen of Dax!

Ariel sensed the change in Lisa. Seeing the confusion in her eyes, she said.

"Gwen has challenged our plans for Coilu too many times. She will not do so anymore."

"What about Frauter?" Lisa asked.

"Without Gwen, he will be easy to deal with."

The way Ariel speaks with such assurance shocks Lisa. She has never heard Ariel doubt any of the Harbingers' actions. For years, she believed that Beulah (as the Ancient of Tunez) had plans to take over all Ocia. Being around Ariel and Peter made her even more impressed with Beulah. She has no idea Beulah does not lead the Harbingers.

"Lisa. Ask yourself this. Who is the better master, a druid who actually advances your cause or an imprisoned magus who needs others to free him?" Ariel asked.

Lisa became nervous. She knows eventually she must start down the path of betraying Mel. Ever since she was told about Pam taking over Ocia city, she has tried to figure out what Beulah is up to. Ariel has told her winning the civil war is not important. She did not say what is important. Thinking about that, she stared into Ariel's faceless cowl and said.

"It is better to stand with those who stand with you, than to be with those who need you to stand."

Ariel liked hearing that. She stood and told Lisa to keep Peter II in line. Ever since his son was stabbed in Vin, Peter II had been cruel to the people inside the city. He had them herded into the north side of the city. He intends to keep them there during winter so they will be too weak to rise against him in the summer. Ariel finds that to be backwards, but she does not care. After she deals with Gwen, she will find a way to get Paul into the city if Razial has not done so by then.

"I shall return in a matter of weeks. Until then, the Ancient shall contact you directly. Make sure you always keep the ring on. You do not want to miss a message from her."

Lisa nodded while rubbing the magical ring Ariel had given her. It is a medium and allows her to be contacted telepathically. According to Ariel, Beulah's messages will be short and to the point, so she must pay attention.

"All shall be ready upon your return." Lisa stood.

Ariel expressed her confidence in her while exiting the room leaving Lisa alone with her thoughts. She wondered how much time she had before she had to leave the Sisterhood.

For her entire adult life, she has been involved in a war for one reason or another. These wars always dealt with forwarding either her cause or her coven's cause. Recently, she has realized all those wars were useless. Beulah has advanced the Sisterhood's cause more in the last six years than Mel had in the previous two centuries. She has grown tired of Mel's calls for war. He wants war against the Fellowship, war against the Theocracy, war against the Order of the Flame, and even war against other members of the Sisterhood!

That is why she has joined Beulah in whatever war she is waging-a war she knows will never pit her against those who are on the same side she is on.

***

Razial rode point while Alena and Kalvin rode just behind him. The others rode in a tangled formation with the bulwarks bringing up the rear. Scar's pack had run off because a small village could be seen just ahead of them. They will rendezvous with the wolves north of the village. Alena's hawks are soaring above them scouting and searching for prey. It is just before noon. The air is crisp. There is a light snow on the ground. Still, winter is a month away. Thick white clouds cover the sky. There is no sign of the sun. However, the day is bright. They are all wrapped in warm coats. Only Fogi Red has his face uncovered.

Razial's mind is on Anjia. She had snuck behind enemy lines a day before his group, which was a week earlier. Before they set off, Razial had talked with Mantak about Anjia. To Kalvin's surprise, Razial found it humorous how Mantak discovered Anjia is Goraan's daughter. What interests Razial the most is Mantak's personal interest in this. When asked, Mantak had said Razial would soon discover why he is so interested in Anjia.

"So, who is this She-Bear?" Adini squeaked.

Like the elves in the group and Fogi Red, the jolems had heard Scar's thoughts when he had thought to Razial that his pack sensed Anjia close by.

"Stop talking just to hear your own voice." Fogi Red said.

Adini scowled at him, then he realized elfin animals call Anjia She-Bear.

"Hey. When you get my age, let us see how much you remember." Adini mocked.

"How old are you two anyway?" Fogi Red asked.

"Now who is talking just to hear themselves talk?" Adini teased.

Razial changed the subject by saying he will meet with Anjia while they see to lodging for the night. Zelia asked him if he was sure that was a good idea.

"You do know she intends to capture you." Zelia stated.

"Not right now." Razial winked.

"I will accompany you." Mantak said. "Havi. Adini. Stay with the others until, if you want, you can join us."

Havi and Adini looked at each other for a moment before Adini told him they would stay with the others.

"It is better for our plan." Havi added.

He referred to the fact that Araceli is acting like a Vinan noble and Fogi Red and the jolems are acting like her slaves, since Vinans usually have dwarf slaves.

Before Razial and Mantak rode off, Alena told him to avoid any trouble. He waved while saying he always tries to avoid trouble. Razial and Mantak tethered their horses in front of the wooden tavern they had seen Anjia enter. Wearing blue hooded cloaks, they entered the tavern. It is empty except for a woman at the bar. Thin, with pale skin and long blond hair, the woman scoffed before saying.

"What is an elf doing in this part of Coilu?"

Razial walked across the room and placed two gold coins on the bar while saying.

"What elf? I see no elf."

The woman smiled. She watched him and Mantak make their way to the stairs. Razial saw Anjia at the top of the stairs. She has on her black burnoose with the hood drawn over her head. The stairs squeaked as Razial and Mantak made their way up. Anjia moved silently through the dark hallway. They followed her into her room. She made her way to Razial's side and asked why he brought Mantak.

"Because like you, I was born a Bear." Mantak said.

The fact that he spoke in ancient elvish confused her and Razial. He called her by her name without the fa' prefix showing he does not want things to be formal between them.

"So, just Mantak huh?" Anjia frowned at Razial.

Razial raised his eyebrows and shook his head. He told her Mantak knows she is Goraan's daughter. He then explained how he found out. That made her smile. She turned to face Mantak and asked.

"So, why do you want to know me?"

She spoke in Tuyakan, still confused by the fact he is so informal with her. The fact he is speaking ancient elvish shows a willingness to act as if they are close. That is why she wants to know why he wants to know her.

"I am quite interested in you because, so little is known about you." Mantak said.

"Are you not under the Canopy? Last I checked, they still want Ja'Goraan."

Anjia's statement intrigued Mantak because Razial did not tell him that Anjia is at odds with Goraan. He had recognized this when she said Goraan's name formally. He asked her why she is at odds with Goraan.

"Have you ever met Ja'Goraan?"

"Our paths have crossed many times."

"And why are you" Anjia pointed at Mantak. "-at odds with him?"

"Because of the things he has done and the choices he has made in the past." Mantak said.

Anjia had not expected an answer. She thought about asking for more details but decided to ask.

"Why does the Canopy want him? I can assure you Ja'Goraan is no ally of Rakaar."

"Of that, we are sure."

Mantak is puzzled by the fact they do not know why Goraan is wanted by the Canopy. He told Anjia he is not at liberty to say why Goraan is wanted by the Canopy. He watched her hug Razial while telling him Goraan is still roaming Giaour and Rogelio has joined the hunt. He knows that concerns her, but Razial remained stoic. Mantak would not mind an encounter with Rogelio.

"Mantak." Anjia said in elvish, surprising him. "Take care of my love I am very unforgiving."

She smiled at Mantak more out of courtesy than affection. She then kissed and embraced Razial before pulling away and saying.

"I must leave before I get into trouble."

Razial caressed her face and smiled. He understood her coded speech. She is leaving because other assassins are close by, and she cannot defend him without making herself a target. His attention went to Mantak, who watched Anjia leave.

"You will never use her against her father." He warned Mantak.

"I would never try. Remember, I have crossed paths with Ja'Goraan, many times, not once have we ever fought."

Mantak's response made Razial smile because although he has many questions, he will not ask them until he knows Mantak better. As they made their way out of the room, Razial warned Mantak about other assassins being close by.

Alena sat to Kalvin's right while Araceli sat across from him. Paul is to Alena's right with Havi and Adini in between Paul and Araceli. The six of them are alone. The others are in their rooms. Kalvin and Paul are talking about how big the inn is.

Made of wood, the inn is cold but well lit. The innkeeper is happy to have their business. He politely served them bowls of stew and bread. The bread is not fresh, but still tasty. To Paul's surprise, the ale is strong. He frowned when Havi had a pitcher sent up to Fogi Red. He asked why the others are not eating with them.

"There is no reason for all of us to feel lazy at the same time." Araceli said.

Kalvin rubbed his beard. His body has warmed, and his beard is making his neck itch. He looked around while Paul argued for them to take around a bout way to the capital in order to avoid any traps their enemies might have set.

With an unkempt beard that is fuller than Kalvin's, Paul does not appear to be the son of an emperor. Paul appears to be just another swordsman. His blue eyes never waver, but they show how he feels. That is why Kalvin knows he is growing angry with Adini and Havi. The jolems are arguing against his idea. Kalvin knows Paul is used to giving orders without any feedback. However, since he was snuck out of Mohr, he has been taking orders from those he sees as his inferiors. Kalvin can only imagine how difficult that must be for him.

Adini told Paul to let him, and Havi worry about their movements. It was clear in Paul's eyes that he had to restrain himself. Araceli seen this. She called Adini to signal for him to ease up.

"What?" Adini continued chewing his food. "He is not a child. His plan is stupid. How can our foes set traps for us when they do not know we are coming?"

Kalvin admitted to himself that Adini has a point. He listened to Havi state that with the elfin hawks and wolves they do not have to worry about falling into traps. Havi continued talking, but Kalvin's attention went to two men, who eyed him while they approached the table. The jolems looked at the men dismissively. Kalvin saw no swords, but he saw daggers under their coats. That is when he realized they were thieves from Doh!

"Kalvin with a K from Anazi?" One of the men asked knowingly.

Kalvin recognized the man but could not remember where he met him. Without hesitation, he drew his sword and pressed the men. The men backpedaled in opposite directions. The innkeeper shouted for them to fight outside. Kalvin continued to fight wondering why no one was helping him. In his peripheral vision, he saw Araceli put an arm out to stop Paul from helping him. He heard Zelia and the others running down the stairs. By then, he was fighting defensively.

"Let him finish this. He started it." Havi said.

That puzzled Kalvin, who at that moment lost the sense of respect he had for the innkeeper. He kicked a chair and caused one of the men to trip. With his heart pounding, he pressed the other man while drawing his dagger. He stabbed the man with his dagger. Still, the man fought on. Kalvin sidestepped his charge, then stabbed him twice in his back. He heard boots running and moved back to see what was going on. That is when he saw the other man run out of the inn.

"Enough!" Alena stood. "Do you want to be healed?"

She moved over to heal the man. Kalvin saw disappointment in her eyes. He has done something wrong.

"Never act against us again." Alena warned.

It took several minutes to close his wounds. While she healed the thief, Araceli explained that Kalvin is not to initiate any fight unless a sibling tells him to. Kalvin simply nodded.

"Now, pay the innkeeper handsomely so this fight goes unnoticed." Alena said.

*

Hours after meeting with Anjia, Razial and Mantak returned to the village. They had bought scraps and meat for the wolves and hawks. It is growing dark. Mantak had hurried him back saying they cannot run the night-run with the wolves. They have less than an hour of daylight left. They tethered their horses on the side of the inn. While they made their way to the front of the inn, Razial sensed that something was wrong. Mantak sensed it too. He stood in the middle of the street and looked around. He saw Tol methodically walking toward him and three other assassins walking from the other side of the street.

"Who are they?" Mantak asked in elvish.

Razial could not make out who the others are because their faces are covered, but he knows Tol. With long wavy brown hair, olive skin, and light brown eyes, Tol is a younger version of his father-Tollok. He is taller than Razial and well built. As a powerful warlock and skilled swordsman, Tol can afford to be confident. Very few can match him. His sword of choice is the long sword which he can wield with either hand or both hands.

Still, Razial is not worried about him. His concern is his father. If Tollok is present, things will be very difficult.

Tollok is a druid, and his swordsmanship is so impressive that his moniker is the Sword as in the Sword of Fulancia. If he wants to fight, it will mean Razial's plan to get Paul to Coilu city will fail.

"I am Tol the Second Sword. Razial and I have something to settle." Tol said.

The other three assassins pulled bows from under their coats. They spread out and nocked arrows. They drew their powers to show they are warlocks. Mantak looked at Razial who shook his head when he heard the familiar sound of Tollok's voice while the others hurried through the inn to the scene.

Havi and Adini arrived first. Then Fogi Red, Raal, and Alena. The others stayed close to the inn door not wanting to spill out in front of it.

"Alena!" Tollok smiled. "It has been far too long."

Four men stood behind him. Each is a powerful warlock. Razial is glad he is not there to fight.

"Tollok." Alena smiled back moving over to embrace him. "Is all well? Tol?"

Tol walked over to greet her, but it was clear he was there to fight. The hood to his black cloak was pulled back and his long sword is visible. He told her to tell those with her to stay back. He walked over to face Razial while Tollok called to her saying.

"We know who you have with you, but Tol wants this chance. If the Avatar wins, we will stand down, for now. If he loses, there is nothing to discuss."

Alena shook her head as she turned to look at Tol. Like Razial, he has a young appearance. Only five years younger than Razial, Tol is still too young to truly harm him with his powers. His sword is another story.

She likes Tol. He and Razial are friends. However, Razial has to pay for breaking the Society's rules.

"Why are we waiting?" Razial asked.

Kalvin watched as Tol drew his long sword and Razial drew his machete sword. They quickly closed the distance between them. They pressed each other as their swords crashed rhythmically.

Their cloaks flowed behind them as they tried to outmaneuver each other.

While Kalvin watched the fight, Mantak kept an eye on the jolems. They could care less about Tollok's warning. They are bound to guard the Gideon-like their fathers were bound to guard the last Gideon. As the fight wore on, the more solemn the jolems became.

"Impressive." Tol said.

Razial had forced him to parry several skillful thrusts. He managed to cut Tol across his left deltoid. They had removed their cloaks and Tol had drawn a dagger. Frozen breath rose from their mouths. Sweat began to bead on their foreheads. Razial slowed his breathing when he called a dagger to him. Tol recognized the dagger as did Tollok.

"So, you have done what the Merciless could not." Tol said.

Mantak stared at Tol wondering what he meant. His line of sight was on Ja'Brahma's dagger, but he could have been talking about Razial wounding him. Mantak thought about it and decided that he was talking about the dagger.

"You are tiring." Razial stated.

Araceli watched as Tol parried several thrusts with one hand, then spun and brought his sword around on his backswing. Razial was forced to step back. Tol pressed him. His sword came at Razial from an overhead angle. Razial was forced to cross his sword and dagger to block the swing. To Araceli's surprise, Tol cut Razial across his ribs. Razial winced in pain. Tol pressed him-a mistake. Razial kicked him, then cut him across his back hand. Tol dropped his sword but managed to stab him in his waist. She knows the wound is shallow because she still sees half of the dagger's blade. Still, his success came at a cost. Razial drove his dagger into Tol's torso two times before putting his sword against Tol's throat.

"It is done." Tollok said.

There was no disappointment in his voice. He had helped raise Razial. He knows how skilled he is. He knows that Tol's desire to duel Razial was the best chance of resolving things without multiple deaths on both sides.

"Until next time, Avatar. You have a long hunt ahead of you." He said.

Razial winced in pain while Tollok led the assassins away. Razial and Tol nodded in respect to each other. They are still friends.

"You have some strange friends, Razial." Zelia said.

Razial smiled at her. They all made their way into the inn. He saw Anjia on her horse. She had witnessed the entire fight.

***

Early, the next morning, Razial entered the siblings' room. They are still beneath their blankets. The gray light of dawn has only just begun to rise in the east. Araceli exhaled in irritation. Zelia looked up with a confused expression. Alena groggily rubbed her face while telling Razial to go back to sleep. She quickly pulled the blankets back up to her shoulders. It was cold and the chill made her shiver. Razial knelt over her. He winced because his wounds are still tender.

"Razial. Go back to sleep before you wake the others." Alena hissed.

Razial looked around. Araceli frowned at him. Zelia rolled over. He shook his head. Then he leaned over and kissed Alena's forehead. After that, he exited the room.

"At least he has ideas to help." Zelia sighed.

"He should wait until the sun is fully up to share them." Araceli stated.

Alena and Zelia giggled. Alena closed her eyes and dozed off. She could hear Razial and Mantak whispering with the jolems. She did not make out what they were saying. She fell deeper into sleep and lost track of time.

After some time, she became aware of her surroundings. She heard Havi playfully curse Raal for being so energetic.

"Early? It is hours past sunrise. Our breakfast is ready." Raal said.

Alena sighed when she heard this. She heard Araceli sit up and rub her arms for warmth. She rolled over. Zelia stated that their bath water better be warm. Early morning light streamed through the cracks in the shutters. Shivering from the chill in the air, Alena put on her boots. They all began to roll their sleeping blankets. Suddenly, she realized that she had not heard Razial's voice. She stood trying to hear a sign of Razial. Her heart began to pound, and her expression changed.

"Alena. What is wrong?" Zelia asked.

She stood holding out Alena's long coat. Alena stared at her.

"He would not dare." Alena hissed.

"Who would not what?" Zelia asked.

"Alena are you alright?" Araceli asked.

Alena did not answer. She took her coat and wrapped it around her shoulders. She opened the door and called to the jolems while speed walking through the inn.

"Do not ask me." Adini said. "I did not do it."

"I need to speak with you both." Alena said.

"What is going on?" Araceli asked.

"You will see. I cannot believe that these two allowed this to happen."

She had realized that she could not sense her hawks. She knows they would not go hunting so early.

"What is wrong?" Havi wobbled before her.

"Again, it was not me." Adini smiled.

Havi asked why they are not fully dressed. He put his Phrygian cap on.

"Where is Razial and who went with him?" Alena asked.

"I do not know. Mantak and Paul." Havi answered dismissively.

"And Scar's pack and your hawks." Adini grinned.

Araceli and Zelia stood in shock. They listened while the jolems explained that Razial had set off with Mantak and Paul and would use Alena's hawks to stay in contact with them.

"Now let us eat breakfast." Havi said when they finished.

"And you three should put your clothes on." Adini added.

"You two could have stopped them." Alena said.

"And we can send you back to Anazi Falls. We made the decision without you. Now eat and bathe." Adini said then walked off.

***

Standing by a window, staring through a crack in the shutters, Ariel stood next to Peter. They wore their Harbinger cowls to protect against the cold. They had snuck into the small town the night before and are ready to act against Gwen. However, Gwen sensed that something was wrong and exited the house she was in. Ariel and Peter's plan was to have a group of wizards storm into the house so they could fight Gwen in a closed area. That plan must change now!

The six wizards Peter hired are walking toward Gwen, who is in the street watching. A light snow is building on the ground. Ariel knows they must do something before Gwen drives the wizards off and they lose this opportunity.

"We must hurry." She said.

She spun on her heels and quickly jogged out of the house. Peter followed her. As they moved through the house, they sensed Gwen, and her servants draw their powers. Gwen is stronger than he had expected. Just before he joined the fighting, Peter thought about how he had told the wizards to link their powers. He is glad they obeyed.

In the street, people ran to avoid the magical battle. Gwen turned to face Peter and Ariel. She did not hesitate. She staggered Peter with a magical blow. Ariel did her best to stand and face her, but she was knocked around until one of the wizards struck Gwen from behind.

Unfazed, Gwen fought with menace in her eyes. The swordsmen a wizard had hired closed in on Gwen and her servants. Peter looked into Gwen's light brown eyes and saw a fearlessness that he had seen in the eyes of the desperate, defiant soldiers on the front lines of fierce battles. She will not go down without a fight.

He saw a swordsman run one of Gwen's servants through. He watched as the man fell lifeless to the ground. He had not used a magically forged weapon, so he died with his victim.

"Come on Harbingers." Gwen growled.

She staggered Peter again. He had been distracted because he had told the wizards to have their men use magically forged swords. Knowing he had to wear Gwen down, Peter lashed out at her with all that he had. He knows Ariel is a lot stronger than he is so the more attention she pays to him the more Ariel can hurt her.

Grimacing in pain, he forced Gwen to focus on him while he yelled.

"Attack Gwen. Focus on her!"

Gwen stumbled under the relentless attack. She knocked Peter down and killed two wizards, but Ariel and the swordsmen are taxing her. She is trapped. There is no escaping. All she can do is inflict as much damage as she can. She cursed herself for sending Frauter and Dawn to Coilu city. She lashed out, growing tired with each passing moment.

"Are we tired Gwen of Dax?" Ariel asked mockingly.

She breathed heavily, but she is far from being tired. Her cowl makes things easier for her. Gwen is wearing down, her servants are dead, and Ariel has two wizards helping her. Peter is too drained to use his powers, so he is using his sword. Ariel had to admit that he is useful when it comes to fighting.

"Stab her deeply." She told Peter.

She wants Gwen's powers drained from healing her. That will make it easier to bind her. With the wizards weakening, they must hurry. Peter stabbed Gwen in the side.

"Again. Stab her again." Ariel urged.

Peter stabbed Gwen in her upper back. She collapsed and Ariel bound her with gleipnir. She will have to reinforce the bind, but first they must get out of the street.

***

Razial dismounted his horse, then began to lead it by its reins. Behind him, Paul and Mantak did the same. The horses had just finished their second gallop and needed to rest.

With Scar's pack trotting ahead of them, they are walking on the trampled snow the wolves left behind. For miles and miles, there is nothing but snow. Even though the sun is high in the sky shining brightly, it is cold. Razial is glad there is no wind because there would be no shelter out on the plain.

Looking through the slit between his skull cap and scarf- which is wrapped around his face, he scanned the horizon while Mantak communicated with Alena's hawks. He can sense by the way the hawks are communicating that all is well with the others.

"Araceli's plan worked." Mantak said.

He explained that an army had stopped the others and that the story helped them avoid suspicion. The army had heard about the fight in the village. That did not surprise Razial.

"It seems Alena is still angry with you." Mantak added.

"With me?" Razial acted ignorant. "I am blaming all of this on you."

They laughed. Paul asked how Mantak communicates with elfin animals so easily. Mantak told him he has communicated with elfin animals for centuries. It is second nature for him.

"Centuries?!" Paul asked excitedly. "How old are you?"

"I will be four hundred years old soon." Mantak answered.

Razial heard Paul gasp in disbelief. He thought about how Mantak had gone along with his plans. Mantak sees the wisdom of getting Paul to Cula where his cousin rules. From Cula, they can wage a better war and get close to Peter II. Still, Razial knows the main reason Mantak had agreed to go along with his plan is because after the fights in the village too much attention would have been placed on their group and they could not risk a high-ranking soldier recognizing Paul.

With his mind on Mantak needing to ask Adini and Havi for permission to go along with the plan, Razial focused on Paul's voice when he asked.

"Razial. What happened to the bearded assassin in Mohr? Was he one of the ones who tried to kill you in Ruug?"

"No. Had he been around, I would be dead and so would you."

Razial did not mean to sound so cold, but he had spoken the truth. As they walked on, Scar's pack fell back and made themselves invisible. They communicated that a group of riders approached. Razial likes how they fell behind him and the others in order to hide their tracks.

He told Paul about the group of riders. Paul stated he hopes the men are Culans. Razial simply hoped they do not have to fight before they were within sight of Cula. He searched the horizon for several moments until he spotted the group. He stopped walking and mounted his horse while saying.

"They are Culan."

Paul cheered. He and Mantak mounted their horses. They all watched as the Culans approached them. Razial smiled when the Culans' horses grew nervous. They can sense the elfin wolves. Paul recognized the riders' leader. Mantak told him to wait until the riders were closer. That way if they must fight no one will get away. Paul went along with that.

"Now." Mantak said.

Paul called out to the man he recognized. The Culans stopped while Razial and Mantak flanked Paul. Paul introduced them to the captain of the Culans. The captain cursed the horses. He then asked who Paul was. Paul unwrapped his face. The captain stared trying to visualize Paul without the rugged beard that he has right now.

"Escort me to Cula. After I have bathed and shaved, you will recognize me." Paul said.

The captain asked why Paul is with only two guards. Razial responded before Paul could.

"I have guarded him since before his wedding."

The captain has no idea who he is, but he has heard about how well he had guarded Paul. He also heard about the killing of the four generals. The one thing they have in common is that the man who is said to have guarded Paul and killed the generals fit Razial's description.

"Very well, Your Majesty. We shall escort you to Cula." He said.

As Razial approached Cula, he thought about its history. Long ago, a duke made himself king and made Cula strong enough to defend itself. The city of Coilu made a pact with Cula and they built a great empire, but as time passed Cula became more of a junior partner. It remains formidable. However, its role in founding what have become known as the lands of Coilu has become mostly forgotten. Paul is impressed by the fact Razial knows this. He had brought it up, so Razial revealed that he knew more than even Paul knew. Paul stared at Mantak, who asked Razial if he knew that Cula was originally spelled with a K. Razial told him he did and he knew who it was named after. Paul asked why Cula is now spelled with a C.

"The truth is too complicated. Suffice it to say the duke was a wizard, a wise wizard and his name was Kula with a K." Mantak said.

That intrigued Paul. He wants more answers, but he knows not to press Mantak for answers.

As they approached Cula's southern gates, Razial reminded him to have the soldiers clear a path for the wolves, who remain invisible. Paul did this as soon as he was told. He feels strange because he never imagined he would ever travel with elfin wolves. He hates to think about how he used to hunt them. He does not know why the Fellowship had ordered the hunt for elfin wolves. Razial told him they would not know that until they caught up to Peter.

An hour later, Paul finished bathing himself and sat regally dressed. Razial and Mantak sat across from him and Kellen-his cousin, an overweight man with a brownish blond beard. He is bald on top of his head with drooping blue eyes.

Mantak senses no distrust from Kellen. He sat listening to him explain that Peter II had doubled Cula's taxes for refusing to help him in the war. Razial could not believe how inept Peter II is as a leader. Leaving Cula's forces intact while most of Coilu's forces are out fighting Paul's forces is one of the worse mistakes Peter II could have made.

"When is your next delivery due?" Razial asked.

His mind is already racing with ideas. He knows the others will arrive within two days. His chance to end the war is at hand.

"Tomorrow." Kellen said. He then turned to Paul. "That is if you do not mind."

Paul is proud, Kellen is willing to throw his lot in with him. He smiled as he realized that he intends to defer to Razial.

"Give me time to think cousin. Do me a favor and escort Mantak to the tower so he can contact some elfin hawks." Paul said to Kellen.

Razial smiled to show he was pleased with how Paul had handled Kellen's question. Alone with Paul, Razial explained what he wanted to do. Paul sat in shock, but he decided to go along with him. Razial has taken him this far. He might as well trust him one more time.

***

Two days later, Mantak instinctively drew his powers when Kellen knocked on the door. It is still dark in his room. He had been in a light sleep when he heard Kellen, and two guards walked up to his door.

Sitting up, he released his powers. He moved across the room and opened the door.

"Mister Mantak. Your friends have been spotted. They are being led to the southern gates and the army will be ready before noon. I have already ordered your breakfast. It will arrive in minutes. I shall rest until you are ready to leave." Kellen said.

"Thank you, Lord Kellen." Mantak replied.

He waited until Kellen and his guards had walked away before he closed his door. He sat on his bed and began to meditate. Razial has put him in a bind. Without saying anything, he took Paul to the city of Coilu. Kellen had given him Razial's message about sneaking in with the taxes. The only good thing is Razial had the smarts to take three warlocks and a witch with him. Razial's plan is to rally the people when Kellen leads the Culan armies against Coilu, which is only a half day's march from Cula.

Mantak had expected something like this from Razial. That is why he had given him an elfin burnoose. Had he not, he would have gone after him.

Although Adini and Havi will be angry, they will not be able to deny Razial's reasoning, a spy in Cula might reveal Paul is in Cula.

A knock on the door meant his breakfast had arrived, so Mantak changed his thoughts.

***

Razial's plan has worked perfectly, so far. He had used the elfin burnoose to make himself invisible while spying on key individuals around the city. Scar's pack and the witch guarded Paul while he was off spying and the warlocks were spreading the word that Paul is in the city.

To make sure the warlocks' work paid off, Razial snuck Paul around and let him meet with key figures in the city's rebellion.

Paul had the men tell those with them to gather whatever weapons they could and to be ready at nightfall. The fact that all the people are in the north side of the city made it easier for Razial. Squads of men are looking for Paul, but it takes them too long to check a location because of all the people jammed into such a small area.

Now, night has fallen over the city. Paul will address those close to them. Standing at the top of a wooden staircase, Paul is watching as more people tried to get into the granary to hear him speak. He glanced at Razial, who impressed him with his actions.

Between him and Razial, is the witch. The three warlocks are among the crowd. The people are transfixed on him. He can sense their emotions as they press closer to each other. He knows they know the war is about to end one way or the other. The guards who had kept them in the north are no longer as plentiful because they have been called to the walls to prepare for the Culans.

"Tonight-" Paul pounded a fist against his chest. "-this war will end. We shall make the traitors pay. I am here to prove that your loyalty has not been in vain."

The people began to cheer. Razial had expected this reaction. He had counted on it. People are easily manipulated into dying for a ruler. He focused on the smell inside the granary. It is a mixture of wheat, dirt, wood, and unbathed humans. He knows Scar's pack is not happy about the smell of the granary.

"I must warn you." Paul went on. "This battle will not be easy, nor will it be swift. Stand fast, and if you must die-die well!"

That made Razial shake his head. He could never live like a common man while nobles live with arrogance and privilege.

"If you wish to leave, go now. There is no room for cowards by my side." Paul drew his sword and held it high why shouting. "For my father. For Coilu!"

***

Standing atop the southern wall, Ariel watched the Culans march through the snow. To her, the slow falling snowflakes seem to be affected by the tension inside the city. As usual, she was unable to get Peter II to see things her way. She had told him to expel the people, but he refused. He is convinced he can defeat the Culans and the people. That might have been true under normal circumstances, but Razial is lurking, and Paul may be inside the city. If he is, she does not need to stay and help defend the city.

With her Harbinger cowl on, she is unaffected by the cold. She looked around. Archers line the walls. Torches have been placed on the crenels to help the archers see better. Ariel does not need such help. She is searching the Culans' ranks. She saw her sister. She stared at Araceli for several moments. A coldness past through her. Araceli does not remember what happened to their parents like she does. She never harbored the same kind of sentiments that Ariel has.

Changing her mindset, Ariel looked at Alena and Kalvin. She smiled as she took note that Kalvin no longer appears to be the fun-loving thief she had met more than a year earlier.

"That is not Paul." One of Peter's servants said.

He used to be Peter's captain. Now, he is the general of the city's army. Ariel stared at the regally dressed decoy next to Kellen. She had seen enough. She told Lisa and Tammy, who are just behind her, they should leave soon. Razial's plan has changed the war, but it has also helped the Harbingers.

"They are about to charge." Peter II said.

"Then you should return to the palace. Paul is inside the city and so is the assassin." Ariel said.

Peter II stared at her as if to say he would not be dismissed like a servant. At over forty years old, he should not be as childish as he is. Ariel ignored him. Her attention went to how she might capture Razial during the fighting.

"Lisa. Help these magicians hold the wall. Then, join me in my chambers." She said as she walked off.

***

While leading the charge toward the southern gates with Araceli and Zelia, Alena saw Ariel walk away. Mantak had told them to let the Culan magicians deal with the arrows.

"Target the magicians on the wall and be ready for when Adini and Havi take the gates." Mantak had said.

He had decided to scale the northern wall alone. He left just after the jolems had dove into the ground shocking Kellen and other Culans. He told them they would not miss Razial's sign to start the attack. He was right. Just after the Harbinger left the battlement, Scar's pack began attacking the archers and magicians on the southern wall. Alena, Zelia and Araceli linked their powers as they charged. They targeted specific individuals as they rode toward the gates.

***

Kellen was still thinking about how the jolems had dove into the ground as if the land was a pond, when he led the charge to take the wall. He had the magicians shield the men with the ladders as they closed in on the wall. He looked around to make sure all was well. He saw the jolems leap from the ground and butcher the guards at the gates. He knows the gates will not hold.

***

Lisa has no idea who Mantak is, but she knows an elf druid with surprise and elfin wolves on his side is too much to handle. She and Tammy had struck several Culan magicians before Mantak struck. The magicians on the wall do not have a chance.

With the Culans at the gates and the people rebelling inside the city, she knows that Coilu is lost.

"Come Tammy." She said.

She knows they have to join Ariel in order to escape. Ariel had made it clear that once Paul was inside the city her objective would be at hand.

"Peter II will lose his life trying to hold this city." Ariel had said to Lisa.

Running down the stairs, Lisa thought about how the Harbingers were planning to win their war with the Magi. She listened to the sound of fighting and could hear that it had not reached the palace yet. She began to hurry because she did not want to be left behind.

***

Less than an hour after the fighting had started, Ariel sat on her bed with the ancient crown of Coilu in her hands. She rolled the crown from hand to hand. Ancient elvish words are engraved on the inner rim of the crown. She will be able to read them in the future.

With the sound of fighting growing closer, she is not worried. She had sent Lisa and Tammy to guard Peter II. She knows that Razial will try to kill him, and she wants to try to capture him. She put the crown inside her cowl and stood. She looked at the scroll on the floor. On the scroll, she had written a fake message.

"Take the crown and the prisoner to Vin. She may be of use to us still."

She had written the message like the Master had instructed her to. It seems strange to her because Beulah is headed to Vin with Gwen. According to Beulah, the message will help them in the future.

As she exited her room, she thought about her sister. She is sure Araceli will survive the fighting unharmed. Her only question about her sister is how she will react to the truth that has been hidden for so long.

***

Razial snuck around the palace-invisible to non-sorcerers. He was shocked when Mantak gave him an elfin burnoose. Elfin clothing is closely monitored by the Canopy. It possesses the same power that elfin animals use to make themselves invisible. Only two members of the Society have elfin clothing: Binu has a cloak and Goraan has a burnoose and a surplice. Binu was given his cloak after risking his life for the Canopy. Goraan never discusses how he obtained his elfin clothing.

With his back against the wall, Razial crept through a hallway looking for a sign of Peter II. Although he cannot be seen, he can be heard and touched. With guards scrambling through the palace, he does not want to fight because someone bumped into him. He can tell by the sound of the fighting that the soldiers are falling back to make their stand around the palace. He saw two guards standing by a door when he sensed the elfin wolves moving toward him. He decided that the guards were guarding his target: Peter II. He threw his daggers before the guards even looked in his direction. The daggers were back in his hands by the time he reached the door. He opened the door ignoring the dying guards. To his surprise, Peter II stood in the middle of the room. Two other men are with him. Razial ignored them and closed in on his target, who gasped when he saw the dying guards by the doorway. He had no clue Razial was closing in on him. Razial stabbed him four times in his torso. One of the men called out to Peter II when he staggered backwards.

"What magic is this?!" The man exclaimed.

All he and the other man saw was Peter II being stabbed by daggers that seem to float on their own. Razial released the daggers confusing the men even more.

Out in the hallway, Razial saw Scar's pack and Mantak. The fighting has reached inside the palace. Razial told Mantak Peter II was dead.

"Good. Now let us get the ancient crown and find the others." Mantak said in elvish.

***

Ariel, Lisa, and Tammy snuck out of Coilu. Ariel had tried to convince Peter II to leave with her, but he refused. Although Tammy is confused, she did not ask any questions. She listened while Ariel explained that she had seen Mantak inside the palace and that Mantak had been wearing elfin clothing. Tammy knows Ariel had shown smarts by leaving. It would have gained them nothing trying to capture Razial with the elf druid close by.

Riding through the snow, they are riding eastward. Ariel told them they would have to hide out.

"They have elfin hawks that will search for us. Once we lose the elfin hawks, we will be safe." Ariel had said.

Tammy is not worried about being chased. The Order of the Flame does not know who she is. She is more concerned with how much Lisa has changed since joining forces with the Harbingers.

She likes Lisa, but she only stays around to find out how much of a role Lisa played in her mother's death-the motivation behind Tammy's impending war against the Sisterhood!

By noon the next day, everything had been settled. There is no more fighting. Most of Peter II's top supporters had either died or escaped so there will be no public executions. Peter II's lifeless body was put in the courtyard for all to see. Alena had sent her hawks to search for the Harbinger. She also scolded Razial for sneaking off. Zelia found Ariel's fake message. They all assumed it refers to Ariel. After they ate lunch, Mantak called a meeting in the throne room. Razial stood near the back wall watching as the others began to spread out. Mantak told Paul to sit on the throne. Kellen, the witch, and the three warlocks stood watching as if the throne might harm Paul.

Araceli chose to stand with the bulwarks-including Kalvin. Raal is close to Fogi Red, Zelia and Alena are in the middle of the room, while Havi and Adini are off to the side staring up at the high ceiling. Mantak is near the front wall watching Scar lead his packmates into the room. He turned his attention back to Paul and said.

"Now, I am going to tell you what to say. It will be in common but an ancient Brahman dialect."

Paul looked around in confusion. He asked Mantak what was going on.

"Trust me. It is better if you do not know." Mantak said.

His response only confused Paul more and made him more nervous than he already felt. He sat back and began repeating the words Mantak told him to recite. The wolves became tense. Ancient elvish words began to glow across the throne's headrest. That is when Mantak recited the ancient words glowing across the headrest. A magical silhouette of the magus Bal appeared. Razial called the daggers to him. The jolems remained calm, so he relaxed. Mantak held up a hand to calm the others.

"Who are you elf?" Bal growled.

Tall, with a heavily muscled body, Bal has strong light brown eyes. His hair is shoulder length and blond in color. His pale skin stands out against his black pants and short sleeve shirt.

"I am Ja'Mantak, and I deny your release here, in Coilu." Mantak said.

"Bal?" Kellen asked.

"Yes. Bal!" Bal boomed. "Bal the magus of Coilu."

He did not look at Kellen because his attention stayed of Razial. He had noticed Ja'Brahma's daggers. He smiled at Razial promising to kill him. Razial smirked at him saying.

"Many have tried. None have managed to do so."

"You dare mock me? A Tuyakan with elf blood. Do you even know what tribe you are from?"

"Of course I do. Why would someone as mighty as you care?"

"Mantak." Adini called. "Do it already."

Bal began to berate Adini and Havi. Mantak used his powers to break the throne sending Bal's powers into a medallion held by his greatest enemy. Bal yelled before his image disappeared. Mantak knows this Champions' War will only get worse.

CHAPTER 8

THE HARLEQUINS

Tina gasped as she ran through the long corridor. Several priests from the Theocracy are chasing her. She had destroyed the throne of Danou, but a Harbinger had taken the ancient crown before she could.

Tired, she must escape the palace. Already, she has fought too much and has no clue where Barthus is. He was supposed to run away with the last true heir of Danou, but she is not sure if he succeeded in getting to the heir.

Stumbling, as she turned into a connecting corridor, she tripped and fell. Trying to get back on her feet, she saw a man's legs. Ready to strike, she had to stop herself when she saw it is Barthus bringing one of his battle axes down on to an unsuspecting priest killing him.

A magical blow from another priest sent Barthus crashing against a wall. She stood and hammered the priest. Before he could try to fight back, she stabbed him with a dagger.

"Are you all, right?" She asked Barthus.

He is covered in blood-none of it his own. Breathing fast, he nodded. They began to run. She asked him about the heir. He told her he had survived an ambush to reach the heir.

"I sent him out of the city to make the rendezvous." Barthus inhaled. "The others are all dead."

That saddened Tina. Days earlier, she was informed about Coilu, where all survived, and Ocia, where none survived. The thrones were destroyed, but the Harbingers now have the Magi's crowns!

"I told you not to come back for me." She scowled.

They had just exited the palace. He smirked at her. With no one chasing them, he removed his bloody overshirt and hung his axes on his belt. Even in the darkness of night, Tina can see his muscles tense while they walk. His reddish-brown eyes go well with his reddish-brown skin.

"Did you think I would obey?" He asked.

Tina did not respond. She followed him alongside a building. She feels like a thief creeping around. She remembered what Lela and Tu'ani had told her. The Harbingers have the map of Svan which means they will soon know how to free the Magi.

Ulina has sent Adini, Havi, Alena, Araceli, and Kalvin to Svan to learn what the Magi must do to obtain their powers. The keepers had also warned Tina about Troggo being released. She will do all she can to avoid northern Giaour. However, those who pursue her will dictate that.

"I have horses waiting for us." Barthus said.

He lifted her through a window. She climbed into the room and looked around while he climbed into the room. She is puzzled by the fact there are no alarms being sounded. She stated this to Barthus, who said.

"It makes perfect sense. the Harbingers do not care to engage us. They want us distracted, so they can free their leader."

Very few know these Harbingers' true goal, Barthus' knowledge is even more rare because he is still a bulwark-by choice. He has been a bulwark for a very long time and has crossed paths with the Harbingers multiple times. Tina told him about the Harlequins and about Lela and Tu'ani going to Brahma city. His response did not surprise her.

"I have never met a Harlequin. Hopefully, I never will."

***

Troggo stood staring at the doorway. He began to think about how modern Gnorans know nothing about the city's founder and namesake. To him, it makes no sense for the Gnorans to have built modern day Gnor around what they call the ancient district-which is the original city.

He finds it embarrassing they do not know why their city was built or who Gnor really was. He met with their king and made it clear he and his people shall remain in Gnor for the near future. The king-who is named Harras, wants no problems with him and assures him the Gnorans will not enter the ancient part of the city.

"Ja'Troggo." The Master called.

Troggo watched him stand by the doorway. He does not know why the Master has returned, but he is willing to play his game until it no longer benefits him.

"Why have you returned?" Troggo asked.

"Why are you angry with me?" The Master asked.

Troggo scowled at him. The Master was once an ally. When his uncle Bahkez an original paladin led the Boars out of Alf-Hiem and formed Ino-Heim, Troggo stood with him until he refused to attack Eloh's servants. That led to Troggo leading a group of warriors out of Ino-Heim. His group became known as Harlequins. They settled in the Gnor Valley attacking Rakaar's and Eloh's servants alike. That is when the Master helped Troggo several times before helping bring about the Harlequins' imprisonment.

"Do you think I am a fool?" Troggo growled in Tuyakan.

The Master knows it is an act of hostility for an elf to talk to another elf in another language without necessity.

"Far from it. Had you been a fool, you would have never been Bahkez's apprentice."

"What do you know about A'Bahkez?"

"Everything. He is your father's twin. He was an original paladin. He and his brother helped imprison Rakaar and, he never approved of your present course of action. Tell me. Am I wrong?"

His response surprised Troggo, who could not deny anything he had said.

"Who are you?" Troggo asked.

"I walk the path of A'Ja'Brahma. That is all you need to know, for now."

Troggo asked him how he knew Bahkez. He stated he knew Bahkez very well and that he should return to the Boar clan because Beulah needed him.

Confused by the Master's openness and growing frustrated about what to do about the Harbingers, Troggo told him to explain why he had come to Gnor.

"You do not care that the queen of the Boars needs you?"

"She is a false queen. Chose-"

"She is the daughter of Bahkez." The Master cut him off.

Troggo stared at the faceless cowl. His red eyes seemed to darken. His jaws tightened. He knows the Master had spoken the truth. The Master seen the unasked questions in Troggo's eyes. He wants to know how the Master knows so much and why he is so secretive. He also wants to know how the Harbingers can help the Order of the Flame if they truly walk the path of Ja'Brahma.

To keep him confused, the Master explained that he had come to ask him to track and kill the last heir to Danou's heroic line.

"The last? Have Humans forgotten about the Six Heroes?" Troggo asked in elvish.

"Why so surprised? We are talking about humans." The Master stated.

He then went on to explain that the heroic lines of Ocia and Giaour no longer exist. He told him the Giaour line died because the last heir had married a woman who cheated on him constantly and that none of her children were his.

"That happened eighty years ago." He added.

He explained the Order of the Flame decided to remove every woman who cheated after that.

"What about the line in Ocia?"

"We eliminated that line only recently. We have plans for the others also."

Troggo asked how he is supposed to track the Danouan heir. While explaining how the Order of the Flame had ruined his plans to kill the Danouan heir, the Master drew his powers and showed

Troggo a magical image of the heir and of Barthus. He then added that the heir is traveling westward across the Giaour lands.

"Doing this will help the Magi." Troggo stated.

"Slightly. It will mobilize the Order of the Flame and motivate the Society to act against the Magi."

Troggo asked who and what the Society is. The Master told him the Society is an entity of assassins that stands alone. Troggo told him the Society sounds impressive. The Master told him they are a force to be reckoned with. He did not tell him Goraan is one of their leaders because that would complicate things.

"What do I get in return?" Troggo asked.

"I will make sure Queen Beulah accepts all Harlequins without penance."

"What about the Order of the Flame?"

"They will not be able to stop your return to Ino-Heim."

"Very well. I will do this."

That pleased the Master so much so that he revealed that by causing the Magi to fail he was given their medallions and that he gave them to their greatest enemy. Troggo said only one elf can claim to be the Magi's greatest enemy.

"I know. That is who I gave the medallions to. As I have said Troggo, I walk the path of Ja'Brahma. Ask no questions. You have a decision to make. I must go now. We shall talk soon. Trust me."

The Master turned and left. Troggo watched him leave. He has a lot of questions, but he will have to wait for answers.

***

Two weeks after leaving Coilu city, Razial found himself alone in the middle of a snowstorm. There are few trees in the area and all he can see for miles-when he could see, is snow covered land. His horse is tired and needs rest. Still, he is happy because at his feet lies the lifeless body of Coilu's former captain of the palace guards. He had killed the man after a long chase.

While traveling to rejoin Xochi, Razial, Mantak, Raal, Zelia, Fogi Red, and the bulwarks were attacked by the captain and a hundred men. The fighting had been fierce, and their numbers might have sustained them had Anjia not joined the fighting. She used her powers and swords to kill many of them causing them to panic. That is when Razial saw the wolf paws around the man's neck. He refused to let him see another day. It took him about an hour to catch the man. When he did, the fight was over almost as soon as it started.

Standing with his horse's reins in his hand, he is not worried about the others. He knows they are quite formidable, especially with Anjia with them. The question now that it is dark, is should he try to locate the others. He knelt and cut the necklace from the man's neck. He rubbed his horse's neck. Scar's pack is drawing closer. The horse is used to them, but they are excited which is making the horse nervous. He called out mentally to the wolves. He used his daggers to clear away some snow and began digging with his daggers. By the time he had finished digging a small hole, the wolves had arrived. They looked at him while he buried the wolf paws. When he finished covering the hole, the wolves rubbed up against him thinking.

"Hawk's-Blood"

It took a short while, but the wolves explained that Anjia was still with the others and that they had been forced to run from another small army which is why they could not search for him.

Knowing that they had to sleep out in the storm, Razial had the wolves clear as much snow as they could while he gathered rocks and branches from a fallen tree. He built a fire close to the opening of the fallen tree. After he put away his flint, the wolves huddled for warmth. He put a blanket over the horse and huddled with the wolves. He began to meditate. He knows the warmth of the fire will not last throughout the night. He decided to ride when the fire dies. He has to keep the horse's blood flowing.

Time slipped by and Razial opened his eyes. The animals are nervous. There is danger nearby. He exhaled, ignoring the cold. The horse reared and neighed in fear. It is terrified. The wolves growled to show they are ready to fight. He tried to calm the horse, but it continued to strain against the tether, so he released it.

"Haarrr!" The shadow-tracker roared.

The wolves looked from side to side trying to locate it. They tried to explain to him that it was a magical troll. He did not understand. His heart began to pound because he knew they could not locate it. Fear swelled inside of him, but he controlled it. Scar trotted forward. Razial and the other wolves followed him. He was shocked by what he saw. The daggers were in his hands and tumbling through the air immediately. The wolves charged from different angles. The shadow-tracker roared standing its ground. It is like a giant troll. It is heavily muscled with thick legs- each as thick as Razial's torso. Its white eyes stand out in contrast with the beast's black fur and skin.

"Rarr!" It roared in pain when the daggers bit into it.

Razial did not hesitate in throwing the daggers again. This time, it leapt out of the way. The wolves must be cautious with its long black claws. Close to the shadow-tracker, Razial threw his daggers with abandon. It deflected them most of the time. He drew his sword and shouted. It clawed a wolf across its back. That angered Razial. He blocked a swing with his sword and ducked a second swing. She-Scar bit it on the back of its neck. He used his sword to try to cut it across its knee. His sword had little effect, but it made the shadow-tracker stumble saving She-Scar. Razial threw his sword at the beast.

Unlike the shadow-tracker, Razial and the wolves have to use more effort to move around in the snow. It jumped around with ease as it tried to kill Razial. For its size, it has amazing speed.

The wolves kept it from reaching him, so he used his daggers to wound it repeatedly. However, not any of its wounds are serious enough to make it stop.

It closed in on him. The wolves pressed it. It managed to kick Razial before it turned its attention to the wolves. Razial tumbled through the snow. Snow went down his shirt causing him to shiver, but he ignored it because he had no time to shake out the snow.

On his hands and knees, he saw the shadow-tracker claw two wolves before kicking Scar causing him to yelp in pain. He ran and leapt on its back-daggers in hand. He stabbed it repeatedly while it tried to turn on him. He slid down and stabbed it in both knees causing it to falter. He continued to stab it, but it is too big.

It clawed him across his back and hit him in his head. He crashed to the ground-dazed from the blow. Blood filled his mouth. The smell of blood is thick in the air which is a bad sign for him. He felt the coldness of the snow but could not react to it. He watched in horror as the shadow-tracker showed its black pointy teeth. It stared at him as if it were shocked, he still lives.

Powerless to defend himself, Razial watched as a flash of sorcery knocked the shadow-tracker to the ground. That brought him back to his senses. The shadow-tracker writhed in pain as strike after strike struck it. Razial jumped on top of it stabbing it.

"Razial'ja!" Ulina called.

He kept stabbing it until Scar ripped open its throat. It disappeared. He felt Ulina healing him immediately afterward. He told her to heal the wolves first.

"I am strong enough, my son."

Ulina was worried. Priato had told her to ride through the blizzard and to trust her instincts. He had assured her she would reach Razial in time to save him.

Using her powers to clear more snow, she thought about how she had wanted to chase the shadow-tracker off. Razial had taken away that option. After finishing their camp, she helped Razial to his feet. He asked her about the others.

"The others are safe. Rest. We will talk soon."

Vishnu had finally learned enough to act against Paul. He had seen Razial leave, but with Mantak around he knew it would have been foolish to act against Razial. He had heard how the Unknown had almost killed Razial and was not surprised to hear that Tol and Tollok had allowed Razial to go through with his plan after he and

Tol had fought. Tol is good, but he cannot match Razial. He is not sure if Tol is better than Tony the Smith. Still, Tol is willing to prove himself and Vishnu likes that.

Just outside the imperial kitchen, he thought about how during the rebellion against Peter II, he had done enough to be noticed so when things settled, he would get a trusted position.

As a food deliverer, he could not have done any better. Paul is having a feast in honor of a Bassaran princess and Vishnu will take the food to the hall where the feast is held. With him are his two apprentices. They are all dressed like servants. They will not take any special action. He has a magical powder that will not affect them. It is poisonous to everyone else.

Two weeks into winter, he is tired of Coilu's paralyzing cold and he must track Razial.

"You three." The kitchen boss barked. "The trays are ready. Hurry up. Do not keep the emperor and his guests waiting."

Vishnu tilted his head and picked up a tray. His apprentices did the same. They made their way the hallways from the kitchen to the hall which is on the second floor. They only have dirks under their shirts. They will kill everyone because Goraan had sent word to the contractor that he wants the princess of Bassar dead. It is not a contract but an order. Goraan says it will help the Society in the future. That is all Vishnu needed to hear.

*

Paul smiled at the princess. Like all Bassarans, she has milky white skin. Her blue eyes are cloudy-not clear. She has long blond hair that has not been cut in years. She is sitting to his right while the rest of his guests are spread around the table.

He had wanted Kellen to be at the feast, but Kellen could not arrive until tomorrow. He had some things to clear up. Although the war is over, the fighting will go on, until everyone realizes that Peter II is dead. Paul had won the war. He has to marry the princess or another high born Bassaran maiden. He does not mind this. He owes the Bassarans a lot for their loyalty. He owes the Partisans as well and does not mind giving them more influence in Mohr.

Of his debtors, he only anticipates problems from the Order of the Flame. They wanted influence throughout his empire. That is not the problem. The problem is they must understand they are beneath him and cannot continue to tell him what to do. It had been difficult for him to take orders from them-while they made their way to Mohr especially from Razial. He knows he can never repay Razial, and he knows it is his pride and ego that make him hate Razial. It is the fact that Razial had treated him as if he were better than him. He hates that.

"Your Imperialness." The princess called. "The food smells delicious."

Her words brought him back to the present. He had been lost in his thoughts and did not notice that the food had been brought in. He smiled at the princess, then he looked around. That is when he saw Vishnu. His heart felt as if it sank in his chest. Vishnu's cold blue eyes are full of confidence. His full black beard is still well kept, and his black hair is pulled back-not a hair is out of place. The last time he had seen Vishnu, Razial had saved him. In a hall full of people, his only thought is none of them can save him.

"Are you all, right? You appear pale." The princess stated.

Paul did not get the chance to respond. Vishnu and his two apprentices began throwing poisonous powder into the air. Those chosen to guard Paul sprang into action. Two of the three warlocks, who had escorted him to Coilu from Cula, drew their powers. The two bulwarks, who were left behind to guard him, leapt forward with their swords in hand. Those who were not affected by the powder moved to the back of the hall.

"Kill them!" Someone shouted.

Paul looked around trying to find something to fight with. The bulwarks battled Vishnu's apprentices while Vishnu fought the warlocks. Paul grabbed a candle holder and told others to cover their mouths. He heard people running toward the hall. That gave him some hope.

"That will do you no good." Vishnu said.

Paul turned to face him. To his horror, he saw the second warlock slide to the floor with a gaping wound in his chest. His eyes went to the first warlock. He lies dead on the floor. Vishnu had killed them with his dirks. Paul thought about how he had only turned his back for a moment and Vishnu had killed both warlocks in that moment.

Having no choice, Paul charged. Vishnu blocked the candle holder with his left dirk before he cut Paul across his chest with his right dirk. Blood streamed from the wound. Vishnu's next swing was blocked, but his fourth swing plunged into Paul's ribs. His final swing opened Paul's throat. He stepped back and looked around. His apprentices had killed the bulwarks and the Bassaran princess. He ignored the people still alive near the back of the hall.

He led the way out of the hall shouting. He called for help just before he saw a group of guards.

"It was thre-three-three magicians with swords and magic. They killed-" Vishnu inhaled. "Emperor Paul is dead."

"Which way did they go?" A witch asked.

Keeping his head down, Vishnu raised a shaking right arm and pointed in the opposite direction he intends to go.

"Back to the kitchen." She said.

*

Ulina had moved Razial to a lone farmhouse where a family let them stay for several days. Razial's horse had been easy to find. She used it to help drag three dears to the farmhouse. She gave the family one to butcher and dry. The wolves ate one and she shared the other with the family.

After leaving the farmhouse, they rode through the snow until the days turned into weeks. During most of their trip, Razial remained silent while Ulina talked openly, in ancient elvish. She told him they did not warn him about the shadow-tracker because it would have changed the choices he made.

To try to get him to see things her way, she told him that they found two more paladins. Although he had asked, she did not reveal that they now know who two of his keepers are.

As they drew closer to Xochi's camp, he asked why she is so open with him.

"After you have finished in Vin, we shall discuss a lot of things. I will try to answer all your questions." Ulina said.

Razial's attention went to the legion of dwarfs that had arrived to hammer Ruug while the rest of Sidney's forces rest. He has no doubt Fogi Red is among the thousands of dwarfs.

Large mounds of snow sprinkle the camps. Thick white clouds blanket the sky. Still, the day is bright. Ulina smiled at him. He ignored that. He asked about Kalvin and the others. She told him all is well with them.

"At least Paul's death has not broken the Mohrans." He said in elvish.

Ulina had told him how it is being said the Fellowship killed Paul. They doubt that is true. She admitted she is equally unaffected by Paul's death as he is. Her concern is him accompanying Xochi to Vin to kill their enemies there.

She told him his targets serve Rakaar, so they were enemies before they chose to stand with Peter II.

"Leaders and followers die, but their cause lives on in others." She said.

Razial smiled. That is part of Ja'Brahma's justification for total eradication of one's enemies.

*

Zelia watched as Razial and Ulina walked toward her and the others. Standing around a fire with Mantak, Raal, Xochi, and the Ratels, Zelia is wrapped in her fur lined cloak. She rubbed her hands together for warmth. Even with gloves on, she can feel the cold.

She noticed Razial still walks with the same confidence he always walks with. There is no sign he was severely wounded by the shadow-tracker. He greeted them all. He asked Raal why he is not with Fogi Red.

"My presence would be disrespectful." Raal said.

Razial nodded in respect. Ulina asked about Sidney. Mantak told her he is with the Mohran generals planning their next action in case Ruug does not surrender. Ulina told Mantak to join her in talking with Sidney. He followed her and his guards followed him. Zelia asked Razial about his trip with Ulina. He said there is not much to say. He looked at her and her twin. There is a softness in her eyes that Xochi does not have. Where Xochi seems stoic-except when she is angry, Zelia seems more empathetic.

He smiled at Zelia when their eyes locked for a moment. He thought about when Kalvin had told him she had been fierce during the fighting inside Coilu.

"She is as powerful as she is beautiful." Kalvin had said.

He had also told Razial that Alena and Zelia had talked about feeling stronger before they reached Cula.

"Why are you smiling?" Zelia asked in Tuyakan.

Razial winked and made her blush when he said. "Looking at you is something to smile about."

Xochi noticed her twin's reaction. She asked Razial if he knew where Anjia was. He smiled and tilted his head in thought. At that moment, he thought about how their cinnamon skin is pale from the weather.

"She is close by. I am sure. Why do you ask?" He asked.

"I have been told she is very jealous." Xochi replied.

He did not respond. He finds it odd that the keepers chose Xochi to accompany him to Vin. She is the one sibling who dislikes him more than Ariel does. He told her she might get the chance to ask Anjia if she is jealous during their trip to Vin. He then said they will leave after he talks with Fogi Red, and he would appreciate it if she would get him a fresh horse. Raal chose to get him a horse after Xochi said she had to take care of some things before they leave.

Although she had remained stoic, he knew his decision to leave so soon had surprised her.

Standing with Zelia, Razial asked her to accompany him to the dwarfs' camp. She agreed and they began to walk. He asked her to tell him about her trip to Ruug. She began with how she and the others had dealt with the men who had attacked their group when he was still with them.

"Anjia helped us even more during the second battle. She will not be soon forgotten. Afterward, she refused to stop searching for you until Mantak told her Keeper Ulina had contacted him saying you had survived the shadow-tracker." Zelia said.

She noticed the men in the background as they passed by, but her focus stayed on him. She knows he cares about Alena and Anjia, but she wants to know more about him. He is indifferent toward most people, but he is not above showing his feelings. He asked how Anjia knew about the shadow-tracker. She admitted she does not know. He held her gaze for several seconds. When they reached the clearing between the main camp and the dwarfs' camp, he told her to tell Xochi to be nice to him. Zelia looked away. He is flirting with her.

"Xochi is not that bad. She knows how important you are. Smile at her."

"Like I smile at you?" He raised his eyebrows playfully.

She smiled then smirked telling him to keep Xochi safe and Xochi will have no choice but to be thankful to him.

"That is the problem. She thinks she must keep me safe. I am the assassin."

"Then listen to her. Let her be in control." She smiled.

Razial nodded. He knows she likes it when he flirts with her. He told himself to stop. He does not want to disrespect Alena.

"That is what I will do. Maybe the next time you see us, Xochi and I will be close friends."

"Now you are asking for a miracle." Zelia laughed on the way to Fogi Red.

***

Vishnu sat at a bar slowly drinking his mug of mead. He is in Cula waiting out a blizzard. After killing Paul, he decided to stay in Coilu because Razial has to stay to help the Order of the Flame solidify their hold in western Coilu. That is why with Kellen in Coilu he has built a stronger network in Cula. To him, it cannot hurt to make the Society's agents in Cula stronger.

By the time he had finished helping them, the weather forced him to stay a little longer. He gave his apprentices permission to pass the night with some women. That is why he is alone in the dimly lit bar. There are few patrons. He is sitting in thought. Unlike others out to get Razial, he is not consumed with the hunt. He is more focused on the Society's push for more power.

"You are not from Cula." A woman said slowly making her way to him.

He took note of her. She has blue eyes, long brown hair, and an aged face. He cannot tell how old she is, but in his mind that is because she is a witch. She is average in height and build. By the way she speaks, he knows she is used to power.

"Your dark hair and beard give you away. Tell me are you part of the Order or better yet, you are part of the Society."

She grinned. Her pale skin seems to glow in the candlelight. He did not look at her because he wanted her to talk more. He has no doubt they are going to fight!

"You are an assassin. I am sure it was you-" She whispered slowly. "-who killed Paul. You want to know how I know?"

She smiled mockingly. Vishnu continued to ignore her. He drank the rest of his mead while she explained that after Paul was assassinated, she decided to track the first unsympathetic stranger to leave the city. She had followed him to Cula and watched him as he networked with the Society's agents. Vishnu sat patiently waiting for her to reveal more.

"Enough about you. I am Elsa. Maybe you have heard of me-Elsa of Pan. My daughter is Yahida. I have been away for many years spreading my cause."

That is what Vishnu had been waiting to hear. Elsa was once the unrivaled leader of Pan-a city full of vicious fighters and magicians. Her daughter took over after Elsa seemed to have disappeared. Vishnu never expected to cross paths with her. She told him she wants Razial dead, which means she must deal with the Society.

"Since it is going to be war between me and the Society, I have decided to get it started. All your associates in Cula are dead. You should join them soon. Many believe that the Fellowship killed Paul and for years to come, they shall believe the same about you."

He never turned to look at her. He pulled the hood to his cloak over his head waiting for her to draw her powers.

"You are confident." She drew her powers.

Attacking, he drew his powers and his sword. Stronger than Vishnu, she was still surprised by how strong he is. His sword made up for the fact his magical strikes cannot match hers. She was forced to shield herself from his sword leaving her open for a physical attack. She heard his boots skip across the floor before his right foot slammed against her head. Dazed by the blow, the sound of footsteps racing across the bar sounded distant. Her two servants pressed Vishnu with their swords. Yahida had made her take the men with her. Now, Elsa is glad she had.

On her hands and knees, she heard two people running down the stairs. She knows they are with Vishnu. She is angry with herself for underestimating him. She saw him kill one of her men.

"Damn you!" She snapped.

She sent him crashing to the floor and his apprentices across the bar. Still lashing out with her powers, she noticed the few others in the bar had taken cover under the tables. Vishnu battled back. His hood is covering most of his face. All she can see is his beard. His apprentices threw daggers at her. She deflected them, but that allowed Vishnu to kill her other guard. His sword cut the man in two.

"Assassin." She cursed. "You cannot beat me."

She walked toward him while exchanging magical blows with him. His apprentices attacked her. She used her daggers to kill them. They will bother her no more.

"Ahrg!" She cried out in pain.

Vishnu stabbed her with his sword. She sent him crashing across the floor. He rolled to his feet and saw her horn shaped daggers in his apprentices' chests. Lashing out as he ran out of the bar, he promised to kill her one day no matter how long it takes.

"We shall make camp here." Peter said firmly. "Tether the horses and remove the packs from the supply horses."

He stood surveying the area. He and his procession are on the downslope of one of the many mountains that make up the Spaves- the mountain range that separates Svan from Ocia and Coilu.

It had taken him quite a while to reach the Spaves. He does not know why Ulina had stopped trailing him, but he is glad she did.

He had met up with his two remaining servants in Pan. While in Pan, he had used his Harbinger cowl to make it seem as if he wore a black hooded robe. He has his servants thinking that he is Peter's master. He did not give them a name to call him. To them, he is the one behind Peter's rise to power. He finds it humorous that they constantly call him master because they think that is what he calls himself.

"Watch the peaks. The Order has sent people after us for sure. Prepare a fire. I shall check below." He said.

They are below the snowline. The ground is rocky. There are shrubs all over the slope. There are trees farther down the slope. The air is fresh and cool, but not cold. He feels strange looking down at the clouds. The Master had warned him that Svan is a magical land. It is home to all Svan animals. It was made by Rakaar and Haar when Rakaar roamed the world.

For Svan animals, Svan is like a prison that keeps the world safe from them-trolls, gnomes, Svan hounds, and Svan eagles. Occasionally, some escape and manage to terrorize those they encounter.

"They will recognize your cowl. They will act against you if they are hungry enough. Those with you must be strong in magic and have strong wills."

The Master had warned referring to the Svan animals. Peter sighed. He knows at the bottom of the mountain lies a humid jungle full of danger. Although he has the map to Bal's dolmen, he will have to follow a moving target. When the Master had told him about that, it was the first time he had heard doubt from the Master.

There was no doubt in the Master's final warning.

"Do not provoke too many trolls."

***

Four days later, Peter and his men decided to rest. Peter stood by a tree. His men wiped sweat from their foreheads. It is hot and humid, but his cowl keeps him comfortable. He told his men to water the horses. The horses are nervous. Already, they have lost a horse to trolls. With his target moving faster than they are, he is growing frustrated.

"Look!" One of his men pointed.

Peter followed his finger and saw a gnome jump on one of their supply bags. It stood grinning, revealing its sharp teeth. Tiny, with a full beard without a mustache, the gnome's Phrygian cap is on the top of his head.

"Having problems Harbinger?" The gnome squeaked.

It disappeared before reappearing next to Peter. Merciless, hateful, spiteful, and bold beings, gnomes can afford to be daring when they want. They can disappear at will and unless one knows when they are going to reappear one cannot harm them.

Peter thought about drawing his powers but decided not to. Instead, he asked the gnome if he knew a faster way to get to his moving target.

"I am a gnome. Of course I know."

Peter took out several gold coins from his pouch. The gnome eyed them wantonly. Peter tossed him a coin and watched him caress it.

"Tell me how the dolmen I seek moves."

"You seek my brother Harbinger. He speaks in riddles, and he knows you are here."

"I seek a dolmen-not a gnome."

"You seek... "

The gnome trailed off then disappeared. Another gnome appeared close to where he was. The second gnome is bigger. His red Phrygian cap and red jerkin match the other gnome's cap and jerkin.

"I heard what was said. You are wrong." The second gnome said.

Several smaller beardless gnomes appeared around him. He told Peter that the other gnomes were his sons. Peter did not respond.

"My sons are hungry, and they shall eat. The question is what will they feed on."

Peter held out a diamond. It is bigger than the gnome's fist. The gnome and his sons became transfixed on the diamond.

"Tell me how to find this brother of yours-the one who talks in riddles." Peter said.

"That is incorrect. You have a map to find him. What you want to know is how to make him find you."

Peter knew the gnome had done him a favor, so he tossed several coins along with the diamond to him. His sons snatched the coins while he grabbed the diamond. He told Peter to go to the sacred tree marked on the map and call out.

"Sacred tree?" Peter frowned. "Call out to who?"

"Just do it. Be sure to have more coins, Harbinger."

The gnome and his sons disappeared. Peter told his men they had rested long enough. He helped them repack their horses. Pushing back the dense foliage and tall grass, Peter exhaled. He has to control his frustration. He pulled out the map to make sure he was going in the right direction. That is when he noticed that his target is next to his present location!

At first, he thought he had read the map incorrectly. He checked again and saw that he was correct. He held up a hand to stop his men. He began looking around. That is when he saw a large gnome-about the size of a Gully dwarf-standing on his horse's saddle.

"Hello Harbinger. Seek and you will find. Ask and you will be answered. It has been far too long since a human dared to enter Svan. I know why you are here. My red brother profited because of your laziness. Give me the gems and receive the riddle you need." The gnome said.

Peter hesitated to give him the large emerald. Dressed in all green, the gnome seems to love the emerald because it is green.

Still, he rubbed his fingertips together signaling he wants more gems. Peter tossed him several diamonds and a sapphire.

"What cannot survive without sunlight, yet rarely touches sunlight. No matter what species, by this word we call them all?"

The gnome disappeared. Peter looked at the map. He no longer has a target to chase. He cannot reach the dolmen until he answers the riddle. The gnome had come to him to prevent other gnomes from profiting. Peter closed his eyes in thought. He has to answer the riddle.

***

Kalvin hates being in Svan. The heat does not bother him. It is the humidity. He is tired of waking up covered in sweat. There are insects everywhere and the foliage limits his vision. The horses are always nervous, and he is tired of trying to calm them. Adini and Havi are the only ones unchanged by entering Svan. They had warned him and the others about Svan. They told Alena and Araceli not to draw their powers unless they say so. They also told them to keep Kalvin between them after they crossed the snow-capped peaks of the Spaves.

"A troll might try to snatch him and run since he has no power to defend himself." Adini had said.

Kalvin hears that warning every time he is too far from either Alena or Araceli. Eight days of trekking through Svan is more than enough for him. The jolems keep a fast pace. Hours earlier, they passed a horse's corpse. Havi is sure it was one of Peter's horses lost to trolls.

"The Harbinger is still days ahead of us. We have to track the gnomes." Havi said.

He and Adini had explained that jolems can track gnomes so long as they see them before they disappear. They are leading their horses by the reins so Kalvin cannot see them because of the foliage. That is why when they stopped, he was surprised. The jolems climbed on to their horses.

"What's going on?" Araceli asked.

Her red hair is frizzy due to the humidity. She looked at Havi as he removed his Phrygian cap. Alena wiped her forehead and sighed before drinking some water. She had braided her hair into two long braids to avoid the hassle of sweat rolling down her back.

"You." Adini pointed. "Come here or we will kill you."

Alena knows he must be talking to a gnome. She and Araceli looked at each other. Neither knows what the jolems are doing. They watched as Havi climbed down to stand before a gnome who was smaller than he is.

"Call to your father." Havi said.

The gnome, dressed in all green seemed to struggle with what to do. Alena had read gnomes dressed in either red, blue, or green. Each gnome is loyal to his father or an uncle-rarely to a brother. Their colors reveal with whom they are aligned. She finds it odd that gnomes usually change allegiances when their brothers take over their family group.

"Hurry up." Havi insisted.

"He told me not to." The gnome shook his head. "He is avoiding you two."

"Call him here or we will. Then, we will kill him."

Havi's threat made the gnome more nervous. He pondered his options. Alena could see him struggling with what to do. Adini seen this too. He tossed him an emerald.

"And we will kill you too." Adini added.

The gnome still struggled. Adini leapt from his horse and drew his dagger. Havi tossed him a coin, but he did not get the chance to respond.

"You two would have spoken my name and lost the ability to age slowly." The large gnome who speaks in riddles said. "You would have waged a lot."

"Yeah." Adini smirked. "Still, you would have been dead."

Alena knows this is not the first time Havi and Adini have talked with him.

"Where is the Harbinger?" Havi asked.

He stood before the gnome, who was almost as tall as he is. He told Havi he has gotten shorter.

"No. You have gotten taller. Now answer the question."

"Give me a gift and I will give you a riddle."

"We will give you nothing!" Adini closed in on him.

Immediately, tens of gnomes appeared. They are of different sizes and ages, but they are all dressed in green. Kalvin drew his sword. Alena and Araceli drew their powers.

"The elf is strong, but I doubt she would survive if we fought." The riddling gnome smiled.

Adini tossed him a pouch full of gems.

"We want two answers." Havi said while waving his finger. "And no riddles."

"Or we will fight." Adini added.

The grimness in his voice was enough for the gnome, who told them Peter was already at the dolmen and there was no way for them to stop him. Havi asked him what they must do to prevent the Magi from obtaining their powers. The gnome's answer amazed Alena, Araceli, and Kalvin.

"The Gideon must duel the Magi to obtain them from Ja'Brahma." The gnome shivered when he said Ja'Brahma's name. "There are your two answers. One day, the gateway will be opened."

"And you better hope we are dead when it is." Havi replied.

All the gnomes disappeared. Havi told the others to get on their horses.

"We have to get out of Svan. We do not want to cross paths with the Harbinger now." He said.

"Why not? We could take the Magi from their dolmens." Araceli said.

"Araceli. Get on your horse. We have to get out of Svan." Adini said.

Alena does not care about the Magi. She asked how Razial can obtain the Magi's powers from Ja'Brahma.

"Razial cannot raise the dead. Was that a riddle?" She asked.

"No. Ja'Brahma is not dead. Razial will have to fight the Magi to obtain their medallions." Adini replied.

"Damn Harbinger. He really is the Master." Havi stated.

He began explaining how during the end of the last Champions' War the Master made a deal to help the Order of the Flame defeat the Magi so long as he could decide who kept their medallions.

"No one ever considered he would give them to Ja'Brahma." Adini stated.

Alena and Araceli looked around in disbelief. They are still in shock from learning Ja'Brahma still lives.

"How is Ja'Brahma still alive? Where is he? Is he still mad?"

"Because he is not dead. In his prison, and yes." Havi said to answer Araceli's questions.

His tone was dismissive, which angered her. She asked how this secret had been kept by the Order of the Flame's leadership. The two jolems can sense her anger, but they do not care.

"Listen." Adini hissed. "We never kept anything hidden. As for it being a secret, the Master knows. All Boars-including the Harlequins-know."

"The Harlequins?" Araceli scowled. "Is that why the Boars left Alf-Heim?"

"Yes. Now let us ride." Adini said.

***

After weeks of riding through southwest Danou, Tina and Barthus managed to escape with the heir of Danou. Riding along a trail in northeast Giaour, they are taking in the scenery. The sun is shining brightly, trees sprinkle the rolling hills, the grass is deep green, and the air is fresh. They had started the day feeling relieved, but their relief did not last long.

While talking about how it felt good to finally have a good night sleep, they spotted several riders dressed in all black. After trailing them for several minutes, the riders rode off. The heir noticed their change in mood. He does not understand how a few riders could worry them so much.

"Surely several riders cannot harm you two." He said.

He has seen them fight and doubts a few riders could out fight a lone Barthus. Tina looked at him while they trotted along. With strong brown eyes, wavy brown hair, olive skin, and a chiseled face he has a typical Danouan appearance. Unlike the remaining heirs of the heroic lines, he knows he is a descendant of the Six Heroes. However, he does not understand his purpose.

During the third Champions' War, the Conclave created the Six Heroes: six men given magical powers and made kings of the six human lands. So long as one of their heirs lives, the Magi cannot release Rakaar's Shadow.

In the beginning, the Six Heroes made things easier for the Order of the Flame. As time passed, that all changed. Their descendants proved to be less honorable and prouder than the original Six Heroes. The Order of the Flame keeps track of them for only one reason and that is to prevent Rakaar's Shadow from being released. Now, only three lines remain: Anazi, Brahma, and Danou. Tina hopes to get back to Anazi Falls with the Danouan heir alive.

"Even if they are assassins, you two could easily deal with them." The heir said to Tina.

She told him she wishes the riders were assassins. That puzzled him. She looked away from him when they reached the top of a hill. She saw two things: one, they are close to a town and two, more riders are riding toward them and one of them is Troggo!

Behind Troggo, is a small army. She hopes the town has already spotted the Harlequins.

"They seem content to fight after we have reached the town." Barthus said.

Although he sounded calm, Tina knows he is ready for combat. He is not intimidated by Troggo's presence.

"Who are they?" The heir asked.

Even from a distance, he can see Troggo's red hair and sense the violent aura he has. -Troggo's presence has uneased him.

"They are elves. Harlequins to be exact." Tina answered.

"Elves? Harlequins? Do not elves and the Order stand united?"

"Not these elves. Barthus ride ahead and warn the townsfolk if they are not aware of the danger they face."

Tina watched Barthus ride off. She hopes Troggo does not know who her ward is.

Minutes later, Tina and the heir arrived in the town. Hundreds of men stood ready to fight. Most of them have farm tools as weapons. Some have quivers of arrows and bows. Barthus told them to stay among their houses and buildings.

"They are skilled warriors, who possess magic, but they prefer to fight." Barthus said.

Tina dismounted her horse. Barthus said they could hide the heir. She told him that was a good idea. Barthus led the heir away. She explained to the people that the Harlequins respect bravery so they-the people, cannot try to surrender. She went to watch the Harlequins arrive. It is about a hundred of them. They began to spread out. Her pulse quickened. She knows she will most likely die. If this is just a raid, she could live.

During raids, Harlequins fight to test-not slaughter. She scolded herself mentally. She knows Troggo is there for the heir.

"It's done." Barthus said when he returned.

Tina turned to look at him. His bald head is glistening with sweat. His red mustache is unkempt as is his beard. He has an unruly appearance. Holding his axes causes his large forearm muscles to bulge. His eyes match his reddish-brown skin. He towers over her, but she is not short. He is just tall. They have been friends for decades even though they are opposites. He had been on his way to Gully when she had asked him to join her in going to Danou. She knows why he was going to Gully and hopes he gets the chance to go there. She does not want to see him die.

"When you get to Gully, tell her I said hello." She smiled.

"I will bring her to see you." Barthus winked.

Troggo dismounted his horse. His warriors are in position around the town. After days of tracking, he has finally caught up to those escorting the heir across Giaour. Truthfully, he does not care about the heir. Most of the Six Heroes had left Eloh's service at the beginning of the fourth Champions' War.

Walking alongside his warriors, he thought about the Master's advice to rejoin the Boars. His warriors drew their yataghans as they moved closer to the town. He can sense the people's fear. They are huddled throughout the town. There is no challenge in attacking this town. That is why he had split his raid party in half. The townsfolk might outnumber his warriors three to one, but his warriors still have an advantage in skill and power.

"You two servants of Eloh can avoid many deaths. Give me the Danouan heir and you all can go free. You do not have much time." He said in Tuyakan.

"We will fight you for him. If we win, he lives." Tina said.

Troggo grinned while his warriors laughed openly. He nodded as he stepped forward. His warriors do not need to be told to stay back. They will take no action unless someone other than Tina and Barthus acts against him. He told them not to renege.

"If you do, we will slaughter this town." He said.

Barthus and Tina quickly made their way before Troggo. Barthus feels strange standing before Troggo because he has never fought anyone and needed help while his opponent is alone.

Where he towers over Troggo, Tina is just as tall as the legendary elf. Her brown eyes show no emotion. Her golden olive skin shines in the sunlight. Her sandy brown hair hangs over her shoulders. Standing with her short cutlass in her left hand and a dagger in her right hand, she does not appear to be a skilled fighter, but he knows better.

"I am ready." Troggo said.

His yataghans remained inside their scabbards. Barthus is known as a great fighter. He is considered the greatest bulwark. His nickname is the Brawler. However, facing Troggo-a powerful ancient elf warrior, he does not have the usual confidence he has just before a fight.

Normally, he would have advised an opponent to draw his weapons. Troggo will get no such warning.

"Very well." Tina sighed.

She sprang forward whirling her cutlass while Barthus swung his axes. Troggo drew his yataghans and deflected their attempts to wound him. He tried to cut Barthus on his backswing, but Barthus blocked his thrust with his other ax. Impressed, Troggo tilted his head while sidestepping Tina's skilled attack. Barthus tried to make him slip, but the grass was dry. Footing will not be a problem for any of them.

Knowing he cannot strike Troggo from distance, Barthus used his axes to press him. That forced Troggo to focus on him which allowed Tina to press him. He leapt back.

"Impressive." He smiled. "You two fight well together."

He recognized he had underestimated them. Already, the fight has lasted longer than he had expected. With his yataghans whirling, he charged. Barthus was cut several times, but Tina managed to cut Troggo across his shoulder. That angered him. He intensified his attack. His yataghans hissed through the air. They rattled against Barthus' axes while Tina kept trying to strike him. Finally, Troggo managed to cut Barthus across his arms causing him to drop his axes. He wounded Barthus several more times before Tina stopped him.

"Ahrg!" He winced.

He had forgotten that Tina wields her cutlass with her left hand. He spun around and attacked. She winced as he cut and sliced her across her torso. He continued to press her expecting Barthus to pick up his axes first. By the time he realized his error, Barthus' right fist crashed against his head. As he fell to his left, he felt Barthus' left fist slam against his back.

Dazed, he rolled on the grass and shook his head while moving away from a determined Barthus.

"Enough of being careless!" He growled angrily.

He threw his yataghans at Tina, then took on Barthus. He deflected several punches and inflicted severe damage with several kicks. However, Barthus managed to land several punches that rocked him.

With the taste of his own blood in his mouth, he threw several damaging combinations. Then kicked Barthus in his leg knocking him down. Tina's cutlass hissed above Troggo's head saving Barthus. He hit her four times in her stomach and chest. Then, in one fluid motion, snatched her cutlass and drove it through her chest.

"No!" Priato shouted.

Troggo recognized Priato's voice instantly. He looked into Tina's dying eyes and nodded in respect. She had forced him to kill her. He looked at Barthus, who stood. He is a short distance from his axes, but he appears to still want to fight. He is no real threat at the moment. Troggo turned to Priato. He was surprised to see Goraan. All his warriors know who Priato is, but only some of them know Goraan.

Goraan is to Priato's right. He eyed the scene. Tina is on her back with her cutlass sticking into her chest. Barthus is standing on weak legs. He is battered and bloodied. Priato told him the fight is over, but he does not want to listen.

"The fight is over, and you get to live." Troggo said.

Priato told Troggo he had killed a member of the Conclave and to call off his warriors. Troggo told him he knows his warriors would never take any action against him. He then added.

"I shall take no actions against Eloh's servants unless I have to."

Goraan listened as Troggo explained that Tina had challenged him and that they had made a deal. Goraan tried to ask Barthus if that is true, but Priato stopped him. He closed his eyes in thought. Troggo smirked at Goraan asking what insignia he is wearing. Goraan knows if Priato were not present Troggo would act to kill him. He noticed Priato's eyes are still closed, so he told Troggo the flaming dagger is Fulancia's sigil.

"Fulancia?" Troggo frowned.

"Barthus." Priato said. "You are with me. Get your weapons. I shall see to Tina's body while you get your horse. Bring the heir also."

Where Goraan and Troggo had spoken in elvish, Priato had spoken in Tuyakan to Barthus. Goraan watched Barthus stare at Tina's body. He is at a loss. He had been making plans when Priato had contacted him. Priato had known exactly where he was and rode to meet with him.

"Come with me and it will make your plans easier."

Priato had said to convince him to accompany him. He never expected to find himself in the middle of a Harlequin army staring at Troggo. This is the first time in centuries he has felt a sense of danger in the lands of Giaour. Still, he remained stoic while Priato talked with Troggo. He has never understood why Troggo still obeys Priato.

During the last Champions' War, he had heard about Harlequins standing down in Priato's presence. This is the first time he has seen it for himself.

"Where is Kitara?" Priato asked in ancient elvish.

"Raiding in Danou." Troggo answered.

They continued to talk until Barthus returned with the heir. Priato closed his eyes and exhaled. He told Goraan the people are nervous and that the heir still must die. That infuriated Barthus but Priato quickly silenced him saying.

"A deal is a deal, unless you want the town to pay."

Although Priato had spoken to Goraan in elvish, he had spoken to Barthus in Tuyakan. He then switched to ancient elvish when he told Troggo to let Goraan settle the matter of the heir dying.

While thinking about Priato switching from language to language, Goraan realized why he had asked him to accompany him. He wants him to kill the heir. He drew his powers and moved his horse so he could look at the people watching what was going on.

"This Danouan noble should be king of Danou. That is true. He has enemies-powerful enemies, who have endangered your town. He is not Giaouran nor are his problems. Ask yourselves why I am here and not anyone from Tali or Giaour city. You have a friend in Fulancia." He said firmly.

Until he had spoken, the Danouan heir had been ignorant of what was going on. Goraan pulled his horse close to him. The man looked up at him. Goraan kept his attention on the people. As soon as the heir turned to look at what he is looking at, Goraan drew his sword and decapitated him. His head rolled back while his body fell. Goraan saw the sadness in Priato's eyes. That is when Goraan noticed Priato had made Tina's body disappear.

Before riding off, Goraan thought about how the townsfolk will never forget this.

***

Razial and Xochi have turned out to be an effective team. They have been so effective that the king of Vin and Peter III are hiding out to avoid being killed. However, with the Society's and the

Order of the Flame's agents scouring for information, Razial and Xochi now know they are hiding in the Baron's Quarters where they will hold a meeting before they split up. The contractor of Vin had a way to get Razial and Xochi into the mansion where the meeting was held.

As he and Xochi climbed out of the basket used to sneak them into the mansion, he thought about the warning Goraan had sent to him. According to Goraan, the Harlequins might come after him in the future. That makes no sense to him, but he knows if Goraan feels as if it might happen then it is likely.

"Thank you all." He said to the four men who had snuck them into the mansion.

They are cousins, who are fiercely loyal to each other. If they make it to Fulancia, they will receive all they were promised. The question is can they keep it? He and Xochi quickly made their way up the stairs. He told her to hide while he used his elfin burnoose to search for their targets.

"Be quick. We leave Vin tonight." Xochi said.

Xochi watched as Razial became invisible. She crept through a hallway and stopped to listen. She heard two men talking about how Peter III would leave in the morning. He is due to meet with the leaders of Dax, who will negotiate on his behalf. Xochi has no idea who the men are. To her, they are in the know and must die. She moved to the room across from where they were.

She cannot afford for them to be found before Razial returns. Her mind began to wander while she waited. She thought about how several crews of assassins are in Vin and Razial has been able to avoid them.

"Xochi." Razial whispered startling her.

He made himself visible while explaining he would guide her to their targets and that all he wants her to do is seal the room, so no one hears when he kills those inside. She thought about telling him to just kill their targets, then she realized why the others must die too.

"Okay, but first we kill the two in that room." Xochi pointed."

Moments later, Xochi drew her powers and sealed the room after Razial had closed the door. Razial began killing those inside the room. His daggers tumbled with deadly accuracy. Xochi drew her sword and helped the process along. The people were in a panic because although they can see her, all they can see of Razial is his daggers moving around killing them. The chaos quickly died down. Xochi dislikes slaughter, but all in the room were enemies. She took note that Peter III had died fighting. Blood is all over. The scene disgusts her, but she knows it had to happen.

With Razial a step behind her, she opened the door. Her eyes quickly adjusted to the darkness of the hallway. Then, her eyes widened in shock. She drew her powers. Razial held his daggers ready to throw because two Harbingers stood before them!

The Harbingers' red cowls appear eerie in the dark. They drew their powers, and magical flashes lit the hallway. Razial's daggers tumbled repeatedly but never found their mark. They were constantly deflected. Xochi strained trying to battle back. She told Razial to run, but he could not. Beulah had already bound him magically.

"How brave of you Xochi. You dislike the assassin, yet you fight to keep him safe. Good luck escaping." Ariel said.

She knocked down Xochi, who had no idea how the Harbingers knew her. Writhing in pain, she forced herself to her feet. She has to find Scar so the elfin wolves can track Razial.

Stumbling as she ran, she had two things on her mind: getting Razial back and figuring out how the Harbingers know who she is, which is made more puzzling because she is a twin.

CHAPTER 9

THE KEEPERS

Zelia stared at Vin. The city is battered. When Ulina was told about Razial's capture, she marched on Vin-leading the legion of dwarfs that had attacked Ruug. The Partisans and dwarfs laid waste to Vin's defenses.

Divided into quarters, Vin was built to sustain attacks. However, Ulina was bent on making Vin an outpost for allies. She refused to allow any infiltration by the Fellowship. Once the city was breached, she showed no mercy. She unleashed the dwarfs, who were their usual brutal selves. The Partisans burned large parts of the city. By the time the fighting had ended, the people of Vin were no longer loyal to their former leaders. Several common captains were chosen to govern the city until Kellen decides who will be the governor. Although it would have been better for Sidney to stay on as emperor, Priato had told Ulina to let Sidney step aside for Kellen. Ulina did not reveal why Priato had said this. After things were settled in Vin she left.

With Razial captured and Xochi in pursuit, Ulina must try to help free him. Before she had left, she had talked with Mantak about Zelia's sudden ability to understand dwarvish. She had told him that she and the other keepers had been expecting that. Zelia had asked several questions, but Ulina did not give any answers. She simply said she would have answers in the future.

"Hey." Fogi Red called Zelia. "I hear you can suddenly understand dwarvish."

She turned to look at him. He smiled at her-something he rarely does. She told him she was told she would soon be able to speak dwarvish as well.

"Fogi Red. Have you heard about Adini and Havi?" Mantak asked as he entered the room.

"Heard what?" Fogi Red asked.

"They are headed here. The Harbinger succeeded and so did they." Mantak held his gaze.

"So how do we stop the Magi?" Fogi Red smirked.

Mantak explained that Razial has to go to Brahma city. He did not give any other details.

"Too bad the Harbingers have Razial." Fogi Red looked away.

"Xochi will find him. She would not be in Suce if she were not close." Zelia said.

She began to think how Tu'ani had contacted her and explained that Xochi had found Scar's pack after Razial was captured, but she had needed Anjia to explain to the elfin wolves what had happened with Razial. According to Tu'ani, Anjia and Xochi are close to acting to free Razial.

"So, we are stuck here until the others arrive?" Fogi Red asked.

Mantak told him that is the case. Fogi Red told him he is off for bed and to wake him for dinner. Zelia watched him wobble out of the room. Her attention went to the room. It is bright because of the sunlight streaming in through the windows that line the outside wall.

Unlike central and northern Coilu, southern Coilu warms up during spring.

"So, we have to help Razial save the world." Zelia stated.

Nodding Mantak said. "If Xochi and Anjia succeed, we shall."

She turned to look at him. She looked into his narrow eyes trying to figure out what he was keeping from her. He smiled at her. He knows what she is doing. To change her mindset, he told her he knows many questioned his interest in Anjia. Then, he explained he would reveal his reason soon. Zelia looked into his eyes. He bid her farewell. She began thinking about how at times she cannot stop thinking about Razial. It makes no sense for her to care so much about him. Then, she began wondering if she was fated to be one of his keepers.

"Alena, Anjia, me, and another." She thought nervously to herself.

***

Ofelia and the others returned from the street market with fresh food-mostly vegetables and rice. They have been inside Brahma city for months. Lela and Tu'ani bought a large estate, and the novices are acting like their servants-which is not far from the truth while the bulwarks are scattered across the city. The siblings are living on their own, but that will change soon.

The keepers have passed themselves off as rich Anazian widows. They rarely give anyone an audience and accept few invitations. However, they have visited the king several times. They had intended to leave the city but decided to stay until Razial arrived. Ofelia hopes the siblings know who killed two members of the Order of the Flame by then. She has no idea Razial has been captured.

Arranging the food in the cupboards, Ofelia and the others began teasing each other about men they passed in the streets. Bernice blushed because Vera teased her about wanting to kiss one of the bulwarks.

Taller than Ofelia, Bernice is not only the tallest of them, but she is the thinnest also. With shoulder length brown hair, greenish-blue eyes, and full red lips, Bernice is pleasant to look at.

Vera is Ofelia's height and has long black curly hair that gives her a girlish appearance. She has light olive skin that tans easily because she has spent most of her life in southern Anazi, but she was born in Gully.

Niri and Lissa are not short for women, but they are shorter than the others. Lissa is the shortest. She has deep brown hair that hangs over her shoulders. Her chestnut eyes are soft and make her appear non-threatening. She has a full bosom and thick legs. Her tan complexion is darker than Niri's olive skin. Niri has strong reddish-brown eyes, long light brown hair, and thick eyebrows. She is the most fit and most curvaceous of them. She was raised in Gully, but like Lissa, she was born in northern Giaour. The one thing they all have in common is they are all in their twenties.

"Vera. Leave Bernice be. She will kiss him one day." Lissa said.

Niri laughed, but she said nothing. She moved around the spacious kitchen restocking the cupboards. Ofelia did the same. It is a nice spring day, and they want to enjoy it, something they cannot do until they are finished.

Putting a sack on the bottom shelf, Ofelia heard a sibling enter the kitchen. She turned to see who it was.

"The keepers have guests." The sibling said.

With that, they filed out of the kitchen. They must be present when the keepers meet with guests. Ofelia checked the gems beneath her belt. (Something she does throughout the day, every day.) She followed Niri through the house until they reached the greeting room, which has a high ceiling and many windows, so it is always bright during the day. With Lela and Tu'ani sitting in their chairs by the empty fireplace, Ofelia and the others spread out behind them. Across from the keepers are Priato and Barthus. Ofelia has read a lot about both. Priato is Eloh's seer and Barthus is said to be the greatest bulwark-something she knows was not lightly written.

"Ah…" Priato smiled. "It was wise of you to bring them."

He spoke in Tuyakan referring to Ofelia and the others. They understood every word. All their practice has paid off.

"Very well. Let us begin. First, discuss Ulina's plan in Coilu if you do not mind." Priato said.

Tu'ani and Lela nodded to signal that was okay. He then told them they could discuss what happened in Giaour and Danou. Ofelia looked at Niri. They are finally going to learn what is going on with Razial and Kalvin.

Talking simultaneously, Lela and Tu'ani explained that Kalvin and those with him had to escape before they were chased out of Svan. Ofelia listened, but kept her focus on Priato, who did not look at the keepers. He seemed to stare off into the distance. That is when she noticed Barthus seemed sad about something. The keepers went on explaining Ulina's actions in Vin and how she expects to have Razial back soon. They all seem happy that they at least know how to stop the Magi. Priato told Barthus to explain all that had happened in Danou. Ofelia listened to the whole story and realized why he was sad. Her sadness became confusion when she heard that Goraan had killed the heir of Danou. She was not the only one confused.

"A'Priato." Tu'ani called. "Why was Ja'Goraan with you?"

"Because I needed him to be."

Priato knows his answer did not satisfy Tu'ani. He debated mentally before revealing more to her and the others.

"Goraan," He sighed. "will gain from this, but so will we. I needed him there so I could test Troggo's fate. Something unforeseen has happened."

They began discussing the Theocracy having spies in the Brahman court and how they have to keep the king and prince alive.

"We cannot allow more of them to die." Tu'ani said.

Referring to those from the Heroic Lines. She then stated they have to secure the court in Anazi. Lela agreed saying.

"I shall tell the Conclave to kill all new guests added to the court's list."

"We should first try to discourage any new courtiers, but if we must kill them, kill them all!" Priato said.

Ofelia could not believe what she had just heard. She never imagined the Order of the Flame would kill so indiscriminately. Not only did this shock her, but it showed her how naive she is.

"With that settled, inform the others Razial shall be freed. He shall face great danger. What we must worry about is him walking the path of Ja'Brahma and..." Priato said with added emphasis. "we must make sure his powers are not released, or he will suffer the same fate as Ja'Brahma."

His sudden switch confused Ofelia for a moment. She quickly figured out what he was talking about. His words made her nervous. She never thought Razial would be so important to their plans. She has no idea what it means to walk Ja'Brahma's path. All she knows about Ja'Brahma is he died at the end of the first Champions' War.

"Keepers. What does it mean to walk the path of Ja'Brahma?" Niri asked.

"That is not for you to know just yet, young Niri." Priato answered.

Barthus then asked how long he had to stay in Brahma. The keepers told him he must stay there until they stopped the Magi. Lela could see the pain in his eyes. He and Tina had been close. She feels sad for him. Seeing Tina killed will haunt him forever. She knows Priato had explained to him there was no way to save Tina without giving Rakaar an advantage, but that did not make Barthus feel any better-neither did hearing that he is fated to become a paladin!

"Very well." Tu'ani drew everyone's attention. "A'Priato. You and Barthus can choose your rooms. We must discuss things with the novices."

***

Binu and Goraan rarely agree on what course of action to take, especially when it comes to how to deal with obstacles in the

Society's path. However, they agree they must take strong actions against all who serve any of the Magi.

The two of them had met with Carpio and plans were made to take on the Fellowship, then the Sisterhood. Although Goraan does not want to work in tandem with the Order of the Flame, he knows tactically it is the best thing to do. Carpio had been impressed by his knowledge of the Order of the Flame's activities. Binu had been impressed also, but he kept it to himself. He knows Goraan is keeping something from him and the other Hilt members. He waited until Carpio left to find out what Goraan is hiding.

Sitting with his legs under him, Binu asked if he wanted to tell him what he did not tell Carpio. Standing paces from Binu, Goraan stared at him. His hair hung over his shoulders and down his back while Binu's is parted in the middle. They know they are trying to relax before they must do what they have to do. With his fingers interlocked behind his back, Goraan turned away from him.

"The Harbingers have Razial. They have promised his safe return soon." He said.

"How did they contact you?" Binu asked.

Although they have shared a lot with the other Hilt members, only they utterly understand what is going on. Binu listened while Goraan explained that a scroll had arrived earlier that day.

"You have known about this before today. How did you learn about Razial being taken?"

"The Harbingers' message arrived today. Before that, I was making plans to act against them. As for how I knew, I have my ways to find out things."

"Like knowing all about the Order of the Flame's plans."

Goraan did not respond. Instead, he told Binu that if the other Hilt members find out Razial has been taken he wants him to stand with him in saying the Society shall take no action against the Harbingers. Binu sat quietly for several moments while Goraan turned to face him. Goraan knows Binu knows how difficult it would be to take actions against the Harbingers. Still, Binu asked a question Goraan has struggled to answer.

"What about when Razial asks for revenge?"

"Hopefully that will not happen, or we will be forced to act against the Harbingers."

Binu asked him why he wanted an alliance with the Harbingers. Goraan grinned while saying.

"You know me too well, brother. I want to help them defeat the Magi."

"You must be careful. The Order of the Flame already believes you are a Harbinger. Ask A'Priato about sending Razial to Alf-Heim. The shadow-tracker is still around."

Goraan understands his thinking. He had told him about the shadow-tracker. He had also informed the Hilt about Priato's vision about sending Razial to Alf-Heim.

"That is the first thing I did when I was told about Razial being captured. A'Priato's words were clear. Razial is to go to Alf-Heim only under one condition or all will be lost." Goraan said.

They both know Priato's visions are never wrong. Goraan told Binu to say what he has to say to him. Binu nodded. He told him Carpio has done a lot of studying of the Champions' Wars and now plans to capture Razial. That made Goraan scowl. Carpio is a stickler for the rules. If he captures Razial, Razial would be his to command for years. They cannot allow that to happen.

"Carpio is no fool. He understands Razial will be needed to stop Rakaar's servants from freeing him." Goraan said.

"That is what bothers me. He has plans that will put us on the front line of the war between the gods. He intends to force Razial to obtain the Gideon's powers." Binu said shaking his head.

Goraan shook his head in thought. Carpio would never purposely endanger Razial, but until it is safe to send Razial to Alf-Heim, he cannot allow Carpio to capture Razial.

Binu looked into Goraan's eyes, and he knew Goraan was thinking of a way to forward their cause and a way to stop Carpio.

***

Razial sat with his back against the back wall of his cell. He is bound and fettered. He can sense the gleipnir used to magically bind him. He does not know if the Harbingers know he cannot wield his powers, and he will not volunteer that information. The Harbingers treated him well. He has a hay mattress and has been well fed. His cell has a magical light that gives off a bluish light. All he has to do is touch it and it comes on. He is confused by Beulah's openness. She apologized for capturing him. She told him his contract conflicts with some of their plans. She also told him that by keeping him in Suce they are keeping him safe from the shadow-tracker.

Hearing several people approaching his cell, he stood and watched as the heavy metal door opened. Beulah entered the cell with two guards. Her cowl floated just above the floor. She has never revealed her name to him. Like all others, he identifies her by her stature. She is a lot shorter than Ariel.

"How is your strength?" She asked in elvish.

"I am well." He replied.

Beulah took note that his wavy hair has grown a lot since he was captured. It no longer lies on his head. It is fluffier than before. Other than that, he has not changed. She treated him more like a guest than a prisoner like the Master had instructed.

She thought about their first conversation. She had told him they had contacted Goraan and informed him why they had captured him. He asked her why they want to avoid problems with the Society. She told him the Society and the Harbingers are like-minded groups saying.

"We do not serve either god. We believe in structure, and we stand against Rakaar's return. Our differences are few and not significant. Where the Society wants to control parts of the world, we want to control the world. Our interests do not conflict."

Razial asked her if they would try to dictate to the Society or allow them to govern themselves. After she had said they would let the Society do what it wants to do in its lands, Razial told her that eventually they would disagree about something, and it would be war. She did not try to deny that.

"I have come to inform you that I shall leave within the hour. You should escape soon. Of that, I am sure. There is a pack of elfin wolves inside the city. I have no doubt they are here for you. As a departing gift, I shall hand over two of your friends to do with as you please." Beulah smiled.

Razial stared at her. His brown eyes are full of curiosity. He watched as several guards brought in a naked and unconscious Gwen. They laid her on the floor by the wall to his right. She is bound and fettered. He senses the gleipnir used to bind her. He stared at her. Her wavy dark hair covers parts of her face. The patch between her legs and her brownish nipples stand out against her pale skin. He sees no bruises, but he knows the Harbingers had made her suffer.

"That is Gwen of Dax the one who sent the shadow-tracker after you." Beulah said.

Razial did not respond. He watched as Ariel was brought in. At first, he did not recognize her. He stared at her red hair and thought about how she was captured. When the guards backed away, he looked closer and that is when he recognized her. Her pale freckled skin is dirty but not bruised. He felt bad for her when he saw the red patch between her legs and pinkish nipples. She is obviously in shock. Her greenish eyes are glazed over and have a blank stare in them.

"I am sure you recognize her. We mean you no harm Razial. Our agents will take no action to prevent your escape." Beulah said.

After she left, Razial moved Ariel on to his mattress and covered her with a blanket. He left Gwen where she lied.

*

Xochi was on her bed with She-Scar at her feet. The other wolves are out with Anjia watching the fortress where Razial is being held. Other elfin wolves joined Scar's pack while they tracked Razial to

Suce. Instead of six members, Scar's pack now has twenty wolves in it. Anjia intends to use them all to free Razial. Xochi had wanted to include several siblings, who are in Suce, but Anjia refused, saying.

"The Order of the Flame has too many spies in its ranks. That is why Razial was captured."

Xochi could not deny that, so she went along with Anjia's plans. Although they have functioned well together, it is clear they are simply tolerating each other.

Lying in her room, Xochi is waiting for Anjia's return. Anjia went to put the wolves in place before she and Xochi to attempt free Razial. It will be noon soon. The room is dark, but that does not bother her. She-Scar sat up quickly and turned back to face her.

"She-Bear." She-Scar thought.

Xochi, like all advanced practitioners of Tuya-Kan, can communicate with elfin animals if the animal projects its thoughts to her. She-Scar quickly moved to the door. Xochi heard Anjia approaching seconds later. She walked over and opened the door. She-Scar made herself invisible. Anjia spun on her heels, and they all set off.

*

Razial sat listening to Gwen, who was telling him how the Harbingers infiltrated the Fellowship and ousted her from power. She was not surprised to hear that Beulah had told him to demand the truth about Ja'Brahma. She had told him how well the Harbingers are at manipulating things so they can get what they want.

After hearing her tale, Razial was impressed by the Harbingers and their actions. Goraan and Binu had warned him several times about how dangerous the Harbingers are. Sitting in the cell with Ariel and Gwen, Razial had to admit they had lived up to their reputation.

"So, why did you not act against the Sisterhood? You knew all of this for years." He asked Gwen.

"I always fight the enemy closest to me. Many betrayed me throughout Coilu. They all wanted more power in the Fellowship. Fools... the Harbingers will cross them all." Gwen hissed.

Razial does not doubt that. The Harbingers have proven they want nothing more than to destroy the Magi and all who serve them. What he does not understand is why they want to free the Magi. Beulah had told him they had already freed the Magi from Bal's dolmen and had plans to release them. She also told him the Order of the Flame needs him to stop the Magi.

Not knowing how true that was, he decided to ask Gwen. Wearing the thin blue dress he had given to her. Gwen appears to be a peasant-not a powerful druidess.

"The Order of the Flame is powerless without you. Another reason I want you dead." Gwen said.

Razial nodded, then asked why she served Bal to serve Rakaar. Shaking her head as if what he had said bothered her, Gwen stared at him and said.

"I do not serve Bal. I stand with Bal. He is the magus of Coilu, and I am from Dax. I am Rakaar's servant first, then a member of the Fellowship."

"So, to you, Bal is only another servant of Rakaar who has more rank than you." Razial said knowingly.

"There is power in order and structure." She replied.

Razial looked away. He checked on Ariel, who was still asleep. Although she has eaten, she remains unresponsive to him. He rubbed her red hair and began thinking about the Magi. He finds them lacking. He would not stand with anyone who always needed him to be free. When they are free, they seem to serve themselves more than they serve Rakaar. Bal is the warrior. Mel is the manipulator, and Cas is the thinker. Rarely do they work together, but when they do, they are effective.

"That one was tortured a lot." Gwen said.

Her statement made him refocus. Beulah had assured him the Harbingers do not torture its prisoners unless they deserve it. She explained they had freed Ariel from the Fellowship. Looking at Gwen, he decided he was going to give her to the Order of the Flame. He still wants to kill her, but he is under contract, and he knows they want her alive.

"Why did the Harbingers not kill you?" He asked.

"Obviously, they want to make you happy." She answered.

Her thoughts went to Frauter. He can track others magically. Something few can do. He is coming for her. She has no doubt about it.

"I could do without you. Had I known the Harbingers intended to give you to me. I would have told them to kill you." Razial said flatly.

That made Gwen smile. At the lowest point in her life, she refuses to appear weak.

"I assure you the feeling is mutual." She glared at him.

Razial did not respond. His mind went to the Harbingers being so sure he would escape today.

*

Anjia and Xochi had snuck into the fortress without incident. Scar and another wolf are with them. They are following them through the fortress. The wolves are invisible, but they can hear their paws trotting across the floor. Scar communicated he senses elves. Anjia began to think they were walking into a trap. However, before she could say anything to Xochi, two guards appeared at the end of the corridor where Razial is. Anjia stopped in her tracks. The guards' faces are covered by their helms, but the wolves can sense they are elves. Anjia stared at them ready to act.

"Hurry." A guard said. "The Suceans will return soon."

They had spoken in elvish which showed they knew she was an elf even though her face is covered. They walked off. Xochi asked what they had said. Anjia told her while jogging to where the guards had pointed. They entered a poorly lit room. In the middle of the back wall is a doorway. Anjia did not hesitate in going down the six stairs. She opened the door at the bottom of the stairs and entered the spacious cell. A sense of relief filled her when she saw Razial. She had her powers drawn by the time Xochi recognized Ariel.

"Areil!" Xochi ran over to her.

Ariel did not respond. Xochi used her powers to free her while Anjia asked who Gwen was.

"She has been in shock for days." Razial said to Xochi. "That is Gwen of Dax. Do you want her dead?"

Xochi stared at him. She helped Ariel to her feet. She had to force herself to believe what he had just said.

"Alive. I want her alive." She answered.

At that moment, she wondered why she and Razial talked to each other in Tuyakan.

"Keep an eye on her. I will follow the wolves. You all follow me." Razial said.

"No. You watch this…" Anjia tilted her head. "Gwen. I will lead us out."

Razial frowned but said nothing. He released his daggers. He had used them to cut his chains after Anjia had broken the gleipnir used to bind him. He cut Gwen's fetters, then told Anjia to lead the way.

"This was too easy. The Harbingers and their games." Anjia said after they left the fortress.

***

Zelia had met Alena and the others out on the road to Vin. Araceli was shocked by the destruction Ulina had inflicted on Vin. She asked why they had destroyed so much of the city.

Zelia told her Ulina was angry about Razial being captured.

"What do you mean, Razial was captured?" Adini asked.

Zelia quickly explained all she had been told about the Harbingers taking Razial. She was surprised by how angry the jolems became. She looked around at the others. Kalvin's bearded face shows his concern. Araceli is puzzled while Alena appears worried.

"What are the others doing about this?!" Havi asked.

Zelia told him about Anjia and Xochi being in Suce and Ulina en route to join them.

"We last made contact two days ago. The next contact is due later today." She said.

"How far away is Ulina?" Adini asked.

Zelia had intended to say something else, but Adini did not give her a chance. She told him she did not know how close Ulina is to Suce. Pulling his horse ahead and increasing its pace, Havi said.

"Well, we will have to find out what Mantak knows."

After watching the jolems argue with Mantak, Alena needs to be alone. She went to her room thinking. For the first time in her life, she had a vision without being close to Anjia. In her vision, Razial and Anjia faced a great danger. The vision did not reveal if either survives. What it did reveal is that Mantak would come close to death-soon!

"Alena." Kalvin called excitedly.

He looked down at her. She still stood by the doorway. He can see that she is thinking about something. Her long hair hung down her back. Her elflocks framed her face. Her skin is no longer pale like it was during the winter months.

"What is it, Kalvin?" She asked.

Her brown eyes focused on him. He stepped closer and said.

"Razial is free. He's with Anjia and Xochi. That's not the best part." Kalvin smiled.

Alena stared at him wondering what could be better than that. "Ariel is with him!" Kalvin smiled.

Hearing that Razial had been freed made her happy. Hearing about Ariel made her giddy. She cannot stop smiling. She touched Kalvin's arm while asking if, he was sure. She knows he is sure but could not stop herself from asking. His blue eyes are wide with excitement. He has an excited grin on his face.

After he settled down, he explained Mantak told him Tu'ani and Lela told Xochi to take Razial to Svelt North. That puzzled her. She remained silent while he told her the Harbingers gave Razial Gwen of Dax as a gift.

"To make peace with him. They gave him Ariel to make him happy." Kalvin smirked.

"Tell her what else Mantak said." Fogi Red approached.

They turned to face him. He ignored their curious stares. He has a flask in his hand. She can smell the ale inside. She looked into his blue eyes and wondered if he had been told that Ja'Brahma still lives.

"What ole Goldie here" Fogi Red pointed at Kalvin. "-does not realize is that Mantak had said all of that in elvish. Yet, he understood every word."

Alena looked at Kalvin, who stared back. He is at a loss. His expression revealed the doubt he felt about what Fogi Red said. Without saying anything, she told herself this is true because he is drawing closer to becoming a paladin. Fogi Red entered her room and walked to the other side while saying Mantak wants to talk to them all about something. Alena thanked him while thinking that Eloh had chosen a good-hearted thief and an exiled king to be paladins.

***

Razial is riding lead as his small procession travels along the trail that leads out of the hills, they had to cross to reach Svelt. To the south, they can see Svelt North in the horizon. They had managed to lose those who had pursued them from Suce. He knows the Sisterhood's agents were the ones who chased them. But he does not care.

Looking around. He thought about how with two supply horses and Gwen tied to another, they are making good time. Although the sky is partly cloudy, it is a bright day, and the weather is warm. The grass, plants and trees that cover the hills are several shades of green.

Scar's pack is off enjoying the hills. Anjia and Xochi keep Gwen between them while Ariel's horse is tied to the supply horses. Xochi stays close to Ariel. Razial does not know when Ariel will come out of her condition, but he knows she will.

His attention went to two individuals riding toward them. It is a man and a woman. The woman is young, and she seems nervous. The man is wearing a cloak, and he is watching Razial.

It had been difficult for Frauter to track Gwen because of the gleipnir and all the maneuvering her captors-first the Harbingers and now Razial-did, but Frauter's persistence has paid off. With Dawn to his right, he is riding along slowly. He had thought about leaving Dawn, but she pleaded to help him. They had almost reached Gwen near Suce, but a small army chased her group. He had stayed close in case he had to help them get away. He was impressed by Razial's ability to lose the small army. What Razial did not know is Frauter had maneuvered so he could approach their group from the south. He had told Dawn to make sure she remains calm and to wait until he acts before, she strikes. The thing he did not count on is Xochi always having a bad feeling around strangers. She watched them as they moved around Razial. Instinctively, her eyes went to Gwen. Gwen remained stoic, but her eyes seemed to recognize Frauter and Dawn. That is all Xochi needed to see. She drew her powers. Anjia turned to glance at her while drawing her own. That is when Frauter drew his powers-surprising them because he is stronger than they are!

"Frauter!" Gwen shouted.

Anjia and Xochi exchanged powerful strikes with him. He was knocked off his horse after breaking the gleipnir that bound Gwen. While all of this happened, Dawn did all she could to keep

Ariel occupied. Ariel had no choice but to act. She could not continue to act traumatized. Gwen and Frauter are too strong. She hammered Dawn while Razial's daggers tumbled repeatedly toward Gwen, who had been wounded by the first two throws before she could shield herself. Razial had targeted her as soon as Xochi drew her powers. Still, she unleashed a flurry of magical strikes trying to kill him. He was knocked off his horse. He struck the ground hard. Blades of grass pricked his face when he rolled over. He sensed the magical exchanges while he hopped to his feet.

"Kill the Gideon, Frauter!" Gwen ordered.

Dawn was struck by Razial's daggers-once in her shoulder and once in her left side. Ariel knocked her down and moved to help Xochi and Anjia. Unlike Frauter, Gwen is overpowering. She forced a game Anjia to a knee while deflecting a barrage of magical strikes from Xochi. Ariel staggered Gwen with several strikes, but Gwen battled back. However, Ariel's actions allowed Anjia to close in on Gwen and hit her in the face knocking her back.

"Damn you, elf." Gwen snapped angrily.

Razial heard this, but his focus was on Frauter. Had there been space between them, Frauter could have hammered him. That is why Razial is staying close to him using his daggers to force him to use his powers to shield himself instead of lashing out. He could not allow Frauter to draw his sword, so he pressed him relentlessly. Frauter used his magically shielded hands to deflect his daggers-which drained his powers.

Their arms moved with amazing speed. Frauter backpedaled while Razial tried to outflank him. They are no longer on the road. They are on the grass. The horses began to panic because Scar's pack was racing to the scene. Razial saw Gwen fighting against the others. To his surprise, she is winning!

He kicked Frauter to the ground and threw his daggers at her. By the time Frauter recovered from being kicked to the ground, Razial had thrown his daggers at Gwen twice.

Dawn staggered to help Gwen. All around her she sensed magical strikes. They seem to affect her eyes. She gasped when she saw the daggers tumble threw the air and strike Gwen in her back. She saw the daggers tumble toward Gwen again. With her powers focused on her wounds she still lashed out at Razial. Gwen wants him dead, and he keeps harming them with his daggers. She watched Frauter knock Razial down after her strikes struck him. That is when she saw that Razial had stabbed Frauter. Sensing something closing in on her, she spun around just in time to see She-Scar leap into the air and tackle her. Panicking, it was all she could do just to keep She-Scar's mouth away from her throat.

She lashed out at She-Scar causing her to whimper in pain as she bounced back. Dawn's relief was short lived. Another wolf bit her leg as she fell back to help Gwen and Frauter.

Gwen is in a rage. She knows this was her best chance to kill Razial. The elfin wolves' arrival ruined it for her. Their actions have changed the tide. Razial stopped fighting Frauter and targeted her with his daggers which struck true every time because she could not shield herself while fighting Anjia, Ariel, and Xochi.

With her wounds draining too much of her power, she cannot continue to battle all three of them at once. Anjia is a lot stronger than she had expected and all of them are well trained in using their powers for combat, especially Anjia.

Knowing her chance had past, she lashed out at all her foes while shouting.

"Damn elfin wolves!"

She moved to help Frauter, who was swarmed by several wolves. They moved to help Dawn. While she picked up Dawn, she remembered something she had heard long ago as a child. An elf had rescued a man in Dax, who had helped the elf. The man asked the elf why he had risked himself and the elf's response was simple:

"Always repay loyalty with loyalty and your servants will be motivated to stay loyal."

With this on her mind, Gwen led Frauter and Dawn into the surrounding wilderness. She knows her foes will not pursue her because neither side is strong enough to defeat the other without dying.

Xochi watched Gwen run off. She already feels the effects of the fighting. Although she is angry about Gwen escaping, she is happier that they did not lose anyone.

*

Hours later, Xochi and Ariel sat inside their room. They had made their way on foot, to Svelt North. They chose an inn to stay in, then Razial and Anjia left for supplies and horses. They had told Ariel and Xochi they would all meet with the Order of the Flame's agents in Svelt North later in the night. Ariel knows they will also check for Society activity so Razial can better avoid those who hunt him. Ariel has not said much since the fight. She wants it to seem as if she only fought on instinct.

Xochi seems unsure of how to talk to her. Ariel knows she is thinking of a way to ease into talking to her.

"Frauter is more capable than I ever imagined." Xochi said.

Ariel sat staring through the window. People are moving around enjoying the sunny day. Now that Xochi has broken the uneasy silence, Ariel will talk.

"He was able to track her no doubt." She said.

"I am going to be sore for days." Xochi stated.

Ariel agreed with her. She too winces with each breath. Gwen is incredibly powerful. The first time she fought Gwen was difficult even though she had had a lot of help. Fighting Gwen with just a small advantage in numbers is not enough. That is what impressed Ariel so much about Anjia. Ariel knew Razial could deal with pain very well, but Anjia has proven she too can deal with pain while fighting.

A smile came to her face as she thought about how well the Master's plan is working. The others genuinely believe she was a prisoner. Her task now is to try to figure out who the spies in the Order of the Flame are. According to Beulah, the Master is sure of only two things about the spies: they are plentiful, and they reach all the way to the Conclave!

***

With his elfin burnoose folded and tucked inside his pants at the small of his back, Razial is dressed in all brown. He has on an oversized V-neck quarter sleeved shirt and suede pants. He has no visible weapon to go unnoticed.

Before opening the door to the smith shop, he saw Anjia as she approached from the opposite direction. She had told him she wanted to avoid any problems until she is fully recovered from the fight against Gwen and the others. She is dressed in a brown dirndl with a gray burnoose over it. She does not need to hide the fact she is an elf, but she wants to. The few elves who live in Svelt have questionable character and she does not want to be confused for one of them.

"It has been a long time since I have seen Tony." Anjia said. "Then, he shall be happy to see you." Razial replied.

"He will be happy to see us." She smiled.

Like all smith shops, it is hot and smoky inside. Tony looked at them and smiled. Tall, with olive skin, he has a full graying black beard that matches his graying black hair. His brown eyes are full of strength. He is well built and like all warlocks, he does not appear to be half of his age. He has been a member of the Society for a long time. He and Vishnu are peers. Very few from their generation still live.

"The Avatar and the Lady." Tony smiled. "What can I do for you two?"

Since he usually talks to them in Tuyakan, they talk back in Tuyakan.

"I need some daggers." Anjia said.

"I need a sword-machete style." Tony finished with Razial, who smiled.

"I also need a bow that can shoot long and short range." Razial added.

"A bow?" Anjia frowned.

Razial winked. Tony said he would return with their weapons. Anjia winced when Razial pulled her close. He apologized while letting her go.

Thinking about the fight with Gwen, he thought about how Anjia had been stronger than she was before. He asked her about her newfound power.

"I do not know what is going on, but before I reached Suce, Goraan sent me a message telling me that I would grow stronger, and I cannot allow that to make me take more risks."

"He contacted you telepathically?" Razial asked.

Anjia nodded, then she asked him why Mantak had given him the elfin burnoose. Razial did not know the answer and told her he thought it was about him having Ja'Brahma's daggers. Tony returned with their new weapons. Razial handed him a hand full of gold coins. Tony tried to give them back, but Razial told him he had too many.

While Anjia put away the four daggers she asked for, she thought about how Tony was still searching for his daughter. As one of Binu's best servants, Tony was given permission to remain in Svelt for as long as he wants.

Long ago, Tony married an Ocian witch, who was at war with the Sisterhood. She forced rivaling covens to join forces against her. Tony freed her but was captured after he had killed two witches Goraan had marked for death. Binu freed him and tried to lead him to his wife, but she was killed just after giving birth to Tony's daughter. Tony never got to see his daughter, only Binu did. That is how Binu had a magical portrait-that allows Tony to keep track of his daughter's appearance-made.

Thinking about that, Anjia asked to see the portrait. Tony showed it to her without delay. She studied it for several seconds before handing it back to Tony. Razial looked at the portrait for a moment. Then admired the craftsmanship of the sword Tony had given him.

The medium length blade seems to meld into the cross guard. The hilt is large enough for either one or two hands. The pommel flares back so he can slide his fingers off with ease. Tony told him he had made the sword specifically for him. Razial thanked him saying he was most pleased with the sword.

Anjia stared at Tony, who looked back at her. They watched Razial slide a finger along the blade. The sharp edge curves like the point of a cutlass.

"Geoffrey is going to try to match this. You know that right?" Razial said.

"Just make sure he gets the chance to see it." Tony said.

Anjia smirked at Tony. At first, she was irritated by Razial's admiration of the sword. Now, Tony has gone along with Razial's focus on craftsmanship. They are talking about Geoffrey because he is considered the second-best blacksmith in the Society behind Tony. Anjia hates it when others argue over great craftsmanship. To her, great is great.

She switched the conversation to Kalvin and what had happened with Gwen before it was time for her and Razial to leave.

***

Days later, Razial and Anjia separated. Goraan sent her to assassinate two targets in Svelt South. The only reason Anjia did not argue is because Goraan had told her Razial would be sent to Svelt South next. He told her to keep that to herself. She had tried to find out how he knew the Order of the Flame's plans, but Goraan told her nothing.

After Anjia left, Razial was told what he must do in Svelt. He was impressed with the Order of the Flame's plans. He now understands why they need an assassin. Although they have many connections, they do not have the widespread connections the Society has.

His targets cover a wide spectrum-from a noble general to a seedy criminal, who is rarely seen. It took Razial several days, with help from Tony, to track the criminal. Once he found him, he killed him. Ariel and Xochi killed several of his associates.

Dealing with the general took some planning. Not only was he high born, but all his captains were fiercely loyal. Again, Razial called on Tony. Tony helped him set things up so Ariel and Xochi could kill the captains while Razial kills the general.

It took him days to get close to the general. He had met with Xochi and Ariel before going after the general. Using his burnoose, he entered the estate where his target was. With the general sitting out in the open, he smiled mentally because he had figured he would need a bow. He watched the general from across the short distance between them. He took aim with his bow and loosed an arrow. He did not watch it fly. He knocked another arrow and loosed it in one fluid motion. Like the first, the second arrow struck true. Both slammed into the general's back. He tucked the bow under his burnoose. He did not expect it to be so easy. He had thought he would have to run away because some servants would witness the general's death. He feels lucky the general was alone. He pulled the hood to his burnoose over his head and began to walk away. As he walked across the grass, he began to feel like he was being watched. He looked around. The sun will not set for at least another hour. The trees around him cast long shadows, but he can see well. Seeing no one, he decided to stop.

"Impressive. Even with the elfin burnoose."

Razial's heart began to pound. He recognized Rogelio's voice instantly. He knows Rogelio can see him even though he is using the elfin burnoose to make himself invisible. He also knows Rogelio is not there to watch him. He is there to hunt him!

"Are you ready to test your fighting skills?" Rogelio asked.

Razial removed his burnoose. He stared into Rogelio's blue eyes. They stand out in contrast to his olive skin and reddish-brown hair. His beard matches his hair.

Well dressed, in all blue, he appears to be a rich mercenary. Taller than Razial, Rogelio is well built and exudes confidence. He removed his long sword. He likes to fight. As a warlock, he is powerful. As a fighter, few can stand against him. That is why his moniker is the Fist.

"Use Ja'Brahma's daggers and I will use my powers." Rogelio warned.

Razial put his burnoose against the small of his back. Rogelio walked up to Razial with absolute confidence. Razial remained stoic. Binu and Goraan taught him a great deal of martial arts. Rogelio will find him no easy mark.

They both tested the grass. It is dry. They do not have to worry about slipping. They charged each other and attacked with abandon. Razial deflected several swings before he was forced to sidestep a powerful kick. He countered with low kicks and a five-punch combination. Rogelio deflected every punch and avoided the kicks.

Trying to get an angle on the attacking Razial, Rogelio smiled. He is calm. A lesser man would have been overwhelmed.

"You" Rogelio countered with a litany of punches. "-have been" Razial was hit in his right side. "-practicing. Good. Still- arhg."

Razial silenced him with a kick to the inside of his left leg causing him to stumble and leaving him open for a thunderous right hand from Razial.

With blood in his mouth, Rogelio nodded while saying.

"No more games."

He pressed Razial. After several minutes, it became obvious Rogelio would win. He had taken more punches than he had expected, but that did not matter. He is about to capture Razial.

Hearing someone behind him, he stopped suddenly.

Razial staggered as he stood wondering why Rogelio had stopped. He tasted the blood in his mouth. His body ached and he felt his face swelling from the blows he had taken.

Rogelio heard footsteps from the left, he turned to see who dared approach. He drew his powers immediately. He does not know who Ulina is, but Razial does.

"Leave now and go on your way assassin. You will not capture or harm Razial today." Ulina said calmly.

She does not know who Rogelio is, but she knows this has to do with the hunt. She can sense how strong he is, but he cannot match power with her.

"Go assassin. I am Fa'Ulina the Blue Keeper. I will not give you another chance to leave peacefully."

Rogelio looked at Razial. He had put up a good fight. Rogelio had to give him that. Ulina's arrival saved Razial. Rogelio would take his chances with an elf close to his age but fighting Ulina is too much. He knows better than that.

"Next time, Avatar." He said as he walked off.

Razial winced as he walked over to Ulina. She offered to heal him, but he told her to wait until they reached safety. They walked in silence until they reached the estate's northern wall. That is when she asked him why Rogelio did not use his powers during the fight. He explained that Rogelio wanted to test him. That is when she realized she had let Rogelio go. She was not happy.

***

The Master and Beulah met in the telepathic realm. As usual, he is concerned about her being targeted while they communicate. He praised her for sending Lisa to Ocia to watch when Peter frees the Magi. He then explained that Troggo was en route to Ocia city. That surprised her. She voiced her concern. He assured her that all they have to worry about is Troggo trying to capture Razial.

"Why would he do that?" She asked.

"To test himself. If I can meet with him before he captures Razial, I can stop him. He wants to force Razial to free A'Ja'Brahma."

Beulah decided to stop trying to figure out what game he was playing with Troggo. However, allowing Troggo to work in concert with the Magi seems counterproductive. The Master told her that Troggo would not be a problem for them. He then told her to prepare Tunez for the Days of Darkness. That made it clear he would eliminate the heirs in Brahma and in Anazi.

With so much going on, she does not understand why he wants to create more chaos. She did not ask any questions. She listened while he explained that they must keep the Order of the Flame occupied while they act to make sure those who serve the Magi are wiped out during this phase of the war.

"Remember, we have to fight in phases. All Champions' Wars are fought and won in phases." He thought to Beulah.

***

Staring at the other twelve members of the Sisterhood's coven, Lisa could not believe what she was hearing. Only Victoria, a one-time rival, who rules Ryalu, stayed out of the conversation about acting against Troggo and Peter.

Standing in a circle, inside Ocia's Great Hall, each coven member has her scepter in hand. Pam has convinced other members that they can take Troggo's and Peter's powers. Lisa looked around to check the protegees' reactions to hearing this idea. Some of them appear bothered while others are too stoic to get a read on. Only Tammy and Victoria's protegee appear against this foolish idea.

Peter is the only one who can free the Magi and Troggo can take on the entire coven by himself. Add the fact he arrived with thirty Harlequins and attacking him is out of the question to a rationally thinking person. Lisa told the others they were being foolish. They quickly turned on her. Victoria sided with her. Lisa stared at her. Her brown eyes held the others in focus. Inside the hall, her toned skin appears darker. Her light brown hair hangs like a mane. Her full lips moved to pronounce each word as she argued against acting against Troggo and Peter. She ignored others' disapproving stares. Although she is short, she is rumored to be the strongest member of the Sisterhood. Something that was not said lightly.

"Many of you know nothing about the Harbingers. Trust me," Lisa said firmly. "We do not want to tangle with them until we have to. As for the elf, Troggo. I am not foolish enough to think about acting against him. Have you all not heard about the Harlequin raids in Brahma, Danou, and Giaour?!"

She looked around to see if what she was saying was sinking in.

"Let us free our master and let him decide what to do next." Victoria said.

She looked at Lisa, who nodded. Several others began to rethink their support for attacking Troggo and Peter. Lisa and Victoria finally stood on the same side. While they watched their coven sisters, Tammy took note that not one of them had brought up Beulah. That is important to her because Beulah had made all of this happen. Troggo and Peter are in Ocia as Beulah's guests.

Acting against Beulah's guests would be beyond foolish.

Another thing Tammy took notice of is the fact that only Victoria seems to understand the Harbingers are dangerous enemies to have. The others are too arrogant to realize they are outclassed by the Harbingers. She turned to face the wooden double doors when Peter pushed them open. He led a group of Harlequins into the hall. His cowl makes it seem as if he is floating across the floor. The Harlequins poured into the hall with some moving to the right while the others moved to the left.

Like all elves, they walk with absolute confidence. They spread out along the wall while Troggo led in another group of Harlequins- some of them carrying the Magi. Troggo cannot help but stand out. His red hair calls attention to it. His black elflocks make his red eyes stand out even more. His eyes met Tammy's. At that moment, she realized she and others had been moving backward to give him room. The coven members no longer stand in the middle of the hall. Peter is in the middle waiting for Troggo.

Troggo watched his warriors stand up the statues that imprison the Magi. He knows the statues impress the humans who came to witness the Magi's return. -He is there for his own reason.

"Do you want to give them their crowns?" Peter asked him.

"Hand the crowns to them." He pointed at several of his warriors.

Peter pulled the three ancient crowns from inside his cowl and handed them to the three Harlequins. Troggo knows his warriors will use the correct crown on the first try. Although the statues are the same grayish color, it is easy to distinguish who is who. Bal is tall and muscular. Mel is taller than average but thin. Cas is average in height and build. The only difference between the ancient crowns is the face shields. Bal's crown-the ancient crown of Coilu, has a sword on its face shields. Mel's crown-the ancient crown of Ocia, has an arrow on its face shields. Cas' crown-the ancient crown of Danou, has a spear on its face shields. (Cas' crown was part of Danou before he claimed it.)

Troggo knows the weapons on the face shields represent each magus' personality. Mel uses a bow because he prefers to act from a distance. That is why he is considered cowardly. Bal's weapon is the sword. He is a fighter. He prefers close combat. There is little finesse in him. His enemies always see him coming. He refuses to change because few can stop him. Cas' weapon is the spear because he is willing to fight from a distance or from up close. He adapts to whatever is going on.

"Begin." Troggo ordered in elvish.

Peter watched as the Harlequins recited the ancient words engraved inside the crowns. The torches began to flicker. Peter slowly made his way out of the hall. Beulah had been very specific in her message when he was given the crowns. He is to leave before the Magi are freed. They might act against him, and the Master does not want to have to deal with them yet.

Peter increased his pace as he walked through the corridor that connects the Great Hall and the palace. He looked around before releasing his cowl and leaving the palace.

While Peter left, Pam watched when the Harlequins placed the crowns on the statues which instantly became flesh. Each magus inhaled deeply. They shook their heads and limbs. She stared in awe. Never in her lifetime did she expect to see Mel free. His long wavy hair gives him a feminine appearance. His pale skin seems to glow. To his right, is Bal whose medium length blond hair hangs to his shoulders. His muscles bulged as he continued to loosen up. To Bal's right is Cas his tan skin appears darker. His short curly hair dangles over his ears giving him a youthful appearance.

"Ja'Troggo. Why are we together?" Bal asked.

"Because the Harbingers brought all three of you together."

"The Harbingers?" Bal and Mel asked.

"Where are they now? Did you attack them?" Mel asked.

"Of course not." Cas interjected. "They freed him."

Troggo did not deny this. Pam listened to him ask the Magi about their intentions. Neither gave him the answer he was looking for. Standing nearly a foot shorter than Bal, Troggo is talking as if he is the giant in the room. He told them to gather their armies and march on Winnin then to Brahma city.

"Why?" Cas asked.

"The Harbingers have plans to bring about the Days of Darkness now that you all are free."

Troggo's answer shocked them all. Pam listened as he explained that he was going to track the Gideon and capture him. Bal asked if he would kill the Gideon.

"I will capture him. You three will have to fight him to obtain your powers."

His common still has a heavy accent, but it is easy to understand him. He spun around and walked off. The Harlequins in the hall followed him out. That is when Pam realized that Troggo is more powerful than she had thought. She led the way before Mel and bowed while Bal and Cas exited the hall.

*

Outside of the palace, Troggo and his warriors left the city like raiders. He had met with the Magi to make sure they did not stray from the Master's plan. He only wants them to obtain their powers because it would free Ja'Brahma. If The Gideon defeats them, Ja'Brahma must remain in his prison.

***

Weeks after Ulina had saved Razial from Rogelio, she called for a meeting in Svelt South. Mantak and the others with him had arrived days earlier. Ulina waited until the entire group was settled inside a farmhouse before explaining the Magi are free so they must reach Brahma city where Razial will take the final stage to become the Gideon.

Like Kalvin, Sidney is at a loss. Ulina thoroughly explained all that is going on and how Razial will have to fight the Magi to stop them from obtaining their powers. Araceli asked about Ja'Brahma. Ulina did not want to address that, but Priato had told her she should. Without going into details, she explained that Ja'Brahma is alive and imprisoned beneath Brahma city. That made Fogi Red ask her a litany of questions.

Razial sat listening. He knows Ulina is leaving a lot out. He looked around and saw how interested Kalvin and Sidney are. They hung on every word she said. His attention then fell on Xochi and Zelia. He can sense the difference in how he looks at them. Next to them are Ariel and Araceli, who can pass for twins. Ariel is listening quietly while Araceli is asking more questions.

Adini and Havi appear uninterested in what Ulina is saying. Raal and Mantak are listening, but Razial is sure they know most of what Ulina is saying. He turned to look at Alena and Anjia. (Ulina had insisted that Anjia rides to Brahma city with them.)

Anjia is unhappy about the fact the Hilt has targeted the king of Brahma, one of his captains, and the king and prince of Anazi. This means whoever put the contracts on these targets paid for guaranteed success!

Making that even worse is the fact Goraan has marked the prince of Brahma for death. Anjia thinks Goraan should have turned down the contracts on those who are heirs of the Six Heroes still he marked the prince of Brahma making her more angry. Razial does not mind this. That is why Anjia is angry with him.

"Razial." Ulina called. "Please take a walk with me while Mantak prepares the others to leave."

The meeting ended with that. He walked out with her to his right. She told him Tu'ani and Lela had things prepared for his return to Anazi Falls. He does not know why they would want him to go back to Anazi Falls, but he remained quiet. She told him he must learn a lot and that he has to start accepting the fact he is the Gideon. He did not look at her while she said any of this. But she got his attention when she said.

"You shall learn everything that happened to Ja'Brahma when you return to Anazi Falls."

The sincerity in her voice made him think. He looked around. They stopped walking. There are no clouds in the sky. Her blue surplice stands out against the deep green of the grass. He looked at her. There is gray in her long black hair that hangs to her waist. Her narrow eyes are soft and caring. She looked into his eyes while telling him how she became a keeper. She then told him about the other keepers of the fourth Champions' War. She was not surprised by the fact he knows Teresa still lives, but she is curious to know what he knows about her.

"Did Ja'Goraan tell you why Teresa put herself in a self-imposed exile?" She asked.

He told her all he knew was Teresa was the fourth keeper and she had left the Order of the Flame after the last Champions' War. Ulina surprised him by what she said next.

"During the last phase of the war, a deal was made. The Harbingers tried to capture the Gideon. They failed. Three of them died. However, so did several paladins. In our weakened state, the Magi decided to press us-a mistake. An army of our best Ratels stormed into the Gnor Valley. This army was led by a brilliant general, who joined his army with a jolem army led by Havi and Adini. They devastated the Gnorans and Winninans. Teresa joined them when they engaged Ja'Troggo and his army. They captured a Harbinger, which led to the Master agreeing to help imprison the Magi, so long as he got to choose who keeps their medallions."

They both smiled at this. There is no denying the genius of the Master's action. She finished her tale by saying along with Tu'ani and Lela she helped the Harbingers imprison the Magi. She told him two Harbingers died during the fighting.

"While we did this, our husband died stopping the Chosen Servant." She said.

Razial saw sadness in her eyes. He also noted there was something missing but said nothing.

"Meanwhile." Ulina continued. "Eloh ordered us to imprison the Harlequins. Teresa, who was busy dealing with the massive armies trying to defeat the Ratels and jolems, disagreed with this. She tried to kill Ja'Troggo, who defeated her. She was saved by the young Ratel general, who defeated an exhausted Ja'Troggo. Months later, that same general, along with Adini and Havi, stopped Teresa from killing the captured Harbinger."

Razial stared into her eyes. He knows she is about to say something important to him.

"Although Teresa and the general agree philosophically, he had to stop her. Teresa exiled herself after that. The general went on to become the youngest ever to join the Canopy before he was banned and is still wanted for questioning. That young general is none other than Ja'Goraan!"

Hearing that shocked Razial. He knows it is true. He stood frozen in awe. He had to force himself to ask.

"Goraan was a member of the Canopy?"

"Yes. We shall talk more later. I shall reveal more as we ride."

CHAPTER 10

ANCIENT HEROES

As instructed, Vishnu infiltrated the court in Anazi. Doing so was not easy. At first, he was denied entry into the palace, but Diana, who had also infiltrated the court, used her influence to get him added to the courtiers' list.

Where he is acting like a rich merchant, Diana is simply being the Arapian noble she is. That is why she was allowed in court so easily. It is widely known she will soon become the queen of Arapia and will need a husband to keep the throne. That makes her the most welcomed courtier in all courts.

Sitting at a long table, Vishnu watched his fellow courtiers as they continued to eat. The king had left the festivities an hour earlier. The prince left a short while afterward. He had made a rendezvous with Diana, who stayed behind with Vishnu and others to hide the fact she is there to kill the prince.

She is on the opposite side of the table-several chairs to Vishnu's left. She is pretty in a plain way. She has elfish features-thanks to her half elf father. Her long dark hair contrasts with her pale white skin. She has round green eyes, full pouty lips, and a full bosom that stands out even more because of her petite size. She is a skilled assassin with magical powers that rival Anjia's, she is more than enough to kill the prince on her own.

"So, tell us sir." A female courtier said. "Is Fulancia truly a lair for murderous bandits?"

She is fond of Vishnu, who finds her attractive. She stroked her dark hair while her soft brown eyes met his blue eyes. Smiling at her, Vishnu rubbed his beard while saying.

"I hope not, or I am a poor judge of character."

"You are quite brave to travel the lands of Giaour without a personal guard." The woman smiled.

Several others looked at Diana to see if she took offense, because Arapia is in Giaour. Diana smiled to show that she did not take offense.

"Well," a male courtier said. "I know parts of Giaour are ruled by wizards and assassins."

"The Assassin Society rules Fulancia. Everyone knows that." Another man stated.

He stared at the others as if he dared them to disagree. Vishnu tilted his head to the woman to show that he has nothing to say in response to the man.

"Well," Diana stood. "I can assure you that is not true in Arapia. Now, if you all would excuse me. I must retire."

She walked out of the hall. Vishnu continued to flirt with the woman for a short while longer before he excused himself. He knows Diana will kill the prince, so he must kill the king.

Creeping along the hallway wall, Vishnu fingered his daggers. He peered around the corner. He saw two guards outside the secret passageway that is in the middle of the hallway's northern wall. Many years ago, the Society had paid a lot to learn about the passageway. However, that one-time payment still pays dividends.

He cleared his mind and exhaled slowly. Knowing he must act quickly. He walked around the corner. The guards turned to face him. He flung his first dagger by the time they set their feet. His second dagger flew toward them while he charged drawing his sword. The first dagger struck true-in the first guard's throat. His companion turned to look at him when he stopped and grabbed his throat. He had never seen the dagger that slammed into his head. Vishnu made sure not to step in any blood as he pressed the spot to open the secret passageway. Part of the wall swung open. He hurried in. He quickly crossed the short distance to the room where the king keeps his mistresses.

"Hey!" The king gasped pulling away from a woman.

His eyes went wide as he sat up with his mouth agape. A sense of realization came over him. Vishnu is not one of his guards and that is all he needed to see. Vishnu used his sword to cut open the shocked king's throat. He turned on the woman, who had been with the king. She held out her hands trying to stop his sword. It cut through some of her fingers and part of her right palm before cutting through her neck.

Had he not needed to pass the night in Anazi, he would not have killed the woman, but he could not take the chance of being chased out of Anazi. He cleaned his sword then moved to pull the guards' bodies into the passageway. Then, he made his way to his room. He has no doubt Diana killed the prince.

***

Tol crept from underneath a table near the back of an empty hall. He had hidden there for hours. Earlier, he and Dario had been attacked inside the palace of Brahma. It was a well-planned attack, but they were too skilled for their attackers.

During the fighting Dario managed to kill his target-the palace guard captain. Tol had to hide because he did not kill his target-the king of Brahma. After the fighting, he came up with a plan to kill the king. He found a rope and snuck his way to the palace's top floor where he hid under the table. Now, it is time to act. He will lower himself to the windows of the king's chambers. It is the only way. The hallway that leads to the king's chambers is too well guarded.

Tying the rope to the table, he kept the rope tight, so it does not slip while he climbs down. He slid out the window and slowly made his way to the window to the king's chambers. He opened the wooden shutters. The sky is growing lighter. It will be dawn soon. He knows he must hurry. His boots pressed hard against the wall. Still, he is slipping. He remained patient as he slowly cut the ropes used to tie the shutters then slid through the opening he made between the shutters. He shook his head in frustration as he entered the king's chambers. Whoever decided to tie the shutters had come up with a good idea.

Flexing his hands to get rid of the numbness in his hands and arm. (His whole left arm had gone numb while he hung on to the rope.) He saw a thick wooden door at the back of the room. He crossed the room and pushed the door. It did not move. Knowing time was against him, he drew his powers and drove his sword through the door. The door fell open. He stormed into the room.

The king and his wife sat up with raised arms. The queen screamed, scrambling off the bed. Tol ignored her. He charged the king, cutting off an arm before he decapitated him. The queen threw things at him. He ran out to face the guards who had entered the front room. They never had a chance. He parried several thrusts then cut the first guard across his legs. As he fell, Tol blocked a thrust on his backswing, then cut open the second guard's throat on his fore swing. He whirled his sword and drove it through the first guard after he hit the floor.

Hearing more guards, he quickly climbed out the window to make his escape.

***

Razial watched the elfin wolves as he rode along. The wolves want to hide their numbers, so they are trotting in two files. He thought about Ulina explaining that Troggo is tracking him, and the Magi are gathering their forces to march on Brahma city.

Alena's hawks have chased off and killed some crows spying for Troggo. None of that bothers him. He is too busy trying to figure out what the other Hilt members are doing going along with Goraan still targeting the prince of Brahma. He knows Goraan will not change his mind, but it is strange to him that no other Hilt member has even tried to change his mind.

He is thinking about this because Ulina had told them about the assassinations in Anazi and in Brahma. The fact Binu has said nothing is enough proof the prince of Brahma should die. Anjia does not see it that way. To her, the fact the prince of Brahma is only thing between the world and Rakaar's Shadow trumps everything. She and Razial debated about whether to warn Ulina about taking them to Brahma city or not. Razial made it clear he did not want her to say anything.

"Razial." Ulina called.

She pulled alongside him. He turned to look at her. Her soft brown eyes met his gaze. She acts motherly to him, and he does not know why.

"Ride with me. I have a tale for you." She said.

Razial looked back at Anjia and winked before riding off with Ulina. He saw Mantak ride alongside Anjia. The others stayed in the same formation with the twins bringing up the rear. He and Ulina did not ride far from the others before he asked.

"This is not about the others growing stronger, is it?"

"No. This is about Ja'Binu." Ulina said.

Surprised, Razial listened while she explained how when the Assassins' Guild existed, they sent warlocks and swordsmen to kill Binu's parents. Upon his return from Alf-Heim, Binu discovered that four kings were behind this because they wanted to keep elves out of western Giaour.

"Ja'Binu asked his friends-his fellow Hilt members, to help him deal with the Assassins' Guild. They arranged their enemies' downfall. Ja'Binu killed the four kings earning his moniker. That you may know." Ulina stared at him. "Now, I shall reveal some things you do not know about Ja'Binu's past."

She then told him several tales about how Binu had been the one who had stopped the Order of the Flame from targeting the Society after they had eliminated the Assassins' Guild. The stories interested him because they involved the other Hilt members also. He had never heard so much about them before they formed the Hilt.

"So, what was the purpose of telling me all of this?" Razial asked.

"Because there is a lot about your leaders you do not know, yet you trust them. I want you to trust that I have your best interest in mind even though I have to keep a lot from you." Ulina said.

Her response to his question made him think about how Goraan and Binu had taught him that only death can prove someone loyal.

"An individual, who starts a journey on faith has proven nothing even after the individual has faced danger and passed an opportunity to betray the cause." Binu had said.

"No matter how many times an individual has proven oneself loyal, it does not prove that individual shall remain loyal. Only after one has died loyal can one be said to have proven one's loyalty to one's cause." Goraan had added.

Razial knows Ulina is not asking for loyalty, but trust. To him, that is not necessary because he is bound by his contract and has no choice but to face the Magi if they ask him to.

Thinking about that made him think about the fact they wanted him to obtain the Magi's medallions from Ja'Brahma. To him, that is still amazing because all his life he believed Ja'Brahma was dead. Discovering that Ja'Brahma is alive and Goraan has known for centuries without saying anything is shocking to him. He began to wonder if any other Hilt member knows Ja'Brahma still lives. He asked Ulina this, but she did not know. He asked her why they had expelled Goraan from the Canopy, but she refused to answer saying.

"Soon, I shall reveal this to you. First, we have to make sure things do not get too far ahead of us. The wrong thing revealed at the wrong time could cause too much harm. Goraan's past" she shook her head. "-is going to surprise you."

She then changed the subject telling him how Rogelio and his associates were seen as targets by the Order of the Flame. As an outlaw in eastern Anazi and western Brahma, Rogelio was feared until he disappeared for years only to reappear in Giaour.

"Had I known it was him in Svelt, I would have tried to capture or kill him!" Ulina hissed.

Razial knows a lot more happened between Rogelio and the Order of the Flame, but he remains curious about Goraan's past. The fact Goraan was a member of the Canopy was shocking so to hear Ulina thinks what has yet to be revealed is more shocking intrigues him.

"Rogelio might be a hero to Fulancia but in the past, he was a source of fear and dread for many."

With that, they rode back to join the others. Razial knows her tales have a purpose, and in the future, he will learn that purpose.

***

The city of Brahma is in chaos. With the assassination of the king and the disappearance of the prince, several factions have formed. Each faction blames the others for all that has happened.

What they do not know is that the prince is safe. The Order of the Flame has taken over guarding him. As the last with heroic blood, he is invaluable. Until they can track his foes, they shall keep him hidden.

Already, Barthus has killed several assassins out to kill the prince. Lela and Tu'ani have decided to take a more active role in the city's affairs. The first thing they must do is give the gems to a group of jolems who have come for them.

Ofelia and the other novices watched from behind Lela and Tu'ani as Chivia led a group of jolems into the room to meet with the keepers, Priato, and Barthus. Ofelia is surprised by the fact Chivia has a pretty face. She has soft brown eyes and long brown hair that hangs over her shoulders and down her back. Ofelia knows men find her attractive even though she is a Gully dwarf.

"A'Priato." Chivia tilted her head in respect.

He smiled at her and the other jolems. The jolems then greeted the keepers and the siblings, who are standing to Ofelia's right against the wall.

Niri looked at Ofelia for a sign of what was going on. Ofelia shook her head. They did not have to wait long to find out why the jolems had come.

"Keeper Lela. Keeper Tu'ani. I have come for the Stones. The elders want to bind the clan chiefs to the old ways." Chivia said.

Although Chivia had spoken in ancient dwarvish, Ofelia understood every word. She had no idea she understood another language, but Priato did. He watched her listen to Chivia finish explaining what had happened in Nibel.

"The danger in Nibel is a lot worse than believed. Several elders tracked and killed an abomination in the mountains." Chivia shook her head.

"Hunting Fogi Red no doubt." Lela stated.

Chivia nodded in response. Lela glanced at Priato. Her mind focused on what Chivia had said. Chivia had referred to the fact several elder jolems had tracked and killed a dwarf wizard. Very few dwarfs can wield magical powers and only members of the Gully Council are allowed to learn. All others either serve Rakaar or will eventually do so.

The question on Lela's mind is has anyone connected the dwarf wizard to Lodi Gold? She asked this and Chivia told her no one had connected Lodi Gold to the dwarf wizard. Lela nodded in while Tu'ani said.

"We will deal with Nibel, soon. First, we have to deal with the Magi."

After that, Priato used telepathy to reveal Ofelia understood all they had said. The keepers told Ofelia to stand before them. Confused, Ofelia still did not realize she had been listening to them talk in ancient dwarvish. The two keepers spoke in common so the other novices could understand them.

"It is time for you to hand over the gems, Ofelia." The keepers pointed.

Ofelia tilted her head in respect. She pulled the gems from under her belt. She had known this moment would come. She had memorized what the keepers had told her about the Stones of Honor. The gems contain a lot of power. When placed upon the gold crowns made to hold them, the Stones of Honor allow the

Gully Council to test and bind individuals, which prevents infiltration and betrayal.

It had taken hundreds of dwarfs to make the Stones of Honor. They cannot be duplicated or destroyed. Anyone can handle them, but their power can only be wielded by dwarfs.

"Thank you." Chivia said. "Do not worry. The keepers will tell you why you can understand me."

At that moment, Ofelia noticed Chivia had switched from ancient dwarvish to dwarvish. She looked at the keepers, who looked at the jolems. She then looked at the other novices. They are anxious to find out what is going on.

"The mountains shall be ready when you all are. If I am needed, just call on me." Chivia walked out of the room.

The keepers waited until the jolems had closed the door before they told the other novices to stand before them. They all looked at each other trying to figure out what was going on.

"Calm yourselves." The keepers said. "By now, you all have realized that you all are important to us. A'Priato has seen important destinies for you all. However, nothing is certain. Some of you are far away from what you are destined to do. Since destiny is controlled by fate, we shall reveal nothing to you. However, Ofelia, your destiny is at hand."

Ofelia's head began to feel warm. She feels as if everyone inside the room is staring at her. She focused on the keepers' mouths while they explained she was to become a paladin. She heard herself gasp along with the other novices.

"You shall continue to grow stronger and soon, you shall not only understand all other languages but speak them as well. Take heart, for others are fated to become paladins also. One of them is Kalvin." The keepers said.

They knew that would not only calm Ofelia but make her happy as well. They then told Barthus he is also fated to become a paladin along with another. Barthus stared at them. He already knew he was fated to become a paladin. He does not understand why he was chosen to become a paladin. To him, paladins are heroes from the past. He has never considered himself a hero.

***

A day's ride from Brahma, Kalvin thought about the tales Ulina had told them about the Champions' Wars. He looked around. The Ratels have rejoined their group. According to Mantak, they had scouted ahead to make sure there were no traps set in the villages they must pass.

It is close to noon, and he expects Ulina to call for a rest soon. He began to memorize what Ulina had told him to memorize about the Champions' Wars.

During the first war, Ja'Brahma tried to kill Haar, but was stopped by the Magi, who were imprisoned after they finished the magical gateway that connects Svan to Gnor. Rakaar made his first Chosen Servant after the Gully Council imprisoned Haar. Ja'Brahma engaged Rakaar repeatedly. His madness controlled him, which is why he went against what Eloh told him to do and tried to kill Rakaar. Only the Chosen Servant's decision to engage Ja'Brahma saved Rakaar. Against Eloh's will, Ja'Brahma killed the Chosen Servant. That is why Rakaar can make more Chosen Servants.

Having no choice, Ja'Brahma's keepers and paladins took action to imprison him. The original Blue Keeper and three paladins died imprisoning Ja'Brahma. That ended the first Champions' War.

The second war began when the Boar clan left the original Alf-Heim. It grew worse after Kan, then Tuya died. Their children and followers were unable to stop a large group of Tuya-Kan exiles from misleading entire tribes of people. That was made worse by the Magi's servant spreading in secret.

The second Chosen Servant freed the Magi, and they burned the original Alf-Heim. Tuyakans and dwarfs saved elves from being wiped out. Half of the Gully dwarfs died during all the fighting that left the original Alf-Heim destroyed.

The next phase of the war intensified when the Wizars (exiled traitors of Tuya-Kan) managed to infiltrate the Hierarchs (the highest level of Tuya-Kan). The Gideon and Chosen Servant died fighting each other. The Gideon's keepers and paladins drove the Magi into hiding, ending the second war.

The third war began when Priato formed the Order of the Flame and the Wizars waged war against true Tuya-Kan while stealing the Stones of Honor. That became known as the Tuyakan Betrayal because to those who did not know Wizars and Hierarchs were the same.

While that went on, Troggo declared war on Eloh's servants. He and his followers left Ino-Heim and became known as Harlequins. With the Wizars wreaking havoc from the shadows and the Harlequins waging an all-out war, Eloh's servants were forced to fight defensively until the elves and dwarfs recovered from the second Champions' War.

Almost all the Hierarchs were killed by the Wizars who almost achieved their goal until the third Chosen Servant pushed the Magi to wage a global war. The Wizars did all they could to slow the Magi while the Harbingers killed the Chosen Servant.

By that point, the Harbingers had gathered enough information on the Wizars to track and kill many of their leaders. The war between the Harbingers and Wizars did not become known to the Order of the Flame until the Master told Priato he would not act against the Wizars who took action to help stop the Magi from opening the Svan and Gnor gateway. Three keepers died sealing the gateway during that time.

Priato and the paladins ended the war by forcing the Magi into hiding while the Six Heroes led an invasion of Winnin, which was partially destroyed during the final battle of the war.

The fourth war began with the Harbingers secretly rebuilding Winnin while Ino-Heim became a force. The Harlequins settled in Gnor after the Denari were imprisoned inside. Priato kept the Wizars in the shadows and on the run. The Denari had been the Wizars' backbone because they had mostly been eradicated from the ranks of the Menna and the Gully.

The Magi forced three of the Six Heroes to join them gaining control of Coilu, Ocia, and Danou. The fourth Chosen Servant made a potion to create Rakaar's Own.

As the war waged on, the Six Heroes' heirs became unreliable and arrogant. They dubbed themselves the Chosen Kings. The Giaouran king was killed by the Theocracy. Those in Coilu, Ocia, and Danou swore allegiance to the magus of their lands while the king of Brahma disobeyed the Order of the Flame choosing to do as he pleased. Only the Anazian heir died a hero.

The Harbingers tried to capture the Gideon when they felt Rakaar's servants could no longer win the war. They failed and a key Harbinger was captured. The Master made a deal to help imprison the Magi and the Harlequins, which ended the war.

With the wars on his mind, Kalvin pulled alongside Ulina, who looked at him knowing he wanted to ask her a question. With her bluish elflocks shining in the sunlight, she asked what was on his mind.

"I was thinking about the Champions' Wars. What happened to the Wizars who were not with the Denari when they were imprisoned inside Gnor?" Kalvin asked.

Ulina sighed while nodding her head. She knows all the Wizars, who were not imprisoned, have never been accounted for. Where some were tracked and killed, many simply scattered in the wind. Their families have remained hidden. She explained it has been decades since the Order of the Flame had a decent lead to a Wizar. She noticed Kalvin had expected a different answer from her.

"You must understand, young Kalvin. We do not always win. Although we have stopped Rakaar's servants from freeing him in every Champions' War, it cannot be said that we won every Champions' War." She tried to clear his confusion.

After saying this, Ulina called for a rest. While the group prepared to make camp, she noticed Anjia and Razial talking in low whispers. She knows they are arguing about something. She called Alena, who had been with Araceli and Zelia.

"Yes A 'Ulina?" Alena replied.

"What is going on between Anjia and Razial?"

Alena followed her line of vision. She saw Anjia walk away from Razial who remained by the tree where they had argued, Anjia made her way to Mantak. Alena turned back to Ulina and said.

"I have no idea, but Anjia wants to reveal something to me and Razial will not allow her to."

"Do you think we should know?"

"Razial would not lead us into danger." Alena shook her head. "He says whatever it is it is for the Society to deal with."

"Very well. Now, that your pets have spotted Harlequins in the area keep an eye on him." Ulina tilted her head toward Razial.

She looked into Alena's eyes. She knows Alena is thinking about something, so she asked her what is on her mind.

"Why is Mantak so interested in Anjia? Surely, he knows she loves Razial." Alena said.

Her question made Ulina smile. She looked at Mantak and Anjia before saying.

"That is Mantak 's secret to tell. Soon, he shall reveal it. Go and bring Razial to me. I have a tale to tell." Ulina smiled.

Moments later, the group gathered around Ulina. Razial sat cross-legged in the grass. He winked at Anjia. She turned away from him. He rubbed her back, and she tried to hide her smile. Satisfied that she was no longer angry with him, he turned to look at the rest of the group. Alena is on her knees to Anjia's left. By her, is Zelia. Xochi and Ariel are just in front of Zelia. Havi and Adini are lying on the grass next to Ariel with their eyes on Ulina. Fogi Red and Raal are to Razial's right with Sidney and Kalvin on the other side of them. Ulina and Mantak are opposite of Raal and the others with the Ratels behind them. Scar and his packmates are running around exploring.

"Lately, I have noticed some confusion about Ja'Goraan." Ulina began. "Havi's and Adini's admiration of Ja'Goraan is not misplaced. You all have heard about Ja'Goraan once being a Ratel general and how well he performed during the last Champions' War. What I have not told you all is that he was once part of the Canopy."

Alena and Anjia turned to look at Razial who sat listening like it was all new to him. They are convinced Ulina had told him that before. To them, this news is more shocking than hearing Goraan was once a Ratel.

"He was the youngest member ever and is the only one to ever be expelled." Ulina said flatly.

She did not go into details, but she did explain that Goraan had hit another member. Anjia asked several questions forcing Ulina to admit that it is believed Goraan is a Harbinger. She then told them he had a small following of elves inside and outside of Alf-Heim. His following became too violent, so the Canopy decided to capture him.

"What stopped you?'" Razial asked.

"Do you know why the Goraan Mountains are named in honor of Ja'Goraan?"

"No."

"Very well. Listen closely. Several members of the Canopy captured Ja'Goraan. He escaped. An army was sent after him. His followers entrenched themselves in the mountains that were then known as the Ciru Range. Six bloody battles were fought. Ja'Goraan survived them all and managed to flee back to Alf-Heim. Months later-"

Razial and all the others who do not know what had happened noticed she had left out something important. No one said anything because it was clear she would not reveal what she had left out.

"-we tracked Ja'Goraan back to the Ciru Range. More fighting ensued. His followers were eliminated, but he escaped. For two years, he evaded us. Then, Carpio led a massive army to drive us out of the mountains. Not wanting things to escalate, we returned to Alf-Heim. Carpio christened the mountains the Goraan Mountains because many of the humans in the area thought Goraan had battled us for ownership of the mountains."

"How long ago did all of this happen?" Kalvin asked.

"Just over four hundred years ago." Ulina answered.

"You say that as if it were just yesterday." Sidney stated.

"For me, it was just yesterday." Ulina smiled.

Anjia listened to that, but her mind is on the Six Heroes. She asked Ulina if there was anything else she could say about them besides what she had said already.

"Nothing more than glorified swordsmen." Havi said.

"They were useless as heroes." Adini stated.

"Yeah. The Conclave should have called them the Six Fools." Havi added.

"No." Adini smirked. "The Six Arrogant Fools."

"You two should learn how to hold a grudge." Fogi Red teased.

"Are you all finished?" Ulina pursed her lips.

With that the jolems fell silent, but the disgust they felt for the Six Heroes remained evident in their eyes.

Since Ulina had nothing new to say, Anjia stated that the prince of Brahma is all that stands between the world and Rakaar's Shadow. She eyed Razial. He ignored her glaring eyes. They know if they enter the city, they will have to target the prince because the Hilt has marked him for death. Razial does not have a problem with that.

Sidney asked about Rakaar's Shadow. Ulina told him to imagine a shadow covering the sky spreading in all directions simultaneously.

"Just imagine seeing the sun covered by a shadow. That is what the world would look like. The weather would turn very cold. Many would starve." Ulina said sadly.

She then told them to water the horses and that they would ride within the hour.

Ariel walked off listening to Araceli talk about how foolish the Society is acting. She told Ariel she believes Goraan is a Harbinger because he would not allow the Society to perform so many contracts that aid Rakaar's servants if he were not. Ariel did not respond. Her mind drifted to how the Order of the Flame killing their father pushed their mother to commit suicide and Daniel taking them in. Araceli was only a child and does not remember it like Ariel does. How Araceli can blame Goraan for how his actions affect others, but not find fault with the Order of the Flame bothers Ariel.

She finds it humorous that it is said Daniel found a loyal servant in her, but what they do not know is that he had found a witch destined to become a Harbinger!

"Araceli. I doubt Goraan would reveal himself so openly if he were a Harbinger." She said to her sister.

"Then, he is at least complicit in all this." Araceli sighed. "Goraan is definitely more involved than we know."

Ariel left it at that. She went about watering her horse and when it was time to ride again, she listened to Xochi suggest how to deal with the Magi. When she finished, Araceli had a question for Ulina.

"Keeper Ulina. Why would Troggo want to capture Razial?"

"Because, like the Harbingers, he wants to free Ja'Brahma. It is believed that if the Gideon frees Ja'Brahma Ja'Brahma's madness would be cured. Others think the Gideon must die to cure Ja'Brahma's madness. Ja'Troggo wants to use Razial to free Ja'Brahma or to allow the Magi to obtain their medallions which would free Ja'Brahma." Ulina said.

That made Ariel think. What drove Ja'Brahma mad was having too much power. He is still connected to all his power even though the Gideon is connected to his power also. She thinks killing the Gideon would disconnect Ja'Brahma from half of his powers, but the Master says she is incorrect. Since failing to capture the last Gideon, the Master is unwilling to take any action against Razial.

"Killing the Gideon is not the answer. We can use him to free Ja'Brahma and to control his madness. Ja'Brahma cannot be cured." Beulah had said to Ariel.

Ariel wonders if Troggo feels the same way.

*

Later, the group stopped for the night. They will reach Brahma city before noon the next day. Alena's hawks had informed them that the Harlequins had separated into several smaller groups and that some were close by. Sidney sat thinking about that while watching the camp. There are several fires burning around the camp so he can see well. He is trying to deal with all he has learned. He has not had time to really deal with all that has happened. He has spent most of his time with Kalvin, who is not as lost as he is.

Sitting around a fire with Mantak, Anjia, and Ulina, Sidney listened to them talk about an assassination that happened years earlier in Ino-Heim. He remembers when he used to think Ino-Heim was a myth.

"Are you sure Anjia?" Ulina asked.

"Of course, I am. I met this elf you speak of in the city of Giaour years past. He was with Rogelio. When I told Ja'Goraan about Rogelio helping him get a ship to Ino-Heim, Ja'Goraan was most displeased." Anjia said.

"But how do you know that it was Ja'Goraan who killed him in Ino-Heim?" Mantak asked.

"I asked Goraan who he is, and Goraan told me that Rogelio should not have helped him and that he was off to kill him."

"How is it that Ja'Goraan has a hand in all that is going on? I believe more that he is a Harbinger." Ulina stated.

Anjia asked her why she said this. Sidney does not understand the others' preoccupation with Goraan. He is confused by the fact Ulina believes Goraan is a Harbinger. He watched Ulina become more solemn. She told Anjia the elf they were talking about was Anjia's grandfather, her mother's father!

"There is more." Ulina said. "He was the link with the elfin wolves. His death is why the elfin wolves lost their ability to become invisible."

Razial locked eyes with Ulina. She did not have to say Goraan knew this before he killed Anjia's grandfather. He knows Goraan knew. He watched the fire flicker in her eyes. She watched a shadow move across his face.

"Take heart, Razial. No elfin animal shall lose its ability to become invisible while you live." She spoke.

Razial stood. He wants to think. He did not see Anjia stop herself from following him when she saw Xochi walk off after him.

"Razial." Xochi called. "May I talk with you for a while?" Xochi asked.

"What about?" He asked.

He did not look back at her. She quickened her pace so she could pull alongside him. With the moon giving off a bright yellowish light, visibility is good. She looked around and saw Scar's pack running around. The night air is cool. They are only a short distance from the others.

"My sister." Xochi answered. "The life debt you say you owe me. I want you to pay it to my sister."

Razial stopped and looked into her eyes. In the dark their color is hidden, but their shape remains cat-like. As pretty as her twin, she does not attract him like Zelia does. He does not know why he always notices that.

"Is that all?" He asked.

"No. I want you to hear something else. She likes it when you flirt with her. Although she tries to hide it. She is trying to fight fate. She will lose."

"She does not flirt with me." Razial countered. "I flir-"

"Come now, Razial." She cut him off. "You are fated to become the Gideon. You will have four keepers. Three bonded to Eloh and one bound to you. I remember the stories my great, great grandmother used to tell me about how she had tried in vain to stop herself from having feelings for the last Gideon. I have no doubt my twin and Anjia are fated to become two of your keepers. That is why Keeper Ulina allows Anjia to travel with us."

Razial did not respond. He sensed the truth in what she said. She went on saying that Alena is most likely another one of his keepers.

"Now, we only have to find one more. Treat my sister well."

Razial nodded. He then looked away when he sensed the wolves' excitement. Other elfin wolves are close by. He stepped around Xochi because the wolves can sense elves!

"What is it?" She asked.

Before Razial could respond, arrows hissed through the air. His sword was in his hand immediately.

"Razial!" Ulina called drawing her powers. "To me."

Xochi moved before him using her powers to deflect the arrows aimed at them. Running footsteps and arrows came from many directions. Razial back up watching the area. He saw tens of dark clothed figures running toward them from the shadows while drawing their powers. Xochi exchanged magical strikes with two foes. Razial sent his daggers tumbling toward them. Unlike all others before them, the Harlequins knew to avoid or draw more power to deflect the daggers.

"Harlequins!" Havi roared.

In an instant, fighting erupted all around the camp. Razial's sword was busy as a group of Harlequins swarmed him and Xochi. Tens of Harlequins battled Ulina, who gave them all they could handle. Mantak and the Ratels met another group of Harlequins head-on. The Harlequins' yataghans hissed through the air as they tried to overwhelm Razial and the others. Razial could not look around because he was too busy keeping himself alive, but he heard when Fogi Red shouted.

"Kalvin. Sidney. Cover my back. Stand back-to-back with me. Raal will get us through this.!"

Hard-pressed, Razial stood his ground. He managed to trip one of his attackers. That is when he heard Troggo say.

"Leave him. The Gideon is mine."

Before that moment, Razial fought with his usual confidence. After Troggo engaged him, he realized he needed help!

Anjia fought fiercely. Her short swords were as busy as her powers. Alena is battling by her side. They are holding their ground. Ulina is close to them. Her bluish sorcery is lighting up the area, but the Harlequins refuse to be driven off so easily.

Ariel and Araceli are fighting back-to-back. They stand over the Harlequins but are hard-pressed. Xochi and Zelia are fighting on the move trying to help all who need it. Adini and Havi helped Razial hold off Troggo while Mantak and the Ratels did all they could to keep the Harlequins from harming Kalvin, Sidney, Raal, and Fogi Red. Time seemed to drag on. Ulina became desperate.

She tried to drive off the Harlequins by lashing out to kill-killing six of them in a short period of time. That allowed Araceli and Ariel to rally around Fogi Red and those with him.

Xochi began to falter. She had kept Razial away from Troggo long enough for the jolems to reach him. However, she was wounded while fighting Troggo. Zelia did not notice until she fell to a knee. That is when she reached to help her up and touched her blood-soaked shirt. Her heart felt as if it had sunk. She knows Xochi must be healed or she will die!

"A Gideon without magical powers." Troggo said. "I never imagined that."

Standing over a dazed Razial, who lay on his back, Troggo prepared to bind him. He had simply outfought him then used his powers to knock him down.

Sensing two powerful magicians running toward him, he looked up. Before he recognized Goraan, Goraan and Rogelio were upon him. Goraan's sai daggers forced him to defend himself while Rogelio used his powers and his sword to keep Troggo backing up. Their actions angered him. He had been close to grabbing Razial before their arrival.

Kalvin's throat burned. Sweat covers his face and neck. He has several critical wounds and many minor wounds. Fogi Red is covered in blood-much of it his own, still he is in a rage. His battle ax whipped and whirled keeping several wounded Harlequins at bay. He and Kalvin are doing all they can to keep Raal, who is lying face down in the grass, alive.

Fogi Red refuses to give an inch, and Kalvin is watching his back. Fighting on pure instincts and desperation, Kalvin swung his sword nonstop. He is afraid if he stops, he will fall to the grass in exhaustion. Unbeknownst to Kalvin and those close to him, Goraan and Rogelio have stemmed the tide. Sidney saw Kalvin get cut across his back and decided they would all die. He charged two Harlequins, stabbing one in her hip and hitting the other in the face.

"Get Raal!" Sidney said.

Fogi Red pulled Raal back while Kalvin stepped forward wielding his sword like a mad man. Sidney felt a sense of relief because his actions had allowed Raal to be pulled to safety. His relief did not last long. A female Harlequin kicked him in his stomach and stabbed him four times in rapid succession. A pained expression came across his face. As he fell backward, he saw Araceli kill his killer. Mentally, he smiled. The fighting is no longer his problem.

After fighting Goraan and Rogelio for several minutes, Troggo decided he could not capture Razial. Although Ulina is close to exhaustion, he is too tired to take advantage of that and he has lost too many warriors. The elfin wolves in Scar's pack have kept Razial upright and there is no way around them. Had those with Razial not been more powerful than he had expected, he would have killed them and captured Razial.

"Until next time Fa'Ulina." He growled.

He disengaged his tiring foes and called a retreat. Then, as quickly as they had attacked, they disappeared into the shadows.

Down on one knee, Razial looked around. He sensed the elfin wolves' sadness. Twelve had died and four others are too injured to move. Goraan is already healing them. Troggo had used some elfin wolves to cover up the fact he was leading an attack on Razial and the others. He had known Scar's pack would focus on the other elf-in wolves before they realized he and his warriors were closing in. Razial shook his head when he saw Kalvin kneeling over Sidney. He heard Kalvin tell him the Harlequins are gone. Sidney laughed then died. That is when Razial saw Mantak bowing in respect to the two dead Ratels. They had died saving him. A short distance behind Ulina, he saw Zelia kneeling by Xochi, who was lying on her back. Ulina walked over to join them while the three other siblings made their way to Xochi. Anjia winced as she made her way to him with a solemn expression.

"How is Xochi?" He asked, keeping his voice low.

Xochi had fought well but Troggo was simply too powerful.

"Let us say good-bye. She deserves that much." Anjia said.

She led the way to where Xochi lies with her head in Zelia's lap. The jolems had said their good-byes. They wobbled off to talk with Goraan. Razial had not seen them until then because others had blocked his view.

"Look at you." Xochi smiled. He smiled back. "Our greatest hope. Remember our talk."

He saw tears stream down Zelia's face. Xochi will not survive. He can only imagine how she feels. Anjia began to heal him while Xochi continued.

"Never forget what I told you, Razial. And thank you for bringing Kalvin into our lives. He is turning out well." She smiled at Kalvin, who smiled back.

A moment later the others left Zelia alone with her twin. Razial watched Ulina walk with purpose toward Goraan, who stood talking with Mantak. He heard Alena tell Ariel she had healed

Raal and Fogi Red. He kept his focus on Ulina because Mantak had moved away while she approached.

"Why are you here Ja'Goraan?" Ulina demanded.

"Just think." Goraan mused with a grin. "I was happy to talk with Mantak, and you have come to ruin the moment."

"I am not that tired, Ja'Goraan." Ulina warned.

"And you are not that foolish either." Goraan growled. "I am here with Rogelio, Anjia, who you now know is my daughter and Razial."

Goraan took note that Mantak had went to say good-bye to Xochi. He and Ulina know Mantak would take no action against him unless he acts first. Adini and Havi feel the same way about him.

"Now if you do not mind A'Ulina, I would like to talk with Havi and Adini before Rogelio, Anjia, and I go to Brahma to await Razial's arrival." Goraan glanced at Razial.

Anjia scowled at Goraan, who paid her no mind. He turned around and began talking to the jolems. Ulina glared at Rogelio, who remained stoic, before walking off. Anjia tried to argue with Goraan, but Razial stopped her. They know exactly what Goraan is doing. Goraan had just given him an order to go to Brahma and kill the prince.

By taking Anjia with him, Goraan is keeping her safe. Razial knows if Goraan had a way to kill the prince, he would have killed him. The Order of the Flame has outplayed him by hiding the prince and allowing the tension to build. He is using Razial to counter their action.

"He wants you to go to Brahma!" Anjia whispered angrily. "He is trying to bring about Rakaar's Shadow."

"Anjia." Razial clenched his teeth. "This is our way. Do not forget that."

"Razial. This is not something he should allow." Anjia growled.

Face to face, arm in arm, they walked in a circle. Razial had to admit that she has a point, but he trusts Goraan. After hearing all the stories about Goraan, he is sure Goraan does not serve Rakaar. Although he has kept it hidden, Goraan is a hero in the war against Rakaar.

Seeing Razial would go along with Goraan's plan, Anjia pulled away from him. Alena walked over to them. She sensed the tension between them. She looked at them but did not get the chance to ask what is wrong because Goraan called to her.

"Alena'fa. It has been far too long. I have missed you."

Alena likes how he speaks ancient elvish so elegantly. Before she could say anything, Anjia said.

"Then you should invite her to ride with us. I am sure she has a lot to say to you."

Goraan sensed the sarcasm in her voice. He smiled at her and Alena.

"Surely, you can convince the Blue Keeper to allow you to accompany us. The Red Keeper and the Yellow Keeper are already there." Goraan looked back at Anjia.

"Go now." Ulina said in elvish.

Anjia frowned at Goraan, who turned to look at Mantak.

"What game are you playing?" Mantak asked in ancient elvish.

"I am playing no game. I am making a point from an assassin-"

Goraan glanced at Anjia. "-to another assassin. It is good to see you well, Mantak."

"We should meet in Alf-Heim, soon." Mantak replied. "Until next time."

Razial realized there is a lot more to Mantak simply crossing paths with Goraan several times. Goraan bid everyone farewell. Kalvin walked over to Razial and asked why Alena was going with Goraan and the others.

"Because Goraan misses her and Anjia wants company." Razial answered.

Adini and Havi told the others to gather the bodies so they could bury them. Mantak stayed close to Razial while they did as the jolems said. In the yellowish moonlight, Mantak appears menacing. Razial looked around when they finished. Fogi Red and Raal are asleep. They had been too tired to help. The elfin wolves all gathered around one of the fires. Those that had arrived with the Harlequins, have joined Scar's pack.

*

Lying on his sleeping blanket, Razial thought about how the others had fallen asleep shortly after the bodies were buried. He knows they would wake with the slightest out of place noise, so he must be quiet when he leaves.

He slowly rose to his feet. Mantak stared at him, but the others remained with their eyes closed. Mantak walked a short distance with him whispering that he does not know why Goraan had taken Anjia, but he knows Goraan wants Razial to go to Brahma. Razial did not respond. Mantak did not need him to.

Mostly mouthing the words, Razial said Goraan probably has a message he only trusts Alena to deliver to Ulina. Mantak nodded, but he senses Razial is trying to misdirect him.

"Why does he want you to go to Brahma?" He asked.

Knowing Mantak knows Goraan want him to go to Brahma city Razial decided not to lie.

"I must go. I will see you tomorrow." Razial said.

"Why must you go? Assassin's business?"

"Yes. Something only, I can do for him." Mantak nodded in response then stepped back.

"Why?" Razial asked.

"Could I stop you without a fight?"

"No." Razial shook his head.

Mantak gestured for him to go. He warned him about the shadow-tracker. Razial nodded as he untethered his horse. He will kill the prince, but he wants answers afterward.

CHAPTER 11

THE AVATAR

As usual, the novices had delivered the keepers' breakfast. However, unlike most mornings, the two keepers had been awake sitting on their beds awaiting their arrival. They told the novices to prepare their private chambers for a meeting.

Bernice started the teasing like always. The room is not big, but it has not been cleaned in several days. Before, the novices spent each morning cleaning the house, but that changed last week when the keepers increased their practice hours so they could better wield their powers.

"Our enemies have intensified their actions. We must do the same." Tu'ani and Lela had said.

Bernice and Vera tied back the curtains, and the room brightened while Ofelia and Niri dusted the rugs. Lissa fluffed and dusted the floor pillows that lined the back wall. Vera began to sweep the wooden floor while Bernice opened the shutters making the room even brighter.

After placing the rugs by the doorway, Ofelia and Niri began washing the walls. There are no tables, only two wooden chairs. To Ofelia, that was odd.

"I wonder what the meeting is about." Lissa grinned.

"The prince. Since he is back in the palace." Niri mused.

"Why would they need to talk about the prince? Every attempt to kill him has failed." Bernice smirked.

Ofelia thought about that. What Bernice had said is true. Since the prince has returned to the palace, several attempts on his life have been made. What very few know is the general, who acted as the prince's steward is not just any other ally to the Order of Flame. He is a bulwark named Dwight. He is second only to Barthus in reputation. Ofelia and the other novices had been shocked to discover that Dwight is the bulwark they had read so much about.

Dwight had taken over the city when the prince went into hiding. Tu'ani and Lela used him to keep the royal family in line while they eliminated several foes.

"I wonder who is coming to the meeting." Lissa said.

"That is not your concern." The keepers said as they entered the room.

They walked through the doorway staring at the room. They told the novices to go meet with the five siblings, who are waiting for them. Ofelia was shocked to hear them say they want Razial found and given an order.

Unlike the other novices, Ofelia knows Razial. The last she was told; he was headed to Brahma to join them. She wants to know what happened.

While they all walked to the front of the house, Ofelia heard Lissa ask.

"I wonder what the order is?"

"Probably for him to follow us home." Niri said playfully.

***

Anjia, Alena, and Goraan sat around a small wooden table eating breakfast. The room they are in is next to the kitchen. Geoffrey's servant cooked and served them breakfast. Rogelio is eating in his room. Goraan had stopped Larry from serving Rogelio saying.

"You are not a servant, little brother. You are one of us. Go and help your father."

Anjia noticed the expression on Larry's face when Goraan called him little brother. Goraan has always known how to handle individuals. She knows Larry will always remember Goraan treating him like an equal.

Looking at Alena, she knows Goraan deeply missed her, but she also knows he wants something from her. She listened for clues of what that something might be while he explained the Society will help the Order of the Flame against the Magi. He gave Alena a lot of information. She and Anjia were shocked by how much he knows about the Order of the Flame's actions. Anjia paid close attention to when he told Alena that Tu'ani and Lela have been outplayed by Rakaar's servants inside the city of Brahma.

"They have allowed the royals and their guests too much leeway and too much time together." Goraan said.

"Maybe because they have been too busy stopping those you have sent after the prince." Alena countered.

Anjia smiled at that. She turned to face Goraan.

"And yet, it was to stop the royals from revolting against Dwight that they brought him out of hiding." Goraan replied.

He let that set in. Then, he told Alena the keepers should have killed Igor, the leader of Pu'um's dignitaries. Alena did not ask why. She knows he has targeted Igor as a servant of Rakaar. She asked him why he wanted the prince dead.

"Because he is in league with the Theocracy." Goraan answered.

That was enough for her. He then told her to tell her leaders not to try to act against him after the prince is killed. She and Alena frowned at him. Anjia told him Razial will find a way not to kill the prince. He shook his head while smirking at her. She can sense how sure he is the prince will die.

"Uncle. A'Ulina will order Razial to protect the prince when they arrive." She said.

Goraan smiled. Anjia looked at her. She sensed that something was wrong. She did not understand the subtle hint Goraan had given to Razial. She asked Anjia what was bothering her. Anija explained that by telling Razial he would be waiting for him in Brahma Goraan had really ordered Razial to kill the prince!

"How?" Alena asked.

"Because he marked the prince for death. I would have had to act against the prince had I entered the city without him and Rogelio." Anjia explained.

"That is why you brought Anjia." Alena trailed off.

She realized he had made sure Razial does all he can to kill the prince by keeping Anjia safe. She asked Goraan why he and Rogelio do not kill the prince.

"Oh, we shall, if he survives the Avatar."

She dislikes it when he calls Razial by his moniker. She knows he does not do so often and when he does it is to make a point. She asked why he is so sure Razial will kill the prince.

"Alena'fa. Have you forgotten who Razial is? I would not doubt it if he snuck away from the others after we left. No one can order him to protect the prince if they cannot talk to him. I will say the prince will be dead in two days." Goraan said flatly.

"You do know that you are making it possible for the Magi to bring Rakaar's Shadow to the world?" Anjia asked sarcastically.

"Oh, now you are worried about the world. You should have thought like that before you became an assassin." Goraan said.

"Did I really have a choice? My father is known as the Merciless."

"And yet, I am the one who told you and Razial not to become assassins. Now, fate has proven me correct."

Alena closed her eyes. She knows Goraan had tried to stop Anjia and Razial from joining the Society. However, his attempts to discourage them only made them rise faster in the Society's ranks. A vision filled her mind. She saw a dark shadow slowly covering the sky while Anjia took actions to help the Order of the Flame.

"Alena." Anjia called.

She sensed Alena was having a vision. Only they know about Alena's visions. Anjia will try to keep it that way until Alena says otherwise.

In her mind, Goraan's arrogance about being able to manipulate Razial had triggered the vision.

"Razial is going to kill the prince." Alena said.

That angered Anjia. She turned on Goraan and told him that Mantak had told her that Goraan had killed his first wife just like he had killed her mother, his second wife.

"What else did Mantak tell you?" Goraan asked.

Alena frowned. She knows what had happened to Anjia's mother. Goraan had killed her for betraying him. She had never heard of Goraan having another wife before that. Hearing he had killed her too was shocking. Anjia's talks with Mantak are a lot deeper than she had expected. Mantak's interest in Anjia intrigues her even more.

"That it is highly likely that you are a Harbinger. This action of yours makes that seem true."

"It always comes back to that." Goraan shook his head.

"Is it true? Are you a Harbinger?" Anjia asked.

"If I were a Harbinger, what would you do about it? What do you know about the Harbingers"

Anjia did not respond. Goraan turned to Alena and said only she has turned out correctly. He then told her it is important for the Order of the Flame to focus on the Magi and those who serve them.

"Ignore the Harbingers. Tracking them is like handling a poisonous snake with oily hands." He said.

"You are a Harbinger." Anjia hissed. "That is why you are so reckless with Razial. You know he is fated to become the Gideon, yet you send him on this task. You allow the hunt to continue, and you refuse to answer my question."

"Do you think Binu, Carpio, Tollok, and Rogelio are Harbingers also?" Goraan stood.

He had finished his food.

"Have you forgotten that I do not lead the Hilt? Then," He paused. "Tell me how we could call off the hunt without losing honor."

He patted Anjia on her head while saying it is good that she is concerned for the world. Anjia looked away from him. He moved around her and caressed Alena's head before he began to exit the room while saying.

"Do not forget what I said about Igor. The prince must die, so we can weed out Rakaar's servant inside the royal house. And I am not a Harbinger."

With that, he was off. Alena and Anjia began to talk about her vision. Anjia listened and wished she could help the Order of the Flame stop Rakaar's Shadow from entering the world.

"Goraan knows too much." She stated.

"True. However, he has never lied to us. Now, let us meet with Lela and Tu'ani. We have to try to stop Razial before he kills the prince." Alena said.

They stared into each other's eyes. They could not be any closer than they are. No matter how angry they are, they can never stop caring about each other.

"You could face a hunt if we are successful." Alena said.

"I am all right with that. I would only have to make it all the way to Alf-Heim where I would pass the hunt." Anjia smiled.

***

Razial saw no point in delaying. After entering the city, he made his way into the palace. He used his elfin burnoose to walk around. He heard the palace guard scrambling around. Something is wrong. Groups of guards moved through the hallways with purpose.

Walking with his back against the wall, his eyes lowered when he saw two Danouan priests. Their white surplices make them appear ghostly. He increased his pace-moving straight at them because he heard a group of guards storming through the hallway behind him.

"What is going on?" The prince asked.

Razial saw no point in delaying. After entering the city, he made his way into the palace. He used his elfin burnoose to walk around. He heard the palace guard scrambling around. Something is wrong. Groups of guards moved through the hallways with purpose.

Walking with his back against the wall, his eyes lowered when he saw two Danouan priests. Their white surplices make them appear ghostly. He increased his pace-moving straight at them because he heard a group of guards storming through the hallway behind him.

"What is going on?" The prince asked.

He is still inside his quarters while the priests are out in the hallway. Razial moved by them unnoticed. He saw the prince approaching him, so he slid to the right.

Average in height, the prince is well built. Dressed regally with a long sword at his right hip-meaning he is left-handed, the prince's short wavy hair is combed back. While staring at the darkness of his hair, a passing thought told him to kill the prince then and there. He pushed the thought away. He is not that desperate.

"What is going on, Dwight?" The prince asked.

Razial crept deeper into the front room.

"Your Majesty. There is an assassin in the city ready to act against you." Dwight said.

"So?" The prince scoffed. "I trust you to keep me safe."

"This time is different, my lord."

"How so?"

Dwight stood with guards behind him and Barthus to his right. Tu'ani and Lela had contacted him and told him Razial is in Brahma to kill the prince. They told him to not to harm Razial and to order Razial to protect the prince.

After stopping multiple assassinations, he feels as though he must tell the prince the truth.

"The Avatar of Death is here for you, my lord. Let me leave Barthus to be your personal guard while I hunt down the assassin."

"No." The prince said dismissively. "These two are my personal guards. You are my general. Deal with this Avatar of Death. I must see to preparing the palace for my inauguration."

Razial heard the prince say this. He decided to kill him upon his return.

"He has no idea, does he?" Barthus asked shaking his head.

Razial heard Barthus say this. He knows he is Barthus the Brawler. He has heard Binu wonder who would win if Barthus and Rogelio fought. For Dwight to be so sure Barthus could stop him shows a lot of faith in the legendary bulwark. Razial has no idea who Dwight truly is.

***

Kalvin and the others had arrived at the mansion just before noon. Although he is disturbed by Razial's decision to sneak off, he is anxious to see Ofelia. While Raal and Mantak looked after the elfin wolves, Fogi Red, Kalvin, and the two jolems sat in the meeting hall. Ulina had sent the siblings in their group to search for Razial. She also sent the Ratels to rest. Kalvin understands why she ordered them to rest. They had suffered a lot to keep Mantak alive. He still feels the effects of fighting the Harlequins, so he can only imagine how they must feel.

Wondering where Ofelia is, Kalvin listened to the others talk.

"You two know Goraan." Fogi Red said to the jolems.

"Why would he help the Magi bring Rakaar's Shadow to the world?"

"He is not helping the Magi. You heard what Alena told the keepers. The prince stands with the Theocracy." Adini said.

"Still, he could simply lock the prince up." Fogi Red said.

"You do know you are a dwarf." Havi smirked.

At that moment, Kalvin realized they were talking in dwarvish. He has become so prolific in understanding languages that he can now speak them. Ancient elvish and ancient dwarvish still escape him, but Ulina assured him he would speak them, soon.

"What are you talking about?" Fogi Red asked Havi.

"Think. How long can you hold the prince? Until he has a son?" Havi asked sarcastically.

"Until we reimprison the Magi." Fogi Red countered.

"Killing the Magi would be easier." Adini countered.

"But killing the Magi would mean the end." Kalvin stated.

The two jolems smirked. Fogi Red agreed with Kalvin. Adini then explained that Rakaar's Shadow will cause famine and panic, but it would not mean the end.

"Rakaar's Shadow goes away when we the Magi die." Adini said.

"Yeah." Havi nodded in agreement.

"You two would say that." Daniel said as he entered the room.

He startled Kalvin. His gray cowl floats as he walks. Kalvin could not help but think of a Harbinger. Before meeting Razial, he had only seen a druid-sibling twice. He has no idea if it were the same individual or not. He had never tried to stare into the faceless cowl before, so it never bothered him that he could not see the druid-sibling's face. Now, it does.

"Stay as you are." The three keepers said entering the room. "We do not have time for protocol."

Mantak and Raal walked in behind them. They sat with the others while the keepers stood in the middle of the room. Without delay, they revealed all who are fated to become paladins saying they are not mistaken and that others will soon be revealed.

"Some of you might die. It takes five paladins to make another paladin, but the Gideon can do so on his own-so long as two others live. Remember, there can only be eight bonded to a Gideon."

The keepers' words shocked Kalvin and Fogi Red, who still does not want to be a paladin.

"What about his keepers?" Mantak asked.

"Three of them are known. Two of them we know. The third we do not know. We do know she will be his fourth keeper-his Gray Keeper. His Blue Keeper and his Red Keeper are perfect for us. His Yellow Keeper still must be found. If Ja'Goraan is seen, act against him. Kalvin. A group of bulwarks await you. Go with them to the palace. Razial will not act against you. Be sure to order him to protect the prince."

Kalvin left with that. He has no idea what they will discuss, which is why he wishes he could stay and find out. He is excited about being fated to become a paladin. Razial had warned him they were involved in something very worldly.

Shaking his head, he thought how Razial had yet to embrace the change in their lives.

***

Razial heard the prince return. The two priests returned with him. He had waited for hours. Although he waited patiently, his stomach did not. He is very hungry. He pulled the hood to his burnoose over his head and used its power to make himself invisible while he crossed the prince's bedroom. He heard the priests walking around lighting candles. He still has not decided if he is going to kill them or not.

"How long will it take them to realize the crown I gave them is fake?" A priest asked.

"They will not know until they try to take it out of the city." The other priest said.

The prince laughed. He stated how he had thought about giving the crown to the keepers himself but decided it would seem better if he allowed the priest to hand it over to them. Their conversation then went to trying to prove the Cardinal, the leader of the Theocracy, is a traitor. With Cas in Danou city the priests hate being in Brahma city, but if they can return with the ancient crown of Brahma, it would be worth it.

Razial thought about how they feel as if the Cardinal is out for power and has moved too far from Cas' ways. He does not care about this information but will pass it on. His focus is on the ancient crown. He will give it to Goraan.

Hearing the prince walking toward the bedroom, Razial exhaled. He walked by the prince. His eyes adjusted to the light. The priests stood facing away from him. They never had a chance. He called his daggers and drove them into the bases of their skulls. Their bodies tensed as their powers tried to pass through his daggers. Their bodies went limp a second later as they fell to the floor. Razial spun around and walked back to the prince's bedroom. The prince had already undressed. He rolled on to his back. Razial walked over to the bed. The prince opened his eyes. He heard Razial's steps. Razial moved quickly. He put a dagger against his throat while pressing his thumb against his eye.

"Where is the crown?" Razial asked between clenched teeth. "This is the last time I will ask."

Razial released his eye and pulled back his burnoose's hood revealing his face to the prince. He wants him to know he is going to die. The only question is how. Looking up at Razial, the prince pointed at a wooden chest against the back wall. Razial stared at him. He watched as fear filled his eyes.

"I swear it. The crown is there!" The prince said.

Razial remained still. Time is on his side. He could kill him then search the entire chamber.

"I swear it." The prince pleaded with his eyes.

"I believe you." Razial said.

He plunged the dagger into his throat and up through his brain killing him. Releasing the dagger, he turned around and picked up the chest. After opening the chest, he saw the crown. Without pause, he put the crown under his shirt. He walked back to the front room. Blood pooled around the priests' heads. He walked past their bodies while pulling the hood over his head.

He stood by the door and listened. Hearing nothing, he opened the door slightly and slid out closing the door behind him. He put his back against the wall as he crept through the hallway. He has to eat so he will go straight to Geoffrey's house. That way he can eat and meet with Goraan at the same time.

***

The next morning, Dwight and Barthus were shocked by the fact no one inside the palace had encountered Razial. After his talk with the prince, he had two guards posted at the bottom of each staircase on the third and second floors. He told them to watch the stairs in three shifts after dinner was served. Ariel, Zelia, and Araceli helped search for Razial but found nothing.

After a short discussion, Dwight and the others decided to do a room-to-room search and to leave four men in the middle of each staircase. It is well past breakfast, and they want to know why the prince is still in his quarters.

Making their way through the palace, Ariel, Araceli, and Zelia all have different mindsets. Zelia is disappointed by Razial's decision to sneak off. She cannot wait to confront him. Xochi had died keeping him safe and he is betraying her memory.

Araceli is surprised by Razial's willingness to kill the prince knowing it will allow the Magi to release Rakaar's Shadow. The fact that does not give him pause is why she had told the keepers to ask if he is possibly in league with the Harbingers. She told them not to just look at Goraan.

Unlike her sister and Zelia, Ariel wants Razial to succeed. It is part of the Master's plan. Where she too feels disappointment, her disappointment is over not already finding the prince dead.

"I wonder why he is still sleeping." Zelia said in Tuyakan.

"He probably got drunk with his priests friends." Araceli said.

"We will have to do something about them, soon." Ariel stated.

They approached the prince's door. Zelia walked ahead and knocked on the door. No reply came. Araceli knocked harder while calling out to the prince. Ariel took a deep breath because she smelled blood in the air. Araceli was about to knock again, but Ariel stopped her. She pushed open the door. The smell of blood filled their nostrils. The sight of the dead priests sprawled on the floor filled their vision. She had to stop herself from smiling. She walked by the bodies and made her way to the prince's bedroom. With no one to see her, she smiled at the sight of the dead prince. His torso was lying in blood. She stopped smiling as she turned around and told her sister to call Dwight and Barthus. Araceli did not say a word. She simply left the room as soon as she saw the prince's body. Zelia shook her head in frustration while saying she will contact the keepers.

The keepers were truly angry about the news of the prince's death. They told Zelia to make sure no one outside of the Order of the Flame finds out about the prince being dead.

"We are on our way. Tell Dwight to be ready for war!" The keepers thought.

They ended contact with Zelia, who told Ariel all they had thought to her. She then told Ariel it would be best if they waited outside the door. Ariel agreed and they quickly left the room, closing the door behind them.

"They do not call Razial the Avatar of Death because it sounds menacing." Ariel said in Tuyakan.

Zelia knows she had said this to tell her not to be surprised Razial had already killed the prince, but something in Ariel's green eyes seems unbothered by what Razial had done.

"He does not care how difficult he has made things for us and the world." Zelia said.

"Zelia. Do not forget he has made things more difficult for himself. He is the Gideon." Ariel replied.

"I doubt he gave that any thought." Zelia scowled.

"Of course he did. Ask him the next time you talk to him."

They fell silent after that because Barthus led Kalvin and Araceli toward them. Ariel stared at Barthus. He is taller than average, but he would not be described as tall. He is shorter than Kalvin, but much bigger and broader. His broad shoulders are heavily muscled, and his muscles are bulging because he is walking with his battle axes in his hands.

"Dwight is behind us. There was no sign of Razial." Barthus stated.

"We are going to need bulwarks to clean this mess without anyone noticing. The keepers are en route to the palace." Ariel shook her head.

Barthus nodded. Kalvin remained silent. He is no longer the in over his head thief Ariel had met when all this had started. He has matured a lot.

Seconds later, Dwight walked through the hallway. Ariel thought about him. He was born in central Brahma and grew up in the capital. His father was an agent for the Order of the Flame which led to him becoming a bulwark. As time went by, Dwight became more integral in controlling Brahma city. Through the decades, he has performed many tasks and led many battles. All the while he has risen in the ranks of the Brahman army.

Before the prince was put into hiding, he had never had any problems with the royal family even though some thought he was in cahoots with another member of the family, who they think was behind the king's assassination.

"How long has he been dead?" Dwight asked.

Zelia looked at him. Medium, in height and build, he has long dark hair. His beard is short with no gray hair, which is impressive because he is over eighty years old!

"Since last night. The keepers want you ready for war." Zelia said.

"Damn!" Dwight shook his head. "The assassin is more of a fool than I thought. Are the keepers sure he is the Gideon?"

No one responded. Araceli stated there is something else going on with Razial. Kalvin stood listening to them bad mouth Razial for several minutes. He knows what Razial has done is wrong to those who serve Eloh, but Razial does not serve Eloh. He is an assassin and had acted under orders from one of his leaders.

Hearing them accuse Razial of having an ulterior motive angered Kalvin. Alena and Anjia had informed the keepers about Razial's intentions beforehand, so the fault lies with them.

"Well." Kalvin said firmly. "We can only blame ourselves. We failed to stop him. Besides, Razial is the one who has to face the Magi."

"Kalvin." Araceli turned to face him. "You cannot defend this. This is too serious!"

"I am not defending him. I am blaming us-not him. You do not blame a snake for being a snake. Razial is an assassin. We wanted him here. We are at fault."

"Well said, Kalvin." Barthus turned to face Dwight. "Call all loyal to you. We will act immediately before the truth comes out. This way it will seem as if you retaliated. We will tell everyone the priests attacked the prince-who we will say is near death and will die tomorrow."

Kalvin could not believe how quickly Barthus had come up with that cover story.

What makes it so impressive is how truthful it sounds. He had never expected Barthus to be such a good liar. His mind began to drift. Razial has put him in a bind.

***

Razial sat eating lunch with Goraan. After leaving the prince's quarters, he encountered an unexpected setback: the guards blocking the stairs. However, he managed to escape notice during the first shift change.

He had arrived at Geoffrey's house late in the night. Still, Geoffrey had his servant make him something to eat. Razial had paid the woman well, four gold coins for her trouble. After he ate, Goraan told him to give the crown to the Order of the Flame. He did not say why.

During breakfast, he explained he is still in the city in case Troggo catches the Order of the Flame off guard. He told Razial half the palace guard is loyal to the Theocracy and will cause Dwight grief when they discover the prince, and the priests are dead. He ended the conversation by saying not to be surprised when the Order of the Flame launches an attack on its foes inside the city.

"They do not see Igor as a threat. Fools." Goraan had said in the morning.

Razial had asked why he does not deal with Igor. Goraan's answer was typical for him.

"Because he is not yet our problem."

Thinking about Goraan's response made Razial think. Goraan is not worried about Rakaar's Shadow because Goraan knows the Order of the Flame will have to kill the Magi if they release Rakaar's Shadow. He does not want the Magi imprisoned. He wants them dead!

To him, it is better to deal with whatever form Rakaar returns the Magi's powers because it gets rid of their servants.

Thinking about that, Razial finished his orange juice. Hearing the servant leading someone through the house they stared at each other. Neither had invited anyone to Geoffrey's house. With Rogelio off seeing to an errand, they smiled because they knew that means it is Anjia.

"So, what now, Ja'Goraan?" Anjia asked in elvish.

Razial turned to look at her. That is when he saw Alena enter the kitchen. Neither looked at him.

"Why would you two do this?" Alena asked.

"Anjia." Goraan said firmly. "You should stop being angry with me when you do not know what is going on. Alena, I will expect nothing but patience from you, from now on. I know what is going on. You two do not."

"Really?" Alena smirked.

She knows not to push Goraan too far. He had expected them to be angry with him, but he would not let them disrespect him.

"So, you are aware that Keeper Tu'ani has planned multiple assaults on nobles, generals, and merchants throughout the city? I guess" Alena's voice was full of sarcasm. "-you also know the shadow-tracker has returned? What about who will be the next leader of Brahma city?"

Goraan stared into her narrow brown eyes. Her yellow skin seems to glow. Her hair is hiding her elflocks, but there is no mistaken she is an elf. He turned his attention to Anjia. She is tanner than Alena. He knows he has disappointed her. She had hoped he would have changed his mind. She had also hoped Razial would disobey him.

"To your questions." Goraan turned to face Alena. "Yes. No. And I do not care."

Alena asked him how he could help bring Rakaar's Shadow into the world. He told her he did not help bring Rakaar's Shadow into the world and that the Order of the Flame could still kill the Magi or stop them from releasing Rakaar's Shadow.

"Understand. I want the Magi dead. This will make your order act to kill them." He said.

"Tell me, Ja'Goraan. Why did you not kill the prince?" Anjia asked, not expecting an answer.

"Because had I killed him, you would have been less of a keeper to Razial. You are fated to become his Blue Keeper."

His words stunned her. Her eyes went to Razial, who shook his head to signal he did not know Goraan would say that. She turned back to Goraan. A weight had been lifted from his shoulders. Her anger disappeared. He had manipulated all this for her sake!

"How long have you known?" She asked.

"Some things I cannot reveal. Sometimes, leaders must give orders they do not want to give."

"How did you know about Tu'ani's assaults?" Alena asked.

"Educated guess." Goraan stood and smiled. "Razial has a gift for your leaders."

He caressed Anjia's and Alena's heads on his way out.

"Wait." Alena said. "Stay and talk with us. The fighting will start soon. I am not due back until dusk."

Goraan looked at Anjia, who tilted her head to show she does not mind if he stays.

While they talked, Razial noticed no one brought up who his other keepers are. He is sure they want to know. He also has a sense Goraan knew who the others might be.

***

Tu'ani did not just deflect the magical strike unleashed at her, she sent it back at the warlock, who had unleashed it. To make matters worse for the warlock, she sent several strikes of her own with the deflected strike. He was sent crashing against the back wall. His bones snapped. Death took him, instantly.

Breathing hard, but slowly, Tu'ani looked around. Four other foes lay dead inside the room. Their bodies are sprawled around the room. She had killed them all. She heard the fighting around the estate end. She hears no sound of fighting which means the mini civil war is over.

With her hair unkept, Zelia walked into the room. Her breasts heaved as she slowed her breathing. Looking at her, Tu'ani could not help but think of Xochi.

"It is done, Keeper Tu'ani." Zelia said.

"And Igor?" She asked.

"His men" Zelia shook her head. "-were too loyal. They died so he could escape."

"Our losses?"

"Ten bulwarks and two siblings have taken their final rest."

"And young Razial?"

"He has minor injuries, but nothing serious. His information paid off. Dwight shall rule until the royal house chooses a new leader."

"You are still angry with him." Tu'ani smiled knowingly. "I know you have tried to fight your feelings, but they have only grown stronger."

"I am not that angry. I simply want him to chan-"

"I am not talking about your anger, child." Tu'ani cut her off. "I am talking about your love for Razial."

Zelia's eyes widened in surprise. She could not believe what Tu'ani had just said. Her heart began to pound. She became nervous. Her mind felt heavy. She wondered if she should deny that she loves Razial or not. Tu'ani gave her no choice.

"The love you feel is not your doing. Its strength is because of fate. You cannot love anyone but him. You shall be his second wife. His Red Keeper."

Zelia could not respond. She simply let what Tu'ani said set in while waiting for her to reveal more.

"I tell you this now because Razial shall know this soon. Let us return to the palace and meet with the others." Tu'ani nodded.

They began to walk out of the mansion. Zelia is impressed by her. She had caught the nobles, who had secretly sided with a royal to push for power, off guard. For three days, the fighting had lasted. Had it not been for Razial, the fighting would have lasted longer.

Igor's forces were held up in secret. The Society discovered their location and Razial led the assault to finish them. Tu'ani and Zelia accompanied him. The fighting had been fierce, but now it is over.

***

Ulina and the other keepers sat around a small table in a dimly lit room. Although they had met after the fighting ended, they decided to meet for breakfast to discuss what to do with Razial. After he had given them the real ancient crown of Brahma, they decided it was time to send him to Anazi Falls. With their enemies under foot, they must decide who will accompany him to Anazi Falls.

"Before we begin, are we still agreed about what we are going to do about the telepathy?" Tu'ani asked.

During her trip back from the fighting, they had contacted her and informed her they had sensed someone using telepathy inside the palace. When Lela went to check it out, she encountered Ariel, who told her she had seen someone sneaking around, but did not know who it was. They decided how to deal with that before they went to sleep.

"Yes." Ulina said.

"It will not change." Lela added.

With that settled, they began talking about setting aside the problems they have with Goraan. They discussed how they will have to tell others to put aside their feelings about Goraan being a Harbinger. They know that will not be easy, but they must trust he is going to help them. The fact he had Razial give them the ancient crown of Brahma will make things a lot easier for them.

They ended their meeting by choosing who would accompany Razial to Anazi Falls.

***

Kalvin sat talking with Razial. They are in Razial's room with Razial sitting on his bed while Kalvin is sitting on a chair by the door. They had just finished talking with Alena and Anjia, who both left only seconds earlier.

The four of them had talked about how it would be better if Alena kept others from talking about the prince's assassination to

Razial. It is why Razial and Barthus are at odds and why others had to stop Razial and Dwight from fighting.

After seeing Anjia and Alena kiss Razial good-bye, Kalvin told him that is not fair.

"What?" Razial asked.

"You have all the luck. Anjia and Alena. Not to mention you will have two more women once you become the Gideon."

"Sometimes, having Anjia and Alena is more trouble than I can handle. As for the other two" Razial paused to think. "-they might cause me more problems. Plus, you have Ofelia and you both are fated to become paladins."

That made Kalvin think. Before he had talked with Ofelia, he had debated whether he should reveal he is to become a paladin to her or not. After he found out she too is to become a paladin, he realized their meeting was no mere coincidence-nor is her being in Brahma.

"Like you and Anjia. You're both assassins and..." Kalvin trailed off.

Razial had confided in him about Anjia being his Blue Keeper, so he lowered his voice not wanting to be overheard. Razial winked at Kalvin for stopping himself from saying what he was going to say. Razial smiled because Kalvin is convinced Alena is going to be his Yellow Keeper.

"Raz." Kalvin smiled. "You truly have the luck of a dwarf building with gold."

Razial shook his head because Sidney used to say that. To him, Sidney had died a senseless death. Had he chosen to stay in Coilu, he would probably still be alive helping the Order of the Flame.

"Too bad Sidney is dead. He was used like a piece in the gods' game." Razial said.

Kalvin's blue eyes held Razial's gaze. Freshly shaved, Kalvin has an experience in his eyes that was not there before they went back to Mohr. He has seen more death and survived more danger than he had expected. Although he does not know as much about what is going on as Razial, he has grown tired of Razial's attitude toward their fate. To him, Razial must stop fighting the fact he is Eloh's champion.

"At least, he died for what he believed in." Kalvin said.

"And only we will remember that. His death was useless. He should have stayed in Coilu."

"Was Xochi's death useless?"

"No. It allowed me to kill the prince."

The sarcasm in Razial's tone made Kalvin clench his teeth. Still, he had a comeback.

"Because you are the perfect tool."

Kalvin's words struck a nerve, but Razial remained stoic.

"Look a woman in her eyes as you kill her. When you can do that without regret, you will be ready to be Eloh's tool. Go visit Ofelia. I am going to talk with the keepers."

Razial extended his hand to show there were no hard feelings. Kalvin stood and clasped his hand around his hand.

"We will talk on our way to Anazi Falls, like we used to. Only we will not be stealing and killing for fortune." Razial said.

Kalvin smiled. They both know things will never be like they used to be.

*

Razial sat listening to the keepers explain that upon his arrival to Anazi Falls Daniel will tell him what to do. They told him he would learn their darkest secret and why they kept it. To him, that makes no sense because he thought Ja'Brahma being alive was their darkest secret.

As for him, having to go to Anazi Falls to awaken the Gideon's powers seems unnecessary. Just another useless action Eloh has him taking. Awakening the powers is risky enough. If the Gideon's powers release his own powers, it would eventually drive him mad!

The thing is, he needs the Gideon's powers in order to defeat the Magi. The keepers went on to explain he must see to a task in Jedan and that if he succeeded it would strengthen the alliance between the Order of the Flame and the Society. They told him Goraan is aware of the task. That made him stare at them in thought.

Lela's long white hair is parted in the middle and hangs over her shoulders. Her strong brown eyes seem darker in contrast with her pale skin. The wrinkles in her skin do not reveal her true age.

Ulina is to Lela's right. Her soft brown eyes stared at him. Her long brown hair is pulled back, so her elflocks' bluish tint stands out against her light olive skin. Easily the thinnest of them, she still has a healthy appearance.

Tu'ani is to Ulina's right. Her tan skin appears dark compared to the other keepers' skin. Her long curly hair hangs down her back and over her shoulders. Her hazel eyes make him think about Zelia. She is grayer than Ulina, but they appear to be peers.

"So, this is where things change." Razial said knowingly.

"Upon your return, you will be able to retrieve the medallions and hopefully stop the Magi." They said in Tuyakan.

He dislikes it when they talk in unison but said nothing. He listened to them discuss how he might be able to stop the Magi from releasing Rakaar's Shadow while he thought about how they stay in the mansion and let Dwight, Barthus, and several siblings control the palace.

They then warned him not to sneak around at night.

"Do not forget on the shadow-tracker's third life only your powers will be able to harm it." They warned.

"But I cannot wield…" Razial trailed off.

He nodded in understanding. Without suffering magical injuries, the shadow-tracker would be that more difficult to kill.

The keepers then told him to beware of the Harlequins, who might try to force him to free Ja'Brahma. He finds that odd. He has never even seen Ja'Brahma's prison.

"What about the Harbingers?" He asked.

"Beware of them. They manipulated this all. They want the Magi dead-which we will have to help them make happen if the Magi go to Winnin and release Rakaar's Shadow. Remember, it is possible that Ja'Goraan is a Harbinger."

With that, Razial stood and bid them farewell. Ulina held up a finger and asked about the hunt. Razial smiled while saying.

"I am sure you all talked to my uncle about that. He assures me this city is safe."

"We would not want any unfortunate incidents to happen while we prepare the city to defend against the Magi." They said.

Razial waved and exited the room. He will leave for Anazi Falls before dusk tomorrow.

***

Alena and Anjia walked behind Razial, who walked at a quick pace. The summer sun bore down heating the city increasingly with each passing hour. They are wearing lightweight burnooses to keep cool and to make it more difficult for people to recognize they are elves.

There are a lot of people walking the streets. Alena can sense how uneasy Razial is around so many people. He cut his hair and is almost bald. Unlike in the lands of Coilu, he fits in in Brahma.

Watching him, Alena thought about how all their actions had brought her and Anjia back together.

"So, why are we following him?" Anjia asked in a whisper.

"Because he has a habit of changing things without noticing. We are simply making sure he reaches the palace and meets with Dwight without incident." Alena smiled.

Anjia smiled back. They are happy to be sisters again. The animosity that once tainted their relationship is gone. They now know the visions she had with Anjia acting against Razial deal with the fact that as Razial's Blue Keeper it is Anjia's duty to make sure he walks the champion's path and not Ja'Brahma's path. The only thing that bothers them is they know her vision will come to pass!

Razial knows Alena and Anjia are following him, but he is acting like he does not. He walked with his mind on something Goraan had said.

"Do not be surprised if the Hilt has a new leader, soon." He can still hear Goraan's voice as he approached the palace.

He looked around and saw an elf walking toward him. It appears as if she had been in the palace. He took in her beauty, her full lips, amber eyes, tan-olive skin, reddish elflocks, and oval face. Her long black hair is pulled back, which is why he can see her face well. His mindset quickly changed when he realized she was dressed in all black. She smiled, but that did not disarm him.

"I am Fa'Kitara." Kitara said in elvish.

Her voice was soft, but full of menace. He did not respond. She did not expect him to. She drew her powers, and he called his daggers to him. By the time she unleashed the pouch of poison, Razial had thrown his daggers. She was impressed by his reaction. Troggo had informed her that he is a warrior, who shows no fear. Still, the way he fights even though he knows he has been poisoned surprised her.

"Impressive." She hissed. "I must admit. You are worthy of the challenge."

She had expected to simply overpower him once he was poisoned. However, he closed the distance and kept his daggers and fists moving toward her. Her strength surprised him. She backed away because she sensed Alena and Anjia draw their powers.

Suffering two punches to her side angered her. She punched and kicked Razial. The poison took effect. He collapsed to the street, but Kitara experienced no relief. Anjia and Alena lashed out at her relentlessly.

All around, people ran away from them trying to avoid the magical strikes from the three battling elves. Kitara battled back with fury. They are just as surprised by her strength as she is by theirs.

Knowing she is pressed for time, Kitara closed in on Alena and fought her physically. Alena can fight, but not as well as Anjia, who tried to force Kitara to focus on her. By the time Kitara had to face Anjia, she had knocked Alena down with two punches to her head. However, fighting Anjia was a lot different. Their hands glowed magically while their arms and legs moved with blurring speed. Their level of martial arts mastery impressed the other. It took Kitara's knowledge of sorcery to give her the advantage she needed to knock Anjia down. Still, she had to exchange several magical blows with Alena, then with Anjia, in order to escape.

"Until next time." She said as she ran away.

She sensed other magicians as she ran. Anjia gave chase as did Alena. They exchanged several magical strikes before several Harlequins, on horseback, arrived. Kitara jumped on a horse, and they rode off.

Anjia and Alena ran back to Razial. Two siblings stood around him. Alena saw two bulwarks on horses. She told them to go after the Harlequins. She called out to her hawks. She wants the Harlequins tracked. Hearing Razial is alive made her feel relieved.

***

Standing with his back against a wall, Kalvin pushed away the disappointment he felt over Ofelia not accompanying the keepers to the palace. He stared at the others. Raal, Mantak, Barthus, Havi, Adini, Zelia, Dwight, Ariel, Araceli, Alena, and Anjia all sat around a long wooden table while Fogi Red sat with his back against the back wall. Like Kalvin, Fogi Red is in a foul mood. Razial being poisoned has ruined their plans. They are all waiting to find out how bad Razial's condition is.

Hearing footsteps, Kalvin turned to face the doorway. A few seconds later, the keepers entered the room. Speaking in unison, they explained the poison would only harm Razial if they tried to move him too much. The more he moves the sicker he would become.

Making that worse, the keepers need months to make an antidote.

"By then, the Magi and their armies would march on us after they have released Rakaar's Shadow." The keepers said.

They went on to explain that the Magi have already informed their servants they are going to release Rakaar's Shadow.

"What can we do to stop them?" Fogi Red asked.

"Their armies are too widespread, and they are gathering more men. They are still in their lands. At best, we could kill one maybe two of them, but one of them would reach Winnin."

"Would we not be able to kill the third magus after that?"

"Are you forgetting how Rakaar's Shadow would spread? He would be able to march on Brahma city when he pleases."

That seemed to satisfy Fogi Red's curiosity but not Kalvin's.

"So, what can we do?" He asked.

"We might have to fight the Magi while an antidote is being made."

They included themselves because he only referred to those who had been in the room before they entered.

The keepers left the room, some others left also. Only the jolems, Raal, and Fogi Red stayed with Kalvin. Adini explained that the Harlequins want them to free Ja'Brahma or let the Magi kill Razial to obtain their medallions which would free Ja'Brahma.

"But if Razial dies before facing the Magi, they can obtain their medallions without freeing Ja'Brahma." Adini said.

Kalvin shook his head in frustration because there was nothing he could do. Fogi Red stated he wished he had his paladin powers.

"What?" Havi squeaked. "I thought you do not want to be a paladin."

"I did not want to be a king." Fogi Red held up a chubby finger. "I did not want to leave the mountains." Another finger. "I did not want to lead the Partisans." A third finger. "And I did not want to be here." A fourth finger. "A lot of good not wanting something has done for me."

His blue eyes filled with contempt. Havi rubbed his own bald head while Adini stroked his own goatee. Kalvin asked why it is important to take the crown to Anazi Falls.

"So, he can survive." Havi said.

Kalvin did not press for more because he and Adini are a lot more open than others are.

"It will also make all known paladins stronger even though you all do not have your powers yet." Adini added.

"I hate Champions' Wars." Havi said.

He slid off his chair and wobbled toward the door. He then told Kalvin to find Mantak and have him lead several wolves to the palace to stand guard inside Razial's room.

***

The next night, Alena and Anjia sat inside a hall talking when Mantak and Zelia approached them. Knowing Zelia will be Razial's Red Keeper Alena spent most of the day trying to get Anjia to accept Zelia. Something she knows will be difficult because she herself felt jealous when she first found out.

Mantak greeted them then Zelia greeted them. A moment later, Daniel called for Alena to join him during the meeting with the royals and Dwight. Alena looked to Mantak trying to get a clue to why Daniel wanted her to sit in during the meeting. Mantak shook his head to signal his ignorance while Zelia told her Daniel had also asked Araceli to sit in during the meeting.

Alena nodded her thanks, then she turned to Anjia and said.

"We shall talk later, my sister."

"Of course." Anjia said.

Zelia senses when they call each other sister they mean it in the truer sense of the word and not just as a term of endearment like many others do. She watched Alena walk off while Mantak asked Anjia if she senses the wolves' uneasiness. She told him she does. They told Zelia there is no danger, but the wolves are nervous about something. Still, they are going to check on Razial.

Zelia followed them with Anjia leading the way. Anjia walked at a quick pace as she scaled the stairs. Mantak told her to calm herself. Anjia smiled, but she did not slow down. As they made their way toward Razial's room, two wolves backed into the room. Looking through the doorway, Zelia saw Razial lying on his back. His skin is pale. He is due to awake in two days. Her focus changed when Anjia and Mantak drew their powers. She looked around Anjia and saw Goraan holding up a finger while saying.

"I have the antidote. Razial will" He paused because many people raced toward the room.

Zelia wanted to draw her powers, but Mantak and Anjia released theirs.

"Make them stand down so I can finish." Goraan finished in elvish.

Zelia stood just inside the room while Anjia stood before Goraan and Mantak moved toward the doorway. Havi and Adini sped into the room and stopped. The three keepers arrived when Havi and Adini looked up and said.

"Goraan?"

They turned on each other waving their tiny fists and frowning while telling each other to stop saying what the other is saying.

"Why are you here, Ja'Goraan?!" The keepers demanded.

Zelia stepped out of the room and told all the others that all is well and sent them back to where they were.

"I hate it when they do that." Goraan said grinning. "Me too." Havi smirked.

"To give Razial the antidote." Goran winked.

"This makes you appear to be a Harbinger. How"

"Begone, so he can finish!" Anjia snapped.

"Keepers." Mantak said respectfully. "Allow me to settle this, please. No harm will befall Razial and as you can see, the wolves will side with Anjia and Goraan."

He had said Goraan's name informally to show he would not act against him. He knows Goraan had noticed this.

The keepers exited the room leaving him, Anjia, Zelia, Adini, Havi, and a late arriving Alena with Goraan.

"You defended me, my daughter." Goraan teased Anjia.

Anjia remained stoic. He did not press his luck. He sprinkled a powder on Razial's chest while reciting a spell in ancient elvish. The powder became smoke then flowed into Razial's nostrils when he inhaled. Razial began to cough and convulse violently. Goraan urged him to fight. Havi asked Goraan how he knew to have the antidote ready. He told Havi he had simply taken the precaution because he knows how tactical Troggo is.

"How can we be sure you are not a Harbinger?" Mantak asked.

"You cannot." Goraan laid Razial on his back. "However, ask yourself if I were a Harbinger would I have freed the Magi and the Harlequins."

"You knowingly helped eliminate the heroic lines."

"Contracts. I did not make that happen. The Brahman prince was my action, but the others I could not have stopped. Too many brothers accepted the contracts."

"You could have warned them. You simply want us to kill the Magi." Mantak countered.

"Have I ever denied that? Again, I did not target the heirs to the heroic lines-only the prince of Brahma. Now, you all know I had good reasons."

"Why did you choose Razial to assassinate the prince?" Havi asked.

"Because he can handle killing the man whose death would bring about the Days of Darkness. Because he is the Avatar of Death."

After saying that, Goraan walked before Mantak and tilted his head in respect. Mantak asked the jolems to escort him and

Goraan out of the palace to make sure Goraan leaves without any problems.

Anjia watched all of this. She knows Mantak has a respect for Goraan that is based on their relationship in the past. As the leader of the Ratels, Mantak most likely knows all about Goraan's time as a Ratel. What she wants to know is why Goraan respects Mantak so much.

***

Kalvin and Ofelia sat talking. He told her about his travels with Razial before they crossed paths with Alena and Ariel. She told him he was foolish for going to Winnin. He did not try to defend himself.

As they talked, Ofelia could sense the conflict he feels about Razial killing the prince.

"Remember, he is hunted because he is your friend. Still, he is an assassin. Do not be like the others-constantly bad mouthing him." She said.

Kalvin looked into her green eyes. She is not overwhelmed by what is going on. Her hand on his arm feels good. Taking in her natural beauty, he thought about how it is meant for them to be in each other's lives. Had he never met Razial, he would have never met her. He does not know how she has infatuated him, but she has a hold on him.

She smiled when he reached out and caressed her long blond hair. She knows he has accepted they are fated to be together. She asked him what he was thinking about.

"Us." He said.

That made her blush. She had not expected him to answer so honestly. Wanting to look away, she could not. His blue eyes held her focus.

"We are fated to be together. Do you not feel the same?"

"Of course." She answered. "There is no doubt about it. It is too bad that we are involved in all of this."

"At least we will be together for the trip to Anazi Falls."

They smiled and kissed while they embraced. Each pulled away feeling slightly embarrassed.

"The next time others bad mouth Razial, we can say not only did Razial's actions get us the real ancient crown of Brahma, but they also brought us together." Ofelia smiled.

Kalvin nodded in understanding because those who criticize Razial ignore that had he not killed the prince they would not have the ancient crown of Brahma. The Theocracy would. That would have prevented Razial from awakening the Gideon's powers until after he faced the Magi-which would have most likely left Razial dead.

"It's difficult for many to give an assassin any credit-only blame. When they get over the fact, he is an assassin, they will be able to see all the good Raz has done." Kalvin said.

Ofelia agreed with that then told him it is strange that they are two of those fated to become paladins after going through so much in life.

"Just think about how we are responsible for keeping the world full of life." Ofelia smiled.

Kalvin smiled at her, but in his mind he thought.

"And we were brought together by the Avatar of Death."

CHAPTER 12

THE HILT

Bal gathered his top servants, including Gwen and Frauter, in Coilu's imperial palace. Gwen wants blood. Bal had to admit she had made many valid points, but with his forces preparing to march to Brahma through Ocia he cannot afford for the Fellowship to be divided, especially with western Coilu refusing to stand with him. He must present a unified front until he obtains his medallion.

Although he is immensely powerful without his full powers, he needs his full powers in order to rule in the way he is used to ruling.

Sitting on a newly made throne, he sat listening to Frauter demand action. He stared at Frauter. Standing almost as tall as Bal, Frauter is physically impressive. His light brown hair is parted in the middle and hangs down his face. His dark eyes are full of menace.

Bal had intended this meeting to be festive. Throughout the hall, there is food and wine. However, everyone present is sitting quietly listening to Frauter, who is stalking around pointing at different rivals saying they stood with Peter and others.

"Peter?" Bal frowned. "Why do you keep talking about Peter?"

Bal's light brown eyes went from Frauter to Gwen when she stood and explained that Peter was most likely a Harbinger and that the Harbingers were behind her ouster from power.

"The Harbingers also freed mighty Bal!" One of Gwen's rivals snapped.

Gwen hates what is happening. Bal told her she had not proven the others knowingly conspired with the Harbingers. That makes her feel as if some are mocking her.

"Gwen." Bal growled. "For now, we have things to do."

"By your law, I do not have to wait. I want revenge, now. You" Gwen pointed at Bal. "are acting more like Mel instead of Bal the Magus of Coilu."

Bal stood with anger in his eyes. Gwen is his favorite servant, and she is right. However, she should trust he will give her revenge when the time is right.

"Silence yourself, Gwen!" He snapped.

She held her ground and Frauter stood by her. He is not trying to disrespect Bal, but it would have made him feel like a coward had he stepped away from Gwen. He reached out to calm her, but one of their rivals called on Bal to remove her from the hall. Gwen spun around while pulling a dagger. She drove the dagger into a man's chest. He had not said a word, but he was the guiltiest. He stared at Gwen in shock while the hall fell silent. She stabbed him again. When she pulled her arm back to stab him a third time, Bal struck her knocking her to the ground.

"Frauter." Bal boomed. "Take her from my presence before I kill her. When she awakens, make it clear that she is to make Mohr mines before I return."

Several rivals called for her death because she had just killed the leader of the Fellowship without permission. Bal quickly silenced them by saying Gwen was right to seek revenge. He then said since she had acted without permission the matter ends with only one death. That made it clear he had intended to let her kill others!

"Ready your forces. We leave within the hour." Bal walked over to Frauter. "Make sure she understands this is over. She should have waited."

Standing with Gwen in his arms, Frauter watched Bal rub her head before he returned to the throne. He knows Bal does not like how things turned out, but he cannot undue things without seeming weak-something he cannot do.

As he walked out of the hall, Frauter thought about how Gwen would not let things end like this. She will never forgive Bal for striking her when she was right.

*

Later in Gwen's room, Dawn was startled when Gwen opened her eyes. She had just sat down. Gwen smiled at her while holding out a hand. Dawn took her hand with both of hers. Dawn's blue eyes are full of happiness. Her shoulder length blond hair is well kept. She is not pretty, but she is far from ugly. She has learned how to use her powers and is no longer too thin. Gwen kissed her cheek then asked.

"Where is Frauter?"

"He is in the front." Dawn stood. "I shall get him."

"No, child." She grabbed her arm. "Frauter!" She called in a playful tone. "Dawn. You are my ward-not just a servant. You must understand that."

"Of course." Dawn tilted her head in respect.

Gwen sat up in her bed and tapped her mattress signaling for her to sit. She heard Frauter walking through her chambers. He smiled when he saw her.

"I am alive. Another mistake on his part. First, he denied me. Then, he struck me without killing me. And now he let me live." Gwen said.

"I thought you were going to get us killed." Frauter said.

They have a pact: to kill whoever kills the other. Had Bal killed her, he would have had to kill Bal.

"Bal says the matter of revenge is over with the death of-"

"So, he died!" Gwen said excitedly, cutting him off. "Good. Now the Harbingers will guarantee the Magi fail?"

Frauter nodded. She told him that she intends to prove herself inside Rakaar's chamber in Winnin. He scowled. He dislikes this idea because no one has ever succeeded, and failure means death!

"Surely there is another way." Frauter held her gaze.

"But no other way that leads to success. Those who serve the Magi are fools. Look how easily the Harbingers outplayed us- the Fellowship. The Sisterhood refuses to accept male magicians, and the Theocracy is too ambitious. There are too few of them and those with them believe they serve Eloh. Trust me. I will enter Rakaar's chamber as Gwen of Dax and exit as Gwen Rakaar's Chosen Servant!"

***

Razial and the others with him had separated before they rode into Jedan. They all met at the tavern Goraan had reserved for them. Razial decided to scout the city while the others rest and eat. Although Alena did not want him to go alone, she went along with it because Anjia told her Razial could better go unnoticed alone. The jolems decided to follow him from underground. They will only reveal themselves if Razial needs help.

"Mmm. That smells good." Kalvin said.

He sat down next to Ofelia opposite Mantak. He smiled at Alena, Anjia, and Zelia, who were all next to each other. Across from them are Daniel, Barthus, and Araceli. The six bulwarks, who are part of their procession, had already eaten and are up in their rooms

Razial and the others with him had separated before they rode into Jedan. They all met at the tavern Goraan had reserved for them. Razial decided to scout the city while the others rest and eat. Although Alena did not want him to go alone, she went along with it because Anjia told her Razial could better go unnoticed alone. The jolems decided to follow him from underground. They will only reveal themselves if Razial needs help.

"Mmm. That smells good." Kalvin said.

He sat down next to Ofelia opposite Mantak. He smiled at Alena, Anjia, and Zelia, who were all next to each other. Across from them are Daniel, Barthus, and Araceli. The six bulwarks, who are part of their procession, had already eaten and are up in their rooms.

With Adini and Havi watching Razial, it is a lot quieter, especially since Fogi Red is still in Brahma. -He has to help plan the future actions in Nibel. Kalvin misses him and Raal. He is going to drink in their honor.

Watching the servants serve the food, Kalvin thought about how Daniel took notice of the way the owner of the tavern treats Anjia like a princess. Daniel knows the owner is a Society agent. That is why he does not bad mouth Goraan in his presence. The fact Daniel is not wearing his gray cowl still shocks Kalvin and the other members of the Order of the Flame. It is rare for a member of the Conclave to reveal oneself to outsiders, but under the circumstances it is understandable.

Kalvin looked at Daniel. His dark curly hair is kept in four braids-two on the top of his head and two on the back of his head. His amber eyes are full of power and his toned olive skin matches southern Anazians and western Giaouran skin tone. Average in height and build, Daniel has dedicated his life to the Order of the Flame. He has been around for centuries and has witnessed Goraan's rise throughout Giaour. Like others, he suspects Goraan of being a Harbinger.

As they began eating, Mantak stated he doubts Goraan is a Harbinger. Daniel stated he disagrees. Then, added.

"One day, we shall capture him and settle the matter once and for all."

Mantak did not respond. It is not his place. Daniel is a member of the Conclave. He is entitled to his opinion. However, his words angered Anjia, who has grown tired of members of the Order of the Flame talking about capturing Goraan.

"Do you honestly want to threaten my father, Daniel?" Anjia's tone was full of menace.

"Maybe you have forgotten just who my father-a former member of the Canopy, has become. He is a member of the Hilt, which includes Tollok the Sword-a swordsman so skilled that by himself he killed a third of Thar's royal guard and with a squad of his men slaughtered the rulers of Osam for killing his favorite assassin. How long has your order wanted him?"

Anjia's voice oozed with sarcasm, but she was not finished.

"Then, there is Rogelio the Fist, who is wanted dead by your order, yet every attempt on his life has failed. Next, there is Carpio the Dagger-a man so dedicated to the Society that he killed his own son for violating our laws. Now to discuss the Hilt's leader: Binu the Killer of Kings. He has killed a target under Alf-Heim's protection. Who can count the kings he has killed? Finally, we are back to my father: Goraan the Merciless. Need I say more? You are well aware of all he has done for and against the Order of the Flame."

Daniel eyed her but said nothing. The others can sense the tension between them. Still, Anjia was not finished.

"The Hilt by itself is dangerous. Add the fact that tens of assassins are ready to do their bidding along with the Fulancian forces being at their command and it is clear no one wants to act against Goraan unless they have to. Now, trust me when I say my father is no Harbinger. I know this because he told me he is not, and he has never lied to me!"

"Okay. Enough of that." Barthus said. "Why are we here?"

Daniel took Barthus' queue to let things stay as they are. He explained the king of Jedan, and several royals are trying to help the Theocracy establish a position in Jedan. He admitted that

Goraan had informed them about the king's role in the plot. Anjia smiled knowingly.

"Striking our targets will be easy. Making sure we deal with all involved is what will take time. Hopefully, we can be on our way after the king's ball." Daniel said.

A moment later, Razial, Havi and Adini entered the room. Havi began eating others' food while Razial served himself some food. Adini climbed on the table. Alena watched the way Zelia greeted Razial after she and Anjia had kissed him. She still has to get Anjia used to Zelia.

***

All five members of the Hilt stood inside their private room, where only they were allowed to enter. Candles burn in front of mirrors in each corner, so the room is well lit. The back wall is covered with shelves full of scrolls written by them.

Each member is standing around the grayish brown marble table shaped in the form of a pentagon. They are dressed in black abbas with a flaming red dagger on the back. It does not matter where they sit and they rarely sit in the same place in consecutive meetings, but they did so during this meeting. Goraan is to Binu's right and Carpio is to Goraan's right. Tollok is between Carpio and Rogelio, who is to Binu's left. They had sat like this when they met to discuss the hunt for Razial. Now, they are meeting to discuss several issues including a proposed contract on Alena.

"Who brought this contract?" Binu asked.

"Diana handed it to me. She refused to let it be forwarded." Carpio said.

"Who is she to stop a contract?" Tollok asked.

"Last I checked, she is a master assassin with rank. This is well within her rights." Carpio said.

"Who marked Alena for death?" Goraan asked.

"The Sisterhood." Carpio answered.

"We shall finish them. I want them eliminated." Goraan growled.

"Goraan." Rogelio called flatly. "All we have to do is turn down the contract. Surely, the Sisterhood had no idea Alena was close to us."

"This is their second mistake, brother. Remember, it was the Sisterhood who tried to target Razial." Binu said. "I agree with Goraan: we eliminate the Sisterhood."

"You two are making this too personal." Tollok said. "There is no need to war with the Sisterhood. We must finish here, in Giaour. Can we do that first?"

"War?" Goraan scoffed. "There will be no war. We will go after their top members and agents. I shall perform a show of force, so they know we are coming for them."

"Really?" Rogelio asked. "Have you forgotten about Mel the magus, who leads the Sisterhood?"

"Razial will handle the Magi." Goraan replied.

"Razial cannot defeat me." Rogelio countered.

That made Goraan laugh. Binu remained stoic. Carpio sensed Goraan's confidence in Razial, but he decided to wait before he asked Goraan to reveal more about what was going on.

"The Sisterhood shall pay for their actions. If you all disagree, I shall punish them myself." Goraan said.

After that, Carpio asked about plans to strike Elsa. Binu explained he had already put a plan in motion, but it is going to take years to succeed. He told them he has a young assassin named Edward, networking throughout northern Ocia. His plan is to establish several areas where they can take actions against Pan and hide out in. He wants to confuse Pan while they track Elsa and her daughter. The others agreed with his plan. Carpio feels as if Edward is a little young for the task but accepts that Binu wants Edward to prove himself.

"Now to this business of making Dario governor of Fulancia. Are you sure about this?" Tollok asked Binu.

"I am surprised you are not holding a grudge after he almost killed Razial in Coilu." Rogelio said.

"Rogelio." Carpio scolded him.

Rogelio's blue eyes took in Carpio while stroking his reddish-brown beard. Carpio has short, matted hair, dark eyes, and a slim build. He has two scars: one just below his left eye and one along his right jaw line. His scars are reminders of the last attempt the Assassins' Guild made to survive. They tried to kill Carpio, who held them off long enough for Goraan and Binu to save him.

A stickler for rules, he dislikes it when they are sarcastic or dismissive to each other.

"There is no need for sarcasm." Carpio finished.

"Well, Dario is one of us and he might not want the position." Tollok said.

"He will have no choice." Binu assured. "We have to find out who can govern when we take over all Giaour."

Carpio agreed with that. Tollok wants to put contractors in power instead of active assassins, but he chose not to push this issue because of all the other changes it would bring about.

"How is any of this going to help us in Arapia?" Rogelio asked.

"We have to make alternative plans if Diana runs out of time."

"I will handle that. As a matter of fact, I have made sure she has enough time to choose her own husband." Goraan said.

The others stared at him. Tollok asked about the ancient crowns that used to belong to the Six Heroes. He then asked why Goraan wants Razial to search for Giaour's ancient crown in Jedan. Goraan explained the crowns were made to keep Svan animals at bay because many Svan animals roamed around when the Conclave made the Six Heroes.

"The crowns can also be harnessed. They are really mediums, powerful mediums. That is why few individuals can possess more than one. Razial is one of those few." Goraan said.

Tollok asked him to explain. He told him that Razial can bind with all the crowns or bind them to others.

"And the Harbingers have these crowns. What are they doing with them?" Rogelio asked.

"If I were a Harbinger, I would know. I do know. They have three ancient crowns. The Order of the Flame has Anazi's, Razial has Brahma's and before he leaves Jedan he will also have Giaour's." Goraan smiled.

He did not reveal that the Harbingers could free Ja'Brahma if they obtain all six crowns. To him, that would serve no purpose. He began thinking about how the keepers disliked having to let Razial have the ancient crown of Giaour, but they had no choice. They had to accept Goraan's deal: he will help them in exchange for the ancient crown.

"Razial is a loyal assassin. We should not allow these keepers to guide him. If he is going to become as powerful as you say, we must control him." Carpio said.

Goraan knows what he is saying. He wants the Hilt to capture Razial so he would be their servant for ten years!

"No more of your clearing the path for him." Rogelio grinned.

"We can train him and control him." Carpio added.

"That would allow us to solidify our hold throughout Giaour and-"

"No." Goraan cut off Tollok. "Binu. Explain why it would be a horrible idea to control Razial."

Binu explained that until all Razial's paladins and keepers are found Razial must be left to his fate. He then warned them how unstable Razial would become if his powers are released. That did not dissuade the others, so they moved on to the next issue: stopping the Theocracy in Giaour and Brahma.

They talked about that for several minutes until they all agreed on the same plan. Goraan then told them if the Harbingers offer them an alliance they should accept it. Carpio asked about their alliance with the Order of the Flame.

"Are not the Harbingers enemies with the Order?" He asked.

"Rivals." Goraan corrected him. "All we have to do is not choose sides."

Binu disliked that idea but did not vote against it. Rogelio asked what will be in it for the Society. Goraan explained how the Society would benefit. Carpio and Tollok liked what they heard and voted with Goraan. Tollok asked why the Harlequins stopped raiding in northeast Giaour while Carpio told Goraan and Binu to explain more about what is going on. Goraan told them Priato is trying to make peace between Troggo and Goraan. If Priato fails, they would have to go after the Harlequins or Troggo would come after them. They all voiced their support for him against Troggo.

He then told them how the Magi would have to die if they release Rakaar's Shadow. He warned them about the Svan animals that would roam the world with Rakaar's Shadow. He handed them several scrolls that explained, in detail, how the Magi are.

"Why have you kept this from us?" Tollok asked.

"Never expected the Magi to return with such little warning." Gorran said.

Carpio stood and stated he thinks Goraan should lead the Hilt because he knows more about what is going on. His dark eyes watched his brothers in arms. They looked at each other. Goraan stated that is not necessary, but Tollok agreed with Carpio. Then, Binu stood and said.

"Carpio is right, Goraan."

Goraan looked around. Tollok tilted his head to signal that Carpio's idea is a good one even though Goraan thinks it is not necessary. His light brown eyes did not waver. His long light brown hair lies on his shoulders. He is simply an older version of his son, but he stands slightly shorter and has a thinner beard.

As the youngest and weakest member of the Hilt, Tollok remains their sword. Goraan has never seen a human who can out fight him with a sword.

"Well." Rogelio stood. "This may not be necessary, but it is the best action tactically."

With all of them standing, Goraan had no choice but to stand and accept. Carpio remained stoic. He is the shortest of the humans, but he is taller than Goraan and Binu. Goraan watched Rogelio brush his reddish-brown hair back. His blue eyes stared at Goraan. Tollok rubbed his hands together. Binu closed his eyes and exhaled. He was the first to hold out his hands-palms up and call his magical dagger to him. The red magical dagger floated above his hands. The others, including Goraan, quickly called their magical daggers. Then, all their daggers began to glow.

Long ago, Goraan discovered a powerful medium that could be used to link a group of sorcerers-telepathically and magically. He used that medium to link himself, Binu, Tollok, Rogelio, and Carpio after they had defeated the Assassins' Guild.

Goraan and Carpio had been close friends while Binu and Rogelio were close. Tollok associated with Goraan and Rogelio. Goraan and Binu had known each other for quite some time back then, so it was only natural for them to form the Hilt. Binu was chosen to be the leader because of his temperament. That is about to change for the first time since the Hilt was formed!

While all their daggers glowed, Goraan's became blue marking him as the leader. When it switched back to red, he felt slightly stronger. Just like that, he became the new leader of the Hilt.

***

Kalvin smiled when he saw his mark: a rich Jedan merchant, who supports the king's plot with the Theocracy. Several personal guards walk around the man, but Kalvin is not worried about that. It is a bright sunny day. People are crowded in the streets trying to buy, sell, and or trade goods. That is all he needs as a distraction. He is an expert pickpocket. He is not worried about being caught.

The night before, he had stolen a general's sword from his side just before Razial killed that general. Razial had to kill the general because he would not attend the king's ball. Kalvin and Barthus had accompanied him while Anjia, Alena, and others killed other targets who would not attend the ball.

Thinking about that, Kalvin walked toward his mark. Overweight and balding, the man is dressed in expensive clothes. His eyes droop, but his face is not fat. Kalvin tripped himself. As he fell the man was startled. He stopped mid stride. His guards moved in. Kalvin patted him down as they both crashed to the ground. While the guards pulled him off their boss, Kalvin lifted the man's keys and coin pouch.

"Peasant!" The man snapped. "Beat him."

"Wait, good sir." Kalvin pleaded. "You dropped this."

He held up the coin pouch. One of the guards helped the man back to his feet and dusted him off. He stared wide-eyed at Kalvin while snatching the pouch from him.

"You are an honest man." He said to Kalvin.

He grinned while handing Kalvin several silver pieces. People stared at them, but no one stopped. Barthus walked between Kalvin and the mark while Kalvin discreetly handed the keys to Daniel. Kalvin stood dusting himself off. The man suddenly stopped and looked back at him. Kalvin had expected that. Along with his guards, he walked back to Kalvin. Several passersby told Kalvin to stop standing in the middle of the street.

"Give me my keys!" The man demanded.

Kalvin held out his arms saying he does not have any keys and that maybe he had dropped them before he dropped his coin pouch. Still, the guards patted him down. Kalvin acted nervous while assuring the man he does not have any keys and that if he were a thief, he would have run off with the coins not keys.

The guards looked at their boss signaling that they did not find any keys. The man shook his head and walked off. Kalvin smiled at Barthus, who walked toward him while he turned around. Barthus matched his stride while they began to gain ground on Daniel, who walked a short distance ahead of them.

"Hopefully, Anjia gets on us the guest list." Barthus said.

He had kept his voice low while speaking in Tuyakan. Kalvin did not respond. He has grown tired of Daniel doubting Anjia. They have been in Jedan for two weeks waiting for the ball. They have learned a lot. Their target list has grown so much that Razial felt the need to remind Daniel that he is in charge.

Two days earlier, a Danouan priestess arrived, and she is being housed in the merchant's-the one who Kalvin stole the keys from, mansion. That is perfect for Razial because the plans to Jedan's palace are also in the same mansion. Razial wants the plans so he can locate the ancient crown of Giaour. He told Kalvin they will steal the plans and kill as many targets as they can at the ball. Daniel dislikes this plan because too many people he wants to kill will not be at the ball and the plan seems too last minute. Razial does not care how Daniel feels about his plan because all their original targets will be at the party-except for the general Razial had killed the night before.

"Do you remember what Keeper Tu'ani told us before we left?" Kalvin asked in Tuyakan.

He feels strange speaking Tuyakan. Understanding it does not bother him. To him, when he speaks Tuyakan it does not seem as if he is really speaking the words. Still, he must speak Tuyakan because Daniel told him to.

"About?" Barthus asked.

"About how it is rare for most paladins to get along with their Gideon."

A grimness came over Barthus. They continued to walk through the street-still gaining on Daniel, while Barthus' mind focused on what Tu'ani had said in response to him saying that he and Razial do not get along very well. He had told her the only person who dislikes Razial more than him is Dwight. That had made Tu'ani smile before she told him that is fitting since the keepers have to prepare Dwight to become a paladin!

"What about it?"

"With you and Dwight feeling the way you feel maybe that proves that things are going well." Kalvin smiled.

Barthus turned to look at Kalvin. He shook his head then said. "Let us be happy Mantak accompanied us."

Kalvin understands his statement. Razial and Daniel have been at odds many times and Barthus has sided with Daniel every time. Only Mantak's calmness has avoided serious problems between them. Things grew more tense after Razial changed Daniel's plans when the priestess arrived. Kalvin hopes Razial's changes work.

Back in the present. Daniel winked at Kalvin when he walked alongside him. He told Kalvin he had done an excellent job in obtaining the keys. Kalvin thanked him. They continued walking. Kalvin saw a beggar trying to get some food from a trader.

Without thinking, he tossed the silver pieces he had gotten only minutes earlier, to the beggar. The beggar thanked him, Kalvin waved to him as he kept walking.

They quickly made their way back to the tavern. It felt cool to be out of the sun. The owner stood by the kitchen's doorway.

"Do you all need anything?" He asked.

"No. Thank you." Daniel said. "Where are the others?"

"The dwarfs are asleep, and the elf is in the back." The man answered.

Daniel thanked him then led the others to the back room. Kalvin thought about how Anjia had told him the owner is a retired Fulancian soldier, who married a woman from Jedan, and that she had bought the tavern for him. Now that his children have grown, he wants to move back to Fulancia. Anjia will make that happen during her return from Anazi Falls.

"Mantak." Daniel said.

Standing near the back window, Mantak greeted them. Daniel showed him the keys while praising Kalvin's skills as a pickpocket. Mantak's narrow eyes glanced at Kalvin. With his hair down, his pointed ears are still visible. His reddish elflocks are not.

He remained by the back window while Daniel stood in the middle of the room and Kalvin and Barthus stayed by the door.

"Razial has changed plans again." Mantak said in Tuyakan.

Daniel grimaced but said nothing. Razial will hear from him soon enough. Mantak explained that Razial had just left with the bulwarks. The bulwarks will act as guards for Ofelia and Zelia, who both were sent-by Razial, to join Ariel and Araceli before they head to the palace to join Anjia, who had made it so that Araceli and Ariel were placed on the guest list.

"So along with Razial, we shall act as guards for Araceli and Ariel." Mantak said. "That change was made because Razial intends to kill the priestess before the ball."

"What about the shadow-tracker." Barthus asked.

"That is why Havi, Adini, Kalvin, and I shall accompany him to the mansion." Mantak said.

"What about the others we should kill?" Daniel asked.

"Killing the priestess and the merchant is the better plan. We cannot kill all of our targets."

Mantak said this to show he agrees with Razial's change. Daniel nodding to show he agrees with this change also.

***

Ofelia and Zelia sat on the bed listening to Anjia explain that the Hilt is like the Conclave. She told them Goraan being made the leader of the Hilt changes nothing in the Society. Ofelia asked why they changed leaders if it changes nothing. Anjia remained stoic while explaining the other Hilt members know Goraan knows more about what is going on and being made leader of the Hilt gives him more leeway to act. She does not want to talk about this, but Alena had spoken a little too loudly while they talked about Goraan becoming the leader of the Hilt.

Sighing, Anjia thought about how Razial does not care about Goraan becoming the leader of the Hilt, but she is suspicious. She stared at the others before saying.

"Where another member of the Hilt can send a small force to do his bidding, Goraan can wage war against whomever-whenever."

"Can he call off the hunt for Razial?" Zelia's hazel eyes filled with hope.

"No." Anjia answered.

"How long before the hunt is over?" Ofelia asked.

"Just over fourteen months remain." Anjia replied.

After that, Ofelia said the Hilt should call off the hunt because Razial is fated to become the Gideon. Anjia said she agrees, but the Society's laws are clear: a hunt cannot be called off under any circumstances.

That made Zelia think. Razial has avoided moving around unless it is necessary because he does not want the assassins in Jedan to find him. She turned to Ofelia, who told Anjia that she had heard about the attack on Razial outside of Ruug.

"That was Dario the Unknown and others." Anjia said.

"Razial almost died." Ofelia stated.

"One almost dies in every battle." Anjia responded.

A knock on the door interrupted their conversation. Their dresses have arrived. Zelia quickly exited the room to answer the door. Ofelia got off her bed while Anjia walked into the next room. She is ready to act if necessary.

Hearing Zelia thank the person who had delivered their dresses, Anjia relaxed. Ofelia noticed this. Much taller than Anjia, Ofelia thought about how firm Anjia is. She makes a good ally even though she keeps them at a distance. How she had convinced the palace captain that they are members of the Sisterhood is beyond Ofelia. If they succeed, it will be because of Anjia.

"The dresses are pretty." Zelia smiled.

She handed Anjia a dress then handed Ofelia one. The dresses are all different shades of blue. They seem expensive. Ofelia walked back to the bed and undressed. She heard Anjia call Zelia. She looked away because it was obvious Anjia wanted to say something private to Zelia.

"Razial is not for you." Anjia said softly in elvish.

Zelia's heart thumped. She does not want to argue with Anjia about Razial. Alena had told her Anjia can be overprotective and not to take it personally if Anjia confronts her about Razial.

"Do not think I have not noticed how you feel. Alena may not mind, but I do!" Anjia said firmly.

Zelia wanted to look away. She wanted to say that Anjia was wrong, but she knew that would be useless.

"I mean you no disrespect, Zelia. It is just you and I are not sisters in any sense of the word." Anjia shook her head.

***

Just before nightfall, Razial, Kalvin, and Mantak snuck into the merchant's mansion. Adini and Havi are waiting outside. Inside a large room, Razial and the others hid against the back wall. Razial is using his elfin burnoose while Mantak is using his surplice. -He promised Kalvin elfin

clothing in the future.

They heard the merchant talking about how having to go to the party is ruining his plans. He entered the room holding a lit candle on a candle holder. Razial called a dagger to him. By the time the man had taken a second step into the room, Razial slammed the dagger into his throat. Mantak moved to the doorway. Kalvin followed him while Razial stabbed the man in his chest as he fell to the floor. Mantak's katana cut through two guards' necks just as they stepped through the doorway.

"We have to get to the master bedroom." Razial whispered.

"Is not the master bedroom usually on the top floor?" Kalvin smiled.

"Well, lead the way Kalvin with a K." Razial teased.

It grew darker as they walked through the mansion. They came across a stairwell and scaled them quickly and quietly. Until they have the plans, Razial wants to use stealth.

As they crept around the top floor, they heard others moving around the mansion. They ignored this and made their way to the master bedroom. Razial had Kalvin steal the keys because he did not know when the man would leave for the party. He watched Kalvin use the keys to open the double doors to the master bedroom. It only took several seconds. They entered the room, closing the door behind them. It is dark in the room, but they can see well. Razial told Mantak that Kalvin has a knack for finding secret panels.

Hearing others moving toward the room, Mantak said.

"Let his knack take effect quickly."

Razial and Kalvin smiled because he is more playful with them.

"Kalvin. Get the plans. Razial and I shall deal with those in the hallway." Mantak said.

He opened the double doors then sped off. Razial followed him, closing the door as he exited. Kalvin heard them fighting while he searched the room. Several moments went by, making him more nervous before he found the panel. He opened it and took out everything including the plans to the palace.

Sensing magic, Kalvin quickly ran across the room and pulled open the doors. His eyes opened wide, and his heart thumped. Standing before him, he saw the priestess. Her white wimple and surplice seem to glow. Her eyes lowered just above her white veil. Immediately, Razial's words echoed inside his mind.

"Look a woman in her eyes when you kill her."

Without pause, Kalvin's sword thrusted forward. The priestess did not see his sword because she was focused on trying to grab him by his throat. Her hands fell short as his sword pierced her chest and exited her back. The blade Binu had given him has never failed him. Her brown eyes stared emptily at him. Kalvin pushed her back, pulling his sword free. With Razial and Mantak still fighting, he must help.

He moved past the priestess' lifeless body-feeling no guilt. He saw bodies in the hallway. Razial's daggers tumbled through the air while Mantak battled two priests.

"We're going to be" Kalvin cut a guard across his back. "-late if you two don't hurry up."

"This cannot be happening!" Havi squeaked.

"Is that so?" Adini asked. "Well, ask this priest if I am really stabbing him."

The two jolems raced up the stairs and leapt into the air. They landed on the priests' backs stabbing them as they slid down the stairs. Mantak moved to finish the remaining guards. His katana served death to those who escaped Kalvin and Razial.

"Hurry. We are late." Adini snapped.

"For two priests, I would say this was worth it." Razial said playfully. "Besides you two got to kill them."

"Yeah. Now, let us hurry." Havi said.

*

Anjia, Alena, Zelia, Ofelia, and Araceli sat together inside the hall watching the other partygoers enjoy themselves. There are more guests than Araceli had expected. With musicians playing and people laughing, the mood is festive. Still, Araceli knows the king and the two priests with him are puzzled by the fact the priestess had not arrived yet.

She heard Alena point out Daniel's target-the palace guard captain. Daniel thanked her. Araceli knows he is unhappy by Razial's latest change. However, this is the first change she agrees with. Not even Barthus minds.

While Kalvin, Razial, Havi, and Adini search for the crown, Mantak will enter the hall and attack. Almost as soon as she thought about it, Barthus said.

"There is Mantak."

Araceli looked around and saw Mantak walking through the hall pushing people out of his way. He has his head covered so no one noticed he is an elf.

Once in the middle of the hall, he attacked, drawing the attention of all the hall's magicians, who did exactly what Razial had said they would do; they drew their powers making themselves easy targets for Araceli and the others.

*

Razial crept along the hall's back wall. He had entered the hall behind Mantak using his elfin burnoose to hide his presence. He knows Barthus, Ariel, and the bulwarks will occupy the guards trying to reach the hall. He did not see Daniel kill his target before following Barthus and the bulwarks out of the hall to fight the guards.

Moving closer to where the king was standing behind a group of magicians, Razial began throwing his daggers, picking off several magicians. That gave Anjia and Alena an advantage, but it also revealed where he is to one of the priests.

"Run!" The priest said to the king.

Forced to use his powers to constantly deflect Razial's daggers, the priest could not use his powers against Razial. The king stumbled as he tried to flee. Magical flashes lit the hall. Every partygoer, who had no interest in the fighting, ran toward the doors. Fear filled the hall. People shouted-some screamed. Razial stayed focused on the priest.

"Get the king." Mantak said in elvish.

He struck the priest and charged him. Razial did not see him deliver the fatal blow with his katana because he had spun around and chased the king. As he closed in on the king, he heard him gasp in fear. Razial tackled him before he reached the doorway. They crashed into a group of partygoers trying to get out of the hall. Razial stabbed him in the head. While standing up, he shouted to Mantak in Tuyakan telling him to meet him at the top of the palace.

*

Kalvin had already obtained the crown of Giaour-along with some jewels he had given to the jolems, by the time the fighting begun. He thought Razial was going to stay with him and the jolems, but Razial decided the others might need his help, so he went with Mantak while Kalvin and the jolems went to get the crown. They had all looked at the palace's plans before they reached the palace so going after the crown seemed easy. However, before he left, Mantak had warned Havi that if they were discovered they would be trapped on the top floor. That is exactly what happened. Kalvin and the jolems are held up in a locked room.

Standing in the middle of the room, Kalvin looked at Adini, who was standing against the back wall with his daggers in hand.

"Open the door and we will die fighting." Havi said playfully.

Kalvin shook his head at him. The guards are pounding on the door trying to break their way in.

"Don't be silly. If they break the door, we're going to die fighting anyway. Now tell me. Am I the only one who disliked this final change?" Kalvin smiled.

"If we survive, yeah." Havi grinned. "If we don't, I knew this plan was daft."

Just after he said this, several magical strikes sent the guards running away.

"Oaky. Open the door." Adini grinned. "And I am telling Razial you two thought his plan was daft."

He opened the door himself. Kalvin and Havi followed him out of the room. Mantak stood a step from the doorway. Razial stood several paces from him. Both are splattered with blood.

Hearing tens of guards running toward them, Adini knew the stairs are blocked. Not wanting anyone else to fight their way to them, he told the others to follow him and Havi.

"It is a good thing we waited." Adini said.

He and Havi raced toward the end of the hallway. Their speed put distance between them and the others. Razial ran past Kalvin with Mantak bringing up the rear. A large group of guards ran after them. The jolems leapt into the air and flew through the window at the end of the hallway. That surprised the others, but Mantak immediately understood what they were about to do.

"Go!" He urged Razial and Kalvin.

Razial jumped through the window. Kalvin did the same. His mind raced. His heart pounded. He held his breath as his arms and legs flailed as he fell through the air. He asked himself why Mantak had not used his powers to slow their fall. Before he could say anything, he crashed into a soft mound of dirt. Dirt filled his mouth as he slid down to the ground. He began spitting when he reached his hands and knees.

Rubbing his eyes, he heard Mantak land. He opened his eyes and saw the jolems had made large mounds of dirt for them to land on. Mantak winked at him. Razial stood looking around making sure all was well.

"Close your mouth and open your eyes next time." Havi teased.

"Let us get inside before we have to fight the shadow-tracker. Unless you all care to test yourselves." Adini laughed.

With that, they raced off leaving the guards looking through the window wondering how they had survived the fall.

*

Hours later, Razial sat in the tavern's back room looking at the ancient crowns of Brahma and Giaour. Although the crowns are almost identical, Razial feels more connected to the crown of Brahma. He looked at the writing inscribed on them. It is not the same. He put them down and began to think.

A moment later, Ofelia entered the room. He can sense that something is on her mind, so he told her to speak her mind.

"Kalvin told me about killing the priestess. He does not seem to regret it." She said.

"That is good." Razial replied.

"No. That is not good." She countered.

She stood firm as if she were willing to fight if she must. She told him Kalvin is not fated to become an assassin and Razial should not keep trying to make him colder.

It was obvious Kalvin had talked with her about how Razial feels Kalvin should become colder, so he did not bother trying to figure out how she knows he feels this way.

"Ofelia. Think about all paladins are tasked with. Kalvin must become colder so do you. Think about how cruel things are during war especially during Champions' Wars. Could you have made some of the decisions paladins past made? Could Kalvin?"

Before he could continue, Anjia entered the room. She told him she had given the tavern owner a hundred coins so he could return to Fulancia. That is when she noticed they had been in the middle of a serious conversation. She excused herself, but Ofelia stopped her. She realized her mistake. Razial was not trying to make Kalvin more like an assassin. He had done Kalvin a favor because paladins are called upon to make a lot of decisions- most of them will be exceedingly difficult and lead to many deaths!

"Thank you, Razial." Ofelia stood. " I now see the wisdom in your actions."

She bade them a good night before leaving them alone to talk.

***

Six weeks after leaving Jedan, Razial and the others entered Anazi Falls. Alena's hawks had delivered a message from the keepers. (With the Magi roaming around, it is too risky for some to use telepathy.) The message simply informed them that a new Brahman leader would be chosen soon and that Osam and Sahkar will send armies to help face the Magi's armies and that the Magi are in Ocia.

"Does anyone ever send us any good news?" Kalvin asked.

He asked this because he does not want anyone to bring up the fact the Magi can release Rakaar's Shadow because of Razial.

"Are the Magi really that foolish?" Anjia asked.

She rode to Alena's right just behind Razial, who rode in the lead. Behind them are Mantak, Kalvin, and Barthus. Daniel, Zelia, Araceli, and Ofelia are behind them. The jolems and bulwarks brought up the rear.

"Why would they combine their armies instead of attacking from three directions?" Anjia finished.

"You really are Goraan's daughter." Havi stated.

"How so?" Daniel asked.

"Daniel. Need I remind you why the Ciru Range is now known as the Goraan Mountains? Enough of your dislike of Goraan." Havi said firmly.

He knows Daniel knows he had said what he had said because Anjia had seen the error in the Magi's tactics like her father would have.

"So, how long are we staying here?" Adini asked.

"Two days." Mantak answered.

He and Razial had already discussed that. Two days is enough time for them to rest.

***

Razial stood with Diana by his side. She pressed against his left side. Her green eyes were full of concern and fear. Short, with large breasts, long dark wavy hair that seems darker in contrast with her milky white skin, she is not beautiful to him, but she is attractive.

Wearing a sleeved dress that hangs past her knees. She has pants that can be seen through the slit on the left side of the dress. A hooded cloak appeared on her. That is when he realized that not only is all her clothing gray, but every piece of clothing is elfin!

"You do not have to do this." She said, looking away from him.

Razial frowned as he looked around. He saw Anjia, Zelia, and a faceless woman circling him and Diana. They are moving from right to left. They are dressed in the same fashion as Diana except Anjia is dressed in all blue, Zelia in all red, and the faceless woman in all yellow.

He can sense the tension from them. Anjia's narrow eyes did not waver and are full of menace. Zelia's hazel eyes seem to search him for a weakness. He looked down at himself. He began to feel as if he were looking at himself from outside himself.

Dressed in all elfin clothing-blue in color, a cloak, a long-sleeved shirt, and pants. He has on a silver war helm with a large onyx embedded in the front. What surprised him the most about how he is dressed is the fact he is armed to the teeth: two daggers, two short swords, two long swords, and a long bow under his cloak.

He does not understand why he feels so much anger toward Anjia, Zelia, and the unknown woman. A wicked grin grew over his face when they said.

"There is no other way."

"No." Diana pleaded. "You do not have to do this."

She looked at him. Sadness filled her eyes as she shook her head. Suddenly, Havi and Adini appeared. They shook their heads. Razial shouted at them telling them Rakaar must die in order to keep the world safe. He tried to stop his rant but could not.

"Do you see why we must do this?" Anjia, Zelia, and the other woman asked.

They drew their powers as a mist filled the area. Suddenly, Kalvin, Ofelia, Araceli, Barthus, Fogi Red, Mantak, and two other faceless individuals appeared. They formed a circle around him. They began to move from left to right. They are all dressed in the same fashion-bluish gray elfin clothes. They also have two silver bracers. He knows those bracers allow them to call any weapon they want. His weapons disappeared and suddenly, he had on the same bracers. Then, one of the faceless individuals became Dwight.

"Make it quick." Diana said before she disappeared.

Adini and Havi walked off telling Anjia to be careful. That made Razial angrier. He began shouting that their actions only make Rakaar stronger.

"It will cost you dearly to defeat me!" He shouted.

He drew his powers-still raging. Dwight's face became blurry. Weapons appeared. Everyone became faceless before the fighting began without pause. He watched the fighting, then realized what was happening. He was witnessing Ja'Brahma's final fight.

As the fighting went on, the Blue Keeper died along with three paladins. Ja'Brahma was bound and his powers were split so the Gideon could come into existence.

Razial sat up in his bed. His pulse raced. He wiped his face. He thought about what had happened. He had been told to put on the crown of Brahma before he fell asleep. His hand went to his head. The crown is not there. He looked around but saw no sign of the crown. He scrambled to his feet. He felt power pulsating inside of him.

"The crown" Mantak whispered from the front room. "-has bonded with you like the daggers."

Razial lit a candle while Mantak made his way into the room.

"Now, you know why you had to sleep alone." Mantak stated.

Nodding, Razial said. "So, that is what happened to Ja'Brahma."

"Yes. And if you follow his path, the same will happen to you. Remember that." Mantak warned.

He did not wait to be asked. He explained that Ja'Brahma went mad because of his anger and power. He told Razial that if his powers are released before he can be trained, the Gideon's powers would drive him mad.

"Unfortunately, we cannot train you until we deal with the Magi. The Conclave and the Canopy want to train those who are fated to become paladins before you are trained." Mantak said.

"What about the Gully Council?" Razial asked.

"Dwarfs may be cautious, but they are not worrisome. Go back to sleep. Enjoy your rest while you can." Mantak advised.

Razial heard his unspoken warning. He had all but told him to take advantage of this time because in the future he will not be able to. He thought about going to talk with Anjia and Alena but decided to heed Mantak's advice.

***

In Giaour, south of the Gnor-Winnin Range, the Harbingers gathered. Beulah, Peter, Tonige, and the Master remained mounted forming a small circle so they could face each other while they talk.

It is close to noon. The sun is high in the sky. Their bright red cowls stand out even more because they are in the middle of a vast grassland. Peter told the others all his spies had told him what had happened in Coilu between Bal's servants. The Master was happy to hear Gwen had a confrontation with Bal. He was unhappy to hear Gwen did not obey Bal and attack Mohr. She and Frauter were seen in Vin. That made the Master think. He remained silent for several moments before saying.

"Gwen is up to something. Whatever it is, it is dangerous. If you can track her, do so and kill her."

Then, still speaking in Tuyakan, he said the keepers will not allow Razial to challenge the Magi until the Magi are marching on Brahma city. To make sure the others understand why they are doing this, he explained that for Razial to duel with the Magi he must enter Ja'Brahma's cell.

"Once inside, he has to explain why he is there. A'Ja'Brahma would then place the Magi into the realm beneath his prison. If the

Magi were with their armies when this happens, it would seem as if the Magi simply disappeared." The Master said.

The others immediately understood why he wants the keepers' plan to work. He told Peter to go to Tunez to help Beulah attack the Magi's armies if Svelt stands against the Magi. Peter did not like this plan and stated how he felt. He told the Master the Magi have hundreds of thousands of men.

"How can we slow them?" He asked.

"Are you afraid Peter?" The Master asked.

"Of course not. I only feel it would be wiser to ambush their forces after they have crossed into the Brahman lands."

Peter's answer would have been good, but for one reason: the Magi must pass through Tunez to reach the city of Brahma. Peter was not listening. The Master had told Beulah to act if Svelt acts. Since Svelt is farther west than Tunez, what Peter is asking for has already been taken in consideration. Peter did not think about that.

"Peter. Make sure Beulah has the help she may need."

"Understood." Peter replied.

Beulah looked at the Master. Although his face cannot be seen, it is obvious to her he has a disappointed expression. She heard Peter say he understands the Master's instructions, but she doubts it. His instructions were given to help her avoid being discovered by the Order of the Flame. If she acts to help Svelt, then it will be seen as a political action. The Order of the Flame would, at best, consider her to be an ally to the Harbingers. Something that would not cause them to act against her.

"What about the assassin?" Tonige asked. "Is Ariel tracking him?"

"I have not changed my mind about him. I want him to live. No. Ariel is not tracking him." The Master answered.

"Troggo has spies throughout the valley and Harras might push his luck." Tonige said.

The Master understands his statement. Harras wants to spread his influence because, like many Gnorans, he dislikes the fact that Winninans control the Gnor Valley and Gnorans are like second class citizens. Harras is foolish enough to try to use Troggo against Tonige. The Master finds that amusing.

"Ja'Troggo is no fool. He will not act against you." The Master said.

He then told them to be ready for the second phase of their plans, telling them things have taken place that will allow them to manipulate the Society even more. He assured them that with the Society in the fold their plans would not fail. He explained they must find out what is going on with Elsa and what Pan is up to. To make sure they understood his point he told them about how the witch in Mohr, who had tried to kill Sidney had stabbed herself with a horn shaped dagger just like the daggers used in the attack on Vishnu in Gula.

"That is no coincidence." He stated.

He dislikes two things about this Champions' War, two things he does not control. First, he dislikes the fact Elsa has reemerge with horn shaped daggers. Second, he still has no idea who the spies inside the Order of the Flame are.

"The sooner Gwen is dead, the better." He said. "Tonige. Look for signs of the Chosen Servant. She is lurking. Why has she not taken her position? I do not know. Now that the assassin has the Gideon's powers, I shall use him to lure her out of the shadows."

"Then, I can have my revenge on him." Peter said.

The Master did not respond. Razial killed his son and grandson as part of his contract. However, neither were truly agents for the Harbingers. Another thing Razial has in his favor is the Master wants to lead him down Ja'Brahma's path.

"Things shall become difficult once the Magi release Rakaar's Shadow. Many Svan animals shall be freed to wreak havoc. Famine will spread. Prepare yourselves for the long haul Tonige."

"Yes."

"Give the Magi no clue about who you really are, or they will kill you. Until next time." He bid the others farewell.

***

Riding along the snow-covered trail that winds through the Goraan Mountains, Kalvin asked himself why he had agreed to Anjia's plan. After leaving Anazi Falls, Anjia explained she needed him to help her obtain something that is important to the Order of the Flame. Daniel and Ofelia did not want him to go with Anjia, but after talking with Anjia and Alena, who knew about the plan, Razial suggested Kalvin go along with Anjia's plan.

"I am fated to become the Blue Keeper, and you are fated to become a paladin, so you might as well get used to trusting me." Anjia had said to him privately.

After that conversation, to Daniel's and Ofelia's dismay, he agreed to go along with Anjia's plan. After the entire group had ridden for several days through the mountains, Anjia, Alena, and Kalvin separated from the others and rode along the high trail that leads to Doh. Kalvin thought about how the low trail marks the border between Giaour and Brahma, while the high trail is above the snow line. So, while the others are traveling along in pleasant weather, he must travel through snow.

"Anjia. You do know how I feel about winter. Do you not?" Kalvin asked.

"Of course. You love it." Anjia teased. "That is why I have decided to call you Kalvin the Warrior of Winter."

She looked back over her shoulder. Kalvin frowned. Both she and Alena giggled. Her long dark hair hung from under her skull cap. Dressed in all black, her pretty tan-yellow face stands out. Her narrow eyes reveal no menace. Kalvin stared at the flaming dagger on her cloak and thought about how she could be very menacing even for her petite size. He knows very few individuals are allowed to wear the black cloak with Fulancia's sigil on it. She is one of the few.

And where few can wear them, all who see them know the wearer is not to be challenged in any fashion.

Anjia's plan is simple. She is going to lead him into Doh, where he is to challenge Doh's leader to a duel. Afterward, he and the leader's champion will head to Doh's treasure house, where they will scale ten-foot ladders to a fighting platform. She has total confidence in him.

"After you have killed him, take the scroll he keeps hidden under his belt." She said.

With Doh just ahead of them, Kalvin looked around. Trees sparsely cover the area. Snow blankets all they can see. Already, they have spotted several scouts, so they are sure all inside the city know they are coming. He sighed, so long as he succeeds, Anjia will give the scroll to the keepers and the Children of Doh will no longer try to kill him.

Minutes later, Alena looked at Anjia while a group of guards led them through the city to meet with their leader. Alena did not need to be convinced to go along with Anjia's plan, because she had a vision of Anjia giving the scroll to the keepers which means Kalvin would succeed.

Walking through the short corridor that leads to the ruler's meeting hall, Alena took notice of how respectful the guards are to Anjia. She also saw how nervous Kalvin was. He does not understand the Children of Doh exist at the Society's leisure. All inside Doh know what it would mean if anything happened to Anjia while she is inside their city. -Goraan would eradicate the Children of Doh!

"Mighty Anjia." Doh's ruler stood. "Alena? You are Alena, are you not?"

"You have a good memory." Alena tilted her head to show she was impressed that he remembers her.

He is not tall. Slightly shorter than Kalvin. He has a bulky build, graying rusty brown hair, and fiery reddish-brown eyes. Alena knows he had fought his way to the top and that is why he leads the Children of Doh. He asked why they came. Anjia stared at several men, who are standing in front of a young boy.

"I distrust them." Anjia said.

"They are young Abel's caretakers." The ruler replied.

Alena stared at the men and the boy. She sensed danger from the boy-Abel. She began to see many scenes from the future, and she realized she could not share this with anyone. Abel will father a son, who will be named Abel as well. He is the reason she sensed danger. The son will be the threat!

"I never imagined you as the type to adopt a child." Anjia said.

"We all have our weaknesses. Now please tell me why you are here with Kalvin."

"Simple. Kalvin tell him why we are here."

Kalvin stepped forward and drew a dagger and pointed it at the ruler, who sighed.

"Very well get the dirks."

He eyed Kalvin. He knows Anjia is behind this challenge. He is simply happy she was not more forceful about trying to settle the matter between Doh and Kalvin.

Anjia told Kalvin to strip off his shirt and boots. She had forgotten to tell him he must fight shirtless and barefoot; Kalvin did not have a problem with it. He followed her and Alena to the treasure house. The coolness of the floor made him feel more alert. He was surprised to find out there would be no spectators. The ruler called his champion.

"I am ready." The man said.

Kalvin stared at the man as soon as he entered the treasure house. He is taller than Kalvin and more muscular, but Kalvin can sense he is not as calm as he appears to be. Looking around the treasure house, he saw bags and chests lining the walls. In the middle of the high ceiling hall, is a ten-foot-high platform in the shape of a circle. It appears to be over ten feet in diameter. Guards with spears began to surround the platform. His opponent began to climb the ladder. Kalvin looked at Anjia, who gestured for him to do the same. Without pause, he climbed the ladder nearest him.

At the top of the platform, he realized that falling off means death!

"I'm ready when you are." His opponent said.

Kalvin knelt to pick up the dirk. He does not mind being a little nervous. He sighed as he stepped forward. Knowing the man is used to being the aggressor, Kalvin pressed him. He easily adjusted to using a dirk instead of a dagger. His opponent calmly deflected and blocked his swings, but that is what Kalvin wanted. He bent forward and sliced open the inside of the man's right knee. The man winced in pain. He had not expected Kalvin to bend down. Kalvin pressed him still. However, the man was not finished. He forced Kalvin back. His situation is desperate. Kalvin felt the air leave his body when he was hit in the chest by the dirk's hilt. To avoid death, Kalvin kicked him in his left knee as he fell to the platform. His opponent fell two paces away from him. Kalvin rolled over so he could fill his lungs with air. He heard his opponent struggling to his feet.

"Aarh!" Kalvin winced.

His opponent had thrown his dirk, and it bit into Kalvin's side causing him great pain. Angry, Kalvin thought about all that had happened to him. Now, he is in Doh fighting a fight to the death because Anjia-an assassin fated to become the next Blue Keeper, wants him to. He thought about losing Sidney and Xochi.

Clenching his teeth, he charged his opponent, who could not hold back his rage driven attack. Kalvin's dirk bit into his torso repeatedly. Then, he remembered the scroll.

"You can raise the ladders now." Kalvin winced.

Anjia and Alena looked at each other and smiled. They watched Kalvin climb down the ladder. Alena told Anjia that she will heal Kalvin's wound. Anjia looked at the ruler of Doh and tilted her head in respect. She did not have to do that, but she remembers something Goraan had told her.

"No one likes to be dominated. So long as everyone knows their place is all that matters."

Kalvin winked at her while she thought about that. She knew he had gotten the scroll. She nodded in response. The ruler of Doh led them out of the treasure house and smiled because he knew his place.

***

Goraan sat alone in the front room of his private chambers. In the past, he always felt Binu had better patience, which is why he preferred Binu as leader of the Hilt. With all that is going on, he must admit it is best he leads the Hilt. Not only does he know more than Binu, but he is also more aggressive and willing to press the issue even if it would cost him a high price and, at best, all he could win is a draw. He is willing to fight that kind of fight just to prevent his foes from winning!

Already, he has taken actions that the others do not agree with, but that does not matter. This war is his to wage. Dario openly governs Fulancia while Tol, who Goraan sent to Jedan, will look after the Society's interest in Jedan. This is important because

Goraan has made a deal with the Order of the Flame to take over Jedan.

Razial group's actions have presented him with an opportunity he could not pass up. Rogelio believes he has done all he has done to make the hunt safer for Razial, but he does not even discuss this type of thinking. Razial does not heed his help to survive.

Still, he must come up with a way to counter the others' plans to capture Razial.

A knock on the door ended his train of thought.

"Enter." He ordered.

Vishnu entered the room. Dimly lit and pleasantly scented, the room made him feel calm. His blue eyes took in Goraan, who gestured for him to sit. After sitting on the floor pillow opposite Goraan, Vishnu rubbed his beard.

"I have a task for you." Goraan pointed.

Vishnu thought about the fact he cannot see his elflocks with his hair down, but he can see his pointed ears. He wondered why Goraan never tried to recruit more elves into the Society. There are elf members of the Society, but few are assassins.

After thinking about how there are tens of elves across Giaour who have never been recruited by the Society, Vishnu cleared his mind.

"I want you to join Edward in northern Ocia, where you two are to kill several targets. He knows who they are. After you have done this, go to the city of Ocia. Learn all you can before you kill Pam the leader of the Sisterhood. I want her dead." Goraan held out a silver ring.

Vishnu took the ring. It is in the shape of a dagger. Goraan explained there are two other rings just like it.

"One has been in use for several years. The other, I shall give to Dario. They are mediums. They will enhance your powers and allow you to use telepathy without much risk. They were made by an elf druidess to keep in contact with her servants." Goraan said.

He told Vishnu not to worry about the druidess, who could use the ring to enslave him because she is not around to do so. Vishnu nodded in response. Goraan then told him the Magi will release Rakaar's Shadow and explained what will happen when they do. He told him to give Edward extra gold, which he would need to stay in the lands of Ocia. He then fully explained all that is going on with Razial. This news shocked Vishnu whose first response was.

"Should we not end the hunt?"

"You know we cannot do that. But that proves why you are worthy of the dagger. One day, you will join the Hilt." Goraan said with a grin.

With that, Vishnu stood and left the room. Goraan knows he will set off in the morning.

CHAPTER 13

THE PALADINS

From atop the temple, Tonige looked over Winnin. His black and gold robe does not protect him from the steady cold wind blowing across the city. He looked at the priestesses and priests he had gathered at the temple. The Magi had surprised them all by sneaking away from their armies and secretly making their way into Winnin.

They are inside the temple preparing themselves to release Rakaar's Shadow. Word of their presence in the city has spread and people are beginning to make their way to the temple. They all want to see the Magi.

Hearing the Magi exit the sacred hall, Tonige knew they would tell him to accompany them to Brahma. A foolish idea, but something they will do, nonetheless.

"Tonige." Cas called. "What news do you have about the half elf Tuyakan?"

Tonige is slightly taller than Cas, whose tan skin made many call him a Tuyakan especially since he has short curly hair.

As a member of one of the many peoples who descend from the Gully Tuya-Kan, Cas' appearance is quite typical and as a former practitioner of Tuya-Kan, he should not use Tuyakan in a derogatory manner.

"He escaped Troggo's plan. He is on his way back to Brahma. He has obtained the Gideon's powers." Tonige said flatly.

The cold air sent a chill across his bald head. He rubbed his hands together for warmth. His beard is keeping his face warm. He watched Bal and Mel stand around the white flames. Bal's pale skin seems to glow. Even beneath his fur cloak, Bal's muscled arms appear big. He kept his growling voice low while saying.

"You sound impressed by this assassin. I remember when Winninans were not so easily impressed."

Tonige ignored him. He knows the Magi are too arrogant for their own good. They have no idea how deadly Razial is. If he were not a Harbinger and did not know what he knows about Razial, he would be disappointed by their attitude toward Razial. However, he is a Harbinger. He wants them to keep underestimating Razial.

A grin came over his face when the Magi began chanting as they drew their powers. They began sending magical flames into the white flames causing them to grow. The people pushed closer to the temple trying to get a better look. The white flames continued to grow until they lit up the night sky.

Tens of minutes went by before the flames returned to their normal size. That is when a thick black smoke began to rise from them. The smoke blew in the wind as it rose high in the sky.

"Tonige." Cas called weakly. "We will leave soon. Gather an army with extra supplies."

"And if you hear anything from these Harbingers" Mel snarled. "-make it clear that we shall deal with them also, so they better remain hidden."

Tonige watched them walk away. Releasing Rakaar's Shadow weakened them. He thought about what Mel had said. *He is trying to intimidate the Harbingers.* That made Tonige remember something the Master had said to him years earlier.

"No one tries to intimidate another unless one does not want to fight."

The Master's words echoed in Tonige's mind. Mel had all but said the Magi do not want to fight the Harbingers-not yet anyway.

***

Like several others fated to become a paladin, Dwight wishes Razial were not fated to become their Gideon. Along with Raal, Fogi Red, and several siblings, Dwight sat listening while the keepers explained the Magi had released Rakaar's Shadow. They explained that a dark cloud will spread a mile every day in every direction until the Magi are killed or the entire sky is covered.

None of that bothers Dwight. What bothers him is the fact they cannot kill the Magi, but the Magi can kill them during the fight for their medallions.

"So," the keepers warned. "-you all must be careful. Protect each other. It will seem like a fantasy, but if you die there you will die."

Dwight looked at Fogi Red, who frowned. *They have talked about being fated to become paladins. Neither wants this, but there is nothing could do to change it.*

"What about you all?" Fogi Red asked. "Why will you all not accompany us?"

"Because we are not his keepers. We cannot accompany him." The keepers said.

They then explained that they wanted to decimate the Magi's armies while Razial leads his paladins against the Magi. Dwight asked what would happen if Razial manages to stop the Magi but dies in the process.

"Pray that does not happen. For if it does, upon their return the Magi would obtain their medallions freeing Ja'Brahma in the process."

Dwight stared at the keepers. Ulina is in the middle while Tu'ani is to her right and Lela is to the left of Ulina. Ulina is slightly shorter than Lela, but she is a lot thinner. He took in Lela's white hair as it frames her face. Her strong brown eyes met his gaze. They stand out against her pale white skin. She seems to know that he is thinking about how he does not want to stand with an assassin, who not only brought about their present situation, but does not serve Eloh either.

"None of this makes any sense." He said strongly. "We have to depend on the man who brought about all of this. We cannot trust Razial. I will not-"

"You will obey." Lela cut him off. "You are a bulwark. You serve Eloh. Eloh chose Razial to be his champion. Razial does not want to be Eloh's Gideon. Trust" Tu'ani and Ulina joined in. "-Eloh has chosen wisely."

With that said, they explained they already have an army gathering, so when the Magi's forces draw close, they will be able to mobilize these forces so they can strike the Magi's forces once Razial acts to obtain the Magi's medallions.

Dwight stood listening. He is not happy but said nothing. Fogi Red asked about Igor. The keepers said they will deal with him when things settle down with the Magi. Raal asked why they had sent Ariel to meet with Razial's group. The keepers told him they had made a deal with Goraan to take over Jedan and they want Ariel to watch over things until the others arrive in Jedan.

Although that was a good response, Dwight and Raal feel as though something is odd about them sending Ariel to Jedan. Dwight's mind then went to how he had kept the royal family from choosing a new leader by forcing them to settle their differences. Still, he knows time is running short.

*

After meeting with the keepers, Fogi Red decided to go to the top of the palace. With Raal standing next to him, he looked out over the battlement toward the southeast. Raal looked down at him. He has stood by Fogi Red from the beginning of the conflict that slowly turned into Nibel's civil war.

Before his mysterious death, Fogi Black had the Gully Council assign Raal to guard Fogi Red because during the last years of his reign Lodi Gold accused him and Fogi Red of being Alf-Heim puppets. That caused a lot of tension throughout Nibel. Many clan chiefs backed Lodi Gold when Fogi Black suddenly died and Lodi Gold continued to say Fogi Red was blinded by elves, who he claimed had killed Fogi Black.

For one hundred fifty years, Nibel has been divided. To avoid making it seem as if Lodi Gold's accusations are true, the Gully

Council has tracked and killed many of his spies throughout the mountains. They have also proven to the mountain chiefs that there are dwarf-wizards running around Nibel!

That was important because it convinced the mountain chiefs to allow limited help from Alf-Heim to put Fogi Red on the throne. Now with him being fated to become a paladin, a lot of things must change. He cannot serve as king and be a paladin.

"Things could be worse." Raal said. "You could be fated to be a clan chief."

Fogi Red did not look up at him, but he smirked in response. His frizzy red beard covers his throat. Like his hair, it has been cut but is still long.

"You should be a paladin. Not me." Fogi Red growled. "Things keep happening that I do not want to happen. Maybe, I should start wanting things I do not want to happen."

That made Raal grin. He thought about how he and Fogi Red were original Partisans, but they have not been in western Coilu in over two years. He stated this to Fogi Red, who said.

"We are too busy saving the world." That made them smile.

"We have made our share of sacrifices. Sacrifice is part of life. Is it not?" Raal asked.

"Not to most humans. They prefer to give power to those who are no better than they are and serve them."

"That is the difference between followers and servants; servants serve that which they see, while followers act on faith for that which they cannot see."

Fogi Red nodded in agreement, then he asked why Raal insists on being his personal guard. They stared at each other. Raal's slanted narrow eyes are full of strength. His medium length brown hair is braided back so his blond elflocks and pointy ears can be seen. Tall, for an elf, Raal rarely expresses his anger, but he did when he said.

"I want to see Lodi Gold's downfall and see you safely on the throne of Nibel."

Fogi Red understands Raal wants revenge because Lodi Gold has caused them a lot of grief.

"Remember, my friend. Revenge is a double-edged blade. It cuts both ways."

***

Kalvin watched as Scar's pack ran off. The wolves do not want to enter Jedan. With Ofelia to his left, Kalvin is riding along at a leisurely pace. Razial and Mantak are riding lead with Anjia, Alena, and Zelia behind them. Araceli and Barthus are behind Kalvin and Ofelia. Daniel and the bulwarks are bringing up the rear with Havi and Adini riding in supply wagons.

Priato, who is in Jedan, had told Daniel to bring supplies to add to the supplies he is taking to Brahma city. The keepers are preparing for the widespread famine Rakaar's Shadow will cause.

"Why is the bear not going with the wolves?" Ofelia asked.

Kalvin turned to watch Tree-Breaker trot off in the opposite direction of the wolves. After the duel in Doh, they came across the giant bear. He had sensed Anjia and Alena. According to Anjia, Goraan had saved Tree-Breaker when he was a cub. At the time, a Giaouran noble was hunting elfin bears in southern Brahma.

Unfortunately for him, Goraan was in the area and had sensed Tree-Breaker's nervousness. Goraan killed the noble and had Anjia lead the orphaned Tree-Breaker to the Goraan Mountains. That had been over eight years ago. Tree-Breaker decided to accompany them on their travels.

"Bears and wolves usually do not get along. However, with Rakaar's Shadow releasing many Svan animals, all elfin animals have a common enemy." Kalvin said.

Ofelia nodded in understanding. In truth, Anjia had explained that to Kalvin when she first told him about Tree-Breaker joining them on their trip back to Brahma after he had asked about Scar's pack getting along with Tree-Breaker.

To make sure he understood her point, Anjia told him to think about all the other elfin wolf packs they have encountered without problems because they know Scar's pack is helping Razial. She also told him elfin animals deter Svan animals from bothering them. Kalvin told Ofelia all of this while they made their way into Jedan.

Inside Jedan, the group split up. Razial and Anjia went to meet with Tol while the others went to meet with Priato and others in the house the Order of the Flame uses as a safe house. While Anjia rested, Razial and Tol met inside Tol's private room. Tol wasted no time in explaining why Goraan had sent him to Jedan. He told Razial about Dario governing Fulancia and there will be no more kings in Fulancia-only governors, who will swear fealty to the king of Giaour!

"After we have taken possession of the throne of course. Still," Tol frowned. "-Fulancia bending a knee to anyone seems odd. Does it not?"

"Somewhat." Razial admitted. "But it is only symbolic."

"I see you are letting your hair grow again."

"Only until I reach Brahma."

Talking in Tuyakan, they talked about Arapia and how Tol thinks Goraan intends to make Razial king of Arapia. That made Razial frown.

"Only you would be disappointed by having to marry Diana." Tol smiled.

"Just imagine how Anjia will react." Razial tilted his head.

Tol raised his eyebrows in response. His long wavy hair hangs over his shoulders. Its light brown color matches his olive skin that appears dull in the dimly lit room. He has a thin beard that makes him appear more like his father. His light brown eyes were full of interest when he asked if it is true that Dario had almost killed him. Razial lifted his oversized shirt and turned around revealing the scar he had from Dario's attack.

Seeing the scar made Tol think about the scars Razial had given him. He rubbed his right ribs to feel the scars left from the two stab wounds he had suffered during their fight. Razial pulled down his shirt and they began talking about all that was going on. Tol wished him luck, then told him to be careful because other assassins are in Jedan. Razial nodded before saying farewell.

"I need to meet with the Order of the Flame." He said while making his way to the door. "If Anjia asks, tell her I will be back before nightfall."

Razial made his way out of the house. He decided to walk. The air is cold, but fresh. He took a deep breath as he walked through the street. It is late afternoon. Shadows are long and the sun is low in the horizon. He has at least an hour of daylight left which is more than enough for him to talk to Alena about Zelia. He wants to smooth things out. He does not understand how Anjia can choose to give the Order of the Flame the ancient map she had Kalvin take but does not want to accept Zelia as his Red Keeper.

As he walked through the street, he encountered fewer and fewer passersby. That makes him stand out more. As he approached the house, he noticed a crew of assassins-four in all. He likes them. They came up under Binu. He watched them approach. Two of them are warlocks-one of whom is an elf. Still, all four are young and lack experience. He does not want to have to kill any of them. He warned them to stand down. They drew their weapons. He had wasted his time trying to avoid a fight.

Their swords leapt toward him skillfully. He stepped back throwing his daggers. They were prepared for that. They deflected the daggers with their swords which only sent them back to him more quickly. He sent the daggers tumbling at them repeatedly until he decided to draw his sword.

The leader of the crew, the elf, pressed him. Razial had to back away while using a dagger to deflect several strikes from the others. Hard-pressed, Razial lowered his eyes as he focused more. He threw his daggers with his left hand trying to create some space. His senses focused on the immediate area. His sword rattled against theirs. Their footwork matched his, but the daggers gave him an advantage. He half spun and threw the dagger at the leader. Unable to disengage, the leader used his powers to shield himself, but he was not strong enough so the dagger bit into his shoulder. Still, Razial's success was short lived. He was sliced across his back. He threw his sword at the two behind him. Then, he began throwing his daggers nonstop. The other warlock was struck twice: once in his side and once in his leg. Then Razial went on the offensive. Using his daggers to block and deflect, he pressed the two closest to him. As he did, he heard someone closing in on the area. He sensed the leader draw his powers and start lashing out. Unable to turn around to see what was happening, he heard Kalvin tell Barthus to duck. He tripped an opponent, then spun around in time to see Kalvin get cut across his chest by the crew's leader.

At the same time, in his peripheral vision, he saw one of Barthus' axes slicing through the air directly toward the crew leader. He shouted for Barthus to stop, but it was too late.

Barthus and Kalvin had been inside the house when they heard the fighting in the street. When they saw Razial was involved, they raced to join in. Barthus had no idea who the four men are, but he knew they were assassins. Although Razial was handling himself very well, Barthus could not take the risk of Razial being hurt.

After knocking one of the men down, Kalvin saved him from a vicious wound by calling out to him. He spun around to avoid the strike and used his momentum to generate more power as he swung his ax at the crew leader. He heard Razial call out to him, but the assassin wounding Kalvin had angered him. His ax cut through the crew leader's magical shield with ease, almost cutting him in two.

"Go!" Razial shouted to the other assassins.

They raced off because several siblings ran to join the fighting. Razial stared angrily at Barthus. Barthus ignored him. That made him angrier. He followed Barthus to the house while one of the siblings began to heal Kalvin.

"Put his body on a pyre or I will!" Razial snapped.

One of the siblings agreed to put the dead assassin's body on a pyre while Razial entered the house one pace behind Barthus, who spun around to face him. He looked down at Razial, who told him he knows he could have avoided killing the crew leader. Barthus disliked how he had spoken with such hostility, so he told him to back away. Razial refused. He told Barthus he should have listened to him.

"He was an assassin." Barthus said coldly. "I had no time-"

"You will have no choice when my contract is over." Razial cut him off.

Barthus understood his threat. He told Razial he was lucky he was fated to become the Gideon. Razial scowled saying Barthus is lucky he is under contract. Others began to enter the house with them facing off in the middle of the room.

"I am no young assassin. You will learn that." Barthus said.

"That is not what Troggo says." Razial shot back.

That angered Barthus, who could not control himself any longer. Mocking him about the time Tina was killed was too much for him. He swung. Razial ducked the fast-moving right hand, then sidestepped the left that followed it. He quickly countered and their fight began in earnest.

Barthus' speed prevented Razial from trying to outmaneuver him with just his footwork, but his kicks staggered Barthus several times. However, he still managed to knock Razial down.

Kalvin stood watching the fight. He watched how Razial stayed close so Barthus could not extend his arms. Still, he paid a price, but his tactic allowed him to hammer Barthus with blows to his head. Barthus was kept off balance by the kicks to his legs. He countered that with several short chopping blows knocking Razial backward.

"Enough!" Priato shouted.

Others entered with shocked expressions. Araceli made her way to Barthus while Alena made her way to Razial. They made sure to stay between Razial and Barthus.

"This ends here and now." Priato said firmly.

"Of course it does. I came here for Alena and Zelia." Razial walked toward the door.

Alena and Zelia followed him out.

***

The next afternoon, Priato ate lunch with Araceli, Barthus, Ofelia, Kalvin, Mantak, and Daniel. Unlike when they rode to Anazi Falls, Daniel is wearing his gray cowl. There is no longer a need to hide the fact he is a druid-sibling.

Sitting with his hood drawn back, Daniel eyed the others while Priato told them tales about past paladins. When Priato finished, he explained that when they reach Brahma the keepers will explain why Razial had to go to Anazi Falls. Araceli asked why they had to accompany Razial.

"Because when so many, who are fated for greatness, are together, it increases the chances of success." Priato answered.

He then told them that many of them would be involved in the keepers' plans for Nibel. That seemed strange to them, but no one protested. Daniel thought about how few from the Conclave knew about the plans for Nibel. To him, they should focus on the Magi before they try to deal with Nibel.

Curious about if things have changed so Razial can be trained in Alf-Heim, Daniel asked if they can send Razial to Alf-Heim with the Magi's medallions.

"As I have said, there is only one way for him to go to Alf-Heim. We must wait for that time to come. None of this has ever happened before. In the past, the paladins were trained and prepared before the Gideon was revealed. All we can do now is trust Razial's choices. Remember, choices control circumstances, circumstances control fate, fate controls destiny. Choose wisely, young paladins, for your choices will affect the world." Priato said to them all.

"Why are you so sure Razial will win?" Barthus asked.

"I am not." Priato answered.

That ended their meeting.

***

Weeks later, they approached Brahma city. The weather is cold. Kalvin looked around their procession Priato was riding in a wagon with Adini and Havi and eight orphans Priato came across.

With six wagons full of supplies Kalvin wondered why the keepers wanted so many supplies.

"Who are they?" Ofelia asked.

Kalvin glanced at her. She is riding to his right. Her face, like his, is red from the cold. He followed her line of vision and saw two riders riding toward them.

"Mantak's guards." He said to answer her.

It had taken him a moment to say the Tuyakan word for guard. Although Tuyakan is easy for him to speak, he still feels odd saying certain words.

"Be back by nightfall." Anjia said firmly in elvish.

Kalvin looked back and saw Mantak and Razial riding to the west. He looked back and saw the Ratels riding to join them. Seeing his confusion, Alena told him they are going hunting for the elfin animals with them. That is when he tried to see the elfin animals. Priato told him that in the future he will be able to see elfin animals even when they are invisible to others. He has not reached that point yet.

"They are holding the gates." Ofelia stated.

"Of course they are. Daniel is leading our group. Would you want to make him angry?" Kalvin asked playfully.

Daniel told Anjia to have the elfin animals stay between the wagons so they can ride faster to the keepers' mansion. Anjia did as he asked. Kalvin hopes they stay respectful to each other for the rest of their time together.

Later, all those fated to become paladins met in a large meeting room. Alena, Anjia, Priato, Havi, Adini, Razial, and Raal sat spread out in the room also. They all listened to the keepers tell the story of how Ja'Brahma was imprisoned.

Araceli finds the story remarkable. She thought about how Ariel would have reacted to the story had she heard it. While she thought about that, she heard Razial say he was not aware of the fact that two paladins did not act against Ja'Brahma.

"Because the vision only reveals how the Gideon was made. It does not reveal the entire tale." Priato said in elvish.

He is speaking more elvish so the future paladins can grasp the language more quickly. After making sure he had understood him correctly, Kalvin asked how the two paladins could not help the others imprison Ja'Brahma. Priato told him they had a good reason. Araceli stared at him when he said this. Her eyes widened when he admitted he had been one of the two original paladins who did not act against Ja'Brahma. She did not know he was that old.

"Who was the other, A'Priato?" Barthus asked.

"The other was my brother Bahkez."

"Bahkez? The same Bahkez who led the Boar clan out of the original Alf-Heim and made Ino-Heim?" Barthus asked with a frown.

"The very one."

Hearing that, Araceli looked around to see how the others were reacting to this news. Mantak seems unaffected. He obviously had heard this news before. Barthus seemed to know some of this, but Araceli does not know how much. Kalvin and Ofelia sat in shock hearing about all of this. Neither fully understood the significance of what Priato had just revealed while Fogi Red had the same curious expression he had at the beginning of the meeting. Dwight sat listening to whomever was talking at the time trying to figure it all out.

"I tell you all this because you all must understand that not getting along at times, is normal. Do not allow your differences to distract you or get in the way. You all shall meet A'Ja'Brahma very soon. He will be mean spirited to you two." Priato pointed at Anjia and Zelia.

Zelia's expression changed, showing she was curious about that. Anjia smirked. Hearing that did not bother her in the slightest manner. Araceli wondered if she were the only one who felt curious about the fact Priato had referred to Ja' Brahma with honor. To her, Priato must have misspoken.

"He will be happy to see us." Havi pointed at himself and Adini.

That made her think about how they talk respectfully about Goraan while others dislike him and mention his name with contempt. That made her rethink why Priato had said Ja'Brahma's name with honor. Now she thinks he might simply like Ja'Brahma where others do not.

"Why would he be happy to see you two?" Barthus asked.

The jolems smirked at him as if he had insulted them. Neither answered because Priato told him Ja'Brahma likes and respects Adini and Havi. That shocked the others. Ofelia gasped before asking.

"You two are that old?"

"No." They answered.

They turned on each other with angry expressions. The others laughed at them.

"You better stop that." Adini pointed at Havi.

"Me?" Havi scowled, then pointed. "You."

"How old, are you two?" Ofelia asked.

They raised their shoulders and tilted their heads to show their ignorance. She found it odd they do not know how old they are. Havi explained Gully dwarfs do not keep track of birthdays. Their children are raised communally and are grouped according to which season they were born.

"Well, which one of you is older?" Kalvin asked.

"Adini is." Havi said.

"They were born in the same season as their fathers were." Priato stated.

Araceli did not understand the significance of that until he explained how rare it is for two jolems to be born in the same season, it has only happened twice: with Adini and Havi and with their fathers.

The others became even more shocked when Priato told them their fathers had stood with Ja'Brahma. Only then did Araceli understand just who Havi and Adini are.

"We were born in the summer." Havi stated.

"During the middle of the third Champions' War" Adini added.

"They" the keepers pointed at Adini and Havi. "-will be around Razial. They will know him better than you all think."

Razial looked at the jolems but did not ask anything. He eyed the keepers for a moment. He thought about telling them to explain what they meant, but Priato asked them to meet with him. They stood and thanked Anjia for giving them the missing piece to the map of Ino-Heim. Razial shook his head and grinned. For decades, Rogelio had wanted the map of Ino-Heim. Anjia has just made sure that does not happen.

"So, all we do now is wait?" Razial asked.

"Wait and learn, young Razial. We wait and learn." Priato said while leading the keepers out of the room.

Ofelia invited Razial to meet Niri, Lissa, Bernice, and Vera. He looked at Anjia. She assured him she would be fine. Alena watched Razial follow Ofelia, who led Kalvin by his hand out of the room. She turned to Anjia, who whispered.

"One of them better not be one of his keepers. That would anger me. Until all are revealed I must accept any new woman in our lives could be his keeper."

Although she spoke playfully in elvish, Alena sensed she was quite serious. Knowing Zelia is fated to be Razial's Red Keeper bothers Anjia. She wants to know why no one has said Alena is one of Razial's keepers. Alena has tried to get her to accept Zelia; however, after leaving Jedan she had a vision that revealed Diana is fated to become one of Razial's keepers and she knows how much that would upset Anjia, more so than discovering the truth about Zelia. Alena wanted to share this news with her but knew it was a bad idea. Razial obviously does not want to tell her yet, so Alena must guard this news until it is time for Anjia to hear it.

While Alena and Anjia talked, Mantak walked through the house thinking. He knew Priato had told them about past paladins for two reasons-not one. The first reason was truly to explain paladins are often at odds with their Gideon. However, the second-unspoken reason was to prepare them for the fact that although the keepers will make the decision if Razial walks Ja'Brahma's path it will be Adini and Havi who will decide when action is to be taken against Razial.

Knowing just where the two jolems would be, Mantak found them in the kitchen-eating. They smiled at him. They could sense he was looking for them and had something serious to say, so they stood atop the table and faced him. Mantak looked around. With only one candle burning, the kitchen is mostly dark. Havi's light olive skin seems ghostly. He chewed while Mantak asked if they are the ones who will give permission to act against Razial if Razial walks the path of Ja'Brahma.

"Of course." They said.

"You!" They pointed at each other.

Mantak laughed when they tackled each other. They fell hard to the floor, blaming the other for saying the same thing at the same time as the other. After wrestling for several moments, they took turns explaining things they have witnessed in the past. Then, they asked him if he knew why no one ever talks about how Winnin was destroyed during the third Champions' War. He stated he does. -The Gideon of that era walked the path of Ja'Brahma. He stated this and they nodded their heads.

"Now, how did he get to Winnin?" Adini asked.

"I do not know." Mantak answered.

They took turns explaining that their fathers had decided to act against the Gideon, but they convinced them to lead the Gideon to Winnin so he could unleash his powers there.

"After a Gideon has unleashed his full powers, is the best time to act against him." Havi said.

Mantak did not respond. He knows why they had told him this story.

***

Gwen had anticipated correctly: the Magi had taken Tonige with them to Brahma. That removed the one individual who could have denied her access to Rakaar's chamber.

Along with Dawn and Frauter, she spent days studying in several different houses-owned by friends in the clergy. Although she is well known by the clergy, she does not get along very well with Tonige. She was close to his brother, but Tonige wanted her to leave Bal's side. It is ironic that was the issue between them and now she is in Winnin to do just that. She would have hated to have to ask him to enter Rakaar's chamber.

With the backing of many in Rakaar's clergy, she entered the temple and made her way to the main hall. As she crossed the hall walking toward the altar, she smiled at Dawn. Dawn's blue eyes are full of worry. Gwen can sense how nervous Dawn is. Gwen caressed her blond hair saying.

"Fret not, child. This is a chance I want to take. Frauter will see that you are well if I fail."

She glanced up at Frauter, who simply smiled. Dawn hugged her before stepping back. Gwen embraced Frauter. He is her son, her brother, her best friend, and her student. She is glad Dawn has joined them. If she fails, Frauter will have someone he can trust.

"I will deal with Bal." Frauter promised.

"Join someone first. Do not get yourself killed trying to kill him."

With that, Gwen walked to the doorway behind the altar. She entered the doorway. She did not look back for fear of losing her nerve. The room is dark. Still, she walked on. A silence took over her as if someone had blocked her ears. She could hear her heart beating. Swallowing sounded loud to her. She began wondering how long it would be before she will be contacted by Rakaar. She quickened her pace.

After what she was sure was about a half hour in darkness, a confused Gwen heard a voice call her name. It quickly became two voices. Then three. Each time her name was called, another voice joined in until it sounded as if hundreds of voices called her. Then, they all shouted.

"Gwen!!"

A light came on as a single voice said.

"Pain is life. Life is a struggle. Struggle leads to freedom."

Her heart felt as if it stopped when she heard heavy breathing behind her. She turned around. Standing before her stood a shadow-tracker. It snarled revealing its sharp black teeth. Its cold black eyes made her want to ball up in fear.

Much smaller than the beast, she waited until it made its move. It seemed to know each passing moment added to the dreadful anticipation she felt. Drawing her powers, she quickly released them-shouting in pain, because they were the source of her pain. Pain raced through every nerve in her body. The shadow-tracker laughed at her, then clawed her across her shoulder. She ran. It gave chase. Having no choice, she struck it with her powers. The more power she used the more pain she felt.

Crying out in agony, she battled the creature. She drew her daggers and began stabbing it. After several moments, she managed to cut open its throat. It fell lifeless.

Shivering in agony, she knelt over the beast. Everything went dark. She struggled to her feet. Each step and each breath felt like torture. Still, she persisted. She tasted her own blood in her mouth. That made her angrier and her anger made her stronger. Slowly, it grew hotter and hotter. Her throat became dry.

"Gwen. Face your fears!" A voice hissed.

Instantly, Beulah and Ulina-the two she hates the most, stood before her. Beulah struck her. Gwen collapsed writhing in pain. She screamed as she drew her powers to shield herself.

Tears filled her eyes.

"She is strong." Ulina mocked joining the fighting.

It was all Gwen could do just to hold on to her powers. Her head became hot from the pain. She started to sweat as she tried to figure out which pain was worse, drawing her powers or being struck by her enemies.

She felt them trying to drain and bind her. She clenched her teeth as she started lashing out. They did not shield themselves, so she began stabbing them. They staggered backward as she rolled to her feet exchanging magical blows. She roared while charging them, then everything went black.

"Why do you serve?" A voice whispered.

Gwen did not respond. Breathing through her open mouth, she stumbled forward.

"Who do you serve?" The voice demanded.

"I-I serve no one. I follow the ways of Rakaar. It is Rakaar, who I worship. It is Rakaar, who I follow." Gwen said.

"Few can stand directly with Rakaar. To do so, one must be strong and loyal-extremely loyal. Go now as a failure or stay and risk death."

"I am here until death takes me or Rakaar finds me worthy. Do you hear me?!" She asked defiantly.

"Another has been chosen. You would be in the way."

"I will be chosen or killed! Have I not faced Eloh's servants for centuries?"

"That, Gwen of Dax was for Bal. Bal is like all the others, who stand with Rakaar."

"I know. He, like all others, refuses to stand together at all times."

After that, the voice asked her about her unwillingness to stand with the Sisterhood. She argued those in the Sisterhood are fools and only fools stand with fools.

"Interesting." The voice fell silent before shouting. "Survive!"

Instantly, she was surrounded by flames. She tightened her jaws in pain. She shielded herself but the pain became intolerable as time passed. She tried using her powers to push the flames away from her but could not.

"You grow weary Gwen of Dax. Many have tried to prove themselves worthy and the few who have made it this far always missed the obvious." The voice seemed to dare her to figure that out.

Her powers began to wane. She began to panic when the heat from the flames began to burn her. She did her best to figure out the hint the voice had given her. Then, it came to her. She began using wizardry. Wizardry does not tax her, and it did not cause her pain to wield.

"Who is the greatest threat to Rakaar?"

The flames disappeared and she was engulfed in blackness again. She stopped herself from screaming the Gideon was the greatest threat. Instead, she said.

"The Harbingers." Gwen answered weakly.

"Ha-ha-ha-ha-ha. You are the first to realize this."

A silhouette appeared telling her the Harbingers are a threat because they are not who they are supposed to be, but that will change. That puzzled her.

The silhouette carried her back to the doorway. She could feel power growing inside of her. Still, she is weak from the test. After she was placed on her feet, she staggered out of Rakaar's chamber. Frauter ran and caught her.

"Frauter." She gasped. "I am worthy."

CHAPTER 14

THE RETURN

Brahma city is under a cloud of fear. Most of its citizens have fled. The Magi's tactic of using fear has worked very well. Instead of marching straight to Brahma city, they attacked all the lands before them. Tens of thousands of people were forced from their lands while the Magi's armies pressed just ahead of Rakaar's Shadow, which caused even more fear than the Magi's armies.

Slowly creeping its way across the sky, Rakaar's Shadow hangs in the horizon spreading dread. Seeing it draw near, is what drove the people in the capital to flee weeks earlier. Reports from Tunez say Rakaar's Shadow has covered most of Tunez. The weather beneath it is said to be cold and storm like at times. Most people have been forced to move to survive. Many went into shock from the dread people feel when they see Rakaar's Shadow hovering in the sky. However, its effects are not as bad at night as they are in the day.

Thinking about this, Razial stood watching the fire flicker in the fireplace. He watched the blue, red, yellow, and orange flames dance around. He could feel the warmth from the fire, but he is not standing close to the fireplace. He is shirtless enjoying the warmth inside. He had been running with the wolves where it is very cold outside.

With so few people inside the city, no one cares if he runs the streets with the elfin wolves, but Tree-Breaker is another story. People are afraid of the giant elfin bear.

Thinking about that made Razial smile. A knock on the door made him look around. His room is well lit. Candles burn in each corner. Rubbing his head, he said.

"Enter."

The door opened and Zelia stood in the doorway. Holding a lamp that revealed how sheer her gown is. A sense of arousal past through him. The way she held his gaze while she entered his room, made him stare at her-taking in all her beauty. He had forgotten how beautiful she was. This new image of her is now frozen in his mind. It will never be forgotten.

"I was told to make sure you are here." She whispered.

Her voice broke the hypnotic affect her body had on him. He was supposed to have returned to the palace after running with the wolves, but he decided to stay in the mansion. Tu'ani had obviously contacted her telepathically. He is sure she had also instructed Zelia to make sure he did not go back out now that it was night.

"Inform Tu'ani that I am foolhardy-not foolish. Is there anything else?" He smiled.

A solemn expression came over her face. Razial had not expected her to have anything serious to say.

"She changed her mind about you before-" Her voice broke.

He stepped close to her. He caressed her shoulder while saying he had changed his mind about Xochi as well. He knew that was who she was talking about. She was not surprised by the fact he had known what she was talking about even though she had not finished her statement. It made her happy to hear he had changed his mind about Xochi before she died.

"Do not worry. I will keep my word to her." He said in Tuyakan while hugging her.

She hugged him with only one hand because she was still holding the lamp. Still, she did her best to press against him to return the affection she feels from him.

"I owe you a life debt. It will be paid." He said.

She smiled as she rubbed his back. Touching him made her feel good. Pressed against each other-her breasts against his chest, a wave of arousal past through them. They felt the other's heart beating. Razial gently pulled away from her. As he did, he saw someone step through the doorway. He was not surprised to see it was Anjia. She looked at Zelia with anger in her eyes.

Sensing the change in him, Zelia looked over her shoulder and saw Anjia. She does not want to antagonize her, but she refuses to cower before her. She leaned forward and kissed Razial on his cheek.

"Thank you." She said in Tuyakan. "Anjia. I have told those in the palace Razial is here."

She strolled confidently by Anjia leaving her alone with Razial. Anjia sighed while closing the door. Razial did not give her time to say anything. He walked to her while whispering.

"Anjia. Why is it you schemed to get the missing piece to the map of Ino-Heim so you could give it to the Order of the Flame, but you do not want Zelia to be my Red Keeper?"

Anjia smiled but her narrow almond shaped eyes were full of frustration. She sighed and her expression became blank. He knows she has something on her mind. He reached out and caressed her face. She closed her eyes enjoying his touch.

"Goraan sent me a message. Somehow, he knows about me giving the keepers the map." Anjia said softly.

That made Razial scowl. She explained that she had met with the keepers to find out how Goraan had found out about the map. The keepers told her they have no idea how Goraan knows. That ended her meeting with them. While leaving the palace, she crossed paths with Priato, who discussed her feelings about having to share Razial with Zelia and others. Priato had made it clear she must realize where Razial must bind with her and his Red and Yellow Keepers, it does not mean he has to be in love with them.

"He loves you. He does not have to love the others." Priato had said. "The bonds they will share will be bonds of convenience. He may grow to care for them, but he will always be in-love with you."

Remembering that made her smile. She embraced Razial telling him she would be nicer to Zelia.

"It is better that she is one of your keepers than someone I dislike."

Razial looked into her eyes dreading the day he must tell her Diana will become his Gray Keeper.

***

The next day in the palace, Razial saw Dwight, Barthus, and a sibling walking toward him from the opposite direction. He knows Dwight and Barthus dislike him, but it does not matter to him. He likes how Dwight is handling all that is going on. He has kept the city's nobles in line and mediated between the royals wisely, making sure no new ruler is chosen until the Order of the Flame's grip on the city is no longer based solely on his position.

They all acknowledged him as they passed by. He gestured in response without breaking stride. He continued walking until he reached the small hall where Priato, Adini, Havi, Chivia, and the keepers all sat around a stone table. Priato introduced him to Chivia. Razial heard about her from Adini and Havi. She is their mother-in-law and leader.

"Where is Mantak?" Razial asked.

"He is a paladin, and some things are not for paladin ears." The keepers said.

That was good enough for Razial. He took a seat next to Priato with his eyes still on the keepers. Havi recognized Razial dislikes it when the keepers talk simultaneously, so he said.

"I hate it when they do that too. It always makes me wonder who is behind their words or their shared thoughts?"

"Be silent!" Chivia hissed at him.

"Razial." Priato called in elvish. "It has come to my attention that some have tried to recruit you to join the Order of the Flame. I have put a stop to that. You are never to join the Order of the Flame unless both paths are walked at the same time. Do you understand?"

"No." Razial answered. "But it does not matter because I will never join the Order of the Flame."

He looked around and recognized the others understood what Priato had said. He did not ask what Priato had meant because he doubted, he would receive an answer.

"Tell us. Has your vision changed since Anazi Falls?" The keepers asked.

Razial lowered his eyes in thought, then explained that Dwight is clear sometimes but cloudy at other times. He told them that whoever the Yellow Keeper is has long dark hair. He then told them sometimes in his vision Priato is replaced by a female elf.

"Do you know who she is?" Priato stated.

"Maybe. In my vision, she never looks at me and sometimes you are both present." Razial said.

He noticed that disappointed Priato while the keepers seemed confused and the jolems appeared stoic. He stated he does not know who the Yellow Keeper is, but she appears familiar to him. He told the keepers he is sure he has seen her but is not sure where or when.

When he finished saying that Chivia asked about the Gully dwarfs in his vision. He told her more and more appear, but they remained distant from him. Chivia simply nodded while Adini stated that means there will be more fighting in the future.

"Now it is time to explain the path of Ja'Brahma." The keepers said.

"First, I must reveal the tale of the clans." Priato said.

He then explained how when he was young, Rakaar was determined to make all humans worship him and to eradicate all elves. Rakaar almost succeeded, but the dwarfs rescued the elves, and two humans built a civilization based on the Creator's original intentions for all humans. That took some of Rakaar's focus from the elves. He saw the danger from these two humans: Tuya and her husband Kan.

As time passed, Ja'Brahma warned Tuya and Kan not to let their descendants stray too far from Tuya-Kan, but it was too late. Rakaar's taint on the world had finally created a way to poison Tuya-Kan making it less of a threat to Rakaar's desire to dominate the world.

Tuya took measures to counter Rakaar's taint telling her three daughters; Menna, Gully, and Denari to always control who can practice Tuya-Kan. Kan became more militaristic after foreseeing the wars that would take place for control of the world.

In the end, Tuya and Kan failed because their daughters were killed by a group of Tuya-Kan exiles, who were tainted by Rakaar's taint. These exiles called themselves Wizars and went about secretly building empires. Their mission was to surpass elves in power and influence.

"While all of this was happening, all elves decided to live in clans. The Wolves remained completely loyal to Eloh. The Hawks became the best learners. The Bears became the strongest in magic. The Panteras became the best fighters while the Boars became fearless warriors.

After decades of war, Ja'Brahma became king of all elves. He decided to take on Rakaar. So, while the dwarfs waited to strike Rakaar's servants and Kan kept his followers from constant warfare,

Ja'Brahma made an edict saying all Rakaar's servants are to be targeted and killed!" Priato shook his head.

Razial could see the sadness in his eyes. Priato finished his tale by saying when Ja'Brahma became Eloh's champion, he (Priato) and Bahkez became Ja'Brahma's paladins.

"For years, we targeted and killed Rakaar's servants until A'Ja'Brahma decided to kill Rakaar!" Priato finished.

After that, the keepers explained that Eloh had often chosen female servants to spread the Creator's true cause which is why elf clans and Tuya-Kan tribes are based on maternal lines. Razial nodded at this, then they explained that Eloh decided to bind Ja'Brahma to three of his most loyal servants-Ja'Brahma's keepers, to empower Ja'Brahma and his servants.

"Since Ja'Brahma was already married, Eloh made his wife the Gray Keeper and to avoid arrogance from setting in, Eloh allowed all male elves to bind with three wives." The keepers said.

Razial frowned. He does not understand what any of this has to do with the path of Ja'Brahma. He did not have to wait long to find out. The keepers went on to explain that the Blue, Red, and Yellow Keepers were bound to Ja'Brahma to control him. He had become too powerful and his philosophy on how the world should be controlled contradicts Eloh's philosophy.

Ja'Brahma wants to kill all enemies-no matter the consequence. Razial sees nothing wrong with that. The keepers could sense it, so they explained that doing this would create a cycle of never-ending warfare. Razial countered by saying that the world is already locked in an eternal war. Their response intrigued him.

"For humans, this is true. Humans are destined to war among themselves and with others. The thing is to keep it balanced. As for dwarfs, war is necessary to clean the bad blood between them. Elves have never warred against elves. Some elves have fought other elves, but there has never been a war fought between only elves."

"So, if humans are doomed to war, what difference does it make if Rakaar is killed?" Razial asked.

He knows everything changed when Ja'Brahma went mad and became determined to kill Rakaar. He wants to know why they are so convinced Ja'Brahma can kill Rakaar and why it would be so bad if he did.

The keepers explained that the power the Creator used to make Rakaar cannot be destroyed, and that power would always return in a different form-a form that might be more difficult to contain.

"Which is why having to kill the Magi has put us in a serious bind. We have no idea how Rakaar will return their energy." The keepers said.

Razial remained stoic, but he knows they avoided saying he had put them in a bind. He realized Goraan must be ready for however the Magi's energy will be returned to the world.

To make sure he knows what they are saying, he asked.

"So, what exactly is the path of Ja'Brahma?"

The keepers explained that the path of Ja'Brahma leads to madness because it always demands action against all enemies no matter what. It calls for one world order where the strong defends the weak. They made it clear that no matter how good that sounds it is ultimately wrong.

"Such a path leads to constant rebelling and corruption." The keepers said.

They spoke with such certainty that he did not question them. He assured them he has no desire to bring order to the world.

"No. You do not. However, your powers-the Gideon's powers, do!" The keepers said.

Razial scowled but remained silent. He began to think. He knows somehow his feelings and actions will decide which path he walks. A smile came to his face because truthfully, he will not decide which path he walks on his own. The others sensed that he finally realizes the danger he is in from himself. He sighed, then asked.

"So, when do we act?"

"I like him." Chivia smiled. "Knowing the dangers he faces. All he wants to know is when do we attack."

Razial winked at her. Her long brown hair over her shoulders. Her brown eyes appear motherly. She does not have the appearance of a blood thirsty warrior, but he knows she is, or she would not be the leader of the jolem armies.

The keepers explained their plan in full, then ended the meeting.

***

Niri teased Ofelia and Kalvin while she checked on the children, who had all fallen ill. Niri's olive skin has lightened with the arrival of winter. She checked for a child's fever while Ofelia told her to be quiet before she wakes the children.

Standing close to Kalvin, Ofelia looked over the room. Five of the orphans Priato brought to Brahma lay asleep. Although the room is dimly lit, she can see Niri's eyes while Niri walked toward the front of the room where she and Kalvin stood.

"Lissa and Vera will not be happy to see Kalvin here. You can bring more water and some food. I will be all right until you return." Niri whispered in Tuyakan.

Kalvin liked her idea, but before Ofelia could respond Priato approached the room. Kalvin stepped away from Ofelia. She and Niri had been told to look after the children and he does not want to get her into any trouble especially since he is supposed to be training with Barthus.

Priato entered the room with his powers drawn. Ofelia offered to help Priato heal the children. He smiled at her saying the children must cure themselves. He is only there to ease their pain.

While he said this, Alena entered. She smiled knowingly at Kalvin. She knows how happy he is to be close to Ofelia. Niri and Ofelia greeted her respectfully. She nodded in response.

"Uncle. Let me." Alena said warmly.

She reached out to touch Priato's arm while drawing her powers. Priato, who leaned over the first child, stood and looked back at Alena with fear in his eyes. He tried to pull away, but it was too late. She touched him and they both began to convulse and shake violently. Magical flashes engulfed them, and the sense of magic grew.

Kalvin heard others scrambling through the palace while he stepped toward them. He glanced at Ofelia and Niri. They drew their powers. As he reached out to grab Alena and Priato, Mantak arrived and told him not to touch them.

Chivia, Adini, and Havi arrived after that. They shook their heads when they saw what was happening. Others arrived.

"No Razial!" Ulina shouted in elvish.

Mantak intercepted Razial making sure he did not touch Alena or Priato.

"What is happening?" Razial asked in elvish.

"They will be fine." Ulina shook her head. "It must run its course."

The flashes stopped. Razial caught Alena while Mantak caught Priato. Ulina assured Razial they would be fine. Tu'ani moved to the doorway and told everyone to return to what they were doing. Kalvin caressed Ofelia's back before leaving the room. He walked by Lela and followed Barthus so they could train.

Although he wants to know what happened, he knows not to ask Barthus because he should have been with him minutes earlier. He heard Ofelia assuring the children that Priato would be fine. Barthus showed no sign of concern, so Kalvin relaxed.

***

Alena awakened hours after Priato, who had visited with the children and returned before she sat up. He smiled at her. She smiled back. He appears saner than she has ever seen him. She did not ask what happened because she knew. Many things have become known to her.

She saw Ulina standing near the doorway. She feels strange because now she knows why she has had visions and why being around Anjia triggered them. Anjia's fate affected her fate to succeed Priato as Eloh's seer.

"Fate has changed things." Priato said in ancient elvish. "This was unforeseen, but in Razial's vision. He does not understand what you and I existing at the same time means."

"And we must keep it from him." Alena said finishing his sentence with him.

They know fate shall make it so that one of them dies soon. He hopes it is him. He has wanted to take his final rest for millennia.

Since they are born immortal, long-lived elves begin hearing what is known as the Call, a growing desire to die, after they have walked the Creator's path for many years. Priato first heard the Call millennia ago, but he cannot answer the Call because being Eloh's seer is his punishment for refusing to act against Ja'Brahma.

"Alena'a." Priato smiled. "Having this ability is a difficult burden, but you shall bear it well. Now brace yourself to talk with Razial. He must not sense what you and I both know." Alena nodded.

She turned to look at Ulina, who knew one of them must die.

***

The next morning, Razial and Alena were awakened by the city's alarm. After it became clear there was no danger, they decided to bathe.

While getting dressed, Alena smiled. He smiled back. She had enjoyed spending the night with him. She did not reveal what had happened. She told him and Anjia, who was present while she talked with Razial, that somehow her powers had interlocked with

Priato's powers-which is true, but not the whole truth. Still, it satisfied Razial and Anjia.

Watching Razial, she realized they would not spend many more nights together. Soon, he must bind with his keepers. A sadness came over her. Razial sensed this and asked what was bothering her.

"Today, you shall defeat the Magi." She smiled.

She kissed him softly on his lips. Truthfully, she had said this trying to convince herself this would happen. However, neither she nor Priato know the outcome of the impending fight between Razial and the Magi.

Leading Razial by his hand, she led him out of the room. They walked close together as they made their way through the hallway. She did not realize how much she missed being close to him. He was surprised by how affectionate she was being. They saw Kalvin and Ofelia as they all began to walk down some stairs. Alena held up her hand to show they were walking hand in hand.

"Hold her hand, Kalvin." She said teasingly in Tuyakan.

Kalvin tried not to smile but could not stop himself. Ofelia blushed. Araceli, who walked close to Barthus, Mantak, and the two Ratels, called out to Alena telling her to stop teasing Kalvin and Ofelia. Alena smiled at her just before she turned into another hallway disappearing from Alena's line of sight before Alena and the others reached the bottom of the stairs. Alena playfully pushed Razial when he told Ofelia to take Kalvin's hand.

"That is Kalvin's job." Alena teased.

They all reached the main floor and headed toward the main hall to meet with the others. Razial grinned when Kalvin nervously took Ofelia's hand. Ahead of them, Anjia talked with Zelia outside the hall's doorway. As they approached the doorway, Anjia beamed with joy. She kissed Razial and embraced Alena. She and Alena held each other for several seconds. Razial winked at Zelia before walking into the hall.

Dwight, Lela, and Ulina already sat around the table while Mantak, Araceli, Barthus, Tu'ani, and Raal stood by the front wall. Ofelia took a seat while Kalvin shook hands with Razial.

"Today might be the day." Razial said.

Kalvin nodded. His mouth watered when he smelled the food. Biscuits, grits, eggs, ham, milk, and juice cover the table. Razial knows Kalvin is ready to eat. They took a seat as Chivia wobbled into the hall. She climbed onto a chair next to Ofelia. Kalvin can sense the impending battle does not bother her in the slightest.

"What are you feeding the others?" Chivia asked.

"Biscuits, honey, and oatmeal. We would do nothing less for your army." Tu'ani and Lela answered.

Chivia nodded. She asked about Adini and Havi while the others sat. Mantak told her they had stayed behind to help Priato explain something to Fogi Red. Tu'ani told them to start eating. Razial did not hesitate in making his plate and eating all he had put on his plate: eggs, biscuits, and grits.

The honey made it all taste that much better. Priato, Fogi Red, Adini, and Havi arrived while he prepared a second plate. Adini grabbed two biscuits and dipped them in honey before making himself a plate.

While everyone ate, Anjia asked why she could not accompany Razial and the others to Ja'Brahma's cell. Ulina told her she already knows only Eloh's seer and the Gideon's paladins can join the Gideon. Anjia wanted to argue out of spite. She hated not being able to accompany Razial into battle. Although Ulina had explained that the Magi's powers would do them no good during the fighting, Anjia wanted to be there to help. She sighed, pushing these thoughts out of her mind.

Several minutes later, the Ratels arrived. They had made sure the elfin animals ate. They accepted the biscuits offered to them but denied more because they had eaten their fill in the mansion.

With everything settled, Priato told the keepers to let Dwight stay back and lead the fighting against the Magi's forces outside the city. The keepers remained stoic for a moment. Mantak knew they communicated telepathically. To make sure he got his way, Priato told them Alena, Anjia, and Zelia could fight with Dwight to make sure all goes well.

"Very well." The keepers said.

"I believe young Mantak has something he wants to say to all present." Priato smiled at Mantak.

"Thank you, uncle." Mantak said in ancient elvish.

He stood and began to walk around the table. He told them he had a tale to share. Razial and Kalvin eyed each other trying to see if the other had any idea about what Mantak was about to say.

Their expressions revealed they are equally ignorant.

"During Ja'Goraan's two centuries as a member of the Canopy, many elves chose to follow his philosophy-as did many followers of Tuya-Kan. Teresa-the current Gray Keeper, shared virtually the same philosophy. She was allowed to defend his actions during his trial. He was cleared, but afterward one of his followers was imprisoned and he struck another member of the Canopy because of this, so he was expelled." Mantak looked at Anjia.

Anjia stared at him while he continued walking around the table and telling his tale. He explained how Goraan began spreading his cause outside of Alf-Heim and with the world still reeling from the fourth Champions' War the Order of the Flame could not make him a priority until his followers became too much of a problem.

"During the battles that ensued in the Ciru Range, Ja'Goraan's wife became pregnant, which is why he snuck out of the mountains, so his child could be born in Alf-Heim."

Mantak's words shocked Anjia. Alena put a hand on Anjia's arm. She too was shocked by what Mantak had said. Hearing Goraan had a wife before Anjia's mother was surprising, but hearing he had a child is shocking. Razial, Alena, and Anjia each listened intently while Mantak explained that Goraan's wife was captured and agreed to help trap Goraan, who refused to allow her to remain a prisoner. He was captured trying to free her.

"However, he and his wife were freed by his followers. His wife then made the mistake of confessing what she had done. Her guilt and her betrayal cost her life." Mantak said sadly.

Anjia can sense how this tale affects him. Still, he went on. He explained that Goraan returned to Alf-Heim to deliver his son to his mother so she could raise her grandson. Anjia became more and more curious about the identity of her half-brother. She told herself she is going to demand to know who her half-brother is if

Mantak tries to keep it from her. Then, it struck her as soon as she calmed down, Mantak is Goraan's son!

Mantak stared into her eyes and recognized she had figured out they are half siblings, so he said.

"Our mothers shared the same fate."

"Because we failed them." Priato stated. "We should have never recruited them against Goraan."

Although Priato was not involved in the plans that led to Goraan's wives betraying him, he included himself. Mantak knows this and made a mental note to share this with Anjia later. He saw a change in Anjia. She began to scowl as realization began to set in. For decades, she has been at odds with her father because of what had happened to her mother. Now, hearing the whole story, she has someone else to be angry with.

"So, my mother would still be alive had you all not made the same mistake that you made over three hundred years earlier!" Anjia said knowingly.

Razial and Alena sat back. They made no attempt to calm Anjia. It would have only made things worse. Ulina told Anjia that her mother had made the decision on her own.

"She wanted him to stop being an assassin. Our mistake was being ignorant of Ja'Goraan's spies in Alf-Heim. Although many doubt this, there is a lot of evidence that Ja'Goraan is a Harbinger." Ulina said firmly.

"Now is not the time to have this debate." Priato said. "We must deal with the Magi, today."

Anjia stood with her eyes on Mantak. A smile came over her face as she walked over to him and said.

"So, you are my father's son."

They embraced and with that, the meeting ended. Razial looked at all present wondering what evidence they have that makes them believe Goraan is a Harbinger. Shaking his head, he began to think how things would be if Goraan really were a Harbinger.

***

Just outside the city of Brahma, the Master sat atop his horse with Beulah and Peter just behind him. They watched as the Magi's massive armies began to spread out. In the sky, Rakaar's Shadow is slowly creeping toward the city. The weather is cold, and snow blankets the ground beneath Rakaar's Shadow. Even though the day is slowly darkening, their Harbinger cowls remain bright. The Master wants the Magi to see them. He has no doubt the Magi gave no consideration to the fact of not reaching the city. Without the power Rakaar gave them, they would have died long ago.

"Troggo is approaching." Peter whispered.

The Master slowly turned to the right. He watched as Troggo, Kitara, and several other Harlequins rode toward his position. He turned back and watched as the Magi's forces closed in on the city.

Even in the darkness, their black banners with white flame sigils stand out. When he first discovered the Magi would wait before attacking Brahma city, he sent Beulah a message telling her to meet him after she had set Tunez's forces in position to steal supplies from the Magi's armies after the fighting began. He wants the Magi to see Harbingers present when they suffer a humiliating defeat. Already, he has plans for their medallions and to bring them back.

"Mighty Fa'Kitara." The Master said. "It is good to see you. Your plan to keep the Gideon from leaving almost worked. Too bad for you, Goraan was prepared for such an action. He truly is a tactician."

He had spoken in ancient elvish, which puzzled Kitara. Troggo asked how the Master knows about Kitara's plan. The Master's response was simple.

"It is time for the Harlequins to return to their clan. Your queen- A'Bahkez's daughter, needs you. Stop your raids." Beulah and Peter trotted off as planned. "Be ready for when I bring back the Magi to die."

Troggo looked back confused by Beulah and Peter leaving. Kitara asked how the Master could be so sure Razial would defeat the Magi. He told her he was prepared to help Ja'Brahma defeat the Magi if Razial fails.

"Remember. It was I who handed A'Ja'Brahma the Magi's medallions." The Master smiled mentally as he began to ride off. "Heed my advice. Rejoin your clan."

Troggo had to stop Kitara from riding after the Master. She stared at him for a moment. The Master's arrogant confidence bothers her. It bothers him as well, but he knows the Master wants them in the fold with him. The fact he wants them to rejoin their clan confuses him. But that is a good thing.

"The Harbingers puzzle me." Kitara stared. "It is as if they are not the same who stood with Rakaar."

That made Troggo think. The Harbingers were once enemies who did all they could to help Rakaar rid the world of elves. At some point, they changed. Now, they are seen as enemies by all who serve the gods.

Watching the city, he felt a cold breeze blow across the area. It will be a grim day in more ways than one. He looked at the city in the distance and saw the keepers standing, among others. He wanted to see Priato but saw no sign of him. He had expected him to be present when the Magi attacked.

*

Razial and the others stared in awe at the lifelike statue that imprisons Ja'Brahma. It is atop a plinth in the middle of a room that appears to be made of marble, but it is not marble. According to Priato, this room is all that is left of the original Alf-Heim.

Before they had set off for Ja'Brahma's cell, Priato had met Razial. He had explained to him that once he awakens Ja'Brahma, a connection will grow between them, and it will give Ja'Brahma some insight into how he thinks. Razial recognized the warning.

After making their way through the dungeon, Havi and Adini led the way through the magical doorway that leads to Ja'Brahma's cell. Fogi Red moved toward a wall and slid a hand across it. Mantak stood next to Razial while Havi and Adini walked up to the statue. Razial overheard Araceli saying the room is made of marble. Ofelia stood behind the jolems staring at Ja'Brahma.

"Why does it seem like the statue is watching us?" Ofelia asked.

"Because he is." Havi answered dismissively. "Remember. He is not dead."

"She thinks it is a real statue." Adini stated.

"What else could it be?" Ofelia asked.

"His prison." Adini answered. "This is his cell, but the plinth keeps him imprisoned when no one else is inside the cell."

"Why did they imprison him in marble?" Araceli asked sliding a hand across a wall.

"This is not marble." Fogi Red frowned shaking his head.

"Then what is it?" Ofelia asked.

"Dwarf rock." Barthus and Fogi Red answered.

"Good thing we are not jolems." Barthus smiled.

"Funny." Adini smirked. "Let us get on with this."

Kalvin heard all of this, but his mind was on the dwarf rock. He asked Priato what dwarf rock is. Priato explained that it is a mixture of magical wood, sand, and crushed rocks bound together by dwarf magic.

"It takes years to make." Priato stated.

"You will see it in Nibel." Adini growled. "Now-"

"Patience you." Priato cut him off.

Razial looked around and realized that the room had its own light source. He decided the jolems are right. It is time to get on with things. He drew his daggers-Ja'Brahma's daggers, and instantly Ja'Brahma became flesh. His piercing brownish marble-like eyes took them all in. His grim expression exudes power. His long brown hair hangs over his shoulders. His black elflocks hang regally to his chest.

Well-built with olive skin and a round nose, Ja'Brahma stands on his plinth like he is in control. Staring at the daggers, the blades reflected in his eyes. All present, could sense his power. Only Priato and the two jolems are not impressed by his legendary presence. His eyes went to Priato, and his expression changed. Something unsaid past between them. Razial sensed it.

"How long has it been?" Ja'Brahma asked in ancient elvish.

"Just over a thousand years." Priato answered.

"He" Ja'Brahma pointed at Razial. "-cannot wield my powers and the Magi are near."

He closed his eyes. He seemed to smell the air trying to locate the Magi. When he opened his eyes, he looked down at Adini and Havi. A smile came across his face. Razial sensed how much he liked them. Still speaking in ancient elvish, he asked why they were in his cell. Priato quickly explained why they were there. Ja'Brahma smiled while nodding his head. He called the Magi's medallions to him while saying.

"It was wise of him to give me these."

"Indeed. Especially since he was the one who freed the Magi." Priato said.

That made the others look around in confusion wondering who they were talking about. Ja'Brahma laugh. He turned to Razial and warned him about his keepers and paladins. He began to rant.

"A'Ja'Brahma." Havi called firmly.

Ja'Brahma nodded, then asked Priato if he was sure Razial was ready to fight the Magi. Priato told him he has no doubt in Razial's fighting skills.

"It does not mean he is going to win, but he is not afraid." Priato replied.

"Very well." Ja'Brahma sighed. "All of you fight well. Be as brave as the great jolem warriors."

He grinned then mentioned Havi's and Adini's fathers' names. He made a gesture with his fist to signal how much he respects their fathers. He waved his hands, and the room began to fade. Razial inhaled deeply to calm himself. Before everything went black, he heard Ja'Brahma warn Priato saying.

"You know what happens if he fails."

A moment later-minus Adini and Havi, Razial and the others found themselves inside a maze of dark caves. Priato explained everything that happens to them happens in the real world. He had warned them before entering Ja'Brahma's cell about this. Razial knows he simply wants to remind them the danger is real.

"Stay close. Mel will try to get Razial alone before he acts." Priato said in elvish.

Razial walked with his sword in hand, something he rarely does. All the others held their weapons ready as well. As they began to walk through the caves, Ofelia pointed at a shadow in an adjoining cave. Instantly, a witch attacked Ofelia, who battled back with her powers. The others moved to help Ofelia and were engaged by a group of witches. Razial's daggers tumbled toward the witches with deadly accuracy. Barthus' axes deflected magical strikes and opened flesh as he pressed forward. The witches shouted Mel's name while they fought. Fogi Red tackled one of them and smashed his hammer against her head. Razial saw this while deflecting a strike, then cutting his attacker on his backswing.

"Razial!" Araceli shouted.

Stone slid across stone behind Razial, but he could not disengage. Two witches attacked him magically and physically. Knowing he had been cut off, Razial remained calm and pressed his attacker. They could not match his speed and were cut down. He heard Mel laughing then turned to his left and saw Mel standing with his bow in his left hand.

Slightly taller than Razial, Mel has wavy brown hair that frames his face. His face seems powdered, and his lips seem lightly painted. Now, he knows why it is said Mel has a feminine appearance.

A sarcastic grin expressed how Mel feels about Razial. He insulted Razial, then said.

"Simple half elf Tuyakan."

Razial ignored him. Still, Mel continued talking saying he would rather have Razial stand with him than fight him. That made Razial smile. Mel is trying to avoid having to fight him. That made him remember what Goraan had told him in the past.

"There are two reasons why someone stronger than you does not want to fight; either one has use for you, or one is afraid" Goraan had said.

Remembering those words, Razial slowly moved toward Mel, who held his bow up and slowly drew back its magical bowstring. An arrow appeared as he took aim. Razial moved side to side as he fired arrow after arrow. Razial sidestepped most of them but had to use his sword to deflect the last arrow.

With no time to stand still, Mel backpedaled while still firing arrows at Razial, who used his sword and daggers to stay alive and to keep Mel on the move. Still, Mel continued to mock him. Razial winced in pain when an arrow pierced his right side. The arrow went through him, but the wound was not fatal.

Angry, Razial threw his sword, then began throwing his daggers forcing Mel, who had made the mistake of celebrating his success, to avoid the daggers, which stopped him from losing arrows at Razial.

Razial closed the distance between them. Mel was on the defensive. Constantly deflecting the daggers only sent them back to Razial faster.

Seeing how things had changed, Mel changed his bow into a long sword. Adequate, at best, with the long sword, Mel was hard-pressed to hold off Razial-a master assassin. Swinging his sword with both hands, Mel forced Razial to cross his daggers to block his overhead swing. He tried to overpower Razial. That cost him.

Razial ducked as he stepped forward butchering Mel. He stabbed him relentlessly while pivoting around him. Mel could not sustain the wounds.

*

The Magi's forces had remained disciplined after the Magi's sudden disappearance. Tonige kept things in order. He sent the generals messages making sure they stuck to the plan. They moved to surround the city, but as they did the jolems struck. Then, Dwight struck, leading a counterattack to hide the fact other armies were riding from the east.

By the time Tonige got the news, the damage was done. Knowing the Magi are fighting against Razial, Tonige could not order a retreat, so he ordered a full assault. Only his army did not charge the walls of Brahma.

With Rakaar's Shadow overtaking the city, Tonige had to admit the Magi had timed their attack well, but they did not consider when Razial would challenge them. They had expected Razial to challenge them during the march on the city. When he did not, they convinced themselves the keepers wanted to wear them down before he challenged them. Tonige would have advised them to attack the walls first, but he wanted them to fail so now he only wants to weaken their armies.

Watching the battle, Tonige thought about how the armies that have arrived to help Brahma will soon be forced to hold near the western wall. He must avoid making it too obvious he wants the Magi to fail, so he sent orders to have some outflank those near the western wall. That will allow the Magi's forces to scale the walls.

*

After defeating Mel, Razial found himself in the lower floors of Uliv's temple. He recognized where he was almost immediately. At first, he doubted himself, but he recognized the walls and heard the others fighting. He did not call out to them to avoid giving away his position. He crept through the corridors at a hurried pace. He heard Barthus call out to Fogi Red in dwarfish.

"Back up and we can hold them back."

Razial increased his pace. The sound of fighting grew louder with each step. Almost running, Razial turned into an adjoining corridor. He saw Barthus, Kalvin, and Fogi Red standing side by side battling a group of Ulivan guards.

Without thinking, he targeted several guards with his daggers. He drew his sword and ran to join the fighting. Using his sword and dagger, he cut down several guards before Kalvin and Barthus finished the last two.

"Cas is in the altar-room." Fogi Red growled. "Lead the way, so we can end this."

Razial could hear the others still fighting, but he knows Fogi Red is right. Dealing with Cas is the best way to get this part of the fighting over with quickly.

As he and the others ran, Kalvin asked him about his wound. Truthfully, he is in a lot of pain, but the task remains at hand. He told Kalvin that he is fine.

They ran down a staircase and were immediately chased by a large group of guards. Running as fast as they could, Razial and the others sped through the hallways. Barthus asked how much farther they must run. Razial explained they have some distance to run.

As soon as they ran into a connecting hallway, Barthus stopped and put his back against a wall. Razial, then Kalvin stopped. Fogi Red growled stopping several steps ahead of Kalvin. They all know what Barthus is about to do. Razial watched as Barthus' axes slammed into the first two guards. Before he turned away the third guard's spear with his left ax and decapitated him with his right ax. He braced himself to be speared by the fourth guard. However, the spear fell short because Razial's daggers slammed into the fourth guard killing him.

Kalvin charged, using a shield to turn away two spears. Razial targeted the next two guards while Fogi Red leapt into the air with his ax held high. Barthus cut through the spears that Kalvin had deflected, and Kalvin ran a guard through just before Fogi Red split another guard's torso down the middle. Blood poured to the ground covering Fogi Red.

"Go Razial!" Barthus shouted. "Kill the magus."

At first, Razial wanted to stay, but he knows better. He targeted another two guards and without watching the daggers strike true turned and ran. His throat is dry. His heart is thumping, but his mind is focused on reaching Cas. He feels the sweat beading on his head and running down his face. With the altar room just ahead of him, he pushed away the pain he felt. He thought about grabbing his sword but decided not to. His eyes stayed on the altar room's doorway which lights up the dark hallway. He increased his pace. He wants to get this over with.

As soon as he entered the altar room, Cas jumped to his feet calling his spear to him. Razial threw his daggers while trying to close in on him. However, Cas did not deflect the daggers. He avoided them making Razial wait longer before they returned to him. That allowed Cas to close the distance forcing Razial to draw his sword. His speed caught Razial off guard. He managed to put Razial on the defensive. The butt of his spear hit Razial's torso several times. Razial staggered backward but regained his balance quickly.

Cas moved in for the kill, but Razial countered and was only speared in his leg. Razial grimaced in pain. Still, he sent a dagger tumbling at Cas. Forced to turn to the side, Cas was not prepared for his next action-throwing his sword. He had to use his spear to deflect the sword which allowed Razial to close the distance. He drew his daggers and slid them across Cas' spear.

That forced Cas to release his spear. As it fell, Razial kicked it causing it to hit Cas, who made the mistake of calling his spear to him. He was stabbed twice in his torso. Still, he fought back. His actions saved him for the moment because Razial threw his daggers forcing him to block them. Razial tripped him sending both his legs up into the air. Razial was on him before he hit the ground. Cas fought to the death. Hitting Razial several times, bloodying his mouth and watering his eyes.

He had not expected Razial to be so lethal-always going for the kill!

*

Outside the city, the battle came to an end. The jolems had been too much for the Magi's forces to overcome. Add the fact all those who had climbed the walls were met by Anjia, Alena, groups of siblings, and tens of elfin animals and they did not have a chance. Tonige's counter action of having all the magicians in the Magi's forces focus on the jolems would have worked had the keepers not joined the fighting when they heard of Cas' defeat.

Tonige informed the generals about Beulah stealing the supplies. Having no choice, the generals called for a full retreat. While they retreated, Chivia ordered her army to kill until exhaustion set in. Zelia watched as this happened. Her mind thought about Razial. She was told he had defeated Mel and

Cas, but there had been no news for hours. She is anxious and worried.

Tu'ani had her watch over Niri, Lissa, Bernice, and Vera, who were put in charge of passing out supplies to their allies.

"Still no news?" Lissa asked.

Zelia knows she is worried about Ofelia. Even in the darkness of night, Lissa's chestnut eyes seem soft and caring.

"No. Ofelia is with Kalvin and Razial. You know how Kalvin feels about her." Zelia said.

She did her best to sound sure and confident although she is just as anxious to hear something about what is going on with the others facing the Magi. The keepers can only sense when one of the Magi is defeated-nothing else. She sighed and watched her frozen breath rise into the air.

*

Razial awakened, startled by the fact he was unconscious. Cas had knocked him out before he died. His head hurts as does his leg and his side from the arrow wound. He stood and saw Mantak, Barthus, Kalvin, and Priato standing around him. They are now in a clearing. Kalvin has an emptiness in his eyes. He is standing on will alone. He has his sword, but he does not have the shield he had. He is covered in blood. He has a lot of minor wounds and some more serious wounds. Barthus is covered in blood. His wounds-including a cut on his head and one across his torso, do not seem to bother him.

"Are you well?" Priato asked.

Razial nodded while looking at a blood splattered Mantak, who was holding his katanas in front of him. Priato told him they are ready to fight Bal. Razial nodded in thought. He knows they are in Pan's Forest where Bal is originally from.

Priato gathered them in a circle and Razial called out to Bal. A moment later, Bal stood before him with two daggers in his hands. Four of his tribesmen stood before the others-one for each of them. Razial thought about asking about those missing but stopped himself. He must focus. Bal is a fighter. He had caught Cas by surprise. Bal will not be so easily surprised.

"You defeated Cas. I am impressed." Bal growled.

He towers over Razial. Where Cas has tan skin, Bal is pale. He has light brown eyes that match his shoulder length dirty blond hair. Heavily muscled, Bal appears built for combat. Razial glanced around. Bal's tribesmen have the same appearance he has. Some are just as built.

"Well. Why are you waiting?" Bal asked.

Razial attacked-swinging his daggers as fast as he could. Bal blocked and deflected his swings. Their daggers tapped against each other rhythmically. Bal's footwork is not as quick or as light as Razial's, but it is perfect, nonetheless.

Razial threw his daggers. Bal did the same. Razial ducked while Bal used his bracers to deflect Razial's daggers. Razial tripped his left leg, but as Bal fell, he pivoted so he could land on his hands. Still, Razial threw his daggers. Bal growled when the daggers bit into his side. He pushed himself back to his feet and called his daggers to him. Razial was upon him without hesitation. He easily blocked Razial's swings, but Razial had expected that. He kicked

Bal in the face, snapping his head back. Razial kicked him again. This time in his side. Bal retaliated by slamming his right fist against Razial's chest knocking him to the ground. Still, as he fell Razial kicked him in his knee. Bal tried to keep his balance while Razial rolled to his feet.

Razial's eyes darted around. He saw Kalvin fighting defensively while Barthus traded powerful blows with his opponent. He moved to reengage Bal, who swung from out wide at him. He ducked and stabbed him several times in his legs before Bal dazed him with a thunderous left hand. While he stumbled backward, Bal stabbed him in his left side. He smiled to gloat. He had expected Razial to stumble. Instead, he clenched his teeth and slammed his daggers into Bal's torso.

Caught by surprise, Bal dropped his daggers, but quickly recovered. He rocked Razial with quick combinations.

Priato stood perfectly still watching the others fight. He knows his opponent is growing impatient. Mantak dealt with his opponent quickly. Priato told him to stand still and not to join the fighting. He did not have to explain why. Bal sees himself as a warrior. Instead of trying to ambush his foes, he prefers to face them on equal terms. Helping others is seen as weakness. Doing so would make Bal call another tribesman to join the fighting.

Priato saw Barthus finish his opponent with a forearm to his head, then crushing his windpipe with the other hand. Priato told him not to help Kalvin. That is when he saw Bal preparing to finish Razial. His eyes went to his opponent. He whipped up his spear while stepping back and twirling his spear-before his opponent could block it-and drove it through him. He then spun on his heels-pulling his spear free and threw it with perfect accuracy spearing Bal in his back. That stopped him from grabbing Razial by his throat, but also allowed another foe to appear before Priato. Priato masterfully kept him at bay.

"Barthus. Help Kalvin. Mantak. Help Razial." Priato said.

Barthus' axes cut down Kalvin's opponent. A moment later, while Mantak inflicted multiple wounds on Bal, two more enemies appeared to engage Barthus and Mantak. They were more than ready. Kalvin gasped for air while they fought around him. He looked up. Mantak is close to another victory. Barthus shows no sign of tiring and Priato is setting up to finish his second opponent.

Razial on the other hand, is staggering and Bal is ready to close in on him. Kalvin charged and ran Bal through. Bal turned to stab Kalvin, who leapt back only to be cut across his back by the tribesman who had appeared to face him for helping Razial.

As he fell, he saw Mantak kill the man who had just cut him. By the time Kalvin looked up, he saw Mantak fighting his third opponent and Razial creeping up on a distracted Bal. Rage and instinct drove Razial. Before Bal could turn around from his failed attempt to stab Kalvin, Razial closed in on him. Unable to focus, Razial did not trust himself to strike accurately, so he stabbed Bal repeatedly in his back.

Instead of targeting the head, Razial went for the spine. Kalvin had given him the chance he needed. He refused to let it slip away.

Wincing and growling in pain, Bal spun around. He refused to lose so easily, but Razial had learned from his prior error. He ducked still stabbing Bal in his legs and swept Bal off his feet. As Bal crashed to the ground, Razial jumped on him. Bal did not just accept defeat. Razial had to block his swings but was still cut deeply across his chest as he drove his own daggers into Bal's throat, killing him.

*

Araceli sat up surprised by the sudden turn of events. One moment she and Ofelia were running through the temple's many hallways, and the next they stood back in Ja'Brahma's cell. She had tripped over Razial, who lay on the floor covered in blood. Ofelia knelt over a bloody Kalvin healing him.

"The medallions belong to him now." Priato said in ancient elvish.

"And he shall have them when he awakens." Ja'Brahma said.

"Mantak." Priato called. "Bring Razial. Araceli. Heal Barthus."

"What about me?" Fogi Red growled. "You all know that I am a king?"

That made Ja'Brahma laugh. Adini and Havi had told him about Fogi Red while the others fought. Watching them all leave, Ja'Brahma smiled. *Another Champions' War has begun in earnest.*

He will be awake for decades at least. He knows those who call themselves Harbingers are doing their best to free him. He does not understand that because true Harbingers serve Rakaar!

***

Alena and Anjia are in the room with Razial. His wounds were healed, but he remains unconscious. He will survive. He just needs time to heal. The side of his left eye is swollen and both sides of his face are swollen and bruised.

Anjia caressed his head. Alena watched her and could not help but think of when they were young.

"He should let his hair grow like when we were young children. It gives him a less threatening appearance." Alena said.

"But it makes him more vulnerable when he fights. It has been a long time since he last had long hair." Anjia smiled.

"Too busy earning his moniker." Alena stated.

Their eyes locked. The same shade of brown, Anjia's eyes have always been narrower than Alena's. Alena's are more slanted while Anjia's are more almond shaped.

Neither of them has slept very well. They have been too busy worrying about Razial. It is close to noon, and they are due to eat lunch with the keepers. Anjia knows Alena wants to talk about something, so she told her to say what she has to say.

"I need you to do me a favor." Alena said.

"Of course. Just ask." Anjia replied.

"I want you to accept Zelia and ..." Alena paused debating if she should tell Anjia about Diana. Then, decided to do so. "I need you to understand something about the Gray Keeper's role."

Anjia stared stoically. Curiosity filled her eyes. It is obvious Alena has to say something that will make Anjia angry. She watched as Alena sat next to her. Alena sighed, then explained how the Blue, Red, and Yellow Keepers are bound to Eloh and the Gideon, which makes them stronger, but the Gray Keeper is only bound to the Gideon. She is incapable of acting against the Gideon. Eloh cannot influence her like he can the other keepers.

"Sister." Anjia said softly. "I have been told all of this before. Why are you saying this to me?"

"To make sure you understand the next Gray Keeper will stand with Razial even when you think he must be stopped." Alena said emotionally.

"You know who it will be." Anjia said knowingly. "Just tell me who it will be."

Alena did not want to answer this, but she had no choice. She looked into Anjia's eyes and said.

"Diana will be his Gray Keeper."

Anjia's expression changed. She shook her head and looked away. She clenched her teeth as she sprang to her feet. She began to pace around. She is visibly angry. Diana had cared about Razial for quite some time. She has been behind the scenes in Arapia for decades. As a member of the ruling house, her family has helped her hide her true age to avoid people discovering she is a witch. Many of her relatives are born magicians, but she is the strongest. She was secretly recruited by Goraan, another problem Anjia has with her. Still, the major problem is that Diana loves Razial.

"How can she be his Gray Keeper?" Anjia snapped angrily. "It is as if fate is mocking me."

"And yet, Razial only loves you of all his keepers." Alena said.

That made Anjia think, but she remained angry. Zelia is one thing. Diana is another matter. Alena began to laugh. Anjia's expression changed. She frowned wondering why Alena laughed.

Seeing this, Alena explained that fate has chosen a group of assassins to center the world's destiny around.

After a moment, Anjia smirked, then said.

"And it all started with Goraan-my father."

"True. We can only hope others realize he is not a Harbinger, or we are in for a serious challenge." Alena stated.

*

After meeting with the keepers, Zelia separated from Anjia and Alena. She went to talk with several siblings. They discussed several ways to better deal with things in Brahma when the people return. She then spent time alone thinking about the meeting with the keepers. That is when she decided to visit Razial. Talking with him for almost an hour before leaving. She stopped in the doorway because she felt a strange sense as if she were being watched. Not wanting to, but feeling as if she had to, she turned around to look over the room. Razial, who lay on the bed, stared at her with a frown.

"What is wrong?" He asked, looking around the room. "What are you looking for?"

"I felt like someone, or something was watching me." She said. "Do you want me to stay?"

"I am fine, Zelia." Razial smiled. "Tell me when Alena and Anjia return, please."

Zelia nodded then exited the room.

"She is getting stronger." Goraan said keeping his voice low as a whisper.

Razial was not startled by his sudden appearance. Wearing his black elfin surplice. Goraan stood by the back wall. His hair is pulled back into one braid. He has a grim expression. Razial began trying to think how long Goraan has been in his room. Zelia had spent most of the time talking about how it is believed Goraan is a Harbinger and how the keepers have taken actions in case they have to act against him.

Razial had listened, but unlike Anjia he does not care if Goraan is a Harbinger so long as he does not violate the Society's rules. He told Zelia that he is with Goraan. She did not respond to that.

"Can you talk?" Goraan asked.

Razial nodded as he rolled to put his feet to the floor. He did not have to ask if Goraan had heard what Zelia had said because Goraan told him he had arrived in the room just before Zelia had. Razial did not notice because he had been lightly sleeping. Goraan told him to call the medallions to him. Razial thought about the Magi's medallions, and they appeared hanging around his neck. That surprised him. Goraan told him to get dressed and to put on his elfin burnoose. Razial does not know why, but he reminded Goraan that he is still under contract.

"You are also being hunted." Goraan countered. "Hurry now. We have to leave before Anjia and Alena return."

He told Razial to release the medallions, then told him he would explain things later. Staring into Razial's eyes, he said.

"What we are about to do is best for you, the Society, and the world."

ELOH AND HIS SERVANTS

ELOH= the god who remains obedient to the Creator

THE GIDEON= Eloh's champion, created after the First Champions' War, has the ability to make paladins so long as two other paladins live

THE KEEPERS= Blue, Red, and Yellow Keepers are bound to Eloh and his champion, the Gray Keeper is only bound to the champion, they guide Eloh's servants and keep them united

THE PALADINS= eight individuals bound to the Creator, they cannot serve Rakaar, their purpose is to help the champion wage war, it takes five paladins to make another paladin

THE ORDER OF THE FLAME

Dwarfs, elves, and humans who serve Eloh, they are well organized even though their leadership is divided into three entities

THE CANOPY= an entity of elves, based in Alf-Heim, they wear brown surplices

THE CONCLAVE= an entity of humans based in Anazi Falls, they wear gray cowls and are known as druid-siblings

THE GULLY COUNCIL= an entity of dwarfs and Gully dwarfs based in Gully city, they wear no special clothing

BULWARK= nonmagician member

SIBLING= magic wielding member

THE ORDER= common name for the Order of the Flame

RAKAAR AND HIS SERVANTS

RAKAAR= the god who wants to rule the world, his clergy is based in Winnin and wear black and gold robes

THE CHOSEN SERVANT= Rakaar's champion, created after Haar was imprisoned by the Gully Council, always a woman to remind Rakaar's servants that the Chosen Servant will stand aside when Rakaar's queen returns, one can earn this position by rite-of-passage also

THE FELLOWSHIP = serves the magus Bal, based in Coilu

THE SISTERHOOD = serves the magus Mel, based in Ocia, only women members

THE THEOCRACY= openly teaches service of Eloh but secretly serves the magus Cas, based in Danou, its clergy wear white surplices, red trim signals rank

POWERMONGERS AND OTHERS

HARBINGERS= nine individuals out to kill Rakaar and free Ja'Brahma, they wear magical red cowls that hide their identities, originally Harbingers served Rakaar, they were his harbingers

HERALDS= individuals vying to become Harbingers, they wear magical red robes

HARLEQUINS= elves who broke away from the Boar clan leaving Ino-Heim to wage war against the gods' servants, their goal is to free Ja'Brahma, they wield yataghans because other elves wield katanas

THE SOCIETY= commonly known as the Assassins' Society, based in Fulancia inside a fortress known as the Stronghold, its five founding members and leaders are known as the Hilt

TUYA-KAN= ancient living practice founded by Tuya and her husband, Kan, they were the first two human druids, practitioners seek to strengthen their connection to the Creator, killing non-servants of Rakaar must be necessary, master practitioners are called **HIERARCHS** while corrupt practitioners are called **WIZARS**

TUYAKAN= a misnomer that used to mean a practitioners of Tuya-Kan, but has come to refer to anyone with a tanned olive or darker complexion

THE PATH OF JA'BRAHMA
continues in book two

HARBINGERS' DESTINY

The hunt for Razial continues. What Goraan has planned remains unknown. Gwen of Dax has become the Chosen Servant, increasing the danger she presents to Razial. Her actions have caught everyone off guard. The Master remains focused. The next phase of the Harbingers' plans is underway.

The Order of the Flame is scrambling around trying to minimize the deaths that will be caused by the effects of Rakaar's shadow, which continues to expand a mile a day in every direction. The Society will use the spread of Rakaar's shadow to their advantage.

Still, it will be the introduction of an imprisoned Harbinger that will change things in the world.

More paladins will be revealed as the Magi's return remain the most pressing issue for the Order of the Flame.

Made in United States
Cleveland, OH
27 November 2024